Richelle M⸱⸱⸱⸱⸱⸱⸱ MA ⸱n Comparative ⸱elis⸱⸱⸱ and a
passion for ⸱⸱⸱⸱⸱⸱ ac⸱ y and humorou⸱ ⸱⸱⸱⸱⸱ently
lives in Sea⸱⸱⸱⸱⸱⸱⸱⸱ ⸱⸱⸱gets up before n⸱⸱⸱ ⸱⸱⸱⸱⸱ll as
writing the ⸱uccubus s⸱⸱es and the 'Da⸱k ⸱wa⸱ vels,
she is the author of the bestselling 'Vompire A⸱ lemy'
series.

Catch up on her late-night musings and updates about
her next novel at: www.richellemead.com

Praise for Richelle Mead

'My kind of book – great characters, dark worlds, and just the
right touch of humour. A great read'
Patricia Briggs, author of *Moon Called*

'Richelle Mead has a way of cutting through the clichés to get
to the heart of her story. This is urban fantasy the way it's
meant to be: smart, clever, magical, meaningful, with great
characters and real heart'
Carrie Vaughn, author of *Kitty and the Midnight Hour*

'With sharp prose and a powerhouse voice, Richelle Mead
took a death grip on my imagination and refused to let go.
I, too, fell prey to the enchantments of her succubus, and
couldn't stop thinking, wondering, and caring about her
until I turned the final page'
Vicki Pettersson, author of *The Scent of Shadows*

'Deliciously wicked! Dysfunctional, funny, and sexy. I look
forward to reading more tempting morsels about this
succubus-with-a-heart-of-gold'
Lilith Saintcrow, author of *Dead Man Rising*

'Take a beautiful ⸱⸱⸱⸱⸱⸱⸱ ⸱⸱⸱⸱⸱ ⸱⸱⸱⸱⸱ ⸱⸱⸱⸱⸱⸱⸱ murder
and plen⸱⸱⸱⸱ ⸱⸱⸱⸱⸱⸱⸱⸱⸱⸱⸱⸱ ⸱⸱⸱⸱⸱⸱njoy the

M⸱⸱⸱⸱⸱⸱⸱⸱ ⸱⸱⸱⸱⸱⸱⸱⸱⸱⸱s

'Sexy, scintillating and sassy!'
Michelle Rowen, author of *Bitten and Smitten*

'An unusually tangible, believable, living story . . .
an engaging read'
Jim Butcher, author of *The Dresden Files*

Also by Richelle Mead

The Georgina Kincaid series
SUCCUBUS BLUES
SUCCUBUS NIGHTS
(published in the US as SUCCUBUS ON TOP)
SUCCUBUS DREAMS
SUCCUBUS HEAT
SUCCUBUS SHADOWS
SUCCUBUS REVEALED

The Eugenie Markham/Dark Swan series
STORM BORN
THORN QUEEN
IRON CROWNED
SHADOW HEIR

and published by Bantam Books

www.transworldbooks.co.uk

Shadow Heir

A Dark Swan Novel

Richelle Mead

BANTAM BOOKS

LONDON • TORONTO • SYDNEY • AUCKLAND • JOHANNESBURG

TRANSWORLD PUBLISHERS
61–63 Uxbridge Road, London W5 5SA
A Random House Group Company
www.transworldbooks.co.uk

SHADOW HEIR
A BANTAM BOOK: 9780553826098

Originally published in the United States of America by Zebra Books,
an imprint of Kensington Publishing Corp.
First publication in Great Britain
Bantam edition published 2012

A CIP catalogue record for this book
is available from the British Library.

Addresses for Random House Group Ltd companies outside the UK
can be found at: www.randomhouse.co.uk
The Random House Group Ltd Reg. No. 954009

Penguin Random House is committed to a sustainable future for
our business, our readers and our planet. This book is made from
Forest Stewardship Council® certified paper.

Printed and bound in Great Britain by Clays Ltd, Elcograf S.p.A.

Typeset in Times New Roman

6 8 10 9 7 5

For my brother Steve,
who helps keep our family on track.

Acknowledgments

Bringing Eugenie's story to a close is bittersweet. She was my first real action heroine—and a fellow redhead to boot. I've had a great time writing her series and am grateful to all the friends and family who have loved me, supported me, and helped me come up with new and terrifying monsters for her to take down! Many thanks go to editor John Scognamiglio at Kensington, who took the chance on Eugenie and helped bring her story to print. Thank you also to my amazing literary agent, Jim McCarthy, for guiding these books every step of the way. And finally, I can't say enough how grateful I am to all the fans that have followed Eugenie on her journeys in both worlds. Your enthusiasm is what continues to make writing such a joy for me.

Chapter 1

I'm sure Ohio's a perfectly nice place, once you get to know it. For me, right now, it was akin to one of the inner circles of Hell.

"How," I demanded, "can the air possibly contain this much moisture? It's like going swimming."

My sister, walking beside me in the late-afternoon sun, grinned. "Use your magic to push it off you."

"Too much work. It just keeps coming back," I grumbled. Jasmine, like me, had been raised in the dry heat of Arizona, so I couldn't understand why she didn't have the same revulsion I did to the monsoon conditions of high summer in the Midwest. We both wielded weather magic, but hers was focused primarily on water, so maybe that explained her blasé attitude. Maybe it was just the resilience of youth, seeing as she was about ten years younger than me. Or maybe, just maybe, it was because she wasn't nearly five months pregnant and hauling around an extra ten pounds or so of offspring who seemed intent on overheating me, sucking my resources, and pretty much slowing down every goddamned thing I did.

It was also possible hormones were making me a little irritable.

"We're almost there," said a polite voice on the other side of me. That was Pagiel. He was the son of Ysabel, one of the bitchiest gentry women I knew—and she didn't even have excess hormones as an excuse. Pagiel hadn't inherited his mother's personality, thankfully, and possessed a knack for crossing between the Otherworld and the human world that rivaled mine and Jasmine's. He was roughly the same age as her, and the fact that I had to have a teenage escort to get me to my doctor's appointments only added insult to the many injuries I'd endured these last few months.

A block ahead, the Hudson Women's Health Clinic stood among its carefully pruned pear trees and neat rows of geraniums. The business was right on the line of the commercial and residential zones of the city and tried to give the appearance that it was part of the latter. It wasn't the pretty landscaping that made me keep coming back to this sauna, walking half a mile each time between the Otherworldly gate and the clinic. It wasn't even the medical care, which was fine as far as I could tell. Really, when it came down to it, this place's biggest appeal was that so far, no one had tried to kill me here.

That cursed wet heat had me dripping with sweat by the time we reached the building. I was used to sweating in the desert, but something about this climate just made me feel sticky and gross. Fortunately, a wave of air-conditioning hit us as we walked through the door. As glorious as it was for me, it was a miracle for Pagiel. I always liked seeing his face when he felt that first blast. He'd grown up in the Otherworld, where fairy—or gentry, the term I preferred—magic could work wonders. He wouldn't blink an eye at magical feats that would make a human gape. But this? Cold air produced by a *machine*? It blew his mind every time. No pun intended.

"Eugenie," said the receptionist. She was middle-aged and plump, with a kindly, hometown air about her. "Back with your family I see."

We'd taken to passing Pagiel off as our brother, for simplicity's sake. Really, though, it wasn't a stretch to imagine us all being related. Jasmine's hair was strawberry blond, mine a light red, and Pagiel's a true auburn. We could have done advertising for the National Redhead Solidarity Group, if such a thing existed. No one at the clinic ever seemed to think it was weird that I brought my teenage siblings along, so maybe that was normal around here.

We took seats in the waiting room, and I saw Pagiel shift uncomfortably in his jeans. I hid a smile and pretended not to notice. He thought human clothes were crude and ugly, but Jasmine and I had insisted he wear them if he wanted to be part of my obstetric security detail. Normally, the gentry favored silks and velvet in their clothing, with flourishes like puffy sleeves and cloaks. Maybe he could have gotten away with that on the West Coast but not here in middle America.

Both he and Jasmine stayed behind when the nurse came to get me. Jasmine used to go in with me, but after an embarrassing incident when Pagiel had tried to attack someone with a Milli Vanilli ringtone, we'd decided it was best if he wasn't left alone. Although, I admit, it was hard to fault his actions.

I went to see an ultrasound tech first. As the mother-to-be of twins, I was knocked into a high-risk category and had to have more ultrasounds than someone with a "normal" pregnancy would. The tech situated me on the table and slathered gel on my stomach before touching it with her paddle. And just like that, all my crankiness, all my sarcasm—all the feelings I'd so haughtily walked in with—vanished.

And were replaced with terror.

There they were, the things that I'd risked my life—and the fate of the world—for. To be fair, the images still didn't look like much to me. They were only sketchy black-and-white shapes, though with each visit, they became increasingly more babylike. I supposed this was a marked improvement, since for a while there, I was certain I'd be giving birth to aliens and nothing human or gentry at all.

"Ah, there's your son," said the tech, gesturing to the left side of the screen. "I was pretty sure we'd be able to spot him this time."

My breath caught. *My son.* As she moved the paddle to get a better angle, his profile flashed into stark relief, small arms and legs and a rounded head that looked very human. This tiny creature, whose beating heart was also clearly visible, hardly seemed like a conqueror of worlds. He seemed very small and very vulnerable, and I wondered not for the first time if I'd made a mistake in continuing this pregnancy. Had I been tricked? Had I been taken in by this innocent façade? Was I even now nurturing the man who prophecy said would try to enslave humanity?

As though sensing my thoughts, his sister stirred on the other side of the screen. She had been a large driving force in my decision to keep this pregnancy. If I'd terminated it in an attempt to save the world from my son, I would've been responsible for ending her life. I couldn't do that to her. I couldn't do that to him, even. It didn't matter what the prophecy said. They both deserved a chance to live their lives, free of what destiny had allegedly dictated for them.

Now, if only I could convince all the people who were trying to kill me of that.

"Everything looks great," the tech told me. She put the paddle away, and the screen went black, shrouding my children in shadows once more. "Perfectly normal."

Normal? Hardly.

Yet, when I was ushered into an exam room to speak to

the doctor, her opinion was the same. Normal, normal, normal. Sure, twins required extra watching, but otherwise, everyone seemed convinced I was the model of a perfect pregnancy. None of them had any idea, not even the tiniest clue, of the daily struggle I went through. None of them knew that when I looked at my stomach, I was tormented with the image of violence done in my name and the fate of two worlds hanging in the balance.

"Do you feel them move yet?" the doctor asked me. "It's around that time."

Images of *Alien* came to mind. "No, I don't think so. How will I know?"

"Well, it'll be pretty obvious in later pregnancy. This early, you start to feel fluttering sensations. Some people say it's like a fish swimming around. You'll know when it happens. Don't worry—they won't be trying to kick their way out. Not at first."

I shuddered, not sure how I felt about that. Despite the changes in my body, it was still easy to regard this as some physical ailment. It was only the ultrasound that reminded me there were actually *people* living inside me. I wasn't sure I was ready to also start feeling them squirm around.

The doctor glanced at her clipboard. "Honestly, everything looks great," she said, echoing the ultrasound tech.

"I'm tired all the time," I countered. "And I keep getting short of breath. And I'm having trouble bending. I mean, I can still do it, but it's not easy."

"That's all normal."

"Not for me." I used to banish ghosts and beat up monsters for a living.

She shrugged. "You have two people growing inside of you. It's going to get worse before it gets better."

"But I have a lot of things to do. My lifestyle's pretty, um, active."

She remained unmoved. "Then you're going to have to adapt."

Despite my whining, I was sent off with a clean bill of health and instructions to book my next appointment. In the lobby, I found Jasmine and Pagiel exactly where I'd left them. She was leafing through a copy of *People* and trying to explain to him both the definition and appeal of reality TV.

Maybe the office didn't bat an eye at my "siblings" because I simply had too many other weird habits. Like, for example, I always paid for each visit in cash. When you tacked on things like ultrasounds, blood work, and other medical testing, the final price tag was pretty high. I always felt like I was one step away from pulling out a Mafia-style suitcase filled with hundred-dollar bills. There was no alternative, however. I couldn't do anything that would allow my enemies to track me. Medical insurance claims would create a paper trail, as would even paying with a check or credit card. For the majority of gentry, none of that was a concern. Most were like Pagiel and could barely grasp the idea of banks or the postal system, let alone using them to track me. Unfortunately, my enemies in the Otherworld had very good connections here among humans, those who knew our systems inside and out. It was because of them I was in Ohio in the first place. Tucson had been compromised.

Another woman, far more pregnant than me, was just entering the office as the receptionist printed my receipt. A gust of wind swept in behind her, and she had to fight to catch the door and make it close. Pagiel, though inept at technology, had been trained in the gentry ways of chivalry and jumped up to help her.

"Thanks," she told him. She flashed the rest of us a cheery smile. "I can't believe how fast the weather turned on us. A cold front came out of nowhere."

The receptionist nodded sagely. "That's how it is this time of year. We'll have storms tonight for sure."

As if I needed another reason to dislike the Midwest. God, how I missed Tucson's unchanging climate. As I walked out with Jasmine and Pagiel, I knew I had an unfair attitude. I was simply feeling the woes of my self-imposed exile. I didn't really hate Ohio so much as I missed Arizona. Once we were back in the Otherworld, I could visit the kingdom I ruled and practically be in a mirror of Tucson. I'd designed it that way. And yet . . . it wasn't the same. I kept blaming everything on the weather, but a place was defined by more than just that. There was a culture and a vibe, driven by its people, that was unique to every location. The Thorn Land was great, but it would never replace my hometown.

"Damn," said Jasmine, trying to pry her hair off of her face. A fierce wind had whipped it right at her as soon as she stepped outside. "That lady wasn't kidding."

I pulled myself from my self-pity enough to note that she was right. The temperature had dropped, and that thick, suffocating air from earlier was now in motion as fronts collided. The cute ornamental trees swayed back and forth, like synchronized dancers. Dark clouds, tinged with a sickly green, gathered above. A chill that had nothing to do with the cool-down ran over my skin. My asshole gentry father, aside from getting me stuck with a prophecy that said his eldest grandson would conquer humanity, had also passed on his prowess with weather magic. I was tuned in to all the elements that made up a storm: the moisture, the air, even the charged particles that heralded lightning. My senses were open to them, and the intensity of all those factors hitting me at once now was a bit overwhelming.

"So much for a candy run," I muttered, peering at the angry sky. I was out of Milky Ways and pretty desperate for some. "We'll be lucky if we don't get drenched before we

reach the gate." Not for the first time, I wished I had a car
during these Ohio trips, but it was pointless. The only real
reason I came here was for the clinic, and it was within
walking distance to the gate that led back to the Otherworld. There'd be no practical way to keep a car here. Plus,
riding in one would probably kill Pagiel.

I'd glanced at the sky, mostly verifying that things
looked as bad as they felt, when something suddenly jerked
me to a standstill. If I scanned to the north, looking above
a stretch of trees, I could see the edge of the storm clouds.
The black ceiling above us only extended a mile, and where
it ended abruptly, I could see sunshine and blue sky. I was
willing to bet the air was stiflingly hot and humid there
too. Looking around, I saw that was the case everywhere.
Directly above us, the sky was dark, but those clouds extended in a very finite, very clearly defined way. It was like
being under a perfectly round dome. All around those hard
edges, sun fought to get through.

My companions came to a halt beside me, and I met
Jasmine's gaze. "I feel it. . . ." she murmured. "I didn't at
first. There was too much going on. . . ."

"Me too," I said. Along with feeling storm elements, she
and I were also sensitive to magic specifically acting on
them. What we were feeling now wasn't a natural occur-
rence. There were so many stimuli that the magic behind it
had remained hidden to me initially—as was no doubt intended. There were Otherworldly forces at work. And with
that realization came another: we'd been discovered. My
Midwest safe house was no longer safe. "Fuck."

Pagiel's young face was grim as he glanced at me. "What
do you want to do?" Pagiel had inherited his mother's magical prowess with air, so he too had probably figured out
something was amiss.

I began walking again. "We've got to get to the gate.
There's no other choice. Once we cross, we're safe."

"Whoever's doing this must know about the gate," pointed out Jasmine. "They could be on the other side waiting."

"I know. But that also means they would've had to defeat all the troops left behind." This gate in Hudson didn't open within the borders of my kingdoms in the Otherworld. It was close enough to my allies, however, that the journey had always seemed worth it in order to get safe medical treatment in the human world. Still, we never made the journey without a considerable and armed escort on the other side.

The wind seemed to increase as we walked, blowing against us and slowing our progress. I could've used my magic to control it but was holding back until faced with the storm's creator—or rather, creators. There were only two people in known gentry history who could singlehandedly summon and control a storm like this. One was my deceased father. The other was me. My bet was that this was the work of a number of magic users, a thought that made me grit my teeth in frustration. A lot of planning would've had to go into this, which meant my enemies had known about Hudson for a while.

Almost as annoying as being found out was having to deal with my own physical limitations. I wasn't crippled, not by any means. I wasn't even waddling. But, as I'd told the doctor, I just couldn't quite do the things I used to. A half mile was not a huge distance, not at all, especially on suburban sidewalks. In my pre-pregnancy state, I could have easily broken out into a run and covered the distance quickly. Now, my best was a half-ass jog, and I was very aware of the fact that I was slowing Jasmine and Pagiel down.

We exited off the main road, cutting through the outskirts of a vast, wooded park. Otherworldly gates were rarely found in heavily populated, urban areas, and this one lay deep within the park's grounds. The trees blocked the direct force of the wind, but the branches were shifting wildly, showering us with twigs and leaves. We were the only ones out here, since most reasonable humans would've long since taken shelter.

"It'll be here," I called to my companions, forcing my voice to be heard above the wind. From the satchel I wore across my body, I produced my wand and an iron-bladed athame. "If they're going to attack, it'll be—"

They attacked.

Five spirits, two water elementals, and another elemental who glowed like a will-o'-the-wisp. Elementals were gentry who could not cross fully into this world in their original forms. They manifested as vaguely anthropomorphic creatures, composed of whatever element most strongly tied to their magic. From the scope of the storm, I suspected more were lurking nearby, but they were probably the weaker ones. It would take all of their power just to maintain these weather conditions, with none left over for fighting. These sent to battle us were the strongest, and the spirits were a backup choice I'd seen frequently. Spirits who hadn't moved on to the Underworld had no care for who ruled humans or the Otherworld. They were therefore easy recruits for the gentry who opposed me.

They weren't the only ones with help from beyond the grave.

"Volusian!" I called. I quickly chanted the words that would summon my undead minion. The sounds were lost in the wind, but it didn't matter. My intent and power were what counted, and within seconds, Volusian materialized. He was shorter than me, with pointed ears, red eyes, and smooth black skin that always reminded me of a salamander's. "The spirits!" I snapped.

Volusian needed no further urging. He hated me. He wanted to kill me, even. But so long as I bound him to my service, he was forced to obey my commands. He attacked the spirits with a fury, his magic flaring bluish white in the shadowy landscape. Jasmine had already set herself on the water elementals while Pagiel took on the will-o'-the-wisp, whom I assumed had some connection to air or the charges in the atmosphere.

And me? I hung back. I hated doing it but had no choice. We'd rehearsed this over and over. The decision to have these twins meant nothing if I let myself get tossed around or—worse—killed. In protecting myself, I protected them, even though it went against every fighter's instinct I had. Fortunately, I wasn't entirely useless. Our attackers wanted me but were too distracted by my allies. This freed me to use my magic to diminish some of the more annoying effects of the weather. It also allowed me to banish the spirits. Volusian was well matched against them, but obviously, the less he had to deal with, the better.

I extended my wand at one of the spirits as it ganged up with another against Volusian. They were translucent, wraithlike creatures who floated in the air and would have been almost impossible to see outdoors in the sun. The shadows and clouds made them eerily discernible. Opening my senses, I reached past this world, past the Otherworld. I brushed the gates of the Underworld, establishing a connection that was solid but wouldn't pull me in. Banishing spirits to the Otherworld was easier and used to be my tactic when I was eliminating them for frightened suburbanites. Spirits sent there could return, however, and I couldn't take that chance anymore. The less of them around to come back for me, the better. It was the Underworld or bust.

I focused my will on my target, using the human magic I'd learned as a shaman to drive the spirit out of this world. The creature shrieked in rage as it felt the Underworld's tug, and seconds later, it dissolved into nothing. I immediately set my sights on a second spirit, briefly allowing myself to assess Pagiel and Jasmine's progress.

To my astonishment, Pagiel had defeated the will-o'-the-wisp elemental already. I hadn't even seen it happen. I had the power to banish elementals back to the Otherworld as well, but for my two sidekicks, physical confrontation was the only option. Pagiel had used his magic to destroy the elemental outright, obliterating it into nothingness. I'd known he was a strong magic user but had never truly seen him in battle until now. He was stronger than Jasmine, I realized. He immediately joined her side against a water elemental, blasting it with a wind that brought it to a standstill while she used her magic to call on the water of the elemental's form and rip it to pieces. Meanwhile, I banished a second spirit.

"Eugenie, go!" cried Jasmine, barely sparing me a glance as she and Pagiel sparred with the last elemental. Volusian was down to one spirit. The odds were in our favor now. None of these attackers would have a chance to break away and come after me.

I grimaced but didn't hesitate. Again, this was part of the plan we'd established. These Otherworldly denizens were here for me. If I was gone, and they weren't destroyed first, they'd likely leave once they realized only Jasmine and Pagiel (and Volusian) were left. I felt like a coward and had to keep reminding myself, *If you die, the twins die.*

I took off at that half jog, continuing to use my magic to lighten the storm and make my passage easier. Ahead of me, a ring of bright yellow buttercups stood out in sharp contrast against the park's green grass. No matter how many times the landscapers mowed them down, the buttercups always returned within a day. They marked the gate.

I was steps away from it when something hit me from my left. The force knocked me over, and I only barely managed to twist my body in a way that minimized the jarring as my knees hit the ground. It had been foolish to think the gate wouldn't be guarded. My attacker was another elemental, seemingly composed of moss and leaves. They decayed and shifted before my eyes, marking just how weak the elemental really was. It could barely exist in this world. The creature's chances of survival were slim, yet it had apparently thought it worth the risk to its life to come and take mine.

I struggled to my feet as it came at me. In one leafy hand, the elemental held a copper dagger, honed to a fine point. Copper was the toughest metal gentry could wield, and even if it wasn't as effective as steel, it could still kill. The elemental's moves were awkward and lumbering, giving me enough time to get to my feet, even in my addled state. I still held the iron athame and felt some satisfaction that pregnant or not, I was faster than this bumbling creature. It swung at me, and I easily dodged, giving me an opening with my athame. The blade made contact, slashing across the elemental's green chest. It shrieked in pain, and I made an instant decision not to finish it off. I didn't have the luxury of playing hero. That injury was more than enough to slow the elemental and let me spring for the gate. I hurried into the ring of buttercups and reached toward the Otherworld. The gate was a strong one that worked at all times of the year and required hardly any effort from someone who knew how to use it. It was another reason we'd selected this area.

The paths between the worlds opened, and I felt a slightly disorienting sensation, like I was being taken apart and reassembled. Within seconds, I found myself standing in the Honeysuckle Land, surrounded by my own soldiers. There was no sign of any foes here, and from the startled looks my guards gave me, my battle-marked state was totally unexpected. They wasted no time in responding, however, and had their weapons drawn the instant the elemental followed me through the gate.

Only, it was no longer an elemental. It wasn't even an

"it." It was a she, a gentry woman no older than myself with brown hair braided into a high bun. She staggered two steps toward me, still holding the copper blade, before falling to the ground. Blood spilled from her chest, showing the severity of the wound I'd given her. It had been done with iron—the gentry's bane—and occurred in the human world, where she was at her weakest. Maybe she could have survived a similar injury in this world, but now, it was too late. The blade fell from her hands as she feebly clutched at her bleeding torso. All the while, her eyes never left me.

"Death . . . to the prophecy. . . ." she gasped out, just before death took her. The light left those hate-filled eyes, and soon she saw nothing. I felt ill.

New arrivals from the gate immediately drew my guards to attention, but it was only Jasmine and Pagiel. They looked as if they'd been in a fight but otherwise showed no serious damage. Jasmine looked at me first, and despite her hard face, I knew she was checking me for injury, just as I'd done for her. It was hard to believe we'd once been enemies.

Satisfied I was okay, she then glanced at the dead woman before meeting my gaze. "Well," Jasmine said, relaxing slightly. "At least you don't have to go to Ohio anymore."

Chapter 2

The layout of the Otherworld defies human physics. There are no straight lines from point A to point B, even when you walk along a road that doesn't seem to curve or fork away. One step forward on a road may take you into a kingdom you thought you'd cleared ten miles back. Most of the kingdoms tended to stay in the same proximity to each other, but there were no guarantees. A road whose quirks you thought you knew by heart might suddenly change without warning.

Fortunately, there were no such surprises today. The road we'd taken to reach the Hudson gate eventually got us back to the Oak Land, with only the expected detours into friendly lands. The Oak Land wasn't one of my kingdoms. It was ruled by my strongest ally, who was also the one who made me the most nervous. Dorian and I had once been lovers and waged an Otherworldly war together. Things had fallen apart when he'd tricked me into a quest designed to conquer a kingdom I didn't want. We'd been quite hostile toward each other for a while, but my pregnancy had changed our relationship. He was one of the advocates of the prophecy that said my father's first grandson would conquer humanity, and so, even though he wasn't the father, Dorian had vowed to aid and protect my children.

Once he'd ascertained I was alive and well, however, he showed little sympathy upon hearing about our ambush.

"I never understood why you had to go to that Ohoho place anyway," he said, pouring a glass of wine. "I say good riddance."

I sighed. "It's Ohio. And you know why I was there. The twins need medical care."

"So you claim. They can receive 'medical care' here. Ours is just as good as humans'. Do you want a glass?" He held up the wine bottle.

I rolled my eyes. "No. And that's exactly the point. Medicine here's not the same at all. Wine's terrible for babies."

Dorian swept into the sitting room to join me, elegantly arranging himself on a love seat that displayed his purple velvet robes to best effect. "Well, of course it is. I'd never dream of giving wine to an infant! What do you take me for, a barbarian? But for you . . . well, it might go a long way to make you a little less jumpy. You've been positively unbearable to live around."

"*I* can't have it either. It affects the babies in utero."

"Nonsense," he said, tossing his long auburn hair over one shoulder. Life would be easier if he wasn't so damned good-looking. "Why, my mother drank wine every day, and I turned out just fine."

"I think you're proving my point for me," I said dryly. "Look, I know you believe everything's fine here and there's no reason I should ever set foot outside the Otherworld, but I just don't feel safe not having this pregnancy monitored by a—human doctor." I'd been about to say "real doctor" but caught myself in time. It was true that I'd watched the gentry perform some amazing feats of healing. I'd literally seen limbs reattached. Yet, despite all the gentry magic, nothing could match the comfort I took in the reassuring numbers and bleeps of medical machinery. I was half human, after all, and had been raised that way.

"You don't 'feel safe,' eh?" Dorian gave me one of his laconic smiles. "Tell me, did the assurance you got from your human doctor today outweigh the potential damage you received when that elemental knocked you around?"

I scowled and looked away. Even though I'd managed to land fairly well when I'd fallen near the gate, I'd still had Dorian's healers check me out when I returned. They'd performed some minor spells on me to relieve bruising and had sworn there was no injury to the twins. They had no diagnostic equipment to prove it, but gentry healers did have an innate sense for such things in the body, just like I was sensitive to the components of storms. I had to take it on faith that the healers were correct.

"We should've been more prepared, that's all," I muttered.

"How much more prepared can you be?" asked Dorian. He still spoke in that easy way of his, like all of this was a joke, but I could see the hardness in his green eyes. "You already traipse through this world with a veritable army at your back. Are you going to start bringing them with you into the human world too?"

"Of course not. We'd never get a hold of enough jeans to outfit them all."

"You risk yourself. You risk them." Dorian pointed at my stomach, just in case there was any question who he meant. "You shouldn't be going to the human world. Honestly, you shouldn't be traveling between kingdoms here! Pick one. One of yours, mine, it doesn't matter. Just stay still *somewhere*, and stay protected until they're born."

"I'm not very good at staying still," I remarked, noting

a similarity between this conversation and the one I'd had when I told the doctor about my physical frustrations.

To my surprise, Dorian's face actually softened into sympathy. "I know, my dear. I know. But these are unusual times. I'll give you this: moving around does make it harder for them to find you. Maiwenn and Kiyo can only monitor so many places at once, so there's something to be said for not staying entirely stationary."

Maiwenn and Kiyo. My heart twisted. We rarely ever spoke those names. Usually we just said "the enemy" or simply "they." But even though there was a large contingent of gentry who wanted to stop Storm King's prophecy, we all knew that two in particular were the real threats. Maiwenn was queen of the Willow Land and had once been a friend. Kiyo was my ex-boyfriend and half human like me.

He was also the father of my children.

Kiyo . . .

If I thought about him too long, my emotions would get the best of me. Even after our romantic relationship had begun to fracture, I'd still cared about him. Then, he'd made it clear that he considered me and the twins acceptable losses to prevent any threat to humanity. I certainly hadn't wanted to see the gentry conquer the human world either, but his actions had left me reeling. It was still a hard reality for me to accept, that I could know someone so well . . . and yet not really know him at all.

"What do you think we should do about the wedding?" I asked, forcing myself to change the subject. "They know I'll be there." Two servants of mine, Rurik and Shaya, were getting married soon, and I was hosting the festivities.

Dorian nodded, eyes narrowed in thought. "They also know all of your allies and a number of others who simply don't want to be on your bad side will be there. So long as we can get you back to the Thorn Land securely, there shouldn't be—"

"I don't care what he's doing! It's imperative I speak to him *now*!"

Dorian and I both flinched at the interruption and turned in surprise toward the source of the angry female voice. Guards standing sentry at the sitting room's door immediately began protests about how Dorian wasn't to be disturbed, but it was clear those explanations were being ignored.

A world-weary expression crossed Dorian's face. "It's fine," he called. "Let her in."

I'd been sprawling on a chaise, nearly as at ease as Dorian, but now I straightened up. I knew who this newcomer was and wouldn't be caught off-guard.

Ysabel came striding into the room, wearing a gown that was elaborate even by gentry standards. I always thought the best term to describe their fashion sense was "Medieval rave." Her dress was made of a heavy silver satin with a crazy V neckline that went nearly to her stomach. A pattern of seed pearls trimmed all the hems and also adorned her long auburn hair. I wondered if she was on her way to some formal event or if she was simply continuing in her efforts to lure in Dorian. She'd been his mistress until he and I were together, but he hadn't resumed things after our split.

Perhaps more astonishing than her attire was that she had company. Trailing in her wake were Pagiel and her formidable and generally unpleasant mother, Edria. The boy had to hurry up to keep pace with the other two and looked miserable. A few moments later, his younger sister Ansonia also entered nervously. She had long hair, almost the color of mine, and looked terrified to be here.

"Your Majesty," exclaimed Ysabel, coming to a halt before Dorian. I couldn't tell if her cheeks were flushed with anger or bad makeup application. Considering the gentry often made their cosmetics out of nuts and berries, neither possibility would have surprised me. "This is unacceptable."

"Mother—" began Pagiel, reaching her side.

Ysabel pointed at me, anger flashing in her eyes. "I refuse to allow her to keep endangering my son! Why, he nearly died today."

"I did not!" exclaimed Pagiel.

Dorian gave Pagiel a calm once-over. "He looks fine to me."

"It was a very close thing," said Edria gravely.

"I don't know," I said, recalling how quickly Pagiel had dispatched his foe. "From what I saw, he had things under control."

"How would you know?" asked Ysabel with a sneer. "*You* ran away."

I felt a blush of my own creeping over my cheeks. My new coddled status still grated on me, as did the knowledge that I had to keep myself out of harm's way while others defended me. No matter how logical it all seemed, I'd never be easy about it.

"Hey, I did my part," I said.

Ysabel had already turned away from me and was addressing Dorian. "It isn't right that my son is risking his life for *her*."

"Agreed," said Edria. Her dark hair was pulled back so tightly that I swore it stretched the skin on her face. Maybe it was the gentry equivalent of a facelift. "He has no stake in this alleged prophecy concerning her son. He owes her nothing."

Pagiel kept trying to interject and was constantly shushed by his mother and grandmother. I felt bad for him, particularly as the only male in that family. His father had died years ago, and Ysabel's father had allegedly been some ne'er-do-well who ran out on them. Pagiel had no one but women around.

Dorian glanced between Ysabel and Edria. "I'm not ordering him to do anything for her. He goes with her by choice."

"But it's not safe," said Ysabel.

Dorian remained unmoved. "And again, I say that he goes with her by choice. Honestly, I'm not really sure what you expect me to do. Your son is a free citizen of my kingdom, and he is of age to make his own decisions."

Ysabel looked on the verge of stomping her feet. "It's dangerous! Isn't it your job to protect your subjects from harm?"

"Certainly," said Dorian. "And at the same time, I must also look after the kingdom's needs. I can hardly protect every soldier in times of war, can I? And even if we aren't technically at war right now, this kingdom is supporting the Queen of Rowan and Thorn. Doing that has certain unavoidable dangers, but there's nothing to be done for it. Hence my use of 'unavoidable.' I can hardly denounce him for voluntarily choosing to assist her. And, in fact, since he's gone above and beyond to keep her safe—as today's skirmish proved—he's actually due for commendation."

Pagiel beamed under his king's praise, but Ysabel's face grew darker. Part of me felt a little sorry for her. After all, she was a mother trying to protect her son. Bitchy or not, she did care about him. At the same time, it was hard for me to give too much credit to someone who'd often used her son for her own gain. After the death of her husband, Ysabel had come to Dorian's court with the sole purpose of seducing a man (preferably the king) who would then provide for her. Bringing Pagiel and Ansonia had been a ploy on Ysabel's part to enhance her own allure. Fertility was a continual concern among the gentry, who didn't conceive easily. Flaunting her two children was Ysabel's attempt at showing off what a good catch she was.

"There, you see?" asked Pagiel triumphantly, finally

getting a word in. "I have the king's support. I believe in what I'm doing. I want to further the prophecy."

I winced a little at that. While I was thankful to those who were helping protect me from Kiyo and Maiwenn, that gratitude was marred by the knowledge that most who aided me did so in the hopes that my son truly would conquer humanity. Gentry and humans had once shared the same world, but the former had eventually left as magic faded and technology rose. Many gentry felt they'd been wronged and deserved a claim back there.

"You're a foolish boy," snapped Edria. "And you have no idea what you believe in. Half of why you do this is because of her sister."

I saw a flicker of embarrassment in Pagiel's features, but he held his ground. It was true that I'd originally gotten to know him when he began showing a romantic interest in Jasmine. Over time, however, he'd become vehemently opposed to those who would threaten unborn children and had taken my side because of that.

"My reasons are my own," Pagiel returned, glaring at his mother and grandmother. "Not yours. This is what I'm choosing to do, and you can't stop me."

The three of them seemed to have forgotten us and had been drawn back into their own private family dispute. Ansonia continued skulking in the back. I was guessing her mother had ordered her here to show family solidarity.

"Pagiel's been amazing," I said, hoping to lend him a little support. "In fact, he's been essential on our trips to the Otherworld. Few other gen—er, shining ones have that kind of power in the human world."

"Power that's being wasted," said Edria with a sniff. "He has more important things to do than be your errand boy."

"Grandmother, you can't talk to her like that!" Pagiel looked mortified. "She's the Queen of Rowan and Thorn."

"I don't care if she's—"

"Enough," said Dorian, raising his hand. Everything about his posture was still easy and relaxed, but there was sternness in his voice that drew everyone's attention. "This conversation is done. There's nothing I can—or will—do. Both of you charming ladies must accept that Pagiel is a man and in control of his own life. Although, if it's any comfort"—he spared me a brief, amused glance—"I doubt he'll be traipsing off to the human world anytime soon, now that Her Majesty's secret hideaway is no longer so secret."

I scowled but made no argument—because he was right.

Pagiel's blue eyes lit up. "I'll help you find a new place," he told me. "I'll check all the gates and see where they lead into the human world."

I smiled indulgently. I was beginning to think Dorian might have a point about staying holed up in this world, but I didn't want to dress Pagiel down in front of Ysabel and Edria. "Thank you, Pagiel."

Ysabel looked ready to explode. "This isn't finished."

"Oh," said Dorian. "I assure you, it is. Now go. All of you."

That commanding tone was back, and after some obligatory curtsies and bowing, the family scurried off.

"They're always so delightful," said Dorian.

"Not the first word that comes to mind for me," I said, watching as the guards shut the door again. I sighed. "Although, I really *do* hate the idea of anyone risking their lives for me. Especially Pagiel. I like him."

"That's the unfortunate thing," said Dorian, smiling. "It's always going to be people you like. Enemies tend not to risk their lives for you. Only your friends are willing to make the sacrifice. Besides, I thought you got over this moral quandary when we went to war against Katrice?"

"I wouldn't say I ever really got over it. Mostly I learned to deal with it."

"That may have to be a permanent philosophy for you."

"Maybe," I agreed. I stood up, stretching to relieve an ache in my back that hadn't been there earlier. Great. One more way my body was falling apart. "I should get back to the Thorn Land now."

Dorian rose with me. "Not yet."

I eyed him warily. "Trying to keep me around?"

"Just being smart. Maiwenn's agents were probably watching this hold, waiting to see if you'd return after their ambush. If they're still in the area, it's best you not take to the roads, escorted or not. That, and they'd also likely expect you to report here and immediately go home. Wait another day or so, and they'll give up and leave."

"I hate intrigue," I muttered, knowing he was right again.

"But you do it so well."

Then, without warning, he reached out and laid a hand on my stomach. I jumped back. "Hey! Ask permission first."

"Just wanted to check in on my little prodigies," he said, unfazed. He stepped toward me again. "May I?"

"They're not your prodigies." I gave a reluctant nod, and his hand returned. "Why bother? I haven't felt them move yet. You certainly can't."

"Even so, I like the connection. We're going to be very close, these two and I. Well, if you'll stop being stubborn and let me adopt them."

It was an offer he kept making me, one that would give my children legitimacy and status in the Otherworld. As queen of two kingdoms, though, they had plenty of status and inheritance through me, without his help. Dorian kept claiming he simply wanted to be a part of our lives. After all the mistrust between us, I was certain there was some sort of attempt at control going on.

"I'm still thinking it over," I said evasively.

He chuckled to himself. "Something makes me suspect you'll be 'thinking it over' for the next twenty years."

Dorian said no more, but his hand didn't move either. He seemed completely entranced by touching me, and I wished I could read what he was feeling. Dorian excelled at disguising what was on the inside. Part of that came from being king, and part of it came from just being . . . well, Dorian. As we stood there, I soon became aware of the warmth of his hand on me and the closeness of his body. It was disconcerting and stirred up too many recollections of our past. I'd been deeply in love with him when he betrayed me; it hadn't been an easy relationship to just let go of. Even now, the memories of our closeness and the intense physicality burned within me. When he started to slide his hand toward the side of my hip, I abruptly pulled away.

"They aren't over there," I said, hoping I sounded more irritable than flustered. I took a few steps toward the door. "I'll stay another day or so and then head back."

He clasped his hands in front of him and nodded. "As you wish. I'm sure I'll see you around. If not, then at the wedding."

"Right," I said. I held his gaze for a few moments and then quickly turned away, afraid of what I might see in his eyes. Having to guess at his emotions was frustrating sometimes, but it wasn't nearly as scary as actually knowing them.

Chapter 3

I didn't take offense that Rurik and Shaya wanted to be married in the Rowan Land, rather than the Thorn Land. Sure, the Thorn Land was where they'd fallen in love while working for me, but I'd known for a while that few gentry shared my love for the endless heat and vast deserts of my primary kingdom. The Rowan Land was still under my rule, though, and even I had to admit it was pretty gorgeous. It was the kind of place that came to mind when you pictured pastoral picnics and idyllic afternoons. Flowers bloomed in abundance, and low, rolling mountains made for a pretty backdrop along the horizon. If I had any issue with the Rowan Land, it was that I simply hadn't wanted to be its queen.

The wedding was held in the vast grounds stretching out beyond the monarch's castle. The castle had been designed by the Rowan Land's last ruler, Katrice, and looked like something straight out of a Bavarian postcard. Magic tied to plants and nature was a common gentry power, and several people must have been hard at work in decorating the grounds. I'd told them they could do whatever they wanted, and they'd taken me at my word. Huge, flowering cherry trees—which hadn't been there a few days ago—lined the courtyard like sentries, showering everything with delicate pink petals. Climbing roses had been coaxed into a natural arch where the couple would take their vows and bloomed in exotic colors I'd never seen in the wild. There were no chairs for the guests, and I'd been told it was tradition to stand for gentry weddings, particularly since the ceremony was usually brief. Off to the sides, kept discreetly away during the ceremony, servants were piling ornate wooden tables with platters of food for the feasting that would follow. Blue morning glories wound their way up the tables' legs, and gentry magic ensured the food stayed hot.

If there was anything that marred this beautiful scene, it was the abundance of soldiers patrolling the area. They weren't easy to spot—at first. Guests were pouring into the area, dressed in the variety of colors and fabrics the gentry so loved. It made it difficult to distinguish anything, but after a minute or so of study, I could pick out the uniforms of both my own soldiers and the ones that Dorian had lent for the occasion. Although they were spread throughout all the grounds, the soldiers were more densely arranged around wherever I was. No surprise, seeing as I was the reason for the extra security. I also knew that all the guests—many of whom were dignitaries and royalty from other kingdoms—had been extensively screened before they were allowed anywhere near the wedding site. I felt a little guilty that my situation put this joyous occasion into lockdown mode, but Rurik and Shaya had taken it in stride.

"This dress makes me look fat," I told Jasmine as we stood near the back of the crowd and watched the last-minute preparations fall into place. She glanced over at me and my efforts to rearrange the folds of my long, gauzy dress.

"You're pregnant," she stated. "Everything makes you look fat."

I scowled. "I think the correct response was, 'No it doesn't.'"

Jasmine shrugged, feeling no remorse for her blunt honesty. "It's not that bad. And it's just in your stomach." She eyed me critically. "And maybe your chest."

I sighed, knowing some of what she said was true. I was so active that I'd really put on no weight that wasn't essential for the pregnancy. And yeah, I knew I wasn't *that* big yet, but standing here—especially next to Jasmine's slim figure—I was again reminded of the hard truth: I was no longer the one in charge of my body.

"Your Majesty?"

A new voice drew me out of my self-pity, and I turned to see a middle-aged gentry woman standing beside me in a velvet gown. She swept me a low curtsy and then straightened up in one graceful motion. Her tawny hair was piled up into an impossibly high hairdo that could only be the result of magical assistance. Rubies glittered at her ears and throat.

"My name is Ilania. I am an ambassador of her royal majesty Varia, queen of the Yew Land. My most gracious and exalted lady sends her well wishes and congratulations on such a joyous occasion."

I wasn't familiar with Varia or the Yew Land, but Ilania's presence didn't really surprise me. Probably only about a third of the guests here were actually friends or family of the happy couple. The rest were those who, knowing of my regard for Shaya and Rurik, had come to get in good with me and make a show of diplomacy and friendship. Some supported Storm King's prophecy; some didn't. Regardless, most—unless they were specifically allied with Maiwenn—wanted to make sure they weren't on my bad side.

"Thanks," I said. "That's nice of you. Both of you." I

groped for diplomatic small talk. "I hope you didn't have to travel too far?"

Ilania made a dismissive gesture, showing what nonsense that was. "No journey would be too far to send my lady's regard. In fact, she has entrusted me with this most precious gift as a sign of her friendship."

Two servants in what must be Yew uniforms appeared, carrying a statue made of a marbleized green and white stone. The statue was a little shorter than me and depicted a unicorn balancing a fish on its nose and a butterfly on its horn. Odd choice.

"Um, thank you. I'm sure Shaya and Rurik will find a great place for this in their bedroom."

"Oh, no." Ilania chuckled. "This is for you, Your Majesty. And actually, we brought two—one for each of your lands. I also have one for King Dorian, whom I'm most excited to meet. Since we don't travel here very often, we wanted to make sure to extend our friendship to as many as possible. Don't worry," she added. "Each of the statues is different. All are made of damarian jade, but we'd hardly give you all identical designs. That would be tacky."

"Right," I agreed, eyeing the unicorn and its friends. "We wouldn't want tacky." Her servants seemed restless, so I directed them inside, with instructions to find a servant of mine who would take the statue—or rather, statues— off their hands. Both my castles actually had storerooms for gifts like this. I'd learned a long time ago that even if I had no intention of displaying or using some royal gift, it was always best to keep it around in case the giver ever paid a visit.

"I can't wait to see what you offer in return," added Ilania. "I'm sure it will be lovely."

I blinked. "Er . . . I'm sorry, what?"

She laughed merrily. "Surely you know about our land's

custom? We exchange gifts to emphasize our bonds of friendships. We'll proudly display the offerings from your kingdoms, just as I know you'll display ours."

"Of course," I said, making a mental note to tell the servants to dredge up some acceptable gifts. Keeping up with gentry etiquette boggled the mind. "We'll make arrangements for you to take them when you leave."

Ilania glanced around us conspiratorially and then stepped in closer to Jasmine and me. "My most gracious queen also has another gift for you—or rather, an offer."

"Oh?" I asked carefully. The gentry loved wheeling and dealing, and I wasn't surprised that a gift and offer of friendship would come with strings attached.

Ilania nodded. "My queen knows of your . . . situation." She gave my stomach a not-so-subtle look, just in case there was any question about what my "situation" was. "As the ruler of many kingdoms, Queen Varia has no interest in the prophecy or any stake in conquering other—"

"Wait," I interrupted. "Did you say she rules other kingdoms? How many is she bound to?" Gaining control of a kingdom in the Otherworld was no small thing. A binding took place between the monarch and the land itself, one that required considerable strength on the ruler's part. It was such a great feat, in fact, that no other monarch besides me had been able to pull it off in recent history. At least, that's what I'd been told. Discovering someone who ruled an additional kingdom—multiple ones, allegedly—was huge.

"She isn't bound to them, not exactly," explained Ilania. "Rather, she rules them. Their own monarchs have agreed to become subject kingdoms to her. So, technically, those monarchs are bound to the land, but they happily acknowledge Varia as their high queen."

I glanced over at Jasmine. She looked just as surprised as I felt. I'd never heard of anything like this, a kingdom willingly subjugating itself to another. The Yew Land and its neighbors were far away from my own, so it wasn't entirely surprising that this hadn't reached me before. Still, it was odd.

Ilania seemed to take our stunned silence for awe. "With so many allies around her, my queen's territory is vast and safe. We know that you're under constant threat here—even in your own kingdom." She paused to allow a couple of soldiers to pass us, proving her point. "My queen would like to extend her hospitality to you and provide a haven in which you can safely have your children. And, in fact, if you so desired, they would be welcome to stay there afterward as long as you wished. My queen's forces and power would ensure no harm befalls them, as would the distance from your enemies."

It was true that my greatest adversaries were, unfortunately, also my close neighbors. I didn't like the rest of her implications, though. Ilania was essentially saying that my own resources weren't enough to keep me and the twins safe but that her overlord queen could.

"Why would she offer this?" I asked, again suspicious of any gentry kindness.

"My queen is also a mother and is appalled to see these constant attacks on you and the unborn. She finds them cowardly and wrong." Ilania smiled sweetly. "And, as I was saying, my lady is well content with her own lands. She has no interest in the prophecy and its promise of conquering the human world. She is, however, interested in maintaining friendly relations with another woman possessed of power and command. It's very dreary for her, having so few equals to talk to."

"I can imagine," I muttered. Around us, harried servants were trying to organize the assembled throng into some type of order. "Look, things are about to get started, so

I have to take my place. Send my thanks back to your queen, but tell her I'm happy to stay where I'm at for now. We've done a pretty good job at keeping me safe so far." Ohio adventures aside.

Ilania curtsied again. "As you wish, Your Majesty. My lady urged me to tell you, should that be your answer, that her offer will still stand if you change your mind."

I reiterated my thanks and then hurried off with Jasmine toward the front of the crowd. "That was weird," Jasmine remarked.

"The offer, not so much," I said. "Everyone's always maneuvering for position around here. But that stuff about other kingdoms? *That's* weird."

I had no time to ponder the Yew Land further because once things got going, they were going. As the presiding monarch here, I had a front-row spot. Dorian stood near me, both because of his rank and connection to the couple. They'd originally been in his service and had come to mine when I'd seized control of the Thorn Land. Other monarchs were arranged accordingly in a complex system of status that I didn't entirely follow but which wedding planners had been agonizing over for weeks. Jasmine, as my relative but not a reigning monarch, was a couple rows away. Beside me, Dorian gave me one of his rogue smiles, and it was hard not to smile back. Whatever animosity existed between us, it was easy to put aside for this occasion, particularly since almost a week had passed since our fight over Ohio. Besides, if anyone was going to be able to give me answers about the Yew Land and its subjugated kingdoms, it would be Dorian.

Gentry religion was never anything I'd managed to get much of a grasp on, particularly since my hold on human religion was already pretty loose. From what I'd learned, gentry beliefs were polytheistic and nature-oriented, with specific practices and doctrine that varied widely by region. A priest of some sort was presiding today, but I'd been told he was mostly there to lend authority as a witness and officiant and that religion would have little role in the ceremony.

Another gentry custom was made apparent as soon as the couple appeared. There was no giving-away of the bride, nor did she even walk the aisle alone. Shaya and Rurik walked together through the crowd, hand in hand, making their way to the arch of roses as equals. Few gentry even bothered with weddings, but those who did regarded them—rightfully—as occasions of great joy and didn't believe white was an appropriately cheerful color. So, Shaya wore a silk gown of deep rosy pink and had given up her usual braids to wear her long black hair loose down her back. It contrasted dramatically with Rurik's pale, blond features, but their expressions of happiness were a perfect match.

The ceremony was as short and sweet as I'd been told it would be, mostly a recitation of the couple's commitment to each other. The two of them getting together was still kind of incredible to me, seeing as they were so different. Shaya was always reserved and responsible. Rurik was arrogant and crude. Yet, somehow, they'd made it work and reached this point.

"Why, Eugenie," said Dorian, once the vows were complete and the crowd had erupted into cheers, "are you tearing up? I never took you for the sentimental type."

"No," I snapped, running a hasty hand across my eyes. "It's just hormones. They make me do stupid things."

"Right," he said, in a tone that clearly told me he didn't believe me at all.

"Your Majesties."

Shaya and Rurik stood before us, bowing low. Custom dictated that the new husband and wife present themselves to their liege lady before they could go on to their family and friends. They'd kind of rolled Dorian into the deal too since they still regarded him as their ruler to a certain extent. I thought the custom was kind of silly. Why should the couple come to us for a blessing? This was about them. We had nothing to do with it. Still, I'd long since learned not to fight against gentry etiquette and surprised Shaya with a big hug.

"I'm so happy for you," I said. She had tiny roses tucked into her hair, and their scent surrounded me. The cherry trees had increased their petal production—through magic, no doubt—so that they rained down around us like confetti. "You look beautiful."

"Thank you," she said, flushing under the praise.

To the surprise of both of us, I hugged Rurik too. "I'm even happy for you. Though I'm not entirely sure you deserve her," I teased.

He nodded. "That makes two of us."

"I wish you many years of joy and fertility," said Dorian, with a genuine expression of pleasure on his face. He always wore a smirk of some sort, so these moments of pure, legitimate delight were rare.

"Are you guys going on any kind of honeymoon?" I asked, realizing it was something I probably should've found out long before this. So much emphasis had been put on preparing for the wedding and its security that I'd never really thought much past today. My question was met with three puzzled looks.

"Honeymoon, Your Majesty?" asked Shaya, clearly unfamiliar with the word.

I was surprised by their surprise. "Er, yeah. It's like a trip . . . a trip you take after you get married. You go away somewhere on a vacation, for a week or two."

"To what end?" asked Dorian with a small, curious frown.

I shrugged. "Well. So you can get away and be alone and . . . well . . . you know . . ."

Understanding flooded their faces. Shaya shook her head. "We're in wartime, Your Majesty. We could hardly dream of doing anything so frivolous."

Typical gentry. They had no problem getting hot and heavy in public, but the idea of a private, romantic getaway was "frivolous."

"Besides," added Rurik with a wink, "why do we need to leave? Plenty of places to do it around here. And in the Thorn Land."

"Ugh," I said, after they'd strolled away. "How in the world did he win her over?"

Dorian chuckled. "Well, I daresay he won you over too. You weren't his biggest admirer when you met."

"That's for damned sure," I said. "But there's a difference between simply learning to get along with someone and vowing to spend the rest of your life with them."

"The way I see it, you can't have one without the other."

"That makes no sense," I countered.

"Love rarely does. It's a magic beyond any in this world." I rolled my eyes, and he extended his arm to me. "Shall we see what delights lie in store among the refreshments? Surely there's something there that even human medicine will allow you to consume."

The mood was too festive for me to give him a hard time, so I let him lead me across the grounds, which wasn't easy. Everyone passing by had something to say to us, whether it was simple congratulations or outright declarations of fealty. We had to carry on our conversation in pieces.

"Have you found another human doctor you can see?" Dorian asked me. "In a new and secure location?"

"Not yet," I said. His wording wasn't lost on me. He'd phrased it as a given, rather than chiding me for what he thought was a foolish errand, as he had last time. I knew it was a great concession for him, and I was willing to give something back. "Honestly, I'm not sure I should. Everything's been going so well . . . with the pregnancy, that is. Like you were saying, whatever help a human doctor can give me might be undone by the dangers I'm risking by venturing out of my kingdoms."

Dorian nodded thoughtfully, with no hint of an I-told-you-so attitude. "Well, you'll choose what's best, I'm sure. Perhaps Roland might be able to suggest something when he next visits."

"Perhaps," I agreed. My gaze drifted to the opposite side of the courtyard, and I felt a smile grow. "And I know Pagiel will go with me anywhere and defend my honor."

Dorian followed where I was looking. Pagiel, bright and full of energy, was holding onto Jasmine's hands and trying to coax her into a dance. Gentry musicians had appeared in a corner and struck up a tune that had many skipping food for dancing. She kept shaking her head, but even I recognized the coy look of someone playing hard-to-get. It was obvious she secretly enjoyed his attentions.

"It doesn't bother you?" Dorian asked.

"Nah," I said as we finally reached the food. "He's a good kid, and at least he's relatively close to her age. Besides, now that I've claimed the honor, I don't have to worry about her getting pregnant first." When I'd first met Jasmine, she'd been involved with a gentry king named Aeson and dead-set on fulfilling our father's prophecy. She, like Rurik, was someone who'd undergone a change for the better.

I meant to ask Dorian about the Yew Land, but the opportunity never really presented itself. Aside from being distracted by those constantly coming up to talk to us, we were also just caught up in the festivities themselves. Both of my kingdoms, as well as Dorian's, had been living in a tense state these last few months, and it was nice to have a break from that. I laughed and cheered with the others when Rurik brought Shaya out onto the dance floor and spun her around. I watched Jasmine and Pagiel flirt with youthful innocence. I even drank some sort of sweet nectar, which the chef had sworn to me wasn't alcoholic. It was served in goblets constructed from tulips, reminding me not for the first time that my life really was a fairy tale— just not always a happy one.

Dorian admired the happy, dancing couples and then gave me a knowing look. "I suppose I'd be wasting my time asking you to dance?"

"You'd have more luck with one of the horses," I said.

He chuckled. "You're smaller than you think, and besides, you keep forgetting how beautiful fertility is to us— not like humans, who seem ashamed of it. You've spent too much time among them."

"That's an understatement," I teased. "I've spent most of my life with them. I can't help but think like a human."

"I know," he said with mock sadness. "It's a habit I keep hoping you'll shake."

I refused Dorian's further invitations to dance, but later, in watching him twirl around with other women, I realized the recent tension wasn't just between our kingdoms. Whether it was my resentment over how he'd tricked me into winning the Iron Crown or simply disputes over how best to protect my twins, it seemed that Dorian and I had been bickering nonstop. It was nice to have just one evening where we were at peace with each other. I was reminded—almost—of how things used to be, back when we were a couple.

It was after midnight when I finally retired from the celebration. Enchanted fireflies had replaced the cherry petals, illuminating those revelers who were still going strong. I slipped away without any big good-byes because I'd learned a long time ago that once you started with one, many more would follow, and it'd be hours before I'd actually get to bed. So, really, only my guards noticed my exit, several of them detaching and following me inside the castle.

When I reached my rooms, I saw that some helpful servant had placed Ilania's statues in there, maybe in case I wanted to decorate with them. Along with the unicorn statue I'd seen earlier, there was also one comprised of five fish balanced gracefully on top of each other. I would have that one sent off to the Thorn Land, since it seemed ironic for a desert kingdom. Tomorrow would be soon enough to put the other statue in storage here, as well as give me the chance to ask Dorian about the Yew Land since I was certain he was staying over tonight. I'd also have to make sure Varia got her token gifts. So much to do, but I was too exhausted to deal with any of it just yet.

Thinking of Dorian reminded me of a comment he'd made. Even though I was ready to fall over, I delayed a moment to summon Volusian to me. The room, which had moments ago been warm and cheery in the summer evening, grew cold and sinister. Volusian appeared in the darkest corner, his eyes glowing red.

"My mistress calls," he said, in his flat tone.

I stifled a yawn and sat on the bed, suddenly feeling smothered by the long dress. "I need you to go to Roland whenever he's up in the morning. Ask him to come see me here when he gets time. Emphasis on the 'when he gets time,'" I warned. The last time I'd sent Volusian with a request to my stepfather, the spirit had simply said, "You must come now." Roland had practically killed himself trying to get to the Otherworld, certain my death was imminent. With Volusian, one had to be specific.

"As my mistress commands," he replied. "Is there anything else?"

"Nope. That's—"

"*What* is that?"

I stared in astonishment, not so much because of the

question itself, but because I could probably count on one hand the number of times Volusian had ever interrupted me. He tended to adhere to his servitude tenaciously (so long as my power was there to hold him) and rarely offered up anything that wasn't asked of him. Equally rare was him soliciting information that wasn't essential to his tasks. It was his way of showing how little he cared about me and my affairs.

"What's what?" I asked, glancing around.

He pointed at the two statues. "Those," he declared, "are damarian jade."

I thought back to my conversation with Ilania. "Er, yeah, I think that's what she called it."

"She?" he demanded. "Who is *she*? And is she here?"

"The ambassador from the Yew Land," I said, still kind of amazed by this conversation. "She's here on behalf of her queen, Varia."

"Varia," he repeated. "She must be Ganene's daughter." There was something chilling about the way he said *Ganene*. The word dripped with venom.

"I wouldn't know," I said. "They just brought me the statues and made an offer of friendship."

"Yes, I'm sure they would," he replied enigmatically. "They excel at that."

I stood up. "Volusian, what do you know about them? Do you know how they've got all these subjugated kingdoms?"

"Subjugated kingdoms? No, but it seems like a reasonable idea, mistress. One you might consider." Volusian had calmed back down to his dry self, if he'd ever truly been upset. It was hard to tell with him.

"Have you been there?" I asked. "To the Yew Land?"

"Not in many, many centuries, mistress."

"But you have been there."

"Yes, mistress."

"What do you know about Varia?"

"I do not know her at all, mistress. As I said, I have not been in the Yew Land for many centuries. Much has undoubtedly changed in that wretched place." His red eyes flicked toward the statues. "Except for their abhorrent taste in art. If my mistress has need, I would gladly destroy those monstrosities and blight their unsightliness from her gaze."

"Very kind. Why do you hate the Yew Land so much?" Before he could answer, another question came to mind. "Volusian, are you *from* the Yew Land?"

He took a long time in responding. I think, had he been able, he wouldn't have answered. The binds that held him were too strong, however.

"Yes, mistress."

He offered no more. I could've grilled him further but thought better of it. Volusian was an old, old spirit. Maybe he was from the Yew Land, but by his own admission, he hadn't been there in recent times, nor did he know Varia. My guess was whatever animosity he held toward that kingdom predated her and was probably of little use to me. What intrigued me, though, was that I had my first real piece of background about Volusian. I'd always known he had done something terrible that had resulted in him being cursed to wander the worlds without peace. I now had a good idea of where his troubles may have started.

"Is there anything else, mistress?" he asked when I remained quiet.

"Huh?" I'd been lost in my own thoughts. "Oh, no. That's it for now."

Volusian nodded in acquiescence, then began to fade into darkness. For a moment, only his red eyes seemed to remain, but then they too disappeared in the shadows.

Chapter 4

Life soon returned to whatever passed as normal in my
world. The many guests and visitors who'd arrived for the
wedding dispersed to their own lands, and true to their
word, Shaya and Rurik continued their duties just as before.
There was little outward sign that much had changed with
them, though occasionally I'd catch them secretly exchang-
ing happy looks.

One guest who didn't leave right away was Dorian. He
kept saying he would. He'd even make comments that
began with, "Well, when I leave tomorrow . . ." But the next
day he'd still be hanging around the Rowan Land. Almost
a week went by before I finally brought the matter up.

I found him out in some of the woods beyond the castle.
While this was still fairly secured land, I was nonetheless
trailed by quiet, discreet guards who kept a distance that
was respectful but still close enough to pounce, should
the need arise. Dorian was engaged in a typically Dorian
activity: hunting. Well, kind of. The forest clearing was
littered with thin, wooden cutouts of various animals.
They were life-size and painted in bright, gaudy colors.
As I approached, I saw Dorian's long-suffering servant,

Muran, nervously holding up a cutout of a pink stag. On the opposite side of the clearing, Dorian focused on them with razor-sharp intensity and drew back a giant longbow. There was a *twang* as he released, and the arrow shot forward, implanting right near the edge of the target's upper body, only a couple of inches from Muran's hand.

"Isn't that kind of dangerous?" I asked.

"Hardly," said Dorian, notching another arrow. "Those animals aren't real, Eugenie."

"Yeah, I know," I said. "The purple polka dots were kind of a giveaway. I was talking about Muran."

Dorian shrugged. "He's still alive, isn't he?" He drew back again, and this time the arrow hit the side of the stag's head, not far from Muran's own. The poor man yelped at the close call, and Dorian gave me an expectant look. "See?"

I had to suppress an eye roll. Those targets were too big and Dorian too good a shot for him to be "accidentally" making such close calls. It was a testament to his skill that he was purposely hitting so near the edges to torment Muran.

"Let's do the rabbit next," suggested Dorian. "I need more of a challenge."

"Y-yes, sire," squeaked Muran. He returned the stag to the pile of other targets and produced a yellow and green striped rabbit that was much, much smaller than the stag. After first pausing to wipe sweat off of his forehead, Muran held out the rabbit off to his side, as far away from himself as he could.

Dorian tsked. "You're tilting it. Use both hands to keep it steady." Doing so, of course, forced Muran to bring the target directly in front of him.

I groaned. "Dorian, why do you do this?"

"Because I can," he replied. He let loose an arrow and

impressively hit one of the rabbit's ears, again only just missing Muran.

"When do you think you might be able to go home?" I asked.

He didn't even look at me as he sized up his next shot. "Are you kicking me out?"

"No, but I do have to go to the Thorn Land soon and commune with it." As part of the bond between monarch and kingdom, it was necessary that I connect to the land periodically. This usually just involved me meditating for a while and reaching out to the land's energy. It was a seemingly small task, but if I didn't do it regularly, both the land and I would suffer. The longest I'd gone without was about a month, and during that time, I'd dreamed nonstop about the land. Possessing two kingdoms now meant twice as many meditation sessions.

"I'm surprised you don't just send your sister," Dorian said. "Seeing as she's getting so good at it."

"Oh, don't start," I said.

I was in a good mood, and the atmosphere between us had been so easy recently that I didn't even rise to the bait. Jasmine and I had discovered that as a quick fix, she could do a type of makeshift connection with the land. Someone had told me that monarchs' children occasionally did this as well in other kingdoms, so maybe the land just recognized some sort of genetic connection. Dorian feared I was opening up the door for Jasmine to conquer my kingdoms, but I was confident she'd long since given up such ambitions. Besides, I'd felt the connection between her and the land when she did it, and it was nothing like what I experienced. The land accepted her as a Band-Aid in my absence but never truly let her into its heart like it did for me. The land was always grateful for my return, and I too pined for it when gone.

"You know it's better if I do it myself," I told him. "And

if I'm right around the corner, there's no reason not to. I mean, you're welcome to stay here if you want, I just thought . . ."

". . . that if you were leaving, there'd be no reason I'd *want* to stay?" he suggested.

I shrugged. That was *exactly* what I'd been thinking, and I now felt a little embarrassed at my presumption. For all I knew, Dorian just liked the change of scenery. I'd given him no reason to want to spend extra time with me.

"Perhaps you're right," he said, hitting the rabbit's tail. "Perhaps I should return home. It'll be harvest time soon."

That brought a smile to my face. "It's *always* harvest time." One of the perks of the Oak Land's perpetual autumn was that trees and plants that normally only bore fruit late in the year were always producing. I'd seen servants pick all the apples from the trees surrounding his castle, only to find those same trees heavy with fruit again in a couple of days.

"Yes, yes, but my people fall apart without me. You'd think they would've learned to manage after all this time, but it's still quite dreadful." He finally lowered his bow and glanced at me. "You want to take a shot?"

I shook my head. "That bow's too big for me. Besides, I don't really get off on shooting animals—even fake ones."

"That's preposterous. You eat them, don't you?"

"Yeah, but there's a difference between killing them for survival and killing them for sport. I know, I know," I added, seeing him start to protest. "These aren't real, but the resemblance is close enough that when I look at them, it's still like taking joy in real animals' deaths."

Dorian looked over to where one of his personal guards stood ready and alert. "Alik, would you remedy this situation? Use the stag, please."

Alik bowed. "Of course, Your Majesty." He strode over to the pink stag and, to my complete astonishment, began hacking away at the stag's neck with his sword. It had the effectiveness of an ax, making me think there must be some magic afoot. That'd be a difficult task with a regular sword, let alone the copper kind favored by the gentry. When Alik completed his work, we were left with a decapitated wooden pink stag.

"There we go," said Dorian, pleased. "It hardly looks real now. Is that better?"

"I don't really know how to answer that," I replied.

Dorian beckoned me over. "Come, I'll help you draw the bow. It's a noble weapon that any good queen should know how to use, regardless of intent."

To my own surprise, I complied, letting him guide my hands to hold the bow in proper position. I'd practiced with smaller bows around here—it was unavoidable in the Otherworld—but nothing resembling this beast. Dorian stood behind me, one hand on my hip and the other on my arm to keep me in the right position.

"Muran," he said. "Prop our headless deer friend against that maple, will you? Then keep an eye on it from over there to make sure it stays upright."

If Muran ever had any fears about his master's regard for him, they were wasted. As I'd suspected before, Dorian's skill was such that his "close calls" with Muran had never truly been any threat. But me and my lack of expertise? We were a different matter—and a dangerous one that could result in Muran actually losing a limb if he held the target again. Dorian was now ensuring his servant stayed out of harm's way.

With Dorian's guidance, I drew back the bow. No, not guidance, exactly. Dorian was actually doing a lot of the work. This would have been a tough draw for me under the best of times, and my recent reduction in physical activity had only made me weaker. I let the arrow go, and it hit the ground before even getting close to the target. My second shot didn't do much better. By the third, my arm felt like it was ready to fall off, and I was just getting frustrated.

"Patience, my sweet," Dorian told me. "This is just something that takes practice."

"All the practice in the world won't help," I grumbled, feeling petulant. "Not so long as I'm incapacitated."

Dorian snorted. "You? Hardly. Now, that deer, yes, he's incapacitated. But I recall seeing you dispatch some wraiths a couple weeks ago. Anyone who witnessed that, including those miserable creatures, would hardly say you were incapacitated."

"I *was* kind of badass," I admitted, lowering the bow. "I just don't have much patience for this . . . state I'm in." Apparently, "state" would continue to be the best way to describe my pregnancy.

"That 'state' will be over before you know it." Dorian took the bow from me and passed it off to a servant. "And until then, you're much more capable of things than you give yourself credit for. Once your little world-conquering bundles of joy are born, we'll train you up to be the best bow-woman in this world."

His bravado made me smile again, and I felt a little silly for my whining. Hopefully, it was just more I could blame on hormones. Inspiration hit me, and I straightened up proudly. "I don't need lessons. I'm already the best shot in this world. And in the others."

Dorian arched an eyebrow. "Oh?"

I glanced over at my fallen arrows and summoned the air currents around them. The air was quick to obey me and lifted the arrows off the ground. One quick motion, and they shot off toward the stag like rockets, embedding themselves in what would have been the poor creature's heart.

"Magnificent," laughed Dorian, clapping his hands. "You really are a natural."

I returned his grin, delighted with my triumph and with . . . well, this. This small moment out in the sunny spring day. This small moment . . . with him. I met his eyes, momentarily caught up in the shades of green that played throughout them, rivaling the leaves that gently rustled around us.

"Eugenie?"

Whatever else might have passed in that moment was lost as I turned and saw Roland Markham approaching with a group of Rowan soldiers. Dorian was forgotten as I hurried over and hugged my stepfather.

"Your Majesty," said one of the soldiers. "Roland Storm Slayer is here."

"So I see," I said. If there was anyone the gentry regarded with as much awe as the mother of Storm King's heir, it was Roland. He had rescued my mother when she'd been abducted to the Otherworld. Later, when Storm King came seeking her and me, Roland had finally put an end to my biological father once and for all. Killing the Otherworld's most powerful, notorious warlord in recent history earned a lot of respect—and wariness. Roland was oblivious to it all, however. In truth, he disliked coming to the Otherworld and had vowed never to return after rescuing my mother. It was only because of me and the dangers I now faced crossing worlds that he had consented to come back. He was incredibly uneasy each time he did, though, and his own nerves distracted him too much to see the nervousness in others here.

"You look good," Roland said, giving me a head-to-toe assessment. He would never let on to it in front of everyone else, but I knew he was checking me for scrapes and bruises the same as he would if I was ten years old. Whenever he was in the Otherworld, he also had a tendency to ignore everyone else and only talk to me.

"So do you," I said. Roland had gone gray but was still lean and muscled, ready for anything that came his way. Tattoos of whorls and fishes adorned his arms, and I took comfort in their familiarity.

"Your, uh, creature said you wanted to talk to me?"

"I do." Glancing around, I saw that between my soldiers, Dorian's guards, and Roland's escort, we'd gathered quite a crowd. Dorian followed my gaze and guessed my thoughts.

"Perhaps we should go inside where we can speak more privately," he said, automatically inviting himself along. A glint of surprise flashed in Roland's eyes, but there was no real reason Dorian couldn't hear what was being discussed.

"I went to your other place first," Roland told me as we walked toward the castle. "The guards there explained where you were at and brought me here." I couldn't help a smile at his use of "your other place." The idea of me being a queen was still unsettling for Roland, and he couldn't quite bring himself to say "your kingdom."

"Then you're fortunate," said Dorian. "This is a much more pleasant land to meet in than that desert wasteland Eugenie usually prefers to spend her time in."

Roland glanced around, taking in the lush greenery, warm breezes, and singing birds. "I don't know," he said. "I think I like the other one better. This one's kind of boring."

"Typical," scoffed Dorian. "Like father, like daughter."

Roland wouldn't admit as much in mixed company, but I knew the comment pleased him. If things hadn't turned out as they had with my Otherworldly involvement, Roland would've been content to ignore my biological heritage for the rest of my life. Blood and the Storm King prophecy meant nothing to him. I had been Roland's daughter for years, and as far as he was concerned, that's how it still was.

The three of us sat down in a small parlor that still bore

the signs of its previous owner's taste in decorating, mainly a lot of doilies and paisley prints. Being "trapped" indoors made Roland uneasy, and he shifted uncomfortably, literally on the edge of his lion-footed velvet chair. Quickly, I explained to him what had happened in Ohio. As he listened, his face grew darker, and all his discomfort at being behind gentry walls faded as his concern shifted to me.

"Damn," he muttered. "I'd had such a good feeling about that one too. How did they find it? There's no way they can have spies in every part of our world."

"They're pretty good at having spies everywhere in *this* world," I pointed out. "We know they regularly watch the borders of my kingdoms—and Dorian's—to track my movements. I'm just usually too well guarded for them to do anything. My guess is someone tracked me to the gate that led to Hudson, and from there, they just staked the town out until they figured out my patterns." It still irked me that pulling that off was something Mainwenn and Kiyo's spies would've had to have done over a long period of time—and I'd never noticed.

"So we need to find another doctor," said Roland. I could already see the wheels spinning in his head as he assessed various locations and what he knew of their Otherworldly connections.

"Well, that's up for debate," interjected Dorian. "These human doctors keep telling her she's fine and healthy. Why does she need to keep seeing them then?"

"To ensure she stays healthy," said Roland evenly. "No offense, but I'm not leaving her in the hands of your medieval medicine."

"I doubt Eugenie appreciates the thought of any of us making decisions for her." That almost made me scoff. Dorian was notorious for making "helpful" decisions on my behalf, so it was comical that he'd now take the high ground about my independence.

"Enough," I said. "Both of you. Dorian has a point— I *have* been getting healthy reports. But . . . it's hard for me to entirely let go of modern medicine."

"'Modern' indeed," said Dorian dismissively.

"Easy enough to talk healthy now," said Roland. "But childbirth's an entirely different matter. You'll want our doctors then. You don't know what can happen."

"Given birth to lots of children, have you?" asked Dorian.

"What's your infant mortality rate around here?" returned Roland. I saw Dorian flinch ever so slightly. Once they were adults, gentry were extremely healthy and hard to kill. Infants were another matter, and that—coupled with the difficulties gentry had conceiving—made having children in general pretty difficult.

"It's irrelevant if she gets herself killed with all this world crossing!" exclaimed Dorian in a rare show of frustration. "If she stays put here and doesn't venture out of her lands, she'll be safe."

I could see Roland starting to get almost as worked up as Dorian. "Putting aside the medical part for a moment, she's hardly safe with her enemies right on her doorstep. Even if she is in her own 'lands,' how long do you think those bastards will leave her alone once they realize she's holing up here?" The "right on her doorstep" part reminded me of Ilania's invitation to the Yew Land and arguments about how I'd be safer once I wasn't actually sharing borders with Maiwenn. I had no intention of accepting that invitation, but Roland's words still drove home the same truth. Staying here might not be wise either.

I expected Dorian to come back with one of his stinging remarks and escalate things further with Roland. It was simply Dorian's nature, plus this was an issue he felt passionately about. I was about to silence them both when Dorian took a deep breath and said, "Look, I don't want to pick a fight with you. I respect you too much, and at the heart of this, our goals are the same. We both just want her safe."

Roland's blue eyes narrowed as he sized Dorian up. I caught my breath, wondering what Roland's response would be. Agreeing with a gentry was not his normal operating procedure.

"Agreed," Roland said at last. "We do want the same thing. Arguing methods is counterproductive."

I exhaled and stared at both men in astonishment. Contrary Dorian and stubborn Roland . . . in agreement? If not for the fact that threats on my life were the source of their accord, I would've reveled in this as a landmark moment of gentry and human peace. Unsurprisingly, this tranquil interlude couldn't last. Guards burst into the room, with Pagiel right beside them. It was almost a repeat of last week at Dorian's, and I half expected Ysabel to be in tow, ready with some new bitchy comment. Pagiel's expression told me, however, that something much direr was at stake.

"What's wrong?" Dorian and I asked in unison.

Pagiel's face grew grim, and I had a feeling he was trying very hard to behave in a calm and controlled manner. A glint in his eye suggested his outrage was so great that he just wanted to burst out with it. "Ansonia," he said.

I cast a quick, questioning glance at Dorian to see if this made any sense to him. His puzzled look said he was just as much in the dark as I was. Pagiel's sister had left shortly after the wedding, and I'd hardly talked to her while she was here.

"What about her?" I asked.

"She was attacked this morning by Willow Land riders on the outskirts of the Oak Land, on her way to see our grandmother."

That got Dorian's attention. He leaned forward. "The Oak Land? *My* Oak Land?" As if there was any other.

"Was she alone?" I asked.

Dorian stood up, his face as furious as Pagiel's. "It's irrelevant. Alone or not, a young girl should be able to ride the length and breadth of my kingdom without feeling threatened by any brigand—let alone militants from another kingdom! Maiwenn has gone too far. This is an act of war! This is—"

"Is the girl okay?" asked Roland, his quiet voice cutting through Dorian's outrage. At first, Dorian looked offended at the interruption, but then he—like me—seemed to realize that we all probably should've asked that immediately.

Pagiel nodded and took another steadying breath before continuing. "She's with a healer now and is recovering. Maiwenn's people beat her up pretty badly but were interrupted when some passing merchants noticed what was happening. By that point, the attackers realized they'd made a mistake and were ready to flee anyway."

Something twisted in the pit of my stomach. "What do you mean 'made a mistake'? What was their intent?"

Pagiel's face was still hard and angry, but I was pretty sure I caught the faintest glimpse of apology in his eyes at what he had to say next. "They had no actual interest in her personally, Your Majesty. They attacked her because . . . because they thought she was you."

Chapter 5

Whatever look came over my face, it was enough to finally crack Pagiel's anger. He blanched and hurried forward, falling to his knees. "Your Majesty, I'm sorry. I shouldn't have said anything—"

"No, no," I said, putting out a hand to stop him. "Don't apologize. You didn't do anything wrong." His words had stunned me, making everything I said and did sluggish. I felt as if I were moving underwater.

Dorian gave me a sharp look. "Neither did you."

"How can you say that?" I exclaimed. "That poor girl was beaten because of me!"

"Not because of you. Because of *them*. Although . . ." He shrugged, his expression considering. "When I think about it, I suppose there is a remarkable resemblance between the two of you. An easy—if stupid—mistake."

"That doesn't help," I grumbled. "Not one bit. All that means is that every girl in our kingdoms with hair like mine now needs to watch her back."

"They were fools to do this," declared Dorian. "Not just because of the violation of my land, but also because they should've known you wouldn't travel alone. If any one of them had half a brain, they would've deduced right away that they had the wrong girl."

"And yet that changes nothing." I sighed and turned back to where a worried Pagiel still knelt before me. "Get up," I told him. "Where is she now? You said she was with a healer. In the Oak Land?"

Pagiel got to his feet. "Yes, Your Majesty."

"I should go see her," I murmured, more to myself than anyone else.

Dorian scoffed. "Oh, yes. That will certainly improve the situation. Go take a jaunt between kingdoms. Expose yourself to more risk."

My temper flared. "What else do you expect me to—" I bit my lip on any other angry protests as I reminded myself we had an audience. Swallowing back all the things I wanted to say to Dorian, I attempted to put on as calm a look as I could for Pagiel. "I'm very sorry this happened to Ansonia. I can't promise immediate retribution for it, but I can promise you it won't ever happen again."

Pagiel nodded, his face growing fierce once more. "I understand. But if you do strike back at some point—"

"Then you can definitely be part of it," I finished, guessing what he was going to ask. I didn't like to encourage revenge, especially in someone so young, but he was certainly entitled to his outrage. "We'll let you know. In the meantime, go back to Ansonia. If there's anything she needs, anything at all, just have her ask Dorian's staff and they'll take care of it." I felt no moral qualms about speaking for Dorian, especially since he ordered my own people around half the time too.

"Thank you, Your Majesty." Pagiel glanced at Dorian. "Your Majesties. I believe my mother is, uh, already working with the servants to ensure Ansonia is comfortable."

Oh, I didn't doubt that in the least. A pang of regret struck me as I recalled that last antagonistic meeting with

Ysabel. I'd been semi-sympathetic to her concerns for Pagiel but had mostly treated her as though she was behaving in a hysterical and exaggerated manner. Whatever she was doing now, no one could accuse her of overreacting. Her daughter's life had been wrongfully threatened.

After a few more conciliatory words from us, Pagiel and the guards who'd entered with him finally left. Once I was alone with Dorian and Roland again, I stood up to walk off my frustration. I paused at the room's window, looking out at the idyllic green grounds below. The Rowan Land looked more like a fairyland than ever before when seen from afar. One didn't notice all the danger and turmoil from this high up.

"Don't beat yourself up, my dear," said Dorian, watching me pace. "There's nothing you could've done. The question is: what are you going to do *now*?"

I glanced back at him in alarm. "What are *you* going to do? You weren't serious about this being an act of war, were you? I mean, we're already kind of at war, but there's no need for some drastic retaliation."

"There's need for *something* drastic," countered Dorian. "Really, Pagiel's interruption follows quite nicely on the heels of what we'd just been discussing. They have us running and slinking in the shadows. Are you really going to do this for the rest of your pregnancy? Are you going to do this *after* your children are born?"

I threw up my hands. "What else is there to do? Are you proposing some invasion of Maiwenn's land?"

Dorian looked remarkably calm, considering the topic. "It wouldn't be unfounded. And it would certainly send a message that they can't keep pushing us around. I don't suppose it's occurred to you that maybe attacking young Ansonia *wasn't* a mistake on their part?"

"What would make you say that?" I came back over to

stand in front of him. Roland watched our exchange in silence. "She has nothing to do with any of this."

"Exactly," said Dorian. "And the next girl attacked won't either. Or the next."

I could hardly believe what I was hearing. "You're saying they're purposely attacking girls who look like me? Even though they know it's in error?"

"I'm not saying for sure that's what they're doing. But it would be an excellent ploy to turn your—our—own people against us, if they feel they're being unjustly targeted."

"Sending our people to war would put a *lot* more of them in danger," I pointed out. Five years ago, I never would have dreamed I'd be having these sorts of discussions.

"Yes," said Dorian. "But danger's a lot easier to face when you're initiating it on your terms, as opposed to exposing yourself to victimization."

"They already went to war once for me. I'm not going to let it happen again," I said adamantly. Last year, Leith— the former Rowan queen's son—had taken it upon himself to become the father of Storm King's heir, whether I consented or not. During my rescue, Dorian had then taken it upon himself to punish Leith—by impaling the prince on a sword. Katrice hadn't taken that news well, starting a war between us that had eventually led to me inheriting this kingdom. I'd hated every minute of that war and had been wracked with guilt over the thought of soldiers dying for me, no matter how many times I'd been assured that my people were willing to defend my honor.

Dorian's look wasn't unsympathetic, but it wasn't exactly warm and friendly either. "War may be on you again, whether you like it or not."

"Enough," I said, raking a hand through my hair. "I don't want to talk about the nobility of war anymore. Ansonia survived, which is what counts. We'll deal with the rest later."

"Don't put it off too long," Dorian warned. "Or you may find others making decisions for you."

"I know," I said.

What I didn't add was that I had no intention of letting any more decisions be made without me, nor would I allow any other girls to be hurt on my behalf. An idea was forming in the back of my mind, one I was pretty sure Dorian wouldn't like. It created a hollow feeling inside me, but from the moment Pagiel had told us about Ansonia, I'd known I had to take drastic action—and not the kind Dorian was suggesting. The answer was so simple, I couldn't believe it had never occurred to me before. With an expression as convincingly bland as one of Dorian's, I glanced over at Roland. "Let's go figure out where my next doctor's going to be. At least that's a relatively simple matter."

Dorian scoffed. "A foolish matter, you mean." But he made no attempts to go with Roland and me, just as I'd thought. He and Roland did exchange very nice, very polite farewells, which I took as a positive sign, considering their past interactions. I wondered how polite things would stay between them if the plan I was formulating actually came to pass.

"Nasty business back there," said Roland, speaking up at last. We were almost to the castle's exit, and I think he felt more at ease now that he was nearly free of the walls. "No easy answers."

"No," I agreed.

"How old is this girl you were talking about?"

"A little younger than her brother. That's Pagiel—the one you just saw." I didn't bother correcting for the rate at which gentry aged compared to humans. Roland would understand.

"There's a dirty feel to all of it," said Roland. He

scowled. "Attacking pregnant women, attacking children. I wish you weren't involved in any of it."

We passed through the gates, back toward the lush grounds that had held the wedding. Two guards silently detached from a group near the door and followed me, keeping that respectful distance they excelled at.

"That makes two of us," I said. "Unfortunately, I'm not just involved—I'm at the heart of it."

I led us out to a cluster of hazel trees and settled down there on the grass. Roland looked surprised at the choice but quickly joined me. The guards, assessing the situation, chose sentry spots that maintained my privacy but would allow them quick access should a bunch of monkey assassins sent by Maiwenn leap down from the trees. Satisfied the guards were out of earshot, I leaned close to Roland and pitched my voice low, just to be safe. As my hands rested on the sun-warmed grass, I felt the Rowan Land sing to me, happy and content.

"I hate to admit it, but Dorian's right about a couple of things. It seems crazy, but this could become a regular tactic of Maiwenn's. And he's also right that me jumping between kingdoms and worlds just exposes me to further attacks." I tipped my head back, taking in the scent of honeysuckle. I couldn't see it from where I sat, but my senses were always attuned to the land's various stimuli. "I was recently approached by an ambassador from a far-off kingdom, who invited me to come hide out with them. They promised security. Their argument was that I'd be away from my enemies' lands and could avoid all the crisscrossing if I just stayed in seclusion within their borders."

Roland's gray eyebrows rose. "And you're thinking of doing that?"

"No," I said. "Certainly not with them, at least. I was thinking . . . I was thinking that maybe the place where I really need to hide and stay put is in the human world." The full weight of it didn't really hit me until I spoke those words. From Roland's expression, I could tell that he understood what a huge thing this was that I was suggesting.

"So not in Tucson," he said, after several thoughtful moments.

"Not in Tucson," I agreed, not entirely able to hide my regret over that. "It'd be the first place they'd look. But I have to assume that somewhere, in all the safe places you've come up with for medical care . . . well, somewhere there must be a place where I could hide and live a 'normal' life until the twins are born."

He nodded slowly. "I can think of a couple of places, but if you did this . . . I mean, don't get me wrong. There's nothing I'd like better than to get you out of this cursed place. But do you know what you're truly asking? If you want to hide out back in our world, then you can't do anything that would risk detection. You can't use your gentry magic. You can't even use your shamanic magic. Any of that could alert some Otherworldly creature wandering our world."

"I know that," I said. That hollow feeling within me intensified.

A faint smile lit his features. "I know you do—in theory. What I worry about is that you're going to stumble across some poor person being tormented by a ghost and do a banishing without thinking twice. It's not easy for you to stand by while others suffer." He gestured around us. "Case in point."

I stared off, knowing he was right. Could I do what I was proposing? Without me realizing it, my hand had moved protectively to my stomach. I could do it for them, I decided. I could do it for all the innocents in Dorian's kingdom and my own. Better to ignore a haunting, I thought, than to allow others to die for a prophecy that probably wasn't even real.

I took a deep breath. "I understand. I'll do it—or rather, not do anything."

Roland studied me for a few more seconds and seemed satisfied with what he saw. "What about all of this? Don't you need to have some kind of regular bonding with this place . . . and the other one?"

"I do," I said. "And that's probably going to be the trickiest part here. Jasmine can do a few quick fixes to tide the land over. I don't know how long the land will accept her, though. If it can't . . . then, well, I'll have to come back or else I'll have caused suffering of a different type. The land will wither otherwise. But, if she and the land can manage it until the end of my pregnancy, I'll just be the only one who suffers. Being away from the land affects me too."

"I don't like the sound of that," he said darkly.

I smiled. "Don't worry. It's nothing physical or dangerous . . . just an intense longing. Like caffeine withdrawal."

He didn't look convinced. "I doubt it's that simple."

"Maybe not," I agreed. "But what about the rest? You said you've got a few places in mind that I could go?"

"I do, though I'll need to make some queries first." In a rare show of affection, he rested his hand on mine. "I wish I could just take you home with me. I'd feel better if you were always in my sight."

I squeezed his hand back. "Even you couldn't take on a gentry army knocking on your door. And we can't risk Mom." I didn't add that if this plan worked out, Roland couldn't see me at all. Wherever I ended up hiding, I'd have to stay there with no connection to my loved ones. Roland and my mother would undoubtedly be watched. Meeting his blue eyes, I knew he'd already thought of this. He didn't like it, but he'd agree to it.

After a bit more discussion, Roland was ready to leave and begin his search. That was his way. If there was a problem to be solved, he didn't want to delay. He wanted to get right on it and take care of business. Now that we'd reached this decision, he was anxious to get me out of the Otherworld and into safety. Once he left, it was time for me to begin my own preparations, starting with the most important piece—Jasmine.

I found her in a nearby rose garden, curled up on a bench with some magazines she'd procured from a recent trip to the human world. After first swearing her to secrecy, I explained the plan Roland and I had concocted. Her reaction wasn't what I'd expected.

"Take me with you," she said immediately.

"I can't," I said. "That's the whole point. I need you here. You're the only person who can cover for me."

"I'm the only one who can really protect you out there," she insisted. After a moment, she made a small concession. "Well, maybe Pagiel too."

I had to work hard to keep my face serious. It was almost cute how she was convinced that out of all the powerful gentry around here, many capable of miraculous feats, only two teenagers could adequately watch over me.

"He can't come. No one I know can, that's the point. I can't even tell anyone where I'm going."

"That's bullshit," she said. The profanity was an amusing contrast to her otherwise ladylike appearance, complete with a flowing ivory gown and flower-bedecked hair. "How will we know you're okay?"

"You won't, but if we can maintain obscurity and anonymity, you can be ninety-nine percent sure I'm fine."

She didn't like that. She didn't like any of that. Seeing how fiercely she wanted to protect me, I marveled at how Dorian continually worried about her wanting to steal power from me. If that had been her intent, you'd think she would jump at the chance to become the lands' caretaker. Instead, she made it passionately clear she only wanted to be by my side.

But finally, after hashing out the same points I'd just made with Roland and Dorian, I was able to convince her. I think the attack on Ansonia helped her accept the decision a little more easily. In growing close to Pagiel, Jasmine had gotten to know his sister as well. Jasmine was as outraged as the rest of us over the attack and didn't want to see any repeats.

"I'll do it," she said at long last. "I don't want to, but I'll do it."

"Thank you. That means a lot." I had to repress the urge to hug her. No matter how close we'd gotten, our sisterly relationship hadn't quite crossed into great shows of physical affection.

She shrugged. "Ah, well. This is nothing. You've got a lot worse ahead."

"Oh?"

"Yup." She gave me a sympathetic look. "I sure wouldn't want to be you when you tell Dorian."

Chapter 6

That made two of us. That realization had been building within me this entire time: I would have to tell him. No one else really needed to be informed. One well-timed crossing to the human world, and no one here would be able to find me. Jasmine could do damage control afterward, telling my staff I was gone. Both kingdoms had seneschals to handle the day-to-day affairs, and everyone was used to Jasmine and Shaya assuming control when I wasn't around. They'd all be shocked, but they'd adapt.

But Dorian? He was an entirely different matter. No matter what had gone down in our past, there was no way I couldn't give him a heads-up that I was about to disappear for a while.

Nonetheless, I put off delivering the news for as long as I could in the following days. He kept hanging around the Rowan Land, and I no longer bothered him about returning to his own home—which normally would've tipped him off that something was afoot. Instead, he reveled in our time together and was an endless source of funny recreational ideas that made target practice on pastel wooden animals seem downright mundane. And without contact from Roland, it was even easier to procrastinate with telling Dorian the news. I simply had no news to tell.

Aside from the constant attempts at entertainment, Dorian also decided he would educate himself on the technicalities of labor and delivery in the human world. Considering my own haphazard knowledge of such matters, I wasn't sure I was the best source, but he insisted that if I was going to keep touting the need for a human doctor, he needed to understand why.

"So what exactly do they do when you have these doctor's visits?" Dorian asked. "They seem pretty frequent."

We were outside, taking in the nice weather, about a week after I'd last seen Roland. "Well," I said, "they, um, check my vitals. Like blood pressure and stuff like that."

"Blood pressure?"

"It's kind of like your pulse. But kind of not," I said lamely. Yeah. I really wasn't the best person to be explaining medical lingo.

Dorian leaned back against a tree. "Well, any of our healers could do that for you. *I* could do it for you even."

"It's more complicated than that. And sometimes, I have ultrasounds at my appointments."

"Ultrasounds?"

And so went the rest of our conversation, with me having to constantly stop and explain what I'd just said. Each time, Dorian had some gentry equivalent for whatever I described. Some were more far-fetched than others, like when he said he was certain gorging on cake all day would achieve the same results as a blood-sugar test. He also had a very complicated explanation about how balancing a chicken in a tree was a well-established gentry method of determining gender. I was almost certain he knew there was no real equivalent to half the things I told him about and that he was making most of this up on the spot. He was simply trying to entertain me with the outlandish. Describing a C-section, however, brought his quips to a halt.

"I don't really know what to say about that," he told me honestly. "It seems very extreme. And dangerous."

"Maybe here it would be," I said, thinking of the gentry aversion to metal. A scalpel might as well be a sword. "Among humans, it's a pretty safe and standard thing. Saves a lot of lives—though I'd rather avoid it if I can. I don't want a scar."

Dorian considered. "Actually, that's the only part I *can* understand. Why not wear a scar of motherhood? Better than a tattoo or some other mark of honor. Let the world know what you've achieved."

I stretched out on my side in the grass. "I'd rather just let the kids speak for themselves."

He smiled and let the subject go. "There've been no more attacks on Eugenie lookalikes, by the way. It seems Maiwenn has more restraint than we thought."

"That's good," I said. The guilt over Ansonia still haunted me. "Beyond good. So you don't need to raze her kingdom just yet?"

"Not quite yet, no. Though I nearly would for what she's put you through." I think he meant it. After all, he'd once run a guy through to defend my honor.

"Well, I'm still doing okay. That's what counts."

Dorian shook his head. "There are lots of ways to be 'okay.' We haven't made a science of stress like you humans have, but even I know all this worry can't be good for you. It's not just your body I want safe. I also want you to be—"

Whatever he wanted was lost as a guard came and announced that Roland was here. The lazy, funny atmosphere with Dorian vanished. A mix of emotions warred within me as I realized what this meant. My days of procrastination were over. Part of me was happy to finally get things rolling. It would ensure the greater good for everyone. The rest of me—the cowardly part—dreaded the consequences that would soon unfold. Dorian wore a kind, sincere look, and I could barely meet his eyes as I mumbled an apology and hurried off to talk to Roland.

"You found a place," I said, once Roland and I were alone.

"I did." He glanced around nervously. I'd taken him to my bedroom, not wanting to risk even my discreet body-guards overhearing something. Still, Roland regarded the room as suspect, as though perhaps there were magical ears within the walls. "Though I'd rather not tell you where until the last minute."

"That's fair," I said, despite the curiosity that burned within me.

"I can tell you that it's a town that has a shaman on hand—and old friend of mine that I trust implicitly. She doesn't know your exact story, of course, but she under-stands there's some danger. She's more than willing to defend you if necessary." He smiled wryly. "And hopefully she'll remove any temptation you have to do shamanic house-cleaning. You see something going on, you just tell her."

The next most complicated part was figuring out how to get me to this secret location. The Otherworld lined up with the human world in a very rough way. It wasn't an exact match, but gates had a geographic similarity. For ex-ample, there was a favorite crossing spot of mine in the Thorn Land that led back to Tucson. One kingdom over, in Dorian's land, there was a gate that opened in New Mexico. Another nearby one went to Texas. That's how it was in this region of the Otherworld; most crossings led to the Ameri-can Southwest. That was why I'd had to travel to the Hon-eysuckle Land to reach the Ohio gate. Roland didn't elaborate, but from what I could gather, his safe house was not in the Southwest, meaning I'd have to travel far in either this world or the human one.

We worked out a reasonably convoluted plan, and then he left again in that way of his, off to make sure everything was in place back on the other side. The plan was for me to leave tomorrow, which was frighteningly close. But in this situation . . . well, the sooner things were implemented, the better.

That evening, not long after Roland had departed, I received a message from one of my servants that Dorian wished to see me in his chambers. I almost laughed at that. It was so typical of him to send *me* a summons in my own castle, as though he were the ruler here, not me. On the other hand, I wondered with dread what this could be about. Despite all our precautions, had he somehow found out about my plan with Roland? Had Jasmine cracked? Had there been magical ears in the walls after all?

Entering Dorian's rooms, I found nothing so sinister. Like most of the larger guest suites in the castle, his consisted of a separate bedroom and sitting chamber. The latter had been arranged with an elaborate table for two, complete with a gold silk tablecloth and candelabra featuring a weird, branching style that seemed to defy all laws of physics. Under normal circumstances, a setup like this would've instantly made alarms go off in my head as I tried to figure out what ploy Dorian had going on. My anxiety over tomorrow's adventure, however, superseded my normal wariness.

He was already seated and gestured me to the chair opposite him. He eyed me as I sat. "I'd so been hoping you'd wear something a bit more formal. Velvet and lace, perhaps. With a plunging neckline, naturally."

"Naturally," I said. I was in jeans and a T-shirt that was one size larger than what I used to wear, no thanks to my expanding waist. "Maybe next time you should let me know this is a formal occasion." A servant swept in through the door I'd just entered, no doubt having waited until my arrival. He set down a platter of quichelike tarts and then scurried off. "What *is* the occasion anyway?"

Dorian sighed dramatically. "A sad one, I'm afraid. To-morrow . . . I'm leaving."

"You are?" For a moment, hope surged in me as I toyed with the idea of sneaking off when he wasn't even around. I wouldn't have to tell him my plans at all.

"Indeed." He swirled around a glass of red wine. For once, he hadn't harassed me about drinking any. "I've enjoyed my time here in your delightful company, but it's time I look to my own kingdom. I also intend to increase security near my borders to discourage that bitch from taking liberties with my people again. Just in case." "That bitch," of course, was Maiwenn.

I picked up one of the quiches. It was heavy with cheese, just the way I loved them. "You just said earlier that you thought she had restraint and wouldn't attack again."

"I do," he said. "I think her people truly did act in error with Ansonia. Even if they didn't, maybe she decided using a scare tactic that attacks innocents is too savage. But it doesn't matter whether they've stopped or not. There was still an incursion on my land, and I have to show I won't allow it again. Maybe I won't raze her lands, but I'll certainly protect mine."

The mention of "innocents" made me think of Kiyo. He hadn't hesitated to come after the innocents that were his own children, but I could see him being responsible for preventing further mix-ups from Maiwenn's people. I was certain he would put a halt to a scare tactic that would endanger those not involved in our dispute. I didn't want to think well of him, not after everything that had happened, but I knew his style.

Course after course of succulent finger foods came, and

we were eating olives stuffed with herbs when Dorian said, "I have another surprise for you." As though on cue, two servants entered. Between them, they were carrying . . . a crib.

I jumped up before they even had a chance to leave. I stared at the crib in wonder. "What is this?"

"What do you think?" asked Dorian, looking very pleased. "Your little warriors need a place to sleep, don't they?"

I supposed they did, but I honestly hadn't given it much thought. Nursery décor and baby registries had been kind of the last things on my mind. I ran my hand along the smooth surface of one of the rails. The entire thing had been carved out of golden oak and polished to brilliance. Elaborate designs of animals and plants had been worked into the wood with painstaking care. Knowing what I did about the gentry, I didn't doubt that most of this had been made by hand.

"This is . . . exquisite," I said at last.

"There's another one coming, but it's still in progress. I wanted to show you this one before I left and see if you approved."

"I . . . yes. How could I not?" I was still in awe at the gift and felt a lump forming in my throat. Whether my emotion was from the thought of a tiny sleeping form inside that crib or simply because of Dorian's kindness, I really couldn't say.

"Excellent," he said, pouring more wine. "I suppose we'll have to have a number of them made, eh? No doubt you'll be hauling those poor children around to both your kingdoms—and to mine, of course. I can hardly spoil them if they don't visit."

I nodded and muttered something in the affirmative. We finished that course, but I was still too overwhelmed to say much that was comprehensible. The last serving of the night was dessert, and I could scarcely believe my eyes when I saw it. It was an elaborate chocolate cake, artfully decorated in the kind of fanciful icing designs the gentry loved. Hazelnuts and chocolate shavings added to the aesthetics, along with . . .

"Are those . . . are those pieces of Milky Way?" Even before the words were out of my mouth, I knew I was right. Chopped up and worked in with the rest of the confectionary wonder were bits of my favorite candy bar. "How on earth did you get those?" Even the gentry had magical limits.

"Young Pagiel acquired some on a recent jaunt to the human world. I remembered how you'd been wanting some." Some warning in my brain said I should be alarmed that Pagiel had made an unauthorized crossing *and* had managed to "acquire" human goods. I wasn't optimistic about his cash resources. "Serving them as-is seemed so primitive, so I had the cook find a more elegant method of preparing them."

"I can't believe you did this." I watched as Dorian sliced the cake, thinking it was a shame to mar such beauty. "Why . . . why did you? What do you want?"

Dorian set a piece of cake on my plate and gave me a look that seemed legitimately perplexed. "Nothing. Well, except to make things pleasant between us again. As I was starting to tell you earlier, I want more than your safety. I want you to be happy. I feel justified in most of my actions—*most*. There are some affairs I haven't treated you well in, and I want to rectify that. This cake is by no means the answer, but if we could manage any sort of trust again . . ." He glanced away briefly, displaying a vulnerability I hardly ever saw in him. "Well. That would make me happier than you can imagine."

Tears threatened to well up in my eyes. *Fucking hormones.* I cast a quick glance at the crib before returning to the cake again. I couldn't take it anymore. "I-I'm leaving," I blurted out. "I'm leaving the Otherworld."

Dorian's face didn't alter in expression as he studied me. "Oh? You found some acceptable but dubiously safe new doctor? I'm telling you, the chicken would be much simpler."

"No," I said, feeling miserable. *If we could manage any sort of trust again, that would make me happier than you can imagine.* Why had he said that, of all things? "For good. Or, well, for a while." I explained to him what I'd worked out with Roland, and throughout it all, Dorian's face still remained damnably calm. I almost wished he'd flip into some burst of rage or mockery. Instead, once I'd finished, his reaction was minimal.

"Well," he said, setting his fork down beside an uneaten piece of cake. "That is unfortunate."

"Unfortunate? That's all you have to say?" I wasn't trying to provoke a fight; I was just surprised.

He paused to sip some wine. "What else is there? It sounds like everything's in place. And clearly you've made up your mind if you've been planning this behind my back all week."

"Is that what bothers you?" I asked. "That I didn't tell you?"

At last, the hint of a smile—but it was a bitter one. "Ah, Eugenie. There are so many things that bother me about this, it's hard to know where to start. I suppose it was foolish of me to try talking about trust again, eh? We're as far from that as ever."

I felt a mix of guilt and anger. "Hey, you're the one who started it! If you hadn't tricked me into the Iron Crown—"

He gave a melodramatic sigh. "Not this again. Please. At least find some other grievance to lay at my feet. That crown saved lives, and you know it."

"You withheld the truth from me."

"And you've withheld this news of your departure from me all week," he pointed out. "One standard for me and another for you?"

"I'm not a hypocrite," I said, even though I kind of was. "Not telling you this doesn't have nearly the impact of the Iron Crown! You just don't like being left out."

"Like I just said, there's a lot more to it than just that," he said coldly. "Like you thinking obscurity is an adequate substitute for the protection of some of the greatest magic users in this world."

"Like yourself?" I guessed.

"Of course." Modesty was never a virtue Dorian really prized. "Do you think I wouldn't rip the earth up around anyone who tried to lay a hand on you?"

"No, but I don't think you can always be nearby."

"I could be," he countered. Some of his earlier anger eased. "I'll stay here in your lands permanently. Oh, I'll have to make the occasional jaunts back to the Oak Land, but far better me traveling than you. Unless, of course, my hair leads to another case of mistaken identity." He tossed some of that glorious auburn hair over one shoulder to make his point. "Of course, with my rugged and manly features, it seems unlikely that kind of error would occur."

"It's not realistic," I said, not falling prey to his charm. "And really, I do think this other plan is the safest option."

"Yet I won't have any idea if you actually *are* safe. You'll be lost among humans."

"You sound like Jasmine."

He sniffed. "Who knew? It appears she and I finally agree on something."

Unlike Jasmine, though, no amount of arguing convinced him of the plan's soundness. He didn't try to talk me out of it; he just stubbornly refused to endorse it. And, as I continued laying out my now well-worn arguments, I could see that patient mask of his growing thinner and thinner. This decision really did agitate him, though I couldn't entirely figure out what bothered him the most. At last, he stood up and cut off some point he was making.

"My dear, this is a waste of time for both of us. We're going to have to agree to disagree, and really, I see no point in my continued presence. It's time for me to go home."

"Tonight?" I asked, standing as well.

"Why not?" He reached for a cloak that was draped over a small table. "As I said before, I'm not the one in danger. I'd thought to stay until tomorrow to enjoy more of your company, but it seems that's futile now."

"I don't understand why you're so upset," I said petulantly.

Dorian approached the door. "Who says I am?"

"You," I said. I would've smiled if anything about this was funny. "Everything about you right now. Your face, your tone, your body language. You're pissed off. I knew you would be. But you can't really fault any of my reasoning."

"No, I suppose I can't," he agreed. He reached the door and regarded me expectantly.

"It's better this way," I said, desperately wanting him to endorse this. "And it's easier on you."

He chuckled. "Do you think that matters? Eugenie, what's 'easy' is of no consequence when it comes to you. I would do anything for you—anything at all—if it only meant you'd—" He cut himself off and abruptly turned away, resting his hand on the door's handle. Yet still he didn't leave.

A bizarre thought came over me, one that made my heart stop for a moment. All this time, I'd assumed Dorian just found me entertaining in his usual perverse way, that he'd liked my attentions and the prestige of being connected to my children. But I'd figured any romantic attachment had died after the Iron Crown. Now . . . now I knew I was wrong.

"Dorian . . . are you most upset because . . ." The words came out awkwardly as I found the courage to speak them. "Are you upset just because you won't see me? Because . . . you'll miss me?" It was a pathetic way to phrase it, but we both knew what I meant.

He glanced back at me over his shoulder, a smile on his face but sadness in his eyes. "Eugenie, do you know what I love about you?" I waited expectedly since Dorian used that rhetorical question in nearly every conversation we had, and his answer was always different. His smile grew, as did the sadness. "I love that *that* is the absolute last conclusion you came to."

He departed, shutting the door firmly behind him and leaving me feeling like an idiot.

Chapter 7

While it was true that nothing could ever fully match the Otherworld's convoluted system of travel, Roland came pretty close with the arrangements he made to get me to his mystery safe location. I left the Otherworld through a gate that opened up in Tucson, knowing that I'd likely be observed. A trip there—though clearly unsafe—didn't raise too much suspicion, if only because my enemies would probably expect me to visit friends and family back there. It was a risk we deemed worthy, in order to cover our larger scheme.

But once I set foot in the human world, the craziness of Roland's plan fell into place. He'd set it up so that my journey used practically every mode of travel imaginable—car, train, airplane, and even bus. Sometimes it would only be a short distance on one of those means of transportation. Sometimes I wouldn't even go in the right direction and would simply zigzag to my next waypoint. Varied means of technology made it difficult for gentry to follow me, and the complex system of reservations and directions made it difficult for humans—like Kiyo—to track me. Roland only stayed with me while I was in Tucson, for fear that he might be used as a way to locate me. He also hoped that by returning home and behaving normally, it might create the illusion that I was staying with him. That meant some Otherworldly creature would undoubtedly come calling, but Roland assured me he could handle it and that they'd leave him alone once the truth was discovered.

So, I did my traveling alone, which I didn't mind so much. There were so many connections to make and so many directions to follow that I had little chance to think about all the problems I'd left behind. Near the end of my second day of travel, I arrived in Memphis. It wasn't my final destination—but was close. Roland wanted me to stay there overnight and for most of the next day. It was a test to see if I'd been followed. If I had been, it seemed likely someone would make a move quickly. If I hadn't, then I could freely continue on to the last stop. Roland had given me the number of a shaman who lived in Memphis to call if I needed help, just in case things went bad. Aside from that, I had nothing else to do but wait out the day in a hotel room and hope we'd shaken any supernatural followers.

After so much time in the Otherworld, I'd hoped the return to modern life would distract me. Cable TV and deep-fried food were certainly things I'd been without for a while. Their novelty was short-lived, however. As I lay on my hotel bed, I just kept thinking about that last conversation with Dorian. Since seeking his protection during my pregnancy, I'd regarded him with nothing but suspicion and wariness. I'd been convinced of ulterior motives and had been certain the only reason he had aligned himself with me now was to further his own plots. The realization that he still had feelings for me—and that I had been oblivious to them—was startling. And troubling, though I couldn't exactly articulate why. I hadn't really allowed myself to think about him in a romantic way in ages, and now . . . despite my best efforts . . . I was.

Self-torment aside, my day in Memphis proved remarkably uneventful—which was all part of the plan. It was as close as I was going to get to confirmation that I hadn't been followed. Around dinnertime of the third day, I boarded a small commuter plane and braced myself for the last stop on this madcap journey: Huntsville, Alabama. I confess, when Roland had told me that's where his safe house was, I hadn't been excited. My stereotypes of Alabama were even worse than my Ohio ones. Roland had been quick to set me straight before I'd left Tucson.

"Don't take this the wrong way, Eugenie," he'd told me. "But you're kind of a snob."

"I am not," I'd argued. "I'm open-minded about a lot of things. And places."

He'd scoffed. "Right. You're like most people from the Western U.S., convinced that anywhere else is beneath your notice."

"That's not true at all! It's just . . . I'm just used to certain things. I mean, Tucson's a lot bigger than Huntsville. I'm just used to that larger-city feel, you know?"

"Right," he'd said, eyeing me skeptically. "Which is why you've been living in a medieval castle with no electricity or indoor plumbing."

It was a fair point, and I'd made no further argument.

Some of my lingering doubts softened as the plane made its descent into Huntsville and I caught sight of a park filled with cherry trees that glowed like gold in the sunset. It was kind of amazing that I could even identify them. We were still fairly high, and unlike the Rowan Land's perpetually pink cherry trees, these had lost their blossoms and were in full leaf. Yet, somehow, I instantly knew the trees for what they were, and I found them comforting. This wasn't the Rowan Land—and certainly not the Thorn Land—but that little reminder of *home* made me feel less alone. I could get through this. Everything was going to be okay.

I was met at the airport by Candace Reed, the local

shaman with whom Roland had set things up. He must have given her my description because she lit up when she saw me and hurried forward to hug me as though we'd known each other for ages. She was about ten years older than me, with dark skin and hair and long-lashed eyes that sparkled with mirth. She wore faded jeans with a red-checked blouse and radiated an air of motherly protection.

"Look at you," she exclaimed, promptly putting her hand over my stomach. I'd noticed this seemed to be acceptable behavior for most people—gentry and human alike—and it normally weirded me out that pregnancy apparently smashed all personal boundaries. Somehow, I wasn't bothered by Candace doing it. "How far along are you, sweetheart?" Before I could even answer, she took my small suitcase from me. "Lord, give me that! We can't have you hauling things around in your state."

The suitcase barely weighed anything and was simply a few essentials my mom had thrown together for me. Something told me that arguing what I was capable of in my "state" with Candace would be a losing battle.

"I told Charles to have your room ready by the time we got home, so he better have listened to me," she continued as we headed toward her car. "You know how men are. He'd be off daydreaming all the time if he didn't have me to keep him in line. Let's hope he didn't burn dinner either. I started it and told him exactly what to do, but knowing him, he probably got distracted. Could be a baseball game on TV or a woodpecker out back. Probably nothing but a pile of ash in the oven now. It's pot roast. Do you eat that? You should, you know. Protein's good for you and the baby. So are the potatoes."

"Babies," I corrected as we reached the car. "I'm having twins."

"Oh. Oh my!" This revelation left her momentarily speechless, and a look of wonder fell over her features, along with a softer emotion I couldn't quite place. "Oh, that's just *lovely*."

She went to put my suitcase in the trunk, and as I sat down in the passenger seat, I caught a glimpse of some familiar tools in the backseat. A silver athame lay near a suede bag, out of which peeked another hilt that I was willing to bet belonged to an iron athame. Near those was a necklace consisting of raw smoky quartz beads. I couldn't help a smile. Candace's chatty Southern charm in no way meant she wasn't a fully active, totally deadly shaman who could combat any creature that messed with us. I wouldn't have been surprised if there was a gun and a wand somewhere in the car too.

Candace had recovered herself when she rejoined me and soon picked up her breezy conversation style. I was happy to let her do the talking. It gave me the chance to take in the sights as we drove to her house. The airport was situated a little outside downtown, and Candace and her husband lived farther out still, though she assured me I could reach the city from her place in a little over a half hour. That wasn't much different from my own house back in the Catalina Foothills near Tucson, and again, I felt a small twinge of reassurance about this new locale.

As we drove away from the airport and the more populous areas, I saw that the trees remained green but that the grass and low plants were yellowing. Candace explained that they were in a drought right now. As much as I loved the dry weather I'd grown up in, there was a part of me that hated to see the land around us so parched for water. It wouldn't be that big a strain on my magic to summon a quick rain shower . . . but, no. I didn't even need Roland's instructions to know how foolish such an act would be. I couldn't attract any attention to myself. These conditions were normal for summer around here; the land would survive without my help. *Just worry about yourself, Eugenie*, I chided myself.

Candace's house was situated on a heavily wooded street. She had neighbors, but they were spread out, giving the illusion that each house on the road was in its own private forest. I'd gotten used to the Rowan Land's greenery, but the castle was set on cleared land, and seeing large trees right outside this house's windows was a world away from what I'd grown up with.

"This is beautiful," I told her as we got out of the car. She'd retrieved her arsenal from the backseat and was going for the suitcase, despite my offers of help. Twilight was casting shadows on everything, but the little house's windows lit up the darkness.

"It is, isn't it?" she said, gesturing me to follow. "We've been here 'bout fifteen years." She took the steps onto the house's wooden porch, which even had a swing for two. A screen door kept insects out and let evening air inside, in an effort to cool the house. As though thinking of this, Candace cast me an apologetic look. "No air-conditioning. It can get pretty hot."

"I'm used to it," I assured her. Compared to my castles, the ventilation here was state of the art. Screens would rock the Thorn Land's world, if I could figure out how the gentry could manufacture them.

Inside, I met her husband, Charles. He was a tall, lanky man with blond hair that was starting to pick up a little white with age. His blue eyes were kind, and his quiet demeanor was quite the contrast to Candace's liveliness. Watching them interact, though, I realized quickly that they balanced each other in a very harmonious way. She passed my suitcase off to him while she checked on the pot roast— which, it seemed, had not turned to ash.

He led me to a room on the second floor, with pine walls

and angled beams crossing over the ceiling. A double bed with a blue and white quilt sat in one corner, but before I could make too many judgments about country living, I noticed a flat-panel TV mounted on the opposite wall. Roland had been right. Never assume anything.

"That's our old TV," said Charles as though apologizing. "We just got a brand-new one for the living room. I hope this isn't too small. . . ."

I laughed. "No, it's perfect. Thank you."

He nodded, looking pleased. "We've got a spare DVD player that I'll hook up for you later." He then proceeded to give me a rundown of their vast channel lineup, reinforcing the fact that even if the Reeds lived out in the country, they still loved their comforts. After a few minutes, Candace interrupted his spiel, calling to us to come downstairs and eat.

The food was exquisite, though it soon became obvious I could never eat enough to satisfy Candace. She was worse than my mom, which was no small feat. Candace continued to dominate the conversation, leaving little room for either me or Charles, but I got the vibe this was perfectly normal and even welcome to them.

"Now," she was saying as she piled a second helping of green beans onto my plate, "I suppose you'll need to get set up with a doctor around here. There's one OB on the road to Mooresville that a friend of mine used to see. That's who I was going to recommend, since it's closer. But seeing as you've got twins—did you know that she's having twins, Charlie?—I suppose you'll probably want to see one of the specialists downtown. We can make some calls tomorrow morning, and Charles can take you to your appointments while I'm working."

"Oh, no, I don't want to cause you any inconvenience," I said. "I'm sure I can get my own car and—"

"It's no inconvenience," Candace interrupted. "He doesn't mind, plus he works at home."

"Still . . ." I felt a little flustered at their attention, especially since the mention of "twins" had made Charles's dreamy expression even dreamier. "That'll interrupt his workday. Besides, once I know the area better, I can probably just find my own place and—" Their solicitous looks turned to shock.

"Why on earth would you do that, child?" asked Candace. "Don't you like it here?"

"I—uh, no. It's wonderful. But I don't want to impose. . . . You've got your own life here. . . ." I faltered, suddenly at a loss. I'd known I'd be staying with them initially when Roland had made these arrangements, but he'd also given me the impression that there'd be no issue with me getting my own place eventually—so long as I stayed in regular touch with Candace.

"Well, that's ridiculous." Candace seemed relieved that inconveniencing her was my only concern. "You'll stay with us as long as you need to, until this trouble's passed." Roland hadn't told her my history, of course, but had simply given a story with elements of truth. He'd painted me as a shaman who'd run afoul of some Otherworldly creatures— not uncommon in this profession—and said that pregnancy made it difficult for me to protect myself. She cast a concerned glance at my plate. "God knows you'll probably starve to death if left on your own."

That seemed to settle the matter for them, and any further protests I might have made were pushed aside when the front door squeaked open. I nearly leapt out of my chair at a potential invasion, but the Reeds' casual attitude kept me in check.

"Hello?" a voice called. "Anyone home?"

A guy my age came into the kitchen. Candace hurried up from the table to grab a clean plate and immediately began piling it with food. "Sit down, Evan," she told him. "Before it gets cold. You can meet our houseguest."

"I'm Evan," he said, in case I'd missed that. He flashed me a grin and held out his hand. Before I could take it, he hastily wiped it on his blue jeans and then offered it again. "Sorry," he said. "I've been working outside all day. Sweat and dirt everywhere."

"Why didn't you say so right away?" exclaimed Candace. "Wash your hands then. We run a civilized house."

Evan complied meekly and walked over to the counter. "I'm Eugenie," I told him.

"Evan is Charles's nephew," Candace explained, taking her seat again. "Lives a couple miles away."

Evan returned with clean hands and joined us. "I just came by to return Uncle Chuck's tools," he said. "But you can't just stop by here and leave without eating—especially around dinnertime."

"So I'm learning," I said.

This made him smile again, and he dug into his food with enough enthusiasm to please even Candace. She started back in with her domination of the conversation, though Evan was a good match for her and kept trying to draw both me and Charles in as well. Evan wasn't quite as lanky as his uncle but had the same blond hair and blue eyes. He had a muscular build that confirmed his earlier statement about "working outside all day," as well as the start of a sunburn, which Candace was quick to scold him about.

"What do you do, Evan?" I asked, when a rare pause in the talking came up. I fully expected anything from farmer to mechanic. I guess I hadn't entirely let go of my stereotypes.

"High school teacher," he said, between bites of potatoes. "At least, I am during most of the year. I've still got another month or so off."

Surprising answer. "What do you teach?"

"Physics," he said. "And shop." Seeing my astonished look, he added, "It's a small school. Some of us do double-duty."

"I guess," I said. "Those seem like polar opposites."

He shook his head. "You'd be surprised. Plus, it gives me an excuse to make lots of field trips to the space center."

"You should take Eugenie there," said Candace. She turned to me. "He's there so much that they should be paying him to give tours. You should talk to them, Evan. You could make a little extra money this summer."

"I'm sure I could take her without seeking compensation from the space center," said Evan patiently. "If she even wants to go."

"Sure," I said, mostly because I wasn't entirely sure yet how I'd be spending my days around here anyway. The irony of my life wasn't lost on me. I hadn't just left behind a shadowy world of mystery and magic; I was now signing on to explore the ultimate triumph of human technology. "That'd be great."

"But don't tire her out," warned Candace. "She's pregnant. With twins."

Evan gave me a once-over. "Really? I can't even tell."

"Flatterer," I muttered, much to his amusement.

"You also can't take her on any of those simulator rides," added Candace. "They're not good for pregnant women."

"That, I know," said Evan patiently.

"Just making sure," she said. "I know how reckless you can be."

Honestly, Evan seemed like one of the least reckless people I'd ever met—rivaled only by Charles. That easygoing nature must run in the family. Both were quick to smile and had a good attitude about everything. Even though Candace harassed them both for various reasons, it was obvious that there was a lot of love in this group, and they were all willing to bring me into their little circle. It was both touching and weird, and I mentioned it to Evan later.

"Your aunt and uncle are so nice," I confessed when we were alone. Charles had entrusted Evan with the spare DVD player to install in my room. "I know she's friends with Roland—my stepfather—but still. They've just gone above and beyond. I didn't expect this kind of welcome."

"That's how they are." Evan's back was to me as he connected a few cables between the TV and DVD player. "They're just naturally good. That, and they'd bend over backward for someone like you anyway."

I frowned. "Because of Roland?"

"Nah." He straightened up and turned on the TV to test it. "Because of the baby. Er, babies."

"What does that have to do with anything?"

Satisfied all was working, he turned around and regarded me with a gentle smile. "They *love* kids and especially babies. They can't have any of their own—though it wasn't for a lack of trying. They went through a lot of heartache, and even though they've sort of accepted things now, I know it still hurts them sometimes."

"I had no idea," I murmured. I rested a hand on my stomach. "I feel kind of bad. Maybe I shouldn't be here. . . ."

"Don't think like that," he chided. "They're not bitter. Like I said, they're good people, and you carrying twins just makes their day. You could stay here as long as you wanted—you and the kids—and they'd be delighted. There's nothing they won't do for you." His words sent a disconcerting reminder of Dorian's constant *What wouldn't I do for you?* quip.

I wondered if Roland had known about the Reeds' childless state when he'd decided on this location for me. Had he guessed their situation would add an extra level of protectiveness?

"I don't know what to say. I just don't feel like . . . I don't know. I'm just kind of overwhelmed by it all. I don't think I can pay them back for this."

"Just accept it and let them take care of you," Evan said with a wink. "That's plenty of payback for them, believe me." He moved toward the door and stifled a yawn. "I've got to head out before I fall over, but I'll give you a call soon if you do want to go check out the space center. And if you don't, then just say so. Don't let Candace pressure you."

"No," I said truthfully. "It sounds like fun."

Evan left, and the rest of the household began winding down. Both Charles and Candace went out of their way to make sure I didn't need anything else before going to bed. I assured them I was fine and then finally shut the door on my little room. With a sigh, I stretched out on top of my bed.

"What have I done?" I murmured, staring up at the pine slats. One day I was the queen of a fairy kingdom, commanding armies and wielding powerful magic. The next, I was out in the country, the darling of a good-hearted family whose only motivations were kindness and affection to others. It left me confused and unsure of what exactly I wanted in the world. And weirdly, for the first time since I'd left the Otherworld and begun my manic journey, I truly felt alone. I'd abandoned a lifestyle that—while dangerous— was familiar and beloved. Now, I was in a much simpler, easier world . . . but I questioned if I'd ever truly feel like I belonged in it.

Dorian's face played through my mind again, and I forcibly pushed him away.

A small fluttering in my stomach made me jerk upright. I sat there in disbelief, staring around foolishly. What was that? Had that been . . . ? Tentatively, I rested a hand on my abdomen, waiting for a repeat. There was none. I tried to remember what the doctor had said about the babies moving. I remembered the fish analogy and—most importantly— her comment that it wouldn't feel like something trying to kick its way out of me.

When nothing else happened, I lay back on the bed. That could have been anything, I decided. Too much pot roast. A muscle spasm. I'd almost convinced myself I'd imagined it when another fluttering in a different part of my stomach left me wide-eyed. I nearly stopped breathing, then told myself that wouldn't be healthy for any of us.

I used no magic but instead expanded my senses so that I could feel the air and water around me. I could hear the hum of insects outside and smell the leaves of the trees outside my window. The world fell into a comfortable harmony as I clasped my hands and rested them carefully on my stomach again. Another flutter answered me, and I realized that maybe, no matter how radically things had changed, I wasn't alone after all.

Chapter 8

I'd thought my biggest obstacle in exile would simply be adjusting to a new area and new people. I was wrong. As it turned out, boredom soon became my greatest enemy in the following weeks.

The Reeds continued to be open and loving in their acceptance of me. For all intents and purposes, I was a member of the family. Evan made good on his promise to take me to the space center and went out of his way to show me all sorts of other interesting sights in the area. Still, he couldn't entertain me nonstop. Even though he was on summer break, he still had lots of home projects of his own to work on during the day, as well as a number of volunteer jobs. Likewise, Charles and Candace had their own commitments to preoccupy them. When evening came, they were quick to gather us all together, but the long daylight hours were left to my own devices.

Surprisingly, jealousy soon became an issue for me as well. Candace might maintain her breezy down-home style and tendency to over-mother while at home, but it was obvious that when it came to her shamanic work, she was all business. Her work sometimes took her quite a few hours outside of Huntsville, and I learned that this region was particularly active for ghosts. Old spirits had a hard time leaving familiar haunts. For whatever reason, gentry and other Otherworldly creatures weren't such an issue, so she rarely used her magic to touch the Otherworld. Her work was mostly restricted to banishing, which made her more of a Ghost Buster than a shaman.

She frequently came home with cuts and bruises from particularly troublesome spirits, and that was what drove me crazy the most. She never complained and took it in stride as part of the job, and Charles would patiently patch her up each time. She was always able to take down any-thing that came her way, but each time she returned home injured, I just kept thinking that if I'd been with her, we probably could've dispatched those ghosts without a scratch. It took every ounce of my willpower to stay silent and let her do her job the way she always had.

I'd wondered initially if Evan knew what his aunt did for a living. Sometimes the shamanic trade was kept under-cover. I quickly learned that not only did Evan know about her job, he also occasionally helped. His skills were pretty minor, but she believed it was good to have a backup. Her profession was well known to a lot of the community as well, who took ghosts and the supernatural as an accepted part of life. The area was rich in history, and a lot of the residents—particularly those in remote regions—had at least one ghost story to share.

Candace found me one afternoon, on a day she'd fin-ished up early. I was reading on the porch, trying with mixed luck to get into a book I'd recently checked out. I hadn't actually used a library in years, but with all my free time, now had seemed like a good time to try to get back into the habit. They helped break up the time when I wasn't working on jigsaw puzzles, which were another old and neglected hobby.

"I was wondering if you could help me out with something," she said, wiping sweat off her brow. The drought hadn't lifted, which also drove me crazy. Charles worked diligently to keep his garden watered and alive, and I had to rein myself in from using magic to help him out. I would've gladly assisted with the manual labor instead, but he wouldn't allow that in my "state."

At her words, a brief surge of hope flared within me. Maybe she wanted me to come help her with a case! Then, as quickly as the thought had come, I promptly dismissed it. I was fairly certain Roland had made it emphatically clear that I was not to assist under any circumstances, and Candace was protective enough to uncompromisingly adhere to that.

"What do you need?" I asked. I racked my brain for any household tasks that needed tending but could think of none that were low-key enough for me to be allowed to do.

"Business is picking up," she said. "And I'm getting lots of calls and e-mails. It's hard for me to keep up with them. Charles tries, but he doesn't always know enough to tell what's a priority and what's not."

A secretary. She wanted me to be her secretary. I was so dumbfounded that I could make no response.

Uncomfortable with my silence, she added, "I figured with your experience, you'd be able to sort everything out and schedule it the right way."

"Of course," I said at last. "Whatever you need."

My acceptance came more from a sense of obligation to this woman who'd done so much for me than any real desire for clerical work. Don't get me wrong—I respected that trade immensely. Back in Tucson, I'd had an administrative assistant named Lara. Her witty personality was enough to make me miss her, but she'd also been amazing at sorting out the day-to-day details of my life and job. Yet, as awesome as I felt she was, my own pride was hurt at being downgraded to phone calls and e-mail. I was one of the most powerful shamans around. I could do things that most of my peers couldn't . . . but this was what I'd been reduced to.

"I know it's not ideal," she said gently. "But I think it's something you'd be good at."

I realized then that her offer came from more than just a need for someone to organize her affairs. Just like with her shamanic skills, I'd underestimated her. She was more observant than she let on. She knew perfectly well that I was bored and restless, so she was trying to do what she could to help me while still maintaining Roland's rules.

"Thank you," I said, genuinely meaning it. "I'll do my best."

A relieved grin spread over her face. "Good. Now that that's settled, tell me how your appointment went."

I smiled back at her obvious glee. I'd found a doctor in Huntsville and had a checkup this morning, continuing to get good marks. "You can see for yourself. There's a folder on the counter with something you might like." The doctor had sent me home with some ultrasound printouts of the twins. Candace hurried back inside, and moments later, I heard a delighted shriek. Laughing, I returned to my book.

When I started working for Candace the next day, I wondered how Lara had managed to do her job for years without going insane.

To be fair, it wasn't like the phone was ringing off the hook. Candace had a separate line for business, and I only got a handful of calls that day. E-mail requests were about the same. Still, I was kind of amazed at the varied personalities I had to deal with. It was easy for me to tell the difference between a major haunting and a minor one, and the latter usually got scheduled out later. Some people didn't take that too well. Equally frustrating were those who didn't even know what they were asking for.

"It's like an occasional knocking in the walls," one man explained to me on the phone. "Usually when the air-conditioning kicks on."

"You have central air?"

"Yup."

"I don't suppose . . . it might actually be something going on with the air-conditioning?"

He considered this for a few moments. "Doesn't seem likely. It's never done it before. I've had this system for years."

"Well," I said patiently, "things wear out over time."

"I dunno. I'm pretty sure it's a ghost."

I sighed. "Have you had any other signs? I mean, have you actually seen an apparition or felt any cold spots?"

"No," he said after another long pause. "But I've sometimes felt warm spots."

"Warm spots?" I asked. "That's not usually an indicator of a spectral presence."

"Well, they're there. Even when the air-conditioning's on, it still feels pretty hot in the house."

I gritted my teeth. "If the air-conditioning's broken, that would explain the noise and why it's not cooling your house."

The guy was obviously still skeptical. "I think it's a ghost. Do you think she can come out and take a look?"

"Yeah, but it might be a while. Her schedule's pretty booked."

"That's okay," he said. "The ghost kind of adds character. Maybe I won't even have her get rid of it."

We scheduled the appointment, and I hung up, thinking bleakly that that had been ten wasted minutes of my life I would never get back. I also found myself again thinking of Dorian. Not that he would do phone customer service, of course. But that customer's personality was exactly the kind Dorian loved to taunt. I could see him nodding along seriously with the guy: "Intriguing. Tell me more about your ghost."

Still, it occurred to me after a few days that I really was making Candace's life easier. I was also helping out Charles, who was relieved to no longer have to deal with air-conditioning ghosts. I decided the annoyance of customer service was a small price to pay for their hospitality.

A week or so into my gainful employment, Evan surprised me with a daytime visit. He was in his usual jeans and T-shirt but had obviously cleaned up and didn't have the typical wear and tear from working outdoors.

"Wondered if you wanted to go see some more local sights," he told me. "There's a plantation south of here that's a historic monument."

I made a face. "Thanks for the offer, but I don't really like the history of those places. It's hard for me to get too excited."

He nodded, his face serious. "The history *is* ugly, but it's an amazing piece of architecture. And sometimes . . . sometimes it's good to have a reminder of the evils of the past."

The comment surprised me. I'd known Evan was neither stupid nor close-minded, but much like with Candace, it was easy to think he was just all laid-back charm. "Okay," I said. I glared at Candace's business phone. "Voice mail can take over today."

We drove deep into the country, about an hour and a half away from Candace's. The land was beautiful, and deep-rooted trees fought fiercely to maintain their green leaves in otherwise yellow and brown terrain. Evan left the windows open, and I leaned back with eyes closed, enjoying the rush of air over me.

A strange longing suddenly welled up in me, filling my

mind with images of desert shrubs and cherry trees in bloom. The Thorn Land and the Rowan Land. How long had it been since I'd been away? Nearly a month? The time seemed both impossibly long and short. The longing within me grew more intense, and in that moment, I would've traded anything for my kingdoms. I'd had those lands call to me before and knew this sudden urgency wasn't coming from them. This was all me, my own body's withdrawal from the Otherworld. If the lands hadn't sought me out, then Jasmine's bonding must be satisfying them. Somehow, that made me feel worse.

"What are you thinking about?" asked Evan. I opened my eyes. "You looked like you were a million miles away."

"Nearly," I said with a small smile. "Just feeling a little homesick."

"I can imagine," he said. "I've traveled a little, but most of my life's been here. Not sure what I'd do if I was suddenly taken away from it."

"Do you plan on staying here for the rest of your life?" I asked.

"Yes," he said without hesitation. "I love the land. I love my house. I even love my students. You always hear about teachers who are relieved when school's out, but me? I miss the kids the whole time. Can't wait to get back into it."

"Do you teach the same thing each term?"

"Pretty much."

"And you don't get bored?"

"Nope. I love the material. And there are always different kids cycling through, so it's new to them each time. That's fun to see."

I shook my head in awe. "That's kind of amazing."

"What, that I like kids?"

I laughed. "No, no. That you're so content with your life. I don't think that's very common."

He shrugged. "When you've got everything you need,

why complicate it? I mean sure, I'd like a family someday, but other than that, I've got a lot of good things going on. People get too caught up in what they don't have and get bogged down as a result. There's joy in the present. It's important to just make the most of these moments we have. Keep an eye on the future, but don't forget to enjoy *now*."

His eyes held mine for a brief moment before returning back to the road ahead. Evan had never made any romantic overtures toward me or behaved in any way that wasn't gentlemanly. That was fine by me. I liked him a lot, but after everything I'd gone through, I was in no way ready to get involved in a new relationship. Nonetheless, I'd gotten the vibe for a while that he wouldn't be opposed to something more developing between us. As his words had just confirmed, though, I'd also gotten the impression that he was more than willing to be patient. He really was content with what we had now.

And that was what was remarkable about him. He was content, at peace with what he had. He wasn't a slacker by any means, but there was none of that burning ambition to shape the world, as I'd experienced too often with Dorian and Kiyo. There were no greater machinations here, just a simple love of life. Things were uncomplicated around Evan, and it occurred to me that maybe that wasn't such a bad thing. *Complicated* had been my operating procedure for so long that I'd never given much thought to living without it. Would it be so terrible to let go of Otherworldly politics and prophecies? Maybe it would be good for me—and my children—to live around people who simply loved unconditionally.

There were no easy answers, certainly none that would present themselves today. We arrived at the plantation shortly thereafter, and it was as magnificent as Evan had said it was. The main building was constructed in Greek revivalist style, sprawling and grand with a veranda that even had pillars. Evan pulled up into a gravel parking lot and then led us toward one of the adjacent buildings, which had obviously been converted into a visitor's center. As we walked toward it, I came to a stop and glanced up in surprise.

"It's finally going to rain," I said.

Evan stopped beside me and glanced up as well. "I didn't hear anything about it. Look—there isn't even a cloud in the sky."

It was true. There was nothing but open blue above us, paired with a merciless sun. Yet, I *knew* there would be a storm before the day was out. I could feel it with every part of my being. The air hummed with it. Remembering Ohio, I had a brief moment of panic that this unexpected storm might be magically induced. I took a deep breath and felt out its true nature. No, this was the real deal. A natural shift in weather that was much needed.

"Just wait," I promised Evan as we continued walking. "You'll see."

He gave me an indulgent smile but made no secret of the fact that he didn't buy it.

A sign at the visitor's center said the plantation was closed today, making me think our trip had been in vain. Evan continued, undaunted, and knocked on the door.

"Wanda?" he called. "You around?"

A few moments later, the door opened, and a tiny gray-haired woman appeared. "Why, Evan. I wondered if you'd make it."

"I told you I would," he said, giving her a quick hug. "Wanda, this is Eugenie. She's staying with Aunt Candy and Uncle Chuck right now. Eugenie, Wanda."

Wanda pushed her silver-rimmed glasses up the bridge of her nose and beamed at me. "You are very welcome here, darling. The house is open if you want to go look around. I know you remember the way, Evan."

"Sure do," he said. "Thanks for letting us come by. I promise not to mess anything up."

"You better not," she teased.

I gave him a look of wonder as we made our way to the house. "Do you know everyone around here?" I'd noticed similar receptions in my time with him, but being given full access to a site like this was pretty remarkable.

He chuckled and opened the front door for me. "It's one of the perks of settling in one place so long. You don't just get to know people—you practically become family."

We spent almost two hours going through the house. It was a huge place, with room after room that had been restored and furnished with period items. Most everything was labeled with small placards too, overloading my brain with more history than I could handle. The plantation's more sinister side and history of slavery continued to bother me, but I could see that Evan was right about the importance of learning about the past.

After finally seeing all there was to see, we returned to one of the grand sitting rooms. I rested on a small bench and admired the setting. Taking in the rich details and lush fabrics, I couldn't help but think this room would've fit seamlessly into some gentry palace. Evan eyed me with concern.

"You up for seeing some of the outside buildings? We can head out if you're tired."

The truth was, I *was* tired. I firmly told myself it was simply from knowledge overload and depressing history— and not because pregnancy was wearing me down. "Let's at least take a quick look," I said, refusing to show any weakness. "It'd be a shame not to after coming all the way out here."

"Okay," he agreed. He held out a hand to help me up, and I accepted. As we walked toward the door, a wave of cold hit me—and it wasn't from the plantation's cooling system, either. In fact, it was exactly the kind of cold spot I'd been trying to explain to that guy on the phone the other day.

"Did you feel that?" I asked, coming to a stop.

Evan gave me a curious look. "No. What was it?"

"A cold spot." Yet, even as I said it, the spot moved, and I was back in the room's previous temperature. I studied the room, looking for some sign of the source. Evan followed my gaze. Even with basic training, he understood the significance of a cold spot.

"There," he murmured, pointing to a corner.

I'd almost overlooked it. In a roped-off alcove filled with furniture, a ghost stood between a clock and a sofa. He was so still and so translucent from the sunlight that he was difficult to spot. He had a forked beard and wore an old-fashioned suit with a bow tie. He watched us warily but made no movements.

"That's an old ghost," I said. "Judging from the clothes. Probably been around since this place was built. Of course, if that's the case, he probably doesn't bother many people—or else someone would've called Candace long before this."

Evan shifted uncomfortably, a small frown wrinkling his forehead. "True. But it doesn't matter. She'd still say he should have been banished a long time ago. It isn't right for him to be tied to this world."

"Also true," I admitted. "We can let her know, and she can come back."

To my surprise, Evan produced a wand from his pocket. It was similar to mine—which I'd left with Roland—save that the gemstones tied to its wooden base were different. "I can do it now," he said.

"You carry a wand with you?" I asked, kind of impressed.

He shrugged. "Aunt Candy says be prepared. You better step away."

I started to say I had nothing to fear from a mild-mannered ghost like this but then remembered that this wasn't my show. Besides, even though this ghost seemed pretty localized, it was better if I didn't draw attention to myself—not that there seemed to be any danger of that. From the way the ghost had now fixed his steely gaze on Evan, it was obvious who had been identified as the threat. I moved to the room's far side.

"Send him to the Underworld if you can," I said.

Evan nodded and extended the wand. I felt its magic fill the room as he attempted to open a gate that would send the ghost away. Before he'd really even opened up past this world, the ghost attacked with a fury that neither of us had expected. Since the ghost had seemed so docile, I'd figured he would take his banishing meekly.

No such luck. He shifted to a flying form and threw himself forward, knocking Evan to the ground and immediately shutting down the tentative gate. Evan had remarkably fast reflexes and rolled to avoid the ghost's next blow. Spying a silver candlestick, Evan leapt up and grabbed it with his free hand and then took a swing at the ghost. It was a smart move. A silver blade was better, but any silver object wielded as a weapon by someone with enough skill and magic to use it correctly could cause damage. Sure enough, though the candlestick seemed to pass harmlessly through the ghost's translucent form, he howled in rage and retreated out of reach.

Evan used the opportunity to attempt his gate. I felt the tingle of magic once more, soon followed by a connection to the Otherworld. With that connection, my earlier need for the Thorn Land and Rowan Land flared up with startling intensity. They were so close . . . but still out of my reach. I bit my lip and forced myself to stay still. Despite the connection,

Evan was taking my advice and sending his senses farther, forming an opening to the Underworld. The ghost snarled as he recognized what Evan was doing. A ghost could come back from the Otherworld sometimes, but from the realm of death, there was no return.

Knowing it was now or never, the ghost struck again. Evan was ready and dodged the blow, still swinging the candlestick defensively. I felt the connection to the Underworld waver, but he was just barely able to keep hold. His near loss was a sign of his inexperience. Neither Candace nor I would've lost a gate that established. Still, he'd pulled it off and began the banishing words. The ghost attacked again, and Evan shifted—realizing too late it had been a feint. Evan moved in the wrong direction, and the ghost quickly picked up a wooden chair and threw it hard at Evan. The chair hit its mark, knocking Evan to the floor once again. The wand fell from his hand, instantly dissolving the connection.

The wand rolled to a central spot in the room, and I moved without even thinking. The ghost was advancing on Evan. I grabbed the wand and quickly cast an opening to the Underworld. As the magic poured through me, I nearly gasped. I hadn't realized just how long I'd gone without it. Shamanic magic didn't have the addictiveness of gentry magic, but it still had a sweet, pleasurable feeling I'd missed.

The ghost turned to me in surprise, not having expected me to offer a challenge. He abandoned Evan but wasn't fast enough to reach me before I spoke the banishing and sent him on. The ghost dissolved before our eyes, screaming in fury as it finally went where it should have long ago. Soon the screams were gone too, and we were alone. I hurried over to Evan, who was already getting to his feet.

"Are you okay?" he asked anxiously.

I almost laughed. "Me? You're the one who just got tossed

around by a ghost. Look at your arm." One of the chair legs had caught his arm at a bad angle, leaving a bloody gash. It likely wouldn't need stitches but was still ugly.

"I'm fine," he said. He righted the chair and gave it a quick survey for damage. There was none, meaning he wouldn't get in trouble with Wanda. "I've never seen a banishing that fast. I don't even think Aunt Candy can do it."

"It just takes practice," I assured him, not wanting to make a big deal of it. Evan knew I had a shamanic background, but I didn't want the extent of my power made that obvious. "Come on—we should get home." I was already looking back on what I'd done with regret. In that moment, there'd been no question. I'd *had* to help Evan. But in doing so, I'd exposed myself.

Candace's grim face confirmed as much when we got back to her place. "That ghost won't tell any tales in the Underworld, at least," she said with a sigh. "And if he was tied to that house, it's unlikely he had contact with anyone who might be after you."

"That's what I was hoping," I said.

"Still. You shouldn't have done it, if only because you and those little ones could have been hurt." Her gaze lifted toward the kitchen, where Charles was bandaging up Evan. "He's got a lot to learn, but he's tougher than he looks."

"I know," I said, feeling terrible. The ride home had given me a lot of time to consider my actions. One of the twins chose that moment to kick, just in case it wasn't obvious that I'd put them at risk. "I just reacted. He was in trouble, and the wand was right there."

Candace's look was almost sympathetic as she rested a hand on my arm. "I know. And I know that's your nature—especially if you're anything like Roland. That man never did know how to stay out of trouble. But for now, you've

got to let go. Next time you fight a ghost, it may tell the
ones who are after you where you're at."

I nodded meekly. Further conversation was put on hold
as Charles and Evan rejoined us. Evan stopped in the doorway to the living room and pointed at the TV set. "That's
where you're from, isn't it?"

I turned and saw a news report on a grocery store robbery in Tucson. The security camera footage was spotty,
frequently going to static, but it showed a few bizarre shots
of what looked like items flying off the shelves. Eyewitness
reports were equally odd, and if I hadn't known it was
completely impossible, I would've thought the store had
been hit by a ghost. But a ghost had no use for money—or,
in this case, food, since that's what had been stolen.

"Weird," I said, once the story ended. If some other type
of Otherworldly creature had been involved, I had no doubt
Roland would deal with it. Knowing that made me feel
even more ineffectual. Roland had theoretically retired, but
my various actions over the last year had forced him to take
on the role of an active shaman once more.

"It is," remarked Candace. "But it hardly fits the usual—"

Her jaw dropped as a low rumbling sound filled the
house. All of us stared at each other in confusion. Another
rumble sounded, just as I saw the living room windows
light up. My senses were suddenly flooded, seconds before
the others realized what was happening.

"It's raining," exclaimed Evan. He hurried to the door,
the rest of us right behind him.

Out on the porch, we watched in wonder as rain poured
down in sheets while lightning ripped apart the sky. A
fierce wind picked up, blowing the rain at us, but nobody
cared. Charles laughed and stepped off the porch, holding
his hands skyward.

"This'll fix my garden right up," he declared.

Evan turned to me in amazement. "You were right. She

said this would happen, Aunt Candy. This afternoon—the sky was clear blue, and she swore there'd be a storm."

Candace smiled and turned to watch Charles, oblivious to the true nature of my insight. "I guess some people just have a knack for the weather."

"You have no idea," I murmured.

Chapter 9

Despite our conclusions that I *probably* hadn't raised any notice in the Otherworld, I still spent the next week on pins and needles. I jumped at shadows, expecting gentry assassins to come bursting through my window at any moment. Candace played it cool and casual as usual, but I noticed she too was more watchful than before. One evening, a friend of hers came by, a wizened woman with an accent so thick I could barely understand her. Candace claimed the friend was visiting for tea, but later, I noticed them walking around the yard. I never asked Candace about it, but I suspected her friend was a witch who had laid some protective wards for us.

My worries continued to be unfounded, and that slow, easy life resumed. Even doing customer service for Candace became more comfortable, and I simply learned to take the silliness in stride. Probably the part of my life that continued to bother me most was my longing for my kingdoms. I would often wake up in the middle of the night with a burning in my chest and tears in my eyes. I'd remember the clean, crisp perfume of the deserts of the Thorn Land or the soft, rolling hills of the Rowan Land. Most of the need was still on my own side, but every once in a while, I'd sense a faint whisper, as though the lands were starting to miss me too.

To my surprise, I also found myself missing Dorian. After finding out I was pregnant, I'd seen him almost every week in the Otherworld. Not having his sarcasm and wit around anymore seemed weird, leaving an empty spot within me. Weirder still was that, aside from that last idyllic week, he and I hadn't really spent much tender or recreational time together. It had always been business, making plans for our kingdoms and figuring out how best to thwart Maiwenn and Kiyo. Nonetheless, I'd simply gotten used to having him around. No matter our personal differences, we worked well as a team.

Occasionally, more troubling thoughts about him would plague me. Lying in bed at night, sweating from the Alabama heat, I'd find myself sifting back farther in my memories, to the time when he and I had been involved. I was rapidly reaching a point in my pregnancy where sex sounded like the least appealing thing ever. But in my memories, it was still easy. There had been a lot of nights in the Thorn Land, when Dorian had been with me and we'd lain in bed in similar kinds of heat, sweaty and restless. Even in those conditions, we hadn't been able to keep our hands off of each other. His skin had felt like fire against mine as he moved in me, his mouth equally hot wherever it touched me. The heat around us had seemed inconsequential to that between us.

Recalling that night did more than just torment my body. It tormented my mind. I still hadn't gotten over the way he and I had parted. *Dorian still cares about me. Dorian maybe even loves me.*

How did I feel about that? How did I feel about him?

Although the weather in Huntsville remained hot, summer was winding down, and with its end, Evan would be returning to school. He began spending more time with me, still in that polite, hands-off way. Sometimes I'd catch him looking at me in a manner that made me nervous, and I feared some outpouring of affection. It never came, showing he was just as patient and content as he'd claimed to be. He further proved the point while we were out fishing one day.

I'd never been fishing before. It wasn't something you really did a lot of in Tucson. We were out on a small, quiet lake ringed in willows, in a no-frills motorboat that had just enough room for us, our catch, and a cooler stocked with Coke, juice, and Milky Ways. Evan was very critical about everything we caught, and it was important to him that we caught no more than we could eat. Anything else was a waste, he declared.

"Uncle Chuck makes a mean batter for these," Evan told me. "We can have a fish fry tonight."

That sounded great to me then and there. I was starving, but then, I always seemed to be lately. My appetite had shot up out of nowhere these last couple weeks, much to Candace's delight. While I certainly didn't try to halt my eating, every extra bite was a reminder that I was going to get bigger and bigger. As it was, my weight had shot up exponentially too. It was still mostly confined to my stomach, but every day, I felt a little slower and a little more uncomfortable.

I finished off a Milky Way to curb my hunger, fully knowing no obstetrician would endorse it as sound nutrition. I chased it with a thermos of cider, giving me a brief flashback to the Oak Land harvest parties. Those bonfires and crisp nights, paired with Dorian's smile, seemed like a lifetime away.

"I think there are some rules about pregnancy and fish," I told Evan, returning to the present. "It's probably in one of the pamphlets the doctors gave me."

"Ah, that'd be a shame," Evan said, casting his line out. A breeze off the water eased some of the heat and ruffled his hair. "If you can't have any now, we'll make sure you have a double helping after the babies come. If you're still here, that is. Have you thought much about it?"

I watched my own bobber drift lazily in the water. As far as I could tell, I was doing exactly what he was with technique, but he kept catching more fish. "Honestly, no. Mostly I'm just trying to get through the pregnancy, but I'll have to figure out the rest soon enough." I sighed. "Do you think I should stick around?" It was a foolish question, I realized, seeing as he didn't have nearly enough background to understand the consequences of that decision.

He shrugged. "Doesn't matter what I think. I like having you here, but in the end you have to do what you want and what you think is best."

I almost laughed. "I don't think anyone's ever said that to me before."

"What's that? To do what you want?" His bobber disappeared in the water, and he gave the line an experimental tug, revealing he'd indeed hooked another fish. Damn. How'd he keep doing that?

"Yup," I said. "I've had a lot of well-meaning people in my life, but most haven't been shy about telling me what they think I should do."

Evan reeled the fish in and deemed its size adequate. "People will always do that—and you said the magic words. *Well-meaning*. Most have good intentions for you at heart, but only you can make the final call."

I thought back to the last time I'd seen Kiyo, when he'd been trying to kill me in an effort to stop our children from being born. That didn't really qualify as "good intentions." Dorian's heavy-handed protection of me had looked out for my well-being, but it had been tainted with his own ambition. If push came to shove, I still wasn't sure if he'd side with me or the prophecy. And yet, even as I thought that, I remembered our last meeting, when Dorian had admitted to having no ulterior motives, save to make me happy and rebuild our trust. It was hard to know what to believe anymore.

Evan assessed our tally for the day and decided we had enough fish. "Don't want to be greedy," he said with a wink. "Need the fish to keep making more fish. Now we'll find out if you're allowed to have the best fried fish in the state."

A little Internet searching back at the house provided info on fish types and local waters that declared I could eat small quantities. Fortunately, the Reeds made an abundance of side dishes and desserts that ensured what I lacked in fish, I could definitely make up for. I went to bed happy and full, still turning over Evan's words about doing what I thought was best. Such a novel concept.

The next day, I was left alone for most of the afternoon while everyone else tended to their own affairs. E-mail and calls were few, though Candace assured me we'd see a surge when summer truly ended and people spent more time inside. So, it was another reading day for me, and I tried to make myself as comfortable as I could on my bed, something else that was becoming more difficult with my size. No breeze came in to cool the afternoon heat, and I mostly found myself growing sleepy.

Suddenly, the temperature dropped sharply in the room, raising goose bumps on my skin. I'd been nodding off but instantly opened my eyes, wide awake. There was nothing natural about this. *Shit*, I thought, sitting up. Here it was, the attack we'd been dreading. And I was weaponless because I wasn't supposed to be practicing any magic. Well, I didn't need tools to use my gentry magic. If they were bringing the fight to me, then there was no need to remain covert—

"Volusian?" I asked in disbelief. Red eyes and a small black body materialized in the room's darkest corner, which really wasn't all that dark this time of day. He glared at the sunlit window in irritation. I'd been a heartbeat away from summoning a storm in the room and immediately stopped myself.

"Mistress," he said in his flat tone.

"What are you doing here?" I demanded. "I commanded you not to come!"

I also hadn't told him where I was, but that made no difference. With his bonds of service, Volusian would always be able to locate me. Still, I figured not giving him any concrete information beforehand would be useful, in the event someone attempted to wrestle control of him from me. Likewise, I'd commanded him to avoid the Otherworld altogether, in the hopes of keeping him off the radars of those who might try to use him.

"Yes, mistress," he agreed. "And were it up to me, I assure you, I would stay out of your presence for as long as possible, unless I was coming to end your life and rip you limb from limb."

"Well, that's very thoughtful," I said. "And yet, here you are."

"Others forced me to, mistress."

I'd nearly relaxed, but this set me on high alert again. Sending my mind out, I tested the magical bonds that kept him under my control, half expecting them to have vanished. But no, we were still solidly connected.

"Rest assured, mistress, I am still enslaved to you," he said, guessing what I'd done.

"Then how the hell did others force you to come here?"

"With enough magic, it is possible to compel me to obey small commands while still bound to you," he explained.

"That would take *a lot* of magic," I said. Commanding Volusian full-time was difficult enough. Overriding that bond—even for a small order—was equally difficult. "I can't think of any one gentry who could pull that off."

"One gentry didn't," said Volusian. "King Dorian and Queen Maiwenn worked together to force me to come to you."

I had to replay his words a few times before I finally believed them. "Dorian and Maiwenn? *Worked together?* They'd never do that. You must be confused."

Volusian's eyes narrowed. "Do I look as though I get easily confused, mistress?"

"No . . . but . . . it doesn't make any sense. . . ."

Oh, sure. Dorian and Maiwenn were both extremely powerful, and I didn't doubt that together, they could send Volusian to me. I also knew they each had valid reasons for it. Dorian had never approved of me running off here, and Maiwenn . . . well, she wanted to kill me. Yet, those reasons didn't exactly mesh with each other enough to explain why those two would unite.

"What exactly did they command you to do?"

"To come to you, mistress, and tell you they have a message for you. They also told me the message—"

"Did they command you to actually tell me the exact message?" I demanded.

"No, but—"

"Then don't," I said, relieved I wouldn't have to magically counteract them. "That's an order."

Volusian's face remained typically expressionless. "My mistress is not curious?"

"No," I lied. I was terribly curious. But, I also didn't want to be swayed by anything those two had to say. I didn't want to hear Dorian's pleas about me coming back, no matter how well-intentioned he might be—partially because I was afraid I might want to give in. I also didn't want to find out what Maiwenn's role was in this. If she'd convinced Dorian to work with her, then maybe she had some song to sing about how she'd seen the errors of her ways and no longer had a hit out on me. I certainly didn't believe that, and honestly, I had a difficult time imagining him buying it either.

Some worried part of me wondered if maybe it wasn't about me and the prophecy after all. What if something had happened to Jasmine? In that case, Dorian would have found a way to tell Roland, and I *had* to believe my stepfather would've gotten that news to me. I supposed the other possibility was that something was wrong with my lands. Maybe they were suffering from my absence more than I'd realized. Yet, when I touched those threads that connected us—even across worlds—I felt nothing particularly concerning. I was still joined to my kingdoms and had sensed none of the desperate longing from them that I had in the past when I'd left them with no caretaker. Honestly, I sensed no emotion at all from the lands. If anything, the connection felt kind of numbed, probably from my absence. Still, it was there, and it was steady.

"No," I repeated. "I can't. I can't hear what they have to say. I've got a good thing going here. This is the right place for me to be, and I can't let anything ruin it right now."

"As my mistress wishes," Volusian replied. "Do you have any further commands for me then?"

"Just the same ones as before. Avoid the Otherworld. Don't come here again. Unless . . ." Inspiration hit. "If they try to summon you, come here immediately if you're able." I didn't know if Dorian and Maiwenn would attempt the feat again, but it would require a complicated set of spells. If Volusian could get to me first, I could probably strengthen our bond to prevent others' influence. "Come to me if *anyone* attempts to summon or compel you. Do you understand?"

"Yes, mistress."

"Then go."

Volusian vanished, and the room instantly returned to its

previous temperature. Still, I couldn't help a small shiver. Dorian and Maiwenn hadn't found me, not exactly, but they'd come much closer to it than I would've liked. I knew sending Volusian away was the smart thing to do, but again, the question nagged at me: *Why would those two work together?* In some ways, that bothered me as much as Volusian's visit. Time and distance had made me start to miss Dorian, and some of the old fondness was starting to return. The thought of him playing some game with Maiwenn made all of my kindly feelings start to crumble. What was he up to?

No matter how hard I tried to push it aside, it was yet another thing to keep me up at night. That, the fear of a gentry attack, and my own pining for my Otherworldly lands continued to wake me up sporadically. I spent my days exhausted, having to nap a lot in the afternoon to make up for what I missed when the rest of the world was sleeping. One night, about a week after Volusian's visit, something else startled me out of sleep, though I couldn't readily figure out what it was.

I lay there in the dark, panicked, stretching my senses to see what had made me wake up. There was nothing magical around, nothing out of the ordinary. I stayed awake for some time, listening and waiting, but still found nothing. I had finally allowed myself to begin to drift off again when a small pain in my pelvis brought me back to alertness. It wasn't the most uncomfortable thing I'd ever experienced, but it certainly got my attention. A lot of the muscles in my abdomen and back tightened as well, and I caught my breath, waiting for it to pass. After several seconds, it did, and my body relaxed.

I rolled to my other side, wide awake now. I had no clock in my room and couldn't say for sure how much time passed, but eventually, I felt that same muscle seizing and pain, only slightly more intense than before.

"Crap," I said aloud.

I eased myself out of bed and turned on the light. I found some drawstring yoga pants that I put on with the oversize T-shirt I'd gone to sleep in. Trudging down the hall, I made my way to Candace and Charles's bedroom door and knocked. She opened it in about five seconds, an athame in one hand and a gun in the other.

"What's wrong?" she asked immediately, peering behind me.

"I'm not sure," I said. "But I think I might be in labor."

"Has your water broken? Are your contractions more than five minutes apart?" Before I could even muster an answer, she turned and yelled, "Charles, wake up! Just like we practiced!"

And to my astonishment, it appeared they really *had* been practicing this. I was glad someone had because I certainly hadn't. Most of what I knew about childbirth came from TV, when people would boil water and make bandages out of sheets. I was pretty sure modern medicine had advanced past that, but I hadn't bothered taking any sort of labor class. There'd been too much else going on, and I figured I could always do it "later." I'd kept telling myself I had plenty of time. In fact, that was the problem.

"It's too early," I said from the backseat of the Reeds' car. Candace had taken it upon herself to drive because she was certain Charles would "follow the speed limit." He rode in the passenger seat, carrying a bag they'd long ago packed on my behalf. "This has to be something else. I'm only . . . what, twenty-nine weeks? I've got eleven more to go."

"Twins come early all the time," said Candace, in a matter-of-fact tone that made me think she'd been doing a lot of reading up on the subject.

"But why would mine?" I argued, knowing I sounded like a petulant child. "I've done everything right. The doctors always say everything's fine with me."

"Sometimes nature has its own ideas," said Charles in that gentle way of his.

Indeed it did. When I was admitted to the hospital, the obstetrician on call was initially optimistic that they might be able to halt this labor and prolong the pregnancy, even though my contractions were picking up in frequency and intensity. Her words relieved me, even though she also mentioned something about future "bed rest" that made me uneasy. Still, that panicked voice inside me kept repeating, *Too early, too early!* If we could delay this, we had to, even if it meant me staying immobile and miserable. Health reasons were key, obviously, but there was also the simple fact that . . . well, I wasn't ready for my new arrivals just yet.

Once I was in a room and the doctor was able to examine me more closely, her story changed. "I'm afraid they're coming whether you're ready or not," she told me, face serious. "I don't know what kind of birthing plan you had, but we're going to have to do an emergency C-section. They're not turned the right way. Pretty common when twins come this early."

Was she kidding? I didn't have *any* plan, let alone a birthing one. My doctor in Ohio had also mentioned caesareans were common with twins. I admired the efficiency of the procedure but wasn't thrilled about being cut open— or the extra recovery time. Still, wasn't this exactly why I'd chosen to come to the human world for delivery? I'd wanted to be in the hands of modern medicine, and this was as modern as it got.

"Okay," I said resolutely. Not that I had a choice. "Let's do what we have to."

Things moved quickly after that. In some ways, that was

good. It gave me little time to worry because someone was constantly giving instructions or doing something to me. I was taken to an operating room with a flurry of activity, Candace by my side in scrubs. An anesthesiologist inserted something in my spine, and like that, all feeling below my waist disappeared. It was strange to say the least, but I was glad to be free of the pain of my contractions.

Whenever I thought of surgery, I thought of being knocked out and waking up later. So, even though I knew this spinal method was better, there was some part of my brain that said it wasn't natural to be awake while people were operating on you. The medical staff erected a small curtain above my waist so that Candace and I couldn't see what they were doing. I could feel it, though—yet had no pain from it. There was just the pressure of a knife in my skin and muscle. I winced.

"Are you okay?" asked Candace worriedly. "Does it hurt?"

"No," I assured her, trying to put on a brave face. "It's just . . . strange."

I had an easier time with the thought of monsters beating me up and tossing me around than calmly allowing a surgeon to cut into me. I wondered if that came from living among the gentry for so long or if it was simply my nature to resist being helpless in the hands of others.

Between the sheets and numbness, it wasn't easy to tell how they were progressing. So, I was caught off-guard when a nurse said, "It's the girl."

She lifted the squirming baby up to give me a quick look, and I felt dizzier than any drug could have made me.

A girl. My daughter. Everything I'd done these last seven months had been for both twins, but she had been the force that initially spurred me to action. Kiyo had given me argument after argument about how her brother was some terrible creature that couldn't be allowed to live, yet I'd been unable to sacrifice her along the way. And now, here she was. I felt worlds away from where I'd been upon first seeing her on an ultrasound.

I had no time for further philosophical musings because they soon spirited her away. Her brother came shortly thereafter, presented to me in the same quick manner.

He made a small, piteous cry, and I tried to remember if the girl had cried or not. Everything had happened too quickly. Again, I got only a brief look before he was whisked away, with explanations of "oxygen" and "NICU." In that momentary assessment, I didn't see any conqueror of worlds. I only saw a baby, a very, very small one, who seemed surprised and upset to have to face what the world had in store for him.

I knew how he felt.

Even with the most intense part over, there was still more to do. There was the afterbirth to deal with, then the stitching and cleanup. My incision was stapled, and I couldn't even fathom trying to explain that to a gentry. The entire process seemed too quick and too neatly wrapped up for its magnitude. Candace stayed as close as they'd let her throughout the whole ordeal, finally returning to my side when I was in presentable shape. She clasped her hands together, face shining.

"Did you see them?" she asked wonderingly. "Oh, Eugenie. They're so beautiful."

They were, I realized. My glimpses had been quick, but those images were etched permanently in my memory. I wanted to see them again, as soon as possible. I was forced to wait, though, while the staff did whatever it was the babies needed in the NICU. Tests were run, and there was nothing I could do but bide my time until the obstetrician sat down with me again.

"They're both nearly three pounds each," she said. "Which is fantastic. Twenty-nine weeks is definitely viable, but it's always better the more weight they've got." That would be Candace's cooking and food agenda, I supposed. "Their lungs aren't as developed as a full-term baby's would be, of course, but we're able to help with that. All in all, they're in remarkably good shape. They'll need to stay here for a while, but at this point, I'm really pleased with the prognosis."

After a little more medical talk, they finally let me go to the twins. I was wheeled down, which seemed like overkill, but the nurses assured me I'd understand once some of my pain medication wore off. Candace and Charles accompanied me. He said something about having called Evan, but I didn't pay much attention. My only thought was that the nurse needed to get me to NICU faster. When we reached it, I wasn't fully prepared for what I found.

The twins were there, each in their own glass-encased bed. They weren't the only things in the box. Each twin was connected to feeding tubes and a ventilator, a world of dizzying machinery. It all seemed too big and too scary for such little people. Something caught in my throat.

"I didn't know there'd be so much . . . stuff," I managed to say.

The nurse had a kind, compassionate face. Exactly what you'd want from someone in this job. "I know the machinery's intimidating, but don't focus on that. Focus on what it's doing. It's helping make sure they'll both get healthy and strong so they can go home with you."

I gave a weak nod and hastily ran a hand over my eyes. Had I really been afraid of these two? And how could anyone have wanted to harm them? They were so tiny, like little dolls, and looked so terribly helpless. I felt guilty and ineffectual, like I should have done something to delay

their birth. Or like I should be doing something *now*. I was
their mother. Wasn't it my job to protect them? I supposed,
so far, I had, but now it was out of my hands.

They didn't look like the downy, cherublike babies on
TV. There was a fragility to their limbs, hands, and feet
that, again, reminded me of dolls. Their skin was pink and
blotchy, yet I could tell I was the parent they'd taken after.
They had my coloring and didn't appear to have inherited
any of Kiyo's features. Small blessings.

"What will you call them?" asked Charles.

Unlike everything else in this ordeal, I actually had an
answer for that. My long days had given me a lot of time to
ponder names, which were a much safer mental challenge
than the rest of my life. It would be nice to say I'd come up
with really symbolic names or names of great people who'd
left some impact on my life. Nope. It was a much simpler
matter than that. I simply gave them names I liked. Ordinary
names. The kinds of names a person shaped—not ones that
shaped a person.

"Ivy and Isaac," I said. I was a fan of alliteration.

Candace and Charles seemed pleased by the choices. I'd
once heard her go off on "the ridiculous things people
name their children these days," so I think she was relieved
I hadn't made up some weird monstrosity for them.

"These are amazing times we live in," she said, looking
down at Ivy. "Imagine having these little ones a hundred
years ago. What would've happened then?"

Or, I thought, what would've happened if they'd been
born in the Otherworld? Because I had to assume they
would've come early there too, in a position not suitable for
natural birth. Dorian had seemed confident of his healers'
magic to handle anything, but I wasn't so sure—especially
considering the gentry track record with infants. I couldn't
believe anything the Otherworld could offer would match

the care the twins were getting now. And I knew in that moment that everything I'd been through—turning my back on the Otherworld, coping with boredom, keeping away from magic—had all been worth it.

I gazed at my children and sighed happily. "We're exactly where we need to be."

Chapter 10

The next few weeks were surreal, and for the first time since coming to Alabama, I no longer worried about the Otherworld or filling my time. Isaac and Ivy consumed my life.

Not that there was much I could do for them. They were in the hands of the doctors and NICU nurses. Initially, I was able to pump breast milk for the twins to supplement the high-calorie formula they were also being fed. I was a little weirded out by being hooked up to a machine, but it was worth it to feel like I was contributing something. In time, it became clear I was one of those women who simply couldn't produce milk very well, and I wondered if it was the result of my half-gentry heritage, since their women often had similar problems. Regardless, after two weeks, I stopped my attempts, and the twins went on a strictly formula diet. Some of the nurses tried to reassure me that the best antibodies came in the early days and that I'd done a good job in giving what I could. I knew current thinking recommended breast-feeding for much longer, however, again making me feel woefully inadequate.

So, my contribution simply became frequent, daily visits. I watched my children and the machines that supported

them, silently counting each breath and heartbeat. I liked
to think that Isaac and Ivy could sense my presence, even
from inside their boxes. Maybe that was just wishful thinking, but it gave me some hope. I was rarely alone in my
visits. One of the Reeds was almost always with me, and I
took comfort from that too.

It was probably one of the most stressful times in my
life, but progress was made in tiny, agonizing steps. The
twins' prognosis remained good, and before long I was allowed to touch them inside their compartments. The first
time I did it, brushing Ivy's hand, was like a miracle un-
folding before me. I was certain I'd never felt anything so
soft. And as the one-month mark neared, I was told Isaac
and Ivy might have to stay for only one more month, based
on their progress. I barely heard that part because it was
immediately followed by two pieces of good news. The
doctors expected the ventilators to come off soon and also
that the twins would be in good enough condition that I
could hold them.

"I can't even imagine that," I said to Evan as he drove
me home that evening. "From the minute they were born,
they've been these fragile, unreal little things. . . . To be
able to hold them . . ." I sighed and leaned my head back.
"I can't wait."

He flashed me a quick smile. "I hope you'll let the rest
of us have a turn." I smiled back. In the beginning, I'd
thought his visits were simply as a kindness to me. Soon,
I'd realized he was coming to regard the twins with as
much affection as his aunt and uncle did. He'd gaze at them
wonderingly, eyes shining as he let himself get lost in
thought.

"Well, there are two of them," I joked. "The problem
might be having enough hands to hold them."

"Not in this family," he said, chuckling. "You're going
to have to fight us off."

We reached Candace and Charles's house, and I felt like I was floating ten feet off the ground. My mood was brighter than it had been in some time, and my physical condition was equally good. Spending so much time sitting and waiting had given me a chance to heal from most of the side effects of surgery. My staples had been removed ages ago, and I'd even gone back on birth control pills out of habit, though sex was pretty far off my radar just now. The waiting and inactivity were probably the only positive parts of the twins being confined to the NICU. I had no doubt that had things been different with them, I would've been out foolishly taxing my body long before its time.

"Looks like a visitor," said Evan, turning the car off.

I followed his gaze. I'd been so consumed by my own joy that I hadn't even noticed a strange car parked in the driveway. It was nothing I recognized, though I did spot a rental sticker on it. I wasn't particularly concerned, since Candace's clients sometimes came by in person. Plus, if there'd been some danger, I knew she would have called us and warned us away.

We walked inside, and I could hear voices from the kitchen. I practically sprinted in, anxious to share the good news with Candace and Charles. Like Evan had said, I had no doubt they'd be lining up to take their turns holding the twins. When I entered the kitchen and saw who was there, though, I came to an abrupt halt. My happy words faltered on my lips, but a few seconds later, a new joy spread through me.

"Roland!"

I hurried into his arms, and he gripped me tightly. Until that moment, I hadn't realized how much I'd missed him. The Reeds had become an adoptive family to me, but they could never replace Roland and my mom. Not having those two around during this part of my life felt strange and wrong sometimes.

When he finally released me, I saw his eyes were wet with emotion. "It's good to see you," he said gruffly. "We've missed you."

"I've missed you too," I said, feeling very young. "And Mom."

Introductions were made with Evan, and then we all sat down at the table. Pictures of the twins were scattered everywhere. The NICU had been no deterrent to Candace, who brought a camera nearly every day.

"I heard the good news," Roland said. "I'm so happy for you. They're beautiful."

"And we got some good news about them today." How could I have forgotten my big announcement? As expected, Candace and Charles were delighted at the thought of holding Isaac and Ivy. "You need to come see them," I added to Roland. "We could go back tonight. Or in the morning. How long will you be around?"

It was at that moment, as the question left my lips, that I realized something. Roland wasn't supposed to be here. That had been an unquestionable part of the plan from its inception. Roland could be tracked, and no matter how much we might miss each other, distance was the safest option. I met his eyes and could tell he knew what I had just realized.

"Not sure," he said vaguely. "But I can definitely make time to see them." His evasive answer didn't surprise me. His presence must mean there'd been some Otherworldly development, and that wasn't a topic we could discuss with the Reeds. A glint in his eye told me we'd talk about it later, and I gave a quick nod of understanding.

Dinner was requisite, of course, and conversation shifted to happier topics, like the twins and Candace's cooking. I couldn't get enough of talking about Isaac and Ivy, yet at the same time, a nagging feeling dimmed some of my joy. Roland being here couldn't be a good thing.

Our chance to talk finally came later when Evan left and Candace and Charles settled down to watch the evening news. Roland and I went on a walk around the Reeds' vast property, ensuring we'd have ample privacy.

"What's going on?" I asked. "I'm glad you're here—you have no idea how glad—but there must be a reason you'd risk someone from the Otherworld following you."

Roland sighed and came to a halt beside a pecan tree. "That's the thing. There's no risk because no one's trying to find you anymore."

I stared incredulously. "What? That's . . . that's impossible. Of course they are. Kingdoms were on the verge of war because of me."

"Not anymore," he said. "They've got bigger things to worry about."

"Bigger things than the divisive prophecy saying my son will lead their armies into conquering this world?"

"Amazingly, yes." He gazed up at the starry sky, gathering his thoughts. "I guess it started . . . oh, I don't know . . . a month or maybe a month and a half ago. It seems the Otherworld—or rather, large parts of it—were struck by a blight."

"What does that entail exactly?" I asked. For some reason, "blight" made me think of barren fields and locust plagues.

"Winter," he said bluntly. "Perpetual winter. And not just any winter—pretty much the worst you can imagine. It came without warning. Steady snow and frigid temperatures that kill people and crops. I wouldn't have believed it until I saw it myself."

"Which kingdoms?" I asked, frowning. Most of the lands remained in a permanent climate—a pleasant one—like mine and Dorian's kingdoms. Some monarchs did have their kingdoms cycle through four seasons, but they did so with the same kind of preparation that we did in the human world, making sure there were provisions put aside for the winter. Maiwenn's kingdom was like this.

Roland's face was grim. "All of them. At least, most of the ones in your 'neighborhood.' Some farther-out ones were spared, but everything you know was struck."

The implications didn't hit me immediately, and when they did, I wasn't sure I believed them. "You don't mean . . . not . . . not *my* kingdoms."

His only answer was a nod.

"That's not possible. I mean, the Thorn Land's a desert! And besides, I would know. . . ." Yet, even as I spoke, I wondered if that was true. Would I know? I had removed myself from the land, leaving it to Jasmine's care. I didn't connect with it in a deep way anymore. All I had was that steady humming that told me my bond to my kingdoms was in place—a bond, I realized, that had felt numb recently. I'd written it off to distance or Jasmine's caretaking. "It's not because of Jasmine, is it? Like, did the land not accept her?"

"You're missing the point again, Eugenie. It's *everywhere.* Yours. Dorian's. Everyone's."

"Dorian's . . ."

That was what really drove the point home. Despite Roland's words, there was some part of me that could still blame my absence for the blight in my own lands. Other kingdoms' suffering could be written off to weak monarchs. But Dorian? Dorian was strong. His bond to his kingdom was rock solid, his control of it absolute. If there was any monarch whose power would protect his land against impossible odds, it would be Dorian, followed closely by Maiwenn.

"Oh my God," I said. "That's what they wanted, isn't it? Dorian and Maiwenn summoned Volusian to come to me with some message, and I sent him away. I thought it was a ploy, but it wasn't—was it? They were trying to tell me about this."

"Most likely," agreed Roland. "I hadn't heard about that. Dorian only recently got in touch with me to convince me to come over and see it for myself. Then he begged me to let you know what was happening."

"Dorian doesn't beg," I murmured, still stunned.

Roland stared off into the shadows, his face troubled. "Under most circumstances, I wouldn't have told you. People can't live in cold like that, and those who survive have no food. You know how I feel about the gentry. But when I actually saw it . . . the death and sickness. Well. I don't know, Eugenie. I don't like them, but no one should suffer like that. Not even the gentry."

I sank down to the grass, mostly because I felt exhausted in mind rather than body. My lands. My kingdoms were suffering . . . had been suffering for a long time . . . and I hadn't known. Maybe I could leave Otherworldly politics behind. Maybe I could even leave my enemies behind. But the land was part of me. I was responsible for it, and I had failed it.

"I don't know what I can do," I said. "Even if I went back . . . I mean, if Dorian and Maiwenn haven't come up with any ideas, I'm not sure I could do better."

"They mentioned something about uniting powers to attempt to break the spell. . . . I didn't really follow that, though." Roland's tone conveyed that even if he pitied the gentry for their suffering, their magic was still something he had no use for. "Dorian also has some ideas about who's responsible."

Of course he would. Even if his own magical attempts proved ineffectual, Dorian wouldn't sit idly by. He'd try to solve this mystery. My knowledge of the situation was limited, but I tried to figure out where his thought process might go. I jumped back to one of Roland's earlier comments, about how some outlying kingdoms hadn't been affected.

"Who isn't under the blight?" I asked. "You said a few weren't."

"The Yew Land is one," said Roland, looking surprised at my leap. "That's who Dorian thinks—"

"—is responsible?" I guessed.

"How did you know that?"

"Because as much as I hate to admit it, I know how Dorian thinks. If some places were affected and some weren't, I'd look at the unaffected ones too."

"That's what Dorian said." Roland didn't look pleased that I could "think like Dorian," and I could definitely understand his dismay. "But that's not all. Apparently, they're making quite a profit off of food. Their land—and I guess their, what, subsidiaries?—are still able to grow and produce food, and they have no qualms about selling it to the stricken lands at very, very high prices."

I was aghast. "That's terrible."

Roland shrugged. "But some of the monarchs are willing to pay, rather than see their people suffer. And it's better than the alternative. . . ."

I looked up sharply at his ominous tone. "What alternative?"

"Stealing."

"From the Yew Land?" I certainly didn't endorse theft but was surprised Roland would care one way or another about gentry stealing from each other.

"No," he said. "From humans. There are gentry who have been raiding our world for food and supplies."

I gaped, unable to immediately form a response. I knew better than to say "that's impossible" again, but it was still hard to believe. "If there were elementals going on food rampages, I think I would've heard about that. They're not exactly subtle, and there are only a handful of gentry who can cross over in true form." Dorian was one, but I knew with absolute confidence he'd never lower himself to that.

"A handful is all it takes," said Roland. "And those are exactly the ones doing this—not the elementals. One of them's that boy . . . the one I saw that day in the Rowan Land, whose sister had been attacked? You know him, right?"

I jumped back on my feet. "Pagiel? No. No way. He wouldn't . . . *no*." Once again, though, I had to question myself. Pagiel was entirely capable of crossing worlds intact. Even though I knew he was good at heart, I also knew he had a fierce, passionate streak about the things he believed in. He'd made it clear—both in his defense of me and his sister—that he didn't care about the dangers involved if it meant doing what he believed was right. And if ever there was a cause that would trigger all his noble impulses, wouldn't it be feeding his starving people?

Yes, Pagiel as an Otherworldly Robin Hood was very much a possibility. With his powers to control wind and air, he'd also be a formidable—

"Oh Lord," I said. A flashback came to me of that weird story in the news about a Tucson robbery. "I saw something about a grocery store in Tucson. That was him, wasn't it?"

"Yes," said Roland. "With a couple cronies. The one good thing is that they're pretty fast and efficient. Most humans don't know what they're seeing when the hits occur, so there hasn't been any mass hysteria about supernatural invaders—yet. And that's the thing. . . ."

I snapped myself out of my dizzying ruminations and focused on him. The lines of his face were hard . . . and filled with sorrow. "What is?"

"Do you know how hard it was for me to come to you? I swore nothing would get me out here . . . no matter how many of those bastards come knocking at my door or tried to get me to tell where you were at." I flinched, wondering just "how many" there had been. "I was willing to maintain the plan, no matter what, for as long as it took to keep you safe . . . and then all *this* came along. Never in a million years could I have foreseen this."

"I don't think anyone could have," I said softly. Roland was usually unshakeable; it was hard to see him so worked up.

"When I saw those people, what they were going through . . . that nearly made me come for you then and there. Then, when I found out what that boy was doing . . . well, that sealed it. We can't have that, Eugenie. You know we can't. If other gentry catch on to what he's doing and realize they too can just march on over and take what they want, you can imagine the chaos that would follow. What's really awful about it all is that in some twisted way, I understand why he's doing it. He's a kid. He sees a problem, and he's trying to fix it. God help me, maybe I'd do the same in his place."

It occurred to me then that Roland's emotion wasn't just because he'd come to me in exile or because of gentry going on rabid shopping trips. Those were upsetting him, but the real problem was that Roland's worldview had been shaken. He'd spent his life in the shamanic trade, crossing worlds and ousting those who didn't belong in ours. His view of the gentry had never been good, and it had worsened when he'd rescued my mother and later seen the way I'd been ensnared in magical schemes. Yet, now, through a weird series of events, against everything he'd always told himself, he'd suddenly come to see the gentry as . . . people.

Having your beliefs radically altered like that—no matter what your age was—could be devastating. I knew that from personal experience.

I hugged him. "It's okay," I said, unable to remember any time in my life when I'd comforted him. "You did the right thing in coming to me. You're right to feel like you do. I feel the same. It's terrible—all of it."

Roland awkwardly patted my back, and I knew he felt embarrassed by his emotions. With another sigh, he stepped back and regarded me wearily. "Yes, but what do we do about it? I can fight that kid off, you know. His hits are in Tucson—probably because of the gates—and I could easily call in a few outside shamans to help me. Still, I think a little reasoning might go farther."

"It would," I agreed. "Especially if it came from me." It was also preferable to Pagiel getting banished. Unfortunately, me "reasoning" with him was easier said than done. "I have to go back."

"Eugenie—"

"I can do it," I said, more to myself than Roland. "I'll be exposing myself, but it'll be worth it—especially now that I'm not pregnant. Except, the thing is, if I leave here and let myself be known again . . ." Here it was, the awful truth that had been building within me since Roland explained about the blight. "If I go to Tucson, I might as well go to the Otherworld while I'm at it. Once I'm out of here, I'm out. If there's some way I can help undo what's been done and save my people—to save everyone's people—then I should do it."

I could tell by his face that he'd been thinking along those lines but wasn't happy about the options either. "They really are distracted," he said. "Your enemies. They'd probably leave you alone if you could help them."

I nodded. "I know. I'm not worried about myself. I'm worried about *them*."

"The twins."

I nodded again.

He took a long time in responding. "Well, the thing is, we can pull you out of here without anyone Otherworldly knowing where you were. And that means no one will know where the twins are either. They'll be safe."

"I know," I said.

"Then what . . . ?"

Something in my stomach sank. "I don't want to leave them, plus I won't be able to contact them or get updates. And if I go to the Otherworld . . . well, you know how these things are. There's no telling how long I'll be gone." The first time I'd gone to the Otherworld, I'd intended to make a quick late-night jaunt. By the time that mess was over, I'd ended up queen of the Thorn Land. "I don't want to be away from them. I know it's silly. They probably don't even know I'm there, but I can't help it. I just feel . . ."

"Like a mother," he said. He put his arm back around me, seeming more at ease as the one doing the comforting.

"I suppose," I admitted. "I didn't think it'd happen. I've spent all these months afraid of them, afraid of what was happening to my body . . . and now that they're here, I can't imagine how I got by without them. Like I said, it's silly . . . especially since I've barely touched them."

"It's not silly at all." He was quiet for a few moments. "You don't have to go, you know. It's a mess, but no one expects you to take care of it."

"*I* do. These are my people—in the Otherworld and in Tucson. How could I ignore them and then try to teach my children to do what's right? I would always know I'd abandoned everyone else. Of course, if gentry start regularly raiding our world, my failure would hardly be a secret." I laughed but found little humor in anything right now. I leaned my head against his chest, like I used to when I was little. "I have to do this. Isaac and Ivy will be okay. No one knows they're here, and Candace and Charles have enough love for quintuplets. If the twins are discharged before I get back, they'll be more than taken care of. It's just . . ."

"What?" he asked gently.

I felt tears start to form in my eyes and willed them away. "I just wish I'd gotten the all-clear on holding them before I left."

"You can wait," he said. "Wait until you can hold them, then go to the Otherworld."

For a moment, I was tempted. Nothing seemed more important in the world—in any world—than having my son and daughter in my arms. But the longer I put off dealing with the blight, the more people would suffer. Plus, I had an uneasy feeling that if I waited much longer, I might never actually leave. My life here had been slow and comfortable, which had been good for me. It was what I had needed. It was what the twins still needed. Staying here, living a sweet, uncomplicated life with them and the Reeds would be easy. I could sink into this life and never look back. . . .

"No," I said. "The sooner I take care of this blight business, the sooner I can come back to Isaac and Ivy."

Roland held me tightly. "I'm sorry, Eugenie. I'm proud of you, but I'm so, so sorry."

"Don't be," I said, pulling gently away. "This is the right thing to do. But before we leave, there's something else we have to do."

He gave me a curious look. "What's that?"

I caught hold of his hand and tugged him forward. "Come meet your grandchildren."

Chapter 11

Leaving was even harder than I'd thought it would be. And believe me, I'd expected it to be pretty hard.

It was one thing to talk of sacrifice with Roland, when I was away from Isaac and Ivy and fired up by the thought of saving the Otherworld and stopping Pagiel from pillaging among humans. Going forward with that decision, in the light of day, proved to be an entirely different matter—especially when I was back at the hospital throughout the following week. It didn't help that the hospital staff kept regarding me like I was crazy. I knew they couldn't imagine any "family emergency" in the world that would be important enough to justify leaving the bedsides of my NICU-bound children. The nurses didn't judge—not openly—but I was certain I could see the disapproval in their eyes.

Or maybe I was just projecting.

The Reeds were equally astonished, but they had enough faith in Roland and me to believe that whatever cause was taking me away must be important. A good part of what delayed my departure was filling out the reams of paperwork that named Charles and Candace as the twins' guardians in my absence. Presuming the twins were discharged before my return, Charles and Candace would be allowed to take

Isaac and Ivy back to their home. Whenever I started discussing money to help cover the costs that such a venture would entail, nobody would listen to me.

"Nonsense," Candace exclaimed as we were eating lunch in the hospital's cafeteria one day. I had just brought up—for the tenth time—the idea of Roland and me pooling funds to buy baby supplies. "I won't hear of it. What are a few baby things here and there? It'll be nothing at all."

I might almost have believed her if I hadn't discovered a book on "baby essentials" lying around their house, with a shopping list in Candace's handwriting tucked inside. Most items—and there were a lot more than "a few"—had had "x 2" written next to them, which didn't reassure me any.

"It's too much," I argued. "You guys can't afford—"

"You have no idea what we can or can't afford," she scolded. "You just take care of whatever it is you need to and get back to them. We'll worry about those little ones. You don't have to."

It was impossible not to worry about them, though. No matter how often I told myself that the twins were out of immediate danger and simply had to fulfill their NICU time, I couldn't help but fear maybe a doctor had missed something. Likewise, although I never doubted the Reeds' love and devotion, I kept imagining worst-case scenarios. Candace had a dangerous job, after all. What if something happened to her? Would Charles be able to care for them on his own? Would he and Evan have to move in together to take care of the twins, like in some wacky sitcom?

These imaginings delayed me day after day until, one afternoon, Roland called me into Candace's home office. He'd been checking his e-mail on her computer and beckoned me over to his side. "Look at this," he said, flipping to a news website.

I leaned over his shoulder and felt my heart sink. "Oh Lord," I muttered. The story was about a group of "hooligans" who had raided and robbed an outdoor farmers market in Phoenix—on horseback. Reports and witnesses were as sketchy as the Tucson theft had been on TV, but there was no doubt in my mind that this had been Other-worldly in origin. The nature of the farmers market had probably made it easier for them. Food, pure and simple, with easy accessibility. "I don't suppose they rode their horses from Tucson to Phoenix?"

"Unlikely," Roland said, leaning back in the chair with a sigh. "Especially since people report that they seemed to have 'vanished.' My guess is they're just using a new gate. I know a couple up in that area."

I nodded along, trying to merge my mental maps of this world and the Otherworld. "There's a Phoenix one in the Willow Land. If hostilities really have been lifted, then Maiwenn would probably let Pagiel use it." I sat down cross-legged on the floor, feeling a quick spark of pride at how quickly I was regaining my flexibility. "I wonder if we should be relieved Tucson isn't the sole target—or worry that Pagiel's spreading out to other gates and other cities."

"We should be concerned that these raids are still going on, period. If you still think you're up for leaving, we should probably do it soon." His tone was hard, all-business, but I saw compassion in his eyes.

"I'm still up for it," I said sadly. "Everything's in place. If you can book us a flight for tomorrow, I'll be ready to go." Every word of that was true, but the finality of it was a hard thing to accept.

Roland made it happen. Candace and Charles sent us off with a huge farewell dinner of chicken and dumplings, though for once, the focus was less on the food and more on tying up all the loose ends and red tape with Isaac and Ivy. The morning of our flight, Roland and I left extra early so that we could make one more visit to the hospital. I don't know if my timing was just lucky or if the staff felt sorry for me, but the nurse declared we'd reached a point where it would be okay for us to hold the twins.

I could scarcely dare to believe my good fortune. The ventilators were off, but there were still lots of cords and tubes to contend with, making everything a delicate balancing act. Roland and I were each given a twin, and after a little while, we switched. Looking down at Isaac, I felt my breath catch. Although still definitely a preemie, he'd put on weight and looked much more "babylike" than he had at birth. Now that they were both a little more developed, I was more confident than ever that they'd taken after me and not Kiyo. It was just as well since they had my last name and would never have any contact with him.

Isaac slept the entire time I held him, making the small movements and coos that infants do in their sleep. He seemed very content, and I again wondered if he was aware of my presence in any way. Maybe that had been naïve of me to imagine when I was on the other side of the glass, but now, in my arms, he must surely feel some sort of subconscious connection . . . right?

So much has been done because of you, I thought. *A world nearly went to war for you, and I had to change the way I lived to keep you safe.* It had been worth it, though, and I dared to wonder if maybe this current tragedy in the Otherworld would leave its residents with a new sense of solidarity that would make the Storm King prophecy seem like an irrelevant fantasy from the past. I didn't know if I'd ever want to bring my children into the Otherworld, but regardless of where they were, I wanted them to live peaceful lives that weren't plagued by war and prophecy.

Ivy was actually awake, a rare treat. Her eyes were dark blue, normal for newborns, and I'd been told we'd have to wait a bit to see what color they settled into. I hoped they'd be violet like mine and continue the trend of the twins not looking like Kiyo.

The visit was too short. I wanted to keep trading twins back and forth with Roland, memorizing every single one of my children's features. Both the NICU and our airline had their own schedules to keep, however, and we eventually had to give Isaac and Ivy back to their warm, enclosed homes. I left with a lump in my throat and hadn't gotten very far outside the nursery when I spotted Evan waiting in the hall, leaning patiently against a wall. I came to a stop, and Roland cleared his throat.

"I'll get the car and meet you up front, okay?" he said.

I nodded as he left and strolled over to Evan. "What are you doing here?" I asked. "Not that I'm not happy to see you."

Evan straightened up, giving me one of his warm smiles. "Here to see you. Sorry I couldn't come by last night—we had some late back-to-school events I couldn't miss. So, I wanted to make sure I caught you before you left."

"I'm glad," I said, surprised at the mix of feelings churning within me. I was still keyed up over my visit with the twins, and seeing him only added to the turmoil. "I would've hated to leave without saying good-bye."

"Well," he said. "It's not really good-bye, is it? You'll be back."

"Of course," I agreed. "I just don't know when."

"Well, you know we'll take care of everything, so don't you worry."

I laughed. "You sound just like your aunt and uncle. Candace keeps saying the same thing."

"Just telling it like it is." He shrugged. "I know you wouldn't go without a good reason. So, take care of what you have to, and know that we're all here for you—and for them." He nodded toward the nursery.

"I know . . . and I'm sorry . . . sorry I have to go. . . ."

Evan gently reached out toward me and placed his

fingers under my chin, tipping my head up so that I had to look at him. "Why are you apologizing? You haven't done anything wrong."

Maybe. The truth was, I wasn't entirely sure why I was apologizing either. Lots of reasons, I supposed. I felt bad for leaving Isaac and Ivy. I felt bad for leaving Evan.

"I just feel like I'm abandoning everyone," I admitted.

"Abandoning would be taking off without leaving any provisions for your children or if you just left on a whim. None of that's true."

That well-worn thought came to me again, of how simple life would be here, with him. The "simple" part had nothing to do with the Southern jokes I'd made when Roland first sent me here. It was all about this family, these people with their unconditional love and willingness to let everyone make their own choices. It was about a lifestyle free of politics and schemes. I took hold of Evan's hand and squeezed it.

"Thank you. For everything. I really appreciate it."

He gave me a quizzical look. "For what, taking you fishing?"

"Yes, actually. And all the other million little activities you took me on. You have no idea how much it all meant to me, how much I needed those."

"Well, geez," he said, turning adorably flustered. I even caught sight of a blush. "I was just worried you were bored left alone at the house all day. If I'd known I was being rated, I would've taken you on a proper date."

I laughed again and gave him a quick kiss on the cheek. "You did, believe me. Countless times."

He blushed further. "I don't know about that. But when you get back, well . . . then maybe . . ."

"Maybe," I agreed, stepping back. Even now, he was still cautious of pushing too hard on my boundaries. "Thanks again . . . and thank you for, well, for them." I pointed back at the NICU. "I know you'll be just as busy with them as your aunt and uncle will be."

Evan smiled. "There's nothing to thank me for when it comes to those two."

Our farewell took some of the sting out of having to leave the twins, but I was left melancholy and wistful for a whole new set of reasons as Roland and I began our journey home.

After a couple connections and layovers, we finally made it back to Tucson in early evening. For the first time in a very long while, I allowed myself to truly focus on something that wasn't the twins. Tucson. How long had it been since I'd been here? Even before my time in Huntsville, I'd had to avoid my hometown for fear of gentry assassins. Looking at the Sonora Desert that surrounded the city, bathed in the oranges and reds of sunset, I felt a surge of joy spread through me. *Home.* Maybe Tucson didn't have the magical pull of my Otherworldly kingdoms, but I'd ached for it nonetheless.

My mother cried out in joy when Roland and I walked into their house. She raced forward, catching me in a tight embrace. I thought I heard a muffled sob and hoped she wouldn't cry because I was pretty sure I'd start crying too. She clung to me for a long time, as though fearing I might vanish again if she let go. When she finally stepped back, she took one look at me and asked, "What happened?" My body wasn't a hundred percent back to its original shape, but it was pretty obvious I was no longer pregnant.

"You're a grandmother," I said, opting for simplicity.

Since it looked like my mom was on the verge of passing out, we all moved to the kitchen table in order to recap what had been happening. Roland and I had plenty of digital pictures to share, and my mother pored over them, a look of wonder on her face that I was pretty sure mirrored mine. She grilled us on the twins' health and the hospital's care, then moved on to an examination of the Reeds.

For her own safety, I didn't tell my mom where the Reeds lived. As I described them, I had a momentary weird feeling as I realized this all read like some sort of real-life fairy tale. Two children, living in obscurity with a childless couple, only to discover later that they were the offspring of a fairy queen.

Once my mother was satisfied Ivy and Isaac were getting quality care, she moved on to much more momlike things. "Did you really have to name her Ivy?" my mother asked. She wrinkled her nose. "It's such a . . . hippie name."

I rolled my eyes. "It's a fine name. And it sounds nice with Isaac."

My mother looked skeptical. "Well. So do Isabelle and Irene."

There was no question I'd stay overnight at their house, but I knew that was probably the only time I could spend in Tucson. My mother would've kept me forever if she could, but Roland and I both knew that I couldn't delay much longer in getting to the Otherworld. I planned on spending most of the next day acquiring gear for the wintry conditions of the Otherworld's blight. Roland shook his head when I told him that night that I planned on getting my down coat from my own house the next day.

"You're going to need more than that," he said ominously. "You need to go all out. Scarves, gloves, boots. Then layer up underneath those."

"This is summer in Tucson," I reminded him, just in case he hadn't noticed the weather right outside his window. "Where am I going to find that stuff?" There was actually a thriving ski trade outside of town in the winter, so getting supplies wouldn't have been that difficult any other time of year.

"It's out there. You're just going to have to do a little bit of hunting."

He was right. Daytime found me on quite the scavenger hunt as I scoured the city for sporting goods stores that had any meager winter stock. Secondhand stores provided some luck as well, particularly for things like sweaters. My Tucson nostalgia was still going strong, so in some ways, I didn't mind driving all over. I was able to see all the familiar sights I'd missed and even grab lunch at one of my favorite hole-in-the-wall Southwest restaurants.

Late afternoon found me back in the Catalina Foothills, heading toward my own house. Just like everything else around here, it had been months since I'd been to the house. I pulled into the driveway and sat in my car for several minutes, taking in the familiar view. It looked exactly the way I'd left it, with its stucco finish and rock garden of a lawn. The house wasn't big—it only had two bedrooms—but there'd been plenty of space for my needs. Plus, it had been *mine*, my own sanctuary, in a way that even the Otherworldly castles weren't, seeing as those always had people coming and going.

I'd gotten a spare key from my parents and let myself inside, relieved the locks hadn't been changed. I'd left the house in the care of my old roommate, Tim. He wasn't the type to make radical changes, but if any Otherworldly denizens had come calling after I left, I wouldn't have been surprised if Tim had taken some extreme security precautions.

When I stepped into my kitchen, however, I came to a total standstill and wished I'd brought a weapon. There was a stranger sitting at my table.

"Who the hell are you?" I demanded.

He was wearing a stiff gray suit and had short, neatly trimmed black hair. His face was turned away from me as he rummaged through a briefcase on the table, but he jumped in alarm at the sound of my voice. He spun toward me, face showing the same panic I felt. After a few moments of study, however, his eyes widened, and his body relaxed.

"Eug?"

I stared, wondering how this guy knew my name, and then . . . I saw it. I gasped in disbelief.

"*Tim?* Is that you?"

He flashed me a grin and settled back in the chair. "Of course it's me. Who else would be here?"

I was dumbfounded and couldn't answer right away. "But you . . . you're wearing a tie." .

He glanced down and scowled at the paisley silk monstrosity around his neck. "Yeah, it's a pain, but my job has a dress code."

"Your . . . your job?" I felt like I'd wandered into some alternate reality and had to seek out a chair of my own at the table, lest I faint out of sheer mental exhaustion.

"Yup," he said with mock enthusiasm. "I'm a productive member of society."

"You cut your hair," I said, reduced to simply pointing out the obvious.

"Another requirement of the job." He absentmindedly smoothed some of his hair back and then brightened. "But they let me wear my headdress."

"Your headdress?"

He jumped up again and disappeared down the hall that led to the bedrooms. While he was gone, I glanced around, looking for any other signs that I had entered a parallel universe. Nope. Everything else was the same. Tim returned shortly, carrying a full, feathered Lakota headdress that reached nearly to the floor. He put it on and grinned at me triumphantly.

"See?"

I looked him over from head to toe, taking in the formal

suit juxtaposed with feathers. "Where exactly do you work?"

"I sell car insurance," he explained.

"And they let you wear all that to work?"

He sat down again and left the headdress on. "They encourage it, actually. They really support the idea of a diverse workplace and wanted to hire as many minorities as they could. And even though there's a dress code, it's really important to them that their minorities express their unique cultural heritage. Wearing this is a way to bring some Native American influence into the workplace."

"But Tim . . . you aren't Native American."

This, at least, was semi-familiar territory. Tim, having few employable skills, had spent most of his life marketing what he did have: coloring and features that looked Native American to those who didn't know any better. He'd rotated through various tribes (usually opting for non-Southwest ones, so as not to get in trouble with the locals) and played the part to help him get laid and sell bad poetry.

"That's never stopped me before," he said, following my very thoughts.

"Yeah, but when it comes to the workplace . . . I mean, if you're getting some kind of benefit, you usually have to show documentation or something. And I *know* you don't have that."

He shrugged. "I seemed so authentic that they didn't even bother doing a background check. There was another guy interviewing for the same position. I think he was full-blooded Apache, but he didn't do *anything* to play that up. Just showed up in a suit. If he'd worn war paint, he might have gotten hired over me."

I groaned. "Probably he was doing something crazy, like—oh, I don't know—relying on professionalism and job skills. What on earth drove you to get a job anyway? I mean, I'm impressed—well, not with the fake Lakota act—but it's not something I expected from you."

"That makes two of us." His earlier enthusiasm dimmed. "It was all Lara's doing. She said if you weren't around, then it was 'immoral' for me to keep living here rent-free." When we'd been roommates, Tim had earned his keep by doing housework and cooking.

I felt a smile creep over my face. "You're still with her?" Tim getting together with my former secretary had been both unexpected and delightful. It was on par with Rurik and Shaya's seemingly mismatched relationship.

"Yup." Tim sighed. "Oh, the things I do for love, Eug. Anyway, yeah, she said it wasn't right to drain your bank account for the mortgage, so I got a job, and she stopped the auto-deductions or whatever. Now we cover it."

"So she lives here too," I mused. I wasn't surprised that Lara had been able to alter my mortgage payment options. She'd always known more about my finances and business affairs than I had. "Where is she? I'd love to see her."

He glanced at the clock. "Still at work. That Enrique guy has her working crazy hours, but at least she pulls a lot of them." That too was welcome news. As my business had dried up, I'd worried about Lara and had introduced her to a private detective who needed clerical help. Apparently things had worked out. "But forget about us. Where have *you* been? Jesus, Eug. It's been, what? Almost half a year? I didn't think you were coming back."

There was legitimate hurt in his voice, and I realized that I hadn't spared much care for friends who might have wondered at my disappearance. Tim knew I was involved with the Otherworld, but he had no idea of the extent of my entanglement. He hadn't even known I was pregnant. I'd taken off before it was obvious.

"It's complicated," I said. "And messy. All I can tell you

is that I had some, uh, things to take care of, and it was better for all of us that I stayed away."

"Without even a hint that you were okay?" Again, the hurt and accusation in his voice took me aback.

"I'm sorry," I said. "I . . . I just didn't think. I can honestly say it was safer for you not to know, but I should've sent some message . . . or even left a note."

"If the visitors we initially had were any indication, I can understand the 'safe' part," he admitted.

"Visitors?" My earlier instincts may have been right after all.

He waved a dismissive hand, like it was no big deal. "Yeah, kind of a random assortment. I don't know what kind of creatures they all were—Lara could probably tell you. Your old man was around a lot and got rid of them, and before long, they stopped coming. I guess they recognized a lost cause."

I hadn't realized Roland had done that for me, though it shouldn't have come as a surprise. He was the kind of conscientious person who would think of things like that. I owed him. If it hadn't been for him, Tim might not be so blasé about his "visitors."

"So, hey, that's taken care of. No harm done. Now. Let's move on to more important things." He stood up and took the headdress off. "What do you want for dinner? It's been a while, but I still remember your favorites. We've even still got a stash of Milky Ways."

I grinned. "I'll take those, but I'm afraid I can't stick around. I've got to get a few things and then head out."

Tim had been about to open a cupboard and stopped. His face fell. "Can't you even stay to see Lara? She'll probably be back in, oh, an hour. Two at most."

I glanced at the clock and felt my own disappointment. "I don't think I can. I'm heading out of town again and still have to figure things out." Aside from my mom wanting to see me tonight, Roland and I had a few logistics to discuss about my Otherworldly trip.

"Damn," Tim said. "You sure do know how to toy with a guy's emotions, Eug."

"I'm sorry," I said, flashing what I hoped was a sympathetic look. "I'll try to be back soon. Honest." I wondered how Tim would feel if he knew that when I did come back, I might have two babies in tow.

He nodded. "Okay. Can I at least help you get what you need?"

"Sure," I told him. "I need to dig out my winter stuff— like, my real winter stuff."

That got a raised eyebrow, and he asked no questions. We were able to locate what I wanted quickly, largely because—despite his many quirks—Tim ran an efficient household and had had everything neatly arranged in storage. Once that was set, it was time for good-bye. Just like all my other partings, I felt guilty over this one. At least I knew Tim didn't *need* me, not like others did. Plus, I was actually able to say good-bye this time, instead of disappearing on him. Surely that had to count for something.

I left him shortly thereafter and headed back toward Roland and Mom's house. Again, I felt that ache in my chest as I took in the gorgeous scenery of the foothills. I loved this area. It was why I'd shaped the Thorn Land in its image. It hardly seemed fair to be leaving here so soon, yet at the same time . . . a thrill of excitement ran through me. Part of my heart might be here in Arizona, but the rest of it was tied up elsewhere, in a place I was burning to see as much as I had been to see this one.

Tomorrow I would return to the Otherworld.

Chapter 12

I felt a little ridiculous when my mom dropped Roland and me off at a gate out in the Sonora Desert. In addition to my down coat, I also had on a turtleneck, sweater, jeans, tights, knee-high boots, gloves, scarf, and knit hat. Roland was similarly bundled up. It was super early in the morning, but the temperature was already on the rise. Fortunately, there were no hikers out yet to see the spectacle we made.

I was riding shotgun, and my mom caught a hold of my hand before I got out of the car. "Be careful," she said. "And don't stay away so long this time."

"I won't," I said, hoping I could keep my word. I gave her hand one last squeeze and then stepped outside, where I was immediately blasted by morning heat. I grimaced, feeling like I was in an oven. "Let's do this."

Roland nodded and headed over toward the gate. To the uninitiated, it simply looked like any other place out there in the desert. We knew what signs to watch for, however, and could even sense the gate's power. It was of moderate strength, meaning it required little effort for us to cross— and was the kind that a wayward person could accidentally get caught up in on a sabbat day. Roland gave me one last questioning look.

"Sure you're ready?"

"Very," I said, not feeling sure at all.

We stepped through, and I felt that familiar and always-disconcerting sensation of being stretched, pulled apart, and reassembled again. Knowing what to expect helped a little, and within moments, I was back to myself—just in time to be nearly knocked over by a blast of wind. I caught hold of the first thing I could, which turned out to be Roland. He steadied me as I regained my footing and stared around in disbelief at what I saw.

White, as far as the eye could see. We stood on one of the main roads that traversed the Otherworld. It was covered in snow that looked like it had been packed down somewhat by wagons, horses, and feet. I wondered also if there was some magic to the road that kept it semi-clear because the snow covering it was nothing compared to the drifts on either side of us, which came nearly to my waist. Also lining the road were trees coated in both ice and snow. There was almost something beautiful to their delicate, lacy appearance—yet at the same time, the trees had a stricken and forlorn feel to them. They were imprisoned, struggling to stay alive.

With nearly everything blanketed in the ice and snow, it was difficult to pick out many features in the land. Even the sky was dreary, covered in white and gray clouds. This could have been any place, really. The unique characteristics that normally identified the various kingdoms were obscured in white, but I didn't need any of them. I knew exactly where we were.

We were in the Rowan Land.

My eyes had a difficult time believing it, but my heart knew. I sank to my knees and rested my palms flat on the ground. There it was, the hum of energy that sang within the land of every kingdom, the energy that made up the bond we shared. It screamed out to me for help . . . and at

"Sure you're ready?"

"Very," I said, not feeling sure at all.

We stepped through, and I felt that familiar and always-disconcerting sensation of being stretched, pulled apart, and reassembled again. Knowing what to expect helped a little, and within moments, I was back to myself—just in time to be nearly knocked over by a blast of wind. I caught hold of the first thing I could, which turned out to be Roland. He steadied me as I regained my footing and stared around in disbelief at what I saw.

White, as far as the eye could see. We stood on one of the main roads that traversed the Otherworld. It was covered in snow that looked like it had been packed down somewhat by wagons, horses, and feet. I wondered also if there was some magic to the road that kept it semi-clear because the snow covering it was nothing compared to the drifts on either side of us, which came nearly to my waist. Also lining the road were trees coated in both ice and snow. There was almost something beautiful to their delicate, lacy appearance—yet at the same time, the trees had a stricken and forlorn feel to them. They were imprisoned, struggling to stay alive.

With nearly everything blanketed in the ice and snow, it was difficult to pick out many features in the land. Even the sky was dreary, covered in white and gray clouds. This could have been any place, really. The unique characteristics that normally identified the various kingdoms were obscured in white, but I didn't need any of them. I knew exactly where we were.

We were in the Rowan Land.

My eyes had a difficult time believing it, but my heart knew. I sank to my knees and rested my palms flat on the ground. There it was, the hum of energy that sang within the land of every kingdom, the energy that made up the bond we shared. It screamed out to me for help . . . and at

is that I had some, uh, things to take care of, and it was better for all of us that I stayed away."

"Without even a hint that you were okay?" Again, the hurt and accusation in his voice took me aback.

"I'm sorry," I said. "I . . . I just didn't think. I can honestly say it was safer for you not to know, but I should've sent some message . . . or even left a note."

"If the visitors we initially had were any indication, I can understand the 'safe' part," he admitted.

"Visitors?" My earlier instincts may have been right after all.

He waved a dismissive hand, like it was no big deal. "Yeah, kind of a random assortment. I don't know what kind of creatures they all were—Lara could probably tell you. Your old man was around a lot and got rid of them, and before long, they stopped coming. I guess they recognized a lost cause."

I hadn't realized Roland had done that for me, though it shouldn't have come as a surprise. He was the kind of conscientious person who would think of things like that. I owed him. If it hadn't been for him, Tim might not be so blasé about his "visitors."

"So, hey, that's taken care of. No harm done. Now. Let's move on to more important things." He stood up and took the headdress off. "What do you want for dinner? It's been a while, but I still remember your favorites. We've even still got a stash of Milky Ways."

I grinned. "I'll take those, but I'm afraid I can't stick around. I've got to get a few things and then head out."

Tim had been about to open a cupboard and stopped. His face fell. "Can't you even stay to see Lara? She'll probably be back in, oh, an hour. Two at most."

I glanced at the clock and felt my own disappointment. "I don't think I can. I'm heading out of town again and still have to figure things out." Aside from my mom wanting to see me tonight, Roland and I had a few logistics to discuss about my Otherworldly trip.

"Damn," Tim said. "You sure do know how to toy with a guy's emotions, Eug."

"I'm sorry," I said, flashing what I hoped was a sympathetic look. "I'll try to be back soon. Honest." I wondered how Tim would feel if he knew that when I did come back, I might have two babies in tow.

He nodded. "Okay. Can I at least help you get what you need?"

"Sure," I told him. "I need to dig out my winter stuff—like, my real winter stuff."

That got a raised eyebrow, and he asked no questions. We were able to locate what I wanted quickly, largely because—despite his many quirks—Tim ran an efficient household and had had everything neatly arranged in storage. Once that was set, it was time for good-bye. Just like all my other partings, I felt guilty over this one. At least I knew Tim didn't *need* me, not like others did. Plus, I was actually able to say good-bye this time, instead of disappearing on him. Surely that had to count for something.

I left him shortly thereafter and headed back toward Roland and Mom's house. Again, I felt that ache in my chest as I took in the gorgeous scenery of the foothills. I loved this area. It was why I'd shaped the Thorn Land in its image. It hardly seemed fair to be leaving here so soon, yet at the same time . . . a thrill of excitement ran through me. Part of my heart might be here in Arizona, but the rest of it was tied up elsewhere, in a place I was burning to see as much as I had been to see this one.

Tomorrow I would return to the Otherworld.

Chapter 12

I felt a little ridiculous when my mom dro[pped] and me off at a gate out in the Sonora Desert. to my down coat, I also had on a turtleneck, sw[eater] tights, knee-high boots, gloves, scarf, and knit [hat] was similarly bundled up. It was super early in t[he] but the temperature was already on the rise. F[or] there were no hikers out yet to see the spectacle

I was riding shotgun, and my mom caugh[t] my hand before I got out of the car. "Be careful[." And don't stay away so long this time."

"I won't," I said, hoping I could keep my w[ord] her hand one last squeeze and then stepped outsi[de] I was immediately blasted by morning heat. I g[ot] feeling like I was in an oven. "Let's do this."

Roland nodded and headed over toward the ga[te] uninitiated, it simply looked like any other place in the desert. We knew what signs to watch for, [I] and could even sense the gate's power. It was of n[o] strength, meaning it required little effort for us to and was the kind that a wayward person could acci[dentally] get caught up in on a sabbat day. Roland gave me [a] questioning look.

the same time, it felt muted. It was like someone beating on glass, desperate to get out but unable to break the barrier. I couldn't break it either and understood more than ever why I hadn't known about the lands' distress while in the human world. The land hadn't been able to fully reach me.

Roland touched my shoulder. "Eugenie, come on. We shouldn't stay out here any longer than we have to."

I knew he was right and reluctantly got back on my feet, surprised to feel myself shaking all over. I suspected it was as much from shock as from the cold.

"I didn't expect this," I said as I began following him down the road. "I mean, visually, yes. Each time you described the blight, I kept picturing this documentary I once saw about Antarctica. This isn't far off, except with less penguins. What I didn't expect was how the land felt. This cold, or rather the magic that's causing it, goes all the way to the land's core. Until now, I thought only I could reach that deep."

"If you're able to reach that far, were you able to get any sense if you could undo the magic?"

"Not just then, no. It seemed like the magic was entrapping the land, and there was nothing I could do to break through." I saw Roland frown but didn't know if that was in disappointment or because of his inability to fully comprehend gentry magic. "Maybe in time, I could find a way."

I wasn't so sure, however. I had to imagine the other monarchs had experienced the same sensations I had, and if they hadn't been able to find a way to crack the enchantment after all this time, it seemed unlikely I'd be able to either.

After a little traveling on the road, the land shifted, and we found ourselves in a different kingdom. I knew instantly that it wasn't mine and was almost relieved to be free of the Rowan Land's pleading. Without that innate connection, though, I couldn't readily identify where we were. It took the sight of some massive oaks in the distance, their leafless branches burdened by snow, to tip me off.

"The Oak Land," I murmured. Dorian's kingdom. Even though I knew he'd been affected, it was still incredible to see the reality. Many of the other kingdoms around here had changed since I became a frequent visitor, but the red-hued, perpetual autumn of his realm had remained constant. It was unreal to see a land that had once flourished in vivid color, now so barren and stark.

"Do you want to see Dorian?" asked Roland.

"No," I said, even though I kind of did. "We'll stick to the original plan and check in with the Thorn Land first. I need to see my own people."

Another shifting of the road took us back to the Rowan Land, and still another took us into the Willow Land. I cringed, expecting an ambush, but the world around us remained frozen and silent. The only change was that in addition to the wind that had been constantly blowing, snow now began falling as well. It stung our faces and eyes and continued when we made our next crossing, into the Thorn Land.

Although the land had its own unique feel, its cry for freedom matched that of my other kingdom. I stared around, watching the snow fall, unable to believe that this landscape had once been a mirror of Tucson.

"We've got to go off the road now to reach the castle," I said. "Usually there's a smaller road or at least a path that splits away, but if there's anything like that . . ." I shook my head at the drifts, unable to differentiate one from another. "Well. It's buried."

Roland eyed the snow, which was as high as three feet in some places, depending on how the wind had blown it. The visible parts of his face were red, and I knew he was as cold as me. "This is going to be fun to walk through. You're sure you know where you're going?"

"Yeah. I can feel where everything is around here, and the castle's that way." I hesitated before continuing. "You probably won't like this, but I can make things a little easier."

The blight's enchantment was too powerful and all-encompassing for me to break or affect on a large scale with my weather magic, but I still had some control over the individual elements. The blight's greater spell had been to simply lay wintry weather on the land. Once in place, that weather behaved like any other. I summoned my magic to me, gathering the air and already gusting wind. Directing it forward, I made the air blast into the snow ahead of us, serving as a magical snow blower to create a more accessible path. Roland scowled but didn't protest. He knew as well as I did that we'd be out here all day if we had to trudge through this mess unaided.

Still, it took us a few hours to reach our destination, and by that point, I could barely feel my limbs. I kept telling my legs to move forward and took it on faith that they'd obey. I was also just exhausted. Even with magical help, we still had to walk through some snow, and I was a long way from being in my former physical shape. Roland, judging from his heavy breathing beside me, was fighting hard too.

The Thorn Land's blocky fortress of a castle came into sight when we were still a good distance from it. The terrain's basic features had remained under the blight, and the land was relatively flat here, making the black stone building show up in high contrast against the snow. We were close enough to be in range of patrolling guards, and one of them soon rode up to us, demanding to know who we were.

"Me," I said, braving the cold to remove my hat and scarf.

It took several moments of staring before his face registered recognition. Even then, it was easy to tell he didn't believe what he saw. "Y-Your Majesty? Is it really you?"

"The same," I said, bundling back up. "Just a little colder."

The guard turned and yelled something. Moments later, another scout rode up and shared his colleague's shock and amazement. "Ride back and tell them she's here," said the first guard. He dismounted and offered his horse to Roland and me. "Go on and get warm. I'll follow on foot."

I started to protest, but the guard was dressed warmly and had probably become more used to this weather than we were. I thanked him and mounted the horse with Roland. My body remembered how to do it without difficulty, and I was again pleased to be regaining my former agility. The horse moved slower with two, but our speed was much better than if we'd been on foot. The guard who'd ridden ahead had long since beaten us, so we found a crowd waiting for us at the castle's entrance.

I climbed down from the horse ungracefully—reminding me I shouldn't be *quite* so cocky yet about my improved athleticism. The clumsy move made me look like an undignified queen, but it was clear none of that mattered once the people caught sight of my face. I heard awed gasps, and one by one, they began falling to their knees in the snow with murmurs of "Your Majesty." I'd never been entirely comfortable with these shows of loyalty in the best conditions, let alone snowy and frigid ones. I was about to urge them to get up when I noticed one person still standing.

"Jasmine!" I exclaimed, rushing forward.

My sister stood wrapped in a fur-lined cloak, her face pale. It flooded with relief when I caught her in a big hug. She returned it with more fierceness than I would've expected, considering we weren't usually so touchy-feely. "Thank God you're back," she said into my shoulder. "Now we can fix all this."

I wasn't ready to tell her yet that I wasn't sure I *could* fix it. Yet, as I finally managed to get everyone to return inside,

I could see from the servants' faces that they too thought everything would improve now that I was back. That faith made me uneasy. I also noted that, aside from the guards who'd been on patrol, Jasmine was the only one in any sort of suitable gentry-style winter attire. The others who had rushed out to see me had been wearing clothing that had clearly been patched together to protect against the cold, with mismatched layers haphazardly arranged. Better than nothing, I supposed.

After a few greetings and nondescript assurances, Roland and I were able to leave the crowd and meet Jasmine in a cozy sitting room. When Aeson, this kingdom's former ruler, had been in charge, the land had undergone seasons, and the castle had been built to accommodate winter. That had made for miserable conditions once I turned the land into a desert, often making this keep feel like a kiln. Now, that design paid off. The sitting room was small, with no windows, and held the heat coming from a blazing fire. I was pretty sure it was the first time I'd ever seen one of the fireplaces in use here.

Jasmine told me she'd sent word "to the others," whatever that meant. She then gave orders for food and drink to the servants before finally settling into a chair. There was a maturity to her that hadn't been there before, likely the result of being forced to take charge of so much so quickly. She kept her cloak on, but I was ready to remove my layers. I was still cold but felt heavy and encumbered. Roland must have felt the same way because he too stripped off his winter wear. We both found chairs and dragged them as close to the fire as possible. Jasmine sighed.

"I don't know if it's because I grew up in the desert or if it's just because this weather's such a bitch, but I swear—" Her jaw dropped as she did a double take at me. "You . . . you're not pregnant!"

I thought it had been obvious right away, but I suppose the coat might have been deceptive. "Nope, not anymore."

"But you . . ." Her words died again, and I could see her mentally crunching numbers in her head. "You shouldn't be due for a few more weeks. Did you—"

"Everything's fine," I said quickly, seeing panic start to overtake her. "They just came early. About a month ago. They needed lots of medical help, but everything looks great for them."

She relaxed, but her blue-gray eyes were still wide. "Then you're . . . wow. You're a mom. And I'm an aunt."

I smiled. "Yup. Their names are Isaac and Ivy." I wasn't going to say a word, not even to her, about their location, but their names were safe enough. That revelation got an even bigger reaction. Jasmine filled with delight.

"You named her after me!"

I frowned, not entirely sure where that leap of logic had come from. Because of shared botanical names? "Well, I—"

"Oh, Eugenie!" She jumped up from her chair and hugged me again, leaving the cloak behind. "You're so awesome. Thanks so much!"

She seemed so happy that I figured it wasn't worth mentioning the plant names were coincidental. Just as my un-layered state had surprised her, I was astonished to look at her now and see how skinny she was. I could feel her ribs when she hugged me.

"What happened to you?" I exclaimed, once she'd sat down again. "You're skin and bones!"

Jasmine glanced down with a scowl and picked at her too-loose dress. "Oh, that. Well, there's not a lot of food anymore. Plus, trying to keep the lands alive takes a lot out of me."

Guilt ran through me. I certainly knew communing with the land took a fair amount of energy, but it hadn't occurred to me until now that doing so in these conditions would be extra taxing—especially since she was just the substitute. Maybe that bonding wasn't solely responsible for her weight loss, but I didn't doubt that keeping the land in check played a role in some of the gauntness in her face.

"Jasmine, I'm so sorry—"

She waved it off. "Don't worry. It had to be done, right? Besides, once it's charged, the land can go a while in these conditions. And you did what you needed. Everything's okay with Isaac and my namesake, which was the whole purpose."

She then proceeded to give us an account of how things had been in both kingdoms. Jasmine didn't use quite the technical language and statistics that Shaya might when describing people and resources, but she did a much better job than I would have expected. In filling in for me, Jasmine had ended up taking on a lot more responsibilities than just being the lands' caretaker. Her report gave me more specifics on the situation here, but the big picture wasn't much different from what Roland had described. As close as Jasmine was to Pagiel, she hadn't accepted any of his stolen goods—though she was undecided on whether what he was doing was wrong.

My kingdoms had, much to her chagrin, done some trading with the Yew Land. We were one of the few kingdoms that had a steady stream of resources unaffected by the cold: a thriving copper supply. We couldn't eat copper, of course, and had no other significant food sources. The crops in both kingdoms favored warm weather, and the animals in the Thorn Land hadn't been able to survive at all. The Rowan Land had some winter-ready game that had provided meat for the people, but even those animals were struggling. With limited food and a lot of copper that no one else could afford to buy, trading with the Yew Land had seemed like the only option.

"I'm sorry," said Jasmine. "I wish we didn't have to—

especially since those bastards are probably responsible for this mess."

"It's okay," I assured her. "You had to feed the people, and the copper was doing us no good."

A servant arrived just then to announce a group of guests had arrived: Dorian, Shaya, Rurik, and Pagiel. "How'd they get here so fast?" I asked, once the servant went to fetch them. Jasmine had said she'd sent word, but even with magical communication, the trip from Dorian's land would've taken a while.

"They were all in the Rowan Land," explained Jasmine. She nodded toward Roland. "He gave us a heads-up that you might be coming one of these days, so Dorian's been hanging out there. He brought Pagiel because he figured you'd want to talk to him."

"He was right," I said. Despite his quirks, Dorian always had a good feel for what I was thinking.

My heart leapt when I saw him. After the dreariness of the blight, Dorian's presence was a breath of life and excitement. He swept in grandly, as though this were an ordinary state visit. He wore his typically rich, brightly colored garments, with the centerpiece being an emerald green cloak made out of satin and adorned with gold embroidery. It matched the green of his eyes and made his long hair look like a wave of fire that gave the illusion of warmth. Neither he nor any of the others were wearing heavy outerwear, so they must have shed it before entering the room. Probably whatever Dorian had for the cold weather wasn't fashionable enough for him.

He held my eyes for a moment, and I was suddenly flooded by a million thoughts. How we'd said good-bye. The memories of his body that had haunted me these last couple of months. The way I'd missed him. And again, the knowledge that he maybe loved me again.

"The wayward queen returns," he said as though none

of those other matters existed. A quick assessment revealed to him what Jasmine had also discovered. "Considerably less of her."

His tone was light, but I could tell that, also like Jasmine, he was uncertain of what had become of my pregnancy and was hesitant to presume.

"That's because I left my children behind," I said. I kept my words light too, but their meaning left an ache inside me. "They were born about a month ago and are doing well."

Shaya looked awestruck. "Truly? They're thriving after being born that early?" She shook her head in amazement. "Human medicine," was all she said on the matter. From the moment I'd met her, she'd been very outspoken about humans "twisting technology," but I think this had made her reconsider the benefits. Probably not enough to handle hearing about my C-section and the NICU, though.

Her awe soon gave way to joy. She embraced me, and even Rurik did too. Dorian and Pagiel didn't, both keeping their distance for entirely different reasons. Once the welcomes were done and we were all seated, Rurik leaned back and sighed with satisfaction.

"Well, then," he said. "Now that you're back, we can get rid of this blight."

There it was again. I grimaced. "Why does everyone think *I* can fix things?"

"You're Storm King's daughter," he replied. "The weather obeys you."

"Not *this* weather," I said. "I mean, the little parts, yeah, but all of it? It's an enchantment that's bigger than just a weather pattern. It's permeated the core of the land . . . corrupted it."

Dorian nodded. "I know exactly what you mean. And I suspected as much—that your formidable capabilities wouldn't be enough to break this."

Rurik seemed undaunted. "Even if it's not a matter of

controlling the weather, can't all of you just . . . I don't know . . . band together and break the spell?"

I glanced to Dorian for this answer. Roland had hinted that something like what Rurik was suggesting had already been attempted. "Several of us monarchs tried to unite our powers and break through," Dorian confirmed. "It was ineffectual, and I didn't get the feeling that we were close—like if we had one more person, we could have managed it. This enchantment is going to require something more, I'm afraid."

"Maiwenn helped you," I said, trying not to sound accusing.

He shrugged. "What is it humans say? 'The enemy of my enemy is my friend.' Right now, the blight is everyone's enemy. Maiwenn wants to end it as badly as we do, and she's a force that shouldn't be easily dismissed."

"She plotted to have me and my children killed!"

"Yes," Dorian said. "I can see where that would bother you."

I arched an eyebrow at that. "Bother" was kind of a mild way to put it.

Shaya's face had initially reflected Rurik's enthusiasm, but now she'd grown grave. "We have to do something. We can't go on like this."

My gaze fell on Pagiel, who was watching me warily. "We also can't raid the human world for food."

He straightened up, and I knew he'd been bracing for this. "Why not? There's plenty of food there! It just sits around. And most of those humans are fat anyway. They don't need it."

I sighed. "That's not the point. Most humans don't even know this world exists. They're not . . . ready for it. Plus, what you're doing is practically an act of war. It isn't morally right."

Pagiel crossed his arms and leaned back. "Morals don't mean much when friends and family are starving to death.

And I don't even think it's wrong. Humans have plenty. We have none. Taking it from them is better than letting the Yew Land abuse us for their food. *That's* robbery right there."

It was hard to argue against his Robin Hood logic, and seeing his stubborn expression, I knew it would take more than a "talking to" to win him over. Dorian, as his king, might be useful, but my guess was that even if he didn't actively condone it, Dorian wouldn't feel the food raids were severe enough to warrant intervention. After all, Dorian was a supporter of the Storm King prophecy. What was a little theft here and there compared to outright invasion? He probably thought Pagiel's raids were an acceptable warm-up act.

Still, Pagiel's words brought up another concern. I glanced around at the others. "The Yew Land. What do we know about them?"

"That they suck," said Jasmine.

"Noted. Anything else?"

Dorian propped his elbow up on the chair's arm and rested his face in his hand. "Everything suggests they're responsible, though we have no hard proof."

Rurik snorted. "No proof? That bitch queen has said she can lift the blight to those who choose to follow her."

"Yes," said Dorian, "but she's very careful with her wording. She doesn't say she can lift it because she caused it. She acts as though she simply has the power to—if we bend the knee."

"Same difference," growled Rurik.

"I concur, but it's irrelevant. We don't know enough about their magic to puzzle this out," said Dorian.

The answer came to me like a slap in the face. "Volusian," I said.

The others regarded me questioningly. "What about him?" asked Dorian. "I assume he's as charming as ever, though *I* wouldn't know since you went to great pains to keep him away."

I ignored the jab. "Volusian's from the Yew Land. That's where he was cursed. It happened a long time ago, but obviously, they've still got some pretty serious magic going on. Maybe he knows something."

Jasmine leaned forward eagerly. "See? I knew you'd know how to fix this."

"I don't know about that. But at least it'll give us a place to start." I stood up and spoke the summoning words. That familiar, cold feeling spread throughout the room, though for once, it was easy to shrug off. After I'd trudged through that Arctic wasteland outside, Volusian's aura felt pretty soft-core. Moments later, Volusian appeared. He inclined his head to me.

"Welcome back, mistress."

Around me, the others shifted uncomfortably. Roland had disapproved of Volusian since the beginning, and for once, he and the gentry agreed on something. None of them liked Volusian either. Dorian had even offered to help me banish him, since the curse was too much for one person to break.

I sat back down. "Volusian, we need to talk to you about the Yew Land."

Volusian's expression remained unchanged, but like before, I got the vibe that his former homeland was nothing he wanted to discuss. "Yes, mistress."

"Is the Yew Land responsible for the blight?"

A pause. Then: "Most certainly, mistress."

The others exchanged surprised looks. I shared the sentiment. With Volusian, such a direct answer was rare. Even though he was compelled to obey me, he excelled at finding ways to evade the truth.

"That's not quite the same as 'yes,'" I pointed out.

"Indeed," Volusian agreed. "I have not been to the Yew

Land in centuries. I have not spoken to Queen Varia. I have seen no spells cast. Without that, I cannot say, 'Yes, they caused it.' This magic that's blighted these lands feels exactly the same as the sorts of spells the Yew people work. It is possible someone else has learned their magic—but unlikely. Hence my answer: most certainly."

"Fair enough," I said. Volusian-logic was wearying sometimes. "I don't suppose then that you know how to break the enchantment."

Volusian's tone remained flat. "Of course I do, mistress. I have known for some time."

I nearly jumped out of my chair. Rurik actually did.

"*What?*" I cried. "Why the hell didn't you tell someone sooner?"

I couldn't be certain, but I thought I saw the tiniest shrug of Volusian's shoulder.

"Because, mistress," he said. "You never asked."

Chapter 13

"God. Damn. It."

It was one of those times—and believe me, there'd been many—when I wished I really could just blast Volusian into the Underworld. Usually those times also just happened to be when I desperately needed him. This was no exception.

I saw anger and disbelief kindling on the others' faces. I knew how they felt and had to remember that this was typical Volusian operating procedure. By the terms of his servitude, he really hadn't done anything wrong. Although I often asked him to give me a heads-up on useful information, he was under no obligation to deliver news I didn't explicitly ask for. In fact, if I had a standing order for him to tell me "anything important," I was pretty sure he would talk my ear off nonstop, just out of spite. His hatred for me and the Yew Land must have put him in quite the bind here. Who should he inconvenience the most?

I gritted my teeth. "All right, Volusian. Tell us about the enchantment."

"The spell originated in the Yew Land," he said. "Obviously. And that's where it's maintained from. I am not familiar with Queen Varia, but I find it unlikely she alone is working magic of this magnitude. Most likely, it is the collaboration of many who have pooled their powers together to establish the enchantment. Even then, a group of magic users could not maintain a spell so vast for so long. There is most certainly a physical component tied into this magic, objects that allow the Yew Land magic users to connect to the afflicted lands."

I didn't entirely follow that last part, but understanding filled some of the others' faces. "We already thought of that," said Dorian. "We destroyed all those ghastly statues the ambassador left behind. It had no effect on the blight."

I'd nearly forgotten about those tacky green and white monstrosities that had been gifted to all of us. Looking back with the power of hindsight, I could see now how those sculptures would absolutely be perfect Trojan horses. Varia could have infused them with magic that maintained the blight spell, and then we'd unknowingly keep them on hand, ignorantly obeying the rules of etiquette. It was the perfect explanation—except that Dorian's words completely contradicted it.

"Because those are not the objects tied to the spell, Oak King," said Volusian. "This type of enchantment required much planning, and Varia and her conspirators would hardly leave the critical components around at your disposal."

"Then what are they?" demanded Rurik.

"The *other* gifts," I murmured. I remembered when Ilania the ambassador had given me the statues, one for each kingdom, and how she'd said she looked forward to seeing what we gave back in return. Needing to match her kingdom's custom, I'd given haphazard orders to send some token back with her. I'd never followed up. I had no idea what my people had given to her. "Ilania made the rounds in all our kingdoms, distributing her crappy art, which then obligated all of us to give her something back." I turned to Shaya. "We sent her with something, right?"

Shaya's eyes were thoughtful. "Yes. We gave her a very rare vase from the Rowan castle's original art collection. Later, she said that she would also like to take back something representative of the Thorn Land, no matter how small, so I made arrangements for that. She was very insistent it be from that land. I believe it was some sort of copper plate, but I can find out for sure."

"No need," I said. "What matters is that we gave her something. And you did too, right?" That was to Dorian. He shrugged.

"Perhaps. I don't pay attention to such trifles."

I repressed an eye roll. Dorian might not keep up on his household's day-to-day affairs, but I had no doubt some wily servant had made sure the rules of etiquette were followed on his liege's behalf. And, in fact, I was willing to bet every monarch in the blighted kingdoms had followed suit.

"That's it, isn't it?" I asked Volusian. Everything was starting to fall together. "All the gifts we willingly gave are what are being used to maintain the Yew Land's spell. They're tied to our kingdoms and were given freely. The 'freely' part must be crucial. Otherwise, she would've just stolen random things. The gifts provide a physical connection to us that the magic's being worked through, allowing the blight to continue so long as she possesses those objects."

"That would be my assumption, mistress."

"And they've probably got those objects under lock and key."

"Another valid assumption, mistress."

"Would destroying these objects break the enchantment?" I asked.

"Of course," said Volusian. "With no tangible tie to your

lands, the Yew magic users would have no way to maintain the enchantment over such a long distance."

Remembering that there was always the potential for information that Volusian wasn't readily providing, I racked my brain for other pertinent details. "Is there any other way to break the enchantment?"

"You could kill or incapacitate the magic users." There was something about the way he said "incapacitate" that made it sound worse than killing. "However, destroying the talismans are most likely the simplest solution. They would all be kept in one place. The magic users can be scattered at any given time, and it is unclear how many are needed for the spell. If Varia has planned well, she will have more on hand than she actually needs, should something happen to one or two of them."

"Well, that's settled then," said Rurik. It was clear he had less patience than I did for Volusian's communication style. "We head over there and break all the gifts."

"'Over there' could mean a lot of things, I'm guessing," remarked Dorian. His voice was lazy and smooth, but there was an eager glint in his eye. What was a recent problem for me had plagued Dorian and the others for a long time. No doubt he was as anxious as Rurik to finally make progress. "Particularly since none of us have been to Varia's realm. Can you provide us with a more specific location within the Yew Land?"

"No," said Volusian. "I am forbidden to cross its borders. The magic that exiled me prevents me from entering."

"Damn," I muttered. Volusian was annoying, but he was good in a fight.

"However . . ." Volusian hesitated, something I had rarely seen, as though deciding whether or not he should speak. "That spell is old. There's probably no one alive from the time it was cast. The spells that bind me to you, mistress, are not as strong as that original curse, but they are powerful in their way—and newer."

I frowned. "What are you saying?"

"One of the most basic and powerful parts of my en-slavement to you is that I must come when you summon me. There is a chance that if you commanded me to come to you in the Yew Land, our bonds would be strong enough to bring me to your side—even within that kingdom's bor-ders." He paused again, this time for dramatic effect. "Or there is the possibility I might not show."

"Well, that ambiguous answer aside, the important part right now is that we really don't have any way of knowing exactly where in the Yew Land these objects are," I said. "So, if we send people after them, it would be a blind mis-sion."

"It's better than nothing," said Rurik.

Dorian smiled at him. "Crudely put, but true. Our lands can't go on like this. We need to take some action, no matter how remote our chances are."

I sighed and leaned back in my chair, watching the flames of the fireplace dance. There were some ugly choices ahead. I didn't believe much in destiny, but I knew then that this was the reason I had returned to the Other-world. "I'll go."

Roland straightened up. "Eugenie—"

"Don't," I said. I gave him a gentle smile. "I know you're worried, but you also knew when I came back that I'd be signing on for something like this."

"Actually," he said wryly, "I was hoping you'd just do some hocus-pocus and fix things in a day."

"I would if I could," I said, a lump forming in my stom-ach. I wasn't an expert on the Yew Land—not yet—but knew the venture we were about to undertake would last a lot longer than a day. It could take us days—even weeks—

to get there. Those were all days I'd have to stay away from Isaac and Ivy.

"I'll go too, of course," said Dorian. "Nothing I love more than a winter's journey."

Rurik and Shaya exchanged glances at this. "Your Majesties . . ." she said carefully. "Is it wise . . . is it wise for you both to go? For either of you to go? The risks . . ."

"I'd rather die trying to save my kingdom than watch it wither around me," said Dorian, in a rare show of fierceness. "If I die in the attempt, the land will simply find someone else to bond with. Perhaps he or she will then be able to succeed where I didn't. Either way, a triumphant ending."

I wasn't so sure I'd call that triumphant, but I could hardly chastise Dorian for going when I was signing up for the same risks. What I was not so open to was Jasmine volunteering.

"Why not?" she asked when I began to protest. "I'm pretty badass, you know."

I shook my head. "That's not in dispute. Someone has to stay and commune with the lands. You're the only alternative."

"Dorian's leaving his kingdom," she pointed out. "And he doesn't have backup."

It was a fair point, one I didn't have a ready answer for. "The land can go well over a month without me," he remarked. "Especially in these conditions."

"Wouldn't it need more help in these conditions?" I argued.

"Oh, it needs you, no question. But the land isn't thriving in its normal way. It's in a kind of stasis. If we're away longer than we expect, you and the land will miss each other . . . but let's face it, the land can't get too much worse if we're a couple weeks late." Jasmine had hinted at that, I recalled now. The laconic smile on Dorian's face contrasted weirdly with his next words. "Besides, these kingdoms won't survive in two months anyway. No harm done."

"Gee, you have a cheery way of looking at everything," I muttered.

He grinned at me and nodded to Jasmine. "On a more practical note, we're going to have to travel through some pretty miserable conditions. Having two weather-working sisters along would be welcome."

It was another good point. Certainly I'd eased my journey with Roland earlier. Jasmine's specialty was magic tied to moisture, which would come in handy with the snow. Dorian's comment also provided cover for something else I'd wanted to bring up. I turned to Pagiel.

"I suppose he's right. And by that same reasoning, we could really use you if your air magic can combat any of this," I said. I hesitated and frowned before continuing. "Although, I hate to drag you into it. If your mother gave me grief for my doctor's visits, God only knows what she'll say about this."

Pagiel's eyes were stormy. "I'm too old for her to tell me what to do! I don't care if it's dangerous. You need me, and I'm going."

It was hard to keep a straight face. Something amusing flashed in Dorian's eyes, and I knew he'd guessed my ruse. Score one for Eugenie and reverse psychology. In truth, I actually wasn't thrilled about exposing Pagiel to this dangerous journey. It was simply a matter of choosing the lesser of evils, however. If Pagiel was with me, he wasn't out attacking humans. I'd been afraid suggesting he go with us to the Yew Land would make him suspicious, but he seemed pretty confident it was all his decision. I hoped this boded well for my future parenting skills.

After further discussion, the only two people not going were Roland and Shaya. Roland, though not a fan of the Otherworld, had volunteered to help. I'd declined the offer and given him a look that said I'd explain later. That was enough for him. Shaya, however, was much harder to convince. Although she was strong and a good healer, I wanted her back here to manage the fragile state of affairs in my kingdoms. Rurik, being the macho but good-hearted husband he was, simply wanted her kept safe. That was what she took issue with.

"I'm not made of glass!" she exclaimed to him. "I used to be a warrior in the Oak Land's royal guard."

"And now you're my wife, so trust me when I say you're better off here," Rurik said. I think he had noble intentions, but the heavy-handed words weren't the best thing he could've chosen. She grew more incensed, and it was only my command that got her to back down. From the way she kept glaring at him, it was clear she held him responsible, and I suspected Rurik would be sleeping on the proverbial couch.

Once the rest of us, along with some handpicked fighters, were committed to go, our meeting dispersed. We planned on leaving tomorrow, and everyone had individual preparations to make. Roland intended to go back to Tucson now and reluctantly agreed to let some of my guards escort him to the gate so that he could go on horseback.

"I'd love to have you in the Yew Land," I told him as I walked him out. "But honestly . . . I'm worried that while Pagiel's gone, some of his cronies might get the same idea about 'shopping trips' to the human world."

Roland grimaced. "I hope it doesn't come to that. He's a bright boy, the kind others follow. . . . Hopefully none of them will have the initiative to act on their own. I'll be on watch, though."

Outdoors, the same bitter cold greeted us. Roland was bundled up again, but I'd foolishly ventured out in just my jeans and sweater. Not far from the door, his escort waited discreetly and patiently. I wrapped my arms around myself.

"Roland . . . if something happens to me . . ."

"Eugenie . . ."

"I know, I know. It sounds pessimistic, but well . . . everything's changed. There are things we have to plan for."

"The twins," he said grimly.

I nodded. "If something happens to me, then I totally trust you to do whatever you think is best. If that means leaving them where they're at, fine. If you and Mom want to take them, fine too. Whatever will give them a good life and keep them safe from my enemies."

Roland's face showed he didn't like this conversation but knew it was necessary. "I hate to echo Dorian, but if something does happen to you, you probably won't have many enemies left to come after them."

"Then something good comes out of this, right?"

He gave his head a rueful shake. "Be careful, Eugenie, so that we never have to find out the answers to any of these things." He hugged me and then shooed me inside. "Get back in there and get warm. If you think about it, send that fiend of yours to me every once in a while with an update."

"I will," I said. It was difficult watching him go. He was my last bit of contact with humanity. I was now once again fully enmeshed in Otherworldly affairs.

Before I returned inside, I caught the attention of a sentry standing a little ways down the hall. She inclined her head politely at my notice. "Your Majesty."

I glanced back at the door and frowned. "When I first ruled here—back when the desert took out all the crops and water—we had refugees showing up here. And for the war too. Why hasn't anyone come this time? They're in just as bad a shape, right?"

The sentry's face fell. "I'd say they're in worse shape, Your Majesty. The blight has killed more people than either of those times. For many, journeying here through these conditions would prove far more deadly than making do where they're at, no matter how miserable."

I thanked her and went upstairs, her words hitting me hard.

Since my party's plan was to depart from the Thorn Land tomorrow, I set out tonight for a quick journey to the Rowan Land to do what I could for it. An escort of guards went with me, and we again rode to save time. I also continued using my magic to clear the snow. Some part of me worried about expending my energy, but I felt strong and couldn't stand to watch the men and horses struggle.

The people in the Rowan castle bore the same looks of hope that their Thorn brethren had. I was glad to give them something positive in these dreary times but worried once more about whether I could deliver. They were equally excited to hear my children had been born safely and were hidden away among humans. The gentry nodded along as though there was nothing weird about this, and thinking once more about fairy tales, I wondered if maybe those stories had some basis in history.

Communing with the land had to be done outdoors, so while my men warmed up inside, I bundled up and sat down in the courtyard. I reached out to the land and received an answer—and better understood what Jasmine and Dorian had described. It took a lot of energy to reach the land's heart and establish any sort of connection, explaining why she'd been wiped out. But, I could also feel what she'd meant about the land not burning through energy very quickly. It needed the power and welcomed my support, but in the blight's hibernation, the land mostly used my energy to keep its core strong. Nothing was being expended on the living, breathing, day-to-day maintenance of the kingdom. This saddened me, but I hoped it would mean the land really could survive a while without me.

Once that was done, we had little time to dally. My men

and I traveled back to the Thorn Land, and there, in the evening darkness, I performed the same type of magical connection with my kingdom. The response was the same, and when I was finally able to trudge into my bedroom, I was certain I'd fall right to sleep. Normally, I felt flustered when servants waited on me, but tonight I was grateful someone else was off packing and taking care of my supplies for tomorrow.

Those same servants had piled the fire high in my room, bringing the temperature to a level that might even be too hot later—but which was wonderful now. The staff had also taken pains to pile my bed with blankets and pillows. What I was pretty sure they had not placed on my bed, however, was Dorian.

I sighed. "What are you doing here?"

He was sprawled on top of the covers, propped up on some of the pillows with his hands resting behind his head. From the way he'd been gazing upward, he had the look of someone lost in dreams and imaginings. Or world-dominating machinations.

"I came to talk to you, of course." He stayed where he was, and I took a chair near the bed's side. "You didn't really think I would accept your cursory explanation about where you've been all this time?"

"You know where I've been. And why I was there."

He managed a half shrug. "Yes, yes. But what about your children? Aren't you going to tell me more about them? I'd hoped Shaya would do the womanly thing and interrogate you in detail, but she let me down. And of course *I* couldn't quiz you on such things in front of the others."

"Of course," I agreed, rolling my eyes. "Wouldn't want to ruin your harsh, manly reputation."

"It would take a lot more than talking about infants to do that, my dear."

I stretched out my legs, surprised at the small aches in them. "Okay. What do you want to know? I'm *not* going to tell you where they are."

"Wouldn't dream of it." He turned his thoughtful gaze back up. "I don't know. Tell me the essentials. What are they like? What are their names? Are they really in good health after being born so early?"

"Their names are Isaac and Ivy," I began.

"Isaac?" he repeated.

"It's a nice name. A human name."

"I'm aware. But it's not the name I'd give to a conqueror of worlds," explained Dorian. He considered. "I would've gone with Thundro or Ragnor. I might just call him Thundro anyway."

"That's ridiculous, and you know it. Their names are Isaac and Ivy. And my son's not going to be a conqueror of worlds."

"So you say. Now go on."

I thought back to his questions and felt my stomach turn queasy as the twins' faces flashed to my mind. "They're like . . . well, they look like me. So far. No trace of . . . *him*. Other than that, it's hard to guess too much what they'll be like. And they're small, of course. Smaller than what's ideal. But everything's there—there and perfect. Plus, they're growing more and more each day. Pretty soon they'll be able to go home." I didn't elaborate on what "home" meant—partially because I wasn't even certain— but did go on to explain what had happened in the NICU. Dorian bore the usual gentry look of surprise and confusion at the technical lingo, but when I was finished, he actually seemed impressed.

"Well, then, it sounds like it's a blessing they were somewhere that could help them get through all of this," he said. "But tell me, how are *you* handling all of it?"

I stifled a yawn. "Not looking forward to a long journey in the snow. Also not excited that we don't know exactly where we're going, but compared to the alternative, I guess it's—"

"No, no," he interrupted, sitting up so that he could meet my gaze. "Not this Yew Land nonsense. I'm talking about being away from Ivy and Thundro. How are you coping with that? It can't be easy, being apart when they're both so fragile."

My answer was a long time in coming. Aside from Roland—who had actually seen how difficult my parting from the twins was—no one had asked much, so far, about how I felt about having to leave them. Everyone had wanted to know about their births and that Isaac and Ivy were safe and accounted for, but my feelings on the matter had never been brought up. I was Eugenie, Queen of Rowan and Thorn, Storm King's daughter. It was expected that I would slip easily into this new adventure and do my duty.

"It's terrible," I said at last, unable to look into his eyes. I hated when he turned all serious. "I didn't want to come back, even when Roland told me how bad things were. Leaving their bedside was probably the hardest thing I've ever done. I'm wracked with guilt over every option. I hate myself for leaving them and would've hated myself for abandoning all of you. I feel split between worlds."

Dorian swung his legs over to the side of the bed. "You've felt that way since the moment I met you."

I thought about it. "I suppose so."

"Well, don't worry. I'll help you settle this blight problem so that you can get back to them soon." He stood up and caught one of my hands in his. "I promise." His lips brushed the top of my hand, and then he released it. I stared dumbfounded as he walked to the door. Before he left, he glanced back at me. "Oh, and for what it's worth? I'm sorry you had to come back under these circumstances, but I *am* glad to see you again."

"Thanks," I said stupidly, unable to formulate anything more eloquent. I wished I could say a hundred other things, like that I appreciated his compassion now and how he'd tried to help me before I left. I wanted to tell him I was sorry for not confiding in him before . . . but the words stuck on my lips.

He left me, and I was amazed. No snark, no innuendoes. Just honesty and sincerity. He'd seen my pain and offered his comfort. I wasn't so sure cleaning up this "nonsense" would be as easy as he'd made it out to be, but the sentiment still meant a lot to me. This wasn't the Dorian I'd left two months ago.

Despite how awestruck his behavior had left me, I couldn't ponder it much longer. We had a big day tomorrow, and my body was exhausted. I had enough presence of mind to strip off my outerwear and then slide into the heavily layered bed. Just before I fell asleep, I thought I caught the lingering scent of apples and cinnamon from where he'd been lying.

Dorian was back to his usual bantering self the next morning. It wasn't biting or sarcastic, though, and I could tell he was actually trying to boost everyone's spirits with his jokes and quips. Although tense, everyone in our party actually seemed excited about our venture. I think they'd been inactive for too long and were grateful just to be doing *something* to try to rectify this problem.

Along with Dorian, Jasmine, Pagiel, and Rurik, I also had two of my own guards and one of Dorian's. All three were strong fighters, and Dorian's man—Alistir—was also a healer. Shaya came out to see us off, and from the way she and Rurik had to be pried apart, it was obvious they'd long since made up their differences from yesterday.

We set out on horseback into another icy, blustery day. Jasmine, Pagiel, and I all wanted to use our magic to facilitate our journey, but Dorian cautioned against it so early on. "The road will be manageable. The horses are strong right now, and so are we. Don't start expending yourselves quite so soon—especially since we don't know if there's worse weather to come."

The path did indeed grow a little easier once we reached one of the main roads, so I heeded his advice. From what they'd told me, the blight could occasionally whip up into ravaging blizzards. That was when we'd likely need magical assistance.

We'd been on the road for about half a day, still maintaining our good mood, when the land shifted over to the Cedar Land. Its king was one of my allies, though I'd rarely spent time here. The snowy landscape looked the same as the others, which is why I didn't really notice when someone stepped onto the road until he was directly in front of us.

I recognized him immediately. I yelled Volusian's summoning words as I climbed off my horse. By the time my feet touched the ground, I had my gun and silver athame out. Striding forward, I drew the air's power around me. It built up, tense and strong, waiting only for my command to be released. I heard swords drawn behind me but paid them no heed as I came to a halt before the newcomer.

It was Kiyo.

The last time I'd seen him, he'd been trying to kill me. He looked exactly the same, with his tanned skin and chin-length dark hair. A North Face coat covered his well-muscled body. He regarded me levelly and didn't flinch, not even when I put the blade to his throat.

"You have no idea what you've just walked into," I said, in a voice that rivaled the cold surrounding us.

The guards were in position around me now, but it was Dorian who spoke up. "My dear, you might not want to skewer him quite yet."

"Why not?" I asked, never taking my eyes off of Kiyo.

Dorian's voice was light and easy. "Because I asked him to join us."

Chapter 14

It took a lot of self-control not to turn around and see if Dorian was joking. My memories of past experiences with Kiyo—like when he'd tried to kill me—were strong enough to make me keep my gaze fixed on him.

For his part, Kiyo remained calm and unmoving, though I didn't doubt his excellent reflexes would take over in an instant if I attacked. His dark eyes lifted from my face and glanced at something behind me, presumably Dorian.

"Dorian," I demanded, "what are you talking about?"

I heard the sound of feet hitting the ground, and a moment later, Dorian made his way to Kiyo's side. "Exactly what I said. I've told you a number of times that this blight is a concern for all kingdoms affected. As such, Maiwenn wanted to help."

"We don't need her help," I growled. "We can take care of this ourselves."

Dorian tugged his cloak closer. It was violet, with ermine trim. Apparently even dangerous conditions required kingly style. "Maybe. Maybe not. I told Maiwenn she could contribute something, and she suggested the kitsune here since his fox form will make an excellent scout. It seemed reasonable to put differences aside and make a truce for the greater good."

It was really hard to know where to start with that. Admittedly, there was some merit to using Kiyo as a scout. He was half kitsune, the son of a Japanese fox nymph. As such, he could shape-shift into a fox at will and would have speed and cold-resistance superior to the rest of us. Useful plan or not, I nonetheless had a few hang-ups about it.

"'Put differences aside?'" I exclaimed. "He tried to kill me! Why does everyone seem to forget that all of a sudden?"

"No one's forgotten that," said Dorian. There was a glint of steel in his eyes, despite his lazy tone. It gave me hope that he hadn't completely lost his mind. "Although, technically he was trying to kill your children. Since they're not here, you can now rest in relative safety."

Kiyo spoke at last. "You have my word, Eugenie. I won't do anything to hurt you on this journey. I just want to put a stop to this blight."

I glanced between each man in disbelief. "Your word means nothing," I said.

Rurik walked over to my side, sword in hand. "My lord Oak King is undoubtedly confused by the politics of diplomacy, Your Majesty," he told me. "Allow me to rectify things by dispatching this miserable creature from the world so that he no longer troubles you and we can be on our way. Decapitation would probably be the most efficient method."

It was the politest tone I'd ever heard Rurik use. It was also the only time in memory that Rurik had sided with me against Dorian. Although Rurik had become my servant a long time ago, he'd always behaved as though he was indulging me while reserving his true loyalties for his former king.

"And I'll do it if he won't," called Jasmine.

If Kiyo was cowed by these threats, he didn't show it. He remained where he was, face earnest. The rest of us, having stopped moving, were all feeling the cold, but Kiyo had a staunch look that said he could stand here all day.

"You're being foolish, all of you," chided Dorian. "Not to mention melodramatic." The irony of Dorian accusing others of being melodramatic wasn't lost on me. "Varia— her subjugated lands aside—only represents one kingdom. We are many. Don't make me start quoting well-worn adages about uniting against an enemy and how turning against each other will only lead to our downfall. Clichés bore me, and standing around is making me cold."

Kiyo looked at me unblinkingly. "I have every reason in the world to help you lift this blight and none to betray you. I'll go scout ahead now." I wasn't so sure about the betraying part, but before I could make any further protest, Kiyo shape-shifted into a small red fox. In the blink of an eye, he turned around and scampered down the road, easily covering the snowy distance.

"This is a bad idea," I warned Dorian.

"Some would argue our entire plan is a bad idea," he retorted.

Our party moved out again, but the earlier energy and good mood were gone. With the exception of Dorian, everyone was either dumbfounded by the turn of events with Kiyo or completely outraged. I saw Rurik trot over to the soldiers from my kingdoms, Keeli and Danil, and murmur something to them that was received with grim nods. I had a feeling they'd either been ordered to never let me out of their sight or to lure Kiyo off alone and decapitate him as soon as the opportunity came. With Rurik, it was hard to say which strategy would appeal to him.

"Volusian," I called. The spirit was still lurking about from when I'd summoned him earlier. "You go ahead too—

but watch Kiyo. Make sure he really is alone and not meeting up with Willow soldiers." Volusian vanished.

Seeing Kiyo stirred up all sorts of troubling feelings. I was angry, absolutely, that I'd somehow just acquired him as an ally, despite my protests. It was also hard not to resent him after everything he'd put me through. He'd tried to kill me and my children. Because of him and Maiwenn, I'd spent the last six months hiding and on the run. Those were things I wasn't going to forgive. I wasn't even sure I could temporarily put them aside "for the greater good."

At the same time, I remembered that Kiyo and I had once been close. We'd shared a connection. I'd loved him. Nonetheless, I'd had a long time to overcome those sentimental feelings, and they certainly wouldn't give me a moment's hesitation if he attacked me again. The other part I kept thinking about was that at the root of all of this, Kiyo was the father of my children. I thought they were wonderful, the most amazing things in either world. Yet, they were half him. What did that mean? Was there good in him? Bad in them?

None of the above, Eugenie, I immediately realized. We were not our parents. Each individual was his or her own person, no matter the heritage. Jasmine and I were proof of that. Kiyo was in no way a reflection of who Isaac and Ivy were or who they'd become.

"You needn't glare like that," remarked Dorian, leading his horse up beside me. "What's done is done."

I fixed the aforementioned glare on him. "Yeah, well, it would've been nice if you'd maybe given me a heads-up on this. But no. Like always, you withheld information and decided to pull the strings without consulting anyone else."

"It was presumptuous, true." From Dorian, that was a big concession. "But I knew you wouldn't like it either way. If you'd had notice, you simply would've had more time to build up arguments. As it is, he's joined us and is now off helpfully scouting in a furry, smelly form. By which I mean his fox form. I know it's hard to tell the difference."

I shook my head, amazed at his nonchalant attitude. "And you think that's it? All is forgiven and he'll just be cool with me having Storm King's grandchildren because we're all united in some super team? That's naïve."

Dorian's face suddenly hardened. "Equally naïve is the thought that I would carelessly allow him to do anything to you or your children. How many times do I have to convince you of my protection? Do you really think that if he comes back here and attempts to harm one hair on your head, I'll allow it? Eugenie, if he so much as looks at you in a way I don't like, Rurik and his conspirators over there won't have a chance to act because I'll have long since run that bastard kitsune through myself." Dorian's tone astonishingly became light and easy again. "Now then. I wonder where we'll be making camp tonight."

He rode off to chat with the soldiers, leaving me in stunned silence.

We rode for most of the rest of the day, giving me a lot of time to think about Dorian and Kiyo, both of whom were troubling for entirely different reasons. Although bundled up, I was starting to feel the cold more and more, especially as the sun began getting lower. The horses marched on steadfastly, but we all knew they couldn't go as long as they normally would in warmer, easier conditions.

Volusian returned and told me Kiyo had done nothing but scout the road as promised. Volusian also made it clear that watching him had been the most boring thing ever and a waste of the spirit's formidable talents. Kiyo himself came trotting back shortly thereafter, shape-shifting back to his human form as our group drew to a halt. He gestured over his shoulder.

"Two more land shifts ahead," he said. "I think they're the Elm Land and Palm Land, but it's hard to tell out here."

Elm and Palm. Neither were lands in my "neighborhood."
In fact, we hadn't been in any of the familiar kingdoms in a
couple of hours. I'd at least heard of these lands—and knew
they weren't Varia's allies—but it was a stark reminder that
our journey was taking us far out of our normal path.

"There's a village just over the second border," Kiyo
added. He hesitated before continuing. "We could possibly
camp there. . . ."

"No possibly about it," said Rurik, urging his horse to a
light walk. "Much better for us to be in some kind of civi-
lization for the night than out here in the open."

Kiyo frowned. "Yeah, but this place . . . well, it's not in
great shape."

Dorian caught on where I didn't. "Do you think they're
desperate enough to attack and take our supplies?"

"No," said Kiyo. He nodded to the armed soldiers.
"These people aren't in good enough shape to face them
either, and I think they know it. I just wanted you to understand what we're walking into."

"Fair enough," said Dorian. "But there are few other
options."

We set out, and all the calm I'd managed to achieve in
Kiyo's absence vanished now that he was with us again. I
think the only thing that made his presence bearable was
that he accompanied us in fox form, since that was a
quicker mode of travel.

The village really wasn't that far over the second border,
which Dorian confirmed was the Palm Land. The settle-
ment sat a little ways off the road and looked like something from the set of *South Pacific*, with lightly thatched
huts that seemed completely absurd against the wintry
backdrop. The palm trees that had given this land its name
were unnaturally big, but that hadn't saved them from the
cold. They were all dead, unable to cling to life as the trees
in the Rowan Land had. Some of the Palm residents came

out to watch our approach; some peered out at us from the safety of their snowy huts. I had a weird flashback to the time I'd first inherited the Thorn Land, when my own villages had suffered from drought.

Some of them had been in pretty bad shape, but they were nothing compared to this. My people back in the Thorn and Rowan lands were on rations right now, but beside these gaunt, starving people, my own kingdoms were practically feasting every day. Likewise, the cobbled-together winter attire I'd seen on my people was downright luxurious next to the pathetic scraps of the Palm Land's residents. The clothing barely covered their bodies. An uneasy feeling spread over me.

"Are my villages like this?" I asked to anyone who would answer. Since my return, I'd only talked to those who worked in my castles, not those who lived elsewhere. Those in the castles always had a little more than those in the villages and towns.

"No, Your Majesty," said Danil, the guard, coming up beside me. "I've been to this kingdom in the past—before the blight. It was prosperous and lush. The weather was so mild that fruit and plants grew in abundance. You could walk outside your home and pick dinner. They had no need to save for winter or trade."

"And so they had nothing when the blight came," I guessed. Things had been far from easy in my kingdoms, but a few things had helped us through this disaster. The Thorn Land had to import a lot of food normally, meaning there were always extra supplies in storage. When the blight had destroyed most of the food found in the wild, there had been some of that backup to go around and share between both of my kingdoms. Likewise, the Rowan Land's more temperate climate meant there'd been warmer clothing and supplies already in production to share back to the Thorn Land, whose residents (like the Palm Land's) would normally never need anything more than the lightest of attire.

"They must be terrified of us," I murmured as we reached the town's center. "Most seem to be hiding."

Rurik glanced at me, just before he dismounted. "Most are probably dead."

He walked ahead to do our negotiating. I wondered if he was our wisest diplomatic choice, but no one else offered protest. I couldn't hear all of the conversation, but someone who seemed to be a leader gestured to some huts while talking to Rurik. The same man also kept glancing warily at our weapons.

"He probably wants to demand food in exchange for lodging," said Pagiel. "But knows he doesn't have a way to stop us if we don't heed his demands."

"I wish we could give them food," I said. I saw a few children's faces watching us from inside the huts, and they broke my heart. I kept thinking of Isaac and Ivy and what it would be like if they too were in these conditions. "I'd take a cut in my rations."

"I'd encourage you to," said Dorian, not unkindly. "That is, if I knew exactly how long our journey will last. The supplies we brought were just a guess. If they were accurately measured out, you shorting yourself a day or two wouldn't matter. But for all we know, we're two weeks low on food. We can't risk it—not when we have the chance to undo the blight altogether."

I nodded, knowing he was right, but that didn't stop me from feeling bad.

Rurik returned, looking puzzled. "They say we can stay in a bunch of huts they have. They're empty." He didn't need to point out the grim reason as to why there was so much empty lodging.

"What do they want in return?" asked Kiyo.

"That's the weird thing," said Rurik. "They didn't ask for anything—just to protect them while we're here."

I raised an eyebrow at this. "Protect them from what, exactly?"

"Well, they weren't exactly clear on that. Mostly all I got from them was 'the storm,'" said Rurik. This, naturally, made all of us glance skyward. Nothing too different showed itself above, and my senses didn't really pick up on any impending blizzard. With the blight's nature, it was hard to say what might happen. "I agreed to whatever they wanted." Rurik glanced at us for affirmation.

"You did fine," I told him. I climbed down off my horse, unsurprised to find my body stiff and sore from riding. I knew I'd adapt in a couple of days, but they were going to be long days. "Let's check out our accommodations."

There were plenty of huts to go around. We each could have had our own, though Jasmine assumed she and I would share. I honestly think she didn't want to leave me alone with Kiyo around. The huts were deceptively small, but as we entered ours, it was obvious this had once housed a family. There was plenty of space and even partitions to create common and sleeping rooms. We had clean cots and a dining table, and mercifully, no personal items of the lost family remained. The walls and roof looked as though they'd been built to keep out any breezes or tropical rain but had little effect on temperature control. A fire pit that had been intended for cooking was going to be our heat source.

We'd barely been in there a minute when a young woman came scurrying in behind us. She looked no older than Jasmine, yet at the same time had a haggard appearance from harsh living that had aged her beyond her years. She knelt by the cooking pit and began to deftly light a fire.

"Oh," I said, "you don't have to bother with that. We know how to make a fire." It was a skill one had to acquire in a world devoid of lighters and kerosene.

"It is no bother, my lady," the girl replied, not meeting my eyes.

"Eugenie. My name's Eugenie."

"I know who you are, my lady."

The fire roared to life and caught so quickly that I suspected our helper probably had some sort of magical fire ability. Definitely a skill to possess in these times.

"What's your name?" I asked.

"Rhona," she said, getting to her feet. With her facing me now, I was able to get a better look and could see just how harshly the blight had treated her. Her cheeks were sunken in, and there were bags under her eyes. The scraps she wore to stay warm were hardly adequate and showed a figure that was mostly ribs. I also noticed she was missing two fingers off of her left hand and wondered if that was the work of frostbite. The hand had bandages on it, indicating a recent injury.

In that moment, I so badly wanted to give her food that my hands began to move of their own accord toward my travel pack. Dorian's words came back to me, and I forced myself to look ahead. Giving her something—even a strip of dried meat—seemed like such a small thing. But what if that meat would keep someone in my party alive when we reached the Yew Land? What if it meant the difference between stopping the blight and failing?

Making a decision, I reached for my pack—and pulled out a sweater.

"Here," I said. "Take this."

Rhona's brown eyes went wide. "Lady, I cannot. It's too fine."

Fine? It was one of the items I'd scraped together at a secondhand store in Tucson, a red wool Christmas sweater with white snowmen on it.

"I insist," I said, summoning my most imperious, queenly voice. "It will be a grave insult if you don't take it."

My bluff worked. Rhona snatched the sweater and clutched it to her chest. "Thank you, my lady. Thank you," she kept repeating. She backed out toward the door, bowing over and over. When she was gone, Jasmine sighed.

"You shouldn't have done that. What if you need it later?"

"I have a couple others. And she needs it a lot more." Noting Jasmine's skeptical look, I added, "How can you see all that and not be affected by it?"

"I try not to see it," she said bluntly. "Or think about it. It's the only way I've gotten by these last couple months." It sounded harsh at first, but then I realized I could understand her reasoning—and didn't like that I could. She tossed her pack unceremoniously on the floor and stretched. "I'm going to go hang out with Pagiel for a while."

I knew Pagiel had his own hut for the night and wondered if I should be attempting some sort of chaperoning. In the end, I let her go without a word. She'd become a lot more responsible in our time together, and besides, who was I to deny her some happiness in these times? I pulled a chair as close to the cooking pit as possible and warmed myself while trying not to ruminate on what Isaac and Ivy were doing right now.

A knock sounded behind me and I called a welcome without even glancing back. A foolish move, as it turned out.

"Eugenie?"

I jumped up and spun around as Kiyo entered. I had set down most of my weapons already but still had an athame in my belt. I pulled it out and held it out between us. "Don't come any closer," I warned.

He shut the door and then held out his hands beseechingly. "I don't want any trouble. I'm just here to talk."

"I have no interest in talking to you," I said. "I don't want to hear any more explanations about how you're on this journey to help us and have buried the hatchet in order to save the world."

"Actually," he said, "that's not why I'm here."

"Oh. Then are you here to apologize for trying to kill me? Because I don't really want to hear that either."

"I'm not really here for that either," he said, crossing his arms over his chest.

Ouch. I'd meant it that I didn't want to hear any pleading, and really, no apology could make up for what he'd done. Still, there would've been something, well, *decent* about an attempt at remorse. "Then I really don't see why you're here." I sat back in the chair, turning it to face him, but kept the athame out. I wasn't about to let my guard down but wanted to project cool confidence.

"I wanted to talk to you about your children," he said. "Word is they were born early."

I gestured to my stomach. "Obviously."

"And they're alive?" The clinically detached way he asked that was shocking.

"Yes," I replied. "Alive and well."

Kiyo sighed in dismay. If he'd said, "That's too bad," I probably would've punched him then and there. Instead he said, "Eugenie, you must know how dangerous they are. Especially the boy."

"No," I said. "I don't know that, actually. What I know is that they're innocents who have come into the world with their whole lives ahead of them, lives which they—not some prophecy—will shape and which I intend to make happy and meaningful."

"That's nice in theory but also naïve. I'm sure your father started out as an innocent too. Look how he turned out."

Anger was kindling in me, far hotter than the blazing cook fire. "They're nothing like him. Neither am I. And nothing you can say will convince me otherwise. It didn't work when I was pregnant. It's not going to work now."

He took another deep breath, like he was waging a mental battle to try to seem reasonable. "I'm not trying to be cruel here. I don't want any of this. I'm just trying to save this world and the human one from a lot of grief and destruction."

"You're not being cruel?" I exclaimed. "You're all but suggesting the death of a child—a baby! And for what? Some prophecy which probably isn't true? These two aren't even going to know about the Otherworld! They're far away from any of this, and I intend to see they stay that way."

A glint of annoyance showed in his eyes. Maybe whatever anger management he'd been practicing wasn't working so well after all. "That's the attitude everyone has when they try to stop a prophecy. You know the old stories. Trying to avert prophecies just makes them happen. Destiny fulfills itself in ways you never expect."

"Our actions and choices shape our destinies," I growled. "Otherwise there's no point in living. I can't believe you don't see that! You were always so reasonable in the past—at least until you decided to kill your own children. You have no business saying my son's the monster here."

He flinched at those words, as well he should have. A funny look came over his face, one I couldn't quite place. It wasn't guilt or chagrin, like I would have expected. Before I could ponder it further, the door opened without a knock and Dorian strolled in as though he'd lived here for years.

"Why, hello," he said cheerfully. "Hope I'm not interrupting anything. I was just passing by and thought I'd see if your charming hovel needed any patching. My magic's quite good at summoning dirt and rocks for convenient household usage."

He had that typically guileless look and tone, but I wasn't fooled for an instant. Dorian hadn't just wandered by. He'd either seen Kiyo come in or heard about it from someone else. My suspicions were confirmed when Dorian put his hands on his hips in a way that opened his cloak and revealed the sword at his waist.

"Everything's fine," I said, with a tight smile. "Kiyo was just giving me his latest explanation about how my son is a terror to be feared."

Dorian scoffed. "Little Thundro? A terror? Hardly, unless perhaps we're discussing diapers."

Kiyo's hardened expression momentarily faltered. "Wait. You named your son Thundro?"

My response was preempted by a high-pitched shriek that split the night and made the hairs on my neck stand up. It was neither human nor gentry. I got to my feet and immediately began grabbing my weapons. Dorian and Kiyo were already moving for the door.

"What the hell was that?" I asked, knowing perfectly well they had no idea either.

Outside, darkness had fallen, with only well-placed torches to give us light. The terrible screech sounded again, echoed by smaller, terror-filled cries from the Palm residents as they scurried for shelter. A flash of red caught my eye, and I grabbed Rhona's arm as she ran past.

"What's going on?" I demanded. Even in the flickering torchlight, I could see she was as pale as the snow around us.

"The storm," she cried. "The storm is coming." She tugged desperately against me, and I released her, more confused than ever. Others hurried past, and within a couple minutes, no one stood outside in the village—except for me and my traveling companions.

"What's going on?" said Rurik, coming to my side. "Are they being raided?"

"I don't know," I said. "They keep saying that—"

I heard the roar again, and this time, its owner came into view. My jaw dropped.

"*That's* the storm?" I asked.

If you could take every stereotype and caricature of the abominable snowman and roll them into one archetypal snow monster, you'd have what was standing before me. It was about twenty feet tall, covered in white shaggy fur. Three curved horns—one on each side and one in the forehead—protruded from its head. Its eyes were large and black, as were the six-inch claws on its hands. When it roared, I caught a glimpse of a mouthful of razor-sharp teeth.

Dorian drew his copper sword. "Rurik, my friend. The next time you barter for our lodging, do get a bit more information on what exactly we're paying."

"Yes, sire," muttered Rurik.

Seeing as we were standing out in the open, I would've thought the Storm—because really, it deserved a capital *S*—would come charging toward us. Instead it stopped by one of the huts and ripped off the building's roof in one fell swoop. I heard screams from within. It occurred to me then that perhaps cold and starvation weren't the only reasons for this place's low population.

Dorian made the smallest of motions, and the ground beneath the Storm began to ripple. It wasn't enough to make the creature fall over, but it did stumble and turn its attention away from the hut and its inhabitants. The fighters in our group—Rurik, Alistir, Keeli, and Danil—wasted no time in charging forward. They stabbed their swords into the Storm's leg—or rather, they attempted to. Whatever the monster's hide was made of, it was too tough and thick for copper to pierce. I wasn't even sure steel would've done it. The Storm glanced down irritably and knocked aside Danil and Rurik with one easy motion. Kiyo, in a large and vicious fox form, was right behind the fighters and attempted to sink his teeth into the Storm's leg. The monster brushed him off as well.

The Storm began stomping toward the rest of us. Dorian slowed it by manipulating the ground again. At the same time, I felt Jasmine's magic flare, and a sheet of snow flew into the creature's eyes, momentarily blinding him. It was clever. Her magic spoke to water, which responded to her even when frozen. Still, I knew this wasn't going to be enough.

"We're just annoying it," I said.

"Can you banish it to the Underworld?" asked Dorian.

"Not easily." Creatures in worlds they didn't belong in— like gentry and spirits—would be pulled into a gate back to their own worlds. I could also force entities somewhere else, like the Underworld, which would bring about instant death. "For something this big, I'd need to mark him with a death symbol. I don't know that I can get close, let alone get the symbol on him. Her. Whatever."

As though proving my point, a brave Keeli jumped forward and again tried to slash the monster with her sword— and again proved ineffectual. This time, at least, she was able to skillfully dodge his angry swat, thanks largely to more distraction from Dorian and Jasmine.

"Eugenie," said Pagiel, touching my arm. "I have an idea." He quickly explained it to me. I grimaced.

"Crude, but it might be effective," I admitted. "Which one?"

We scanned the village, and I cursed the night since it limited the range of what I could see. "That one," said Pagiel, pointing. "It's the biggest."

"Okay." To Jasmine and Dorian, I said, "You guys do more of the same so it doesn't realize what's happening."

I drew up the full force of my storm magic, forcing every air molecule I could (figuratively) get my hands on to obey me. Beside me, I felt Pagiel summon up his own air magic. Its feel was similar to mine, and we were able to sync up our forces. Joined with him, I was surprised at how strong he was. Maybe I shouldn't have been since Ysabel was pretty adept with air too. I was still stronger, but having his backup made me feel almost godlike.

Together, we ripped one of the dead palms from the ground, doing it in a way that left the roots behind and created a splintery end. Even among its unusually large kin, this palm was pretty huge. Careful to match each other, Pagiel and I used the air to lift up the palm and turn it on its side so that it hovered in a parallel line to the ground.

"We have to make this count," I said. "We need a hurricane- or tornado-worthy blast here, or it's just going to knock him over. Set your aim and get ready. On the count of three?" Pagiel quickly nodded, lines of tension all over his face as he tried to keep up with me magically. "One. Two . . ." The air crackled with tension as I readied to unleash it all. "Three!"

Pagiel and I released the tree. It flew forward toward the Storm with insane speed. Not only that, it was backed by a lot of force. Maybe it wasn't honed to arrow sharpness, but when something that big, that fast, and that forceful hits you, it does some damage. Especially when it's aimed right for the chest.

Amazingly, we got the tree to pierce that tough hide. Pagiel's hope had been that the tree would go straight through him, but we weren't quite that good. Nonetheless, the tree lodged in the Storm's chest and heart, which was more than enough to kill the beast. It gave another roar, though this was of a very different nature than before. This was a death knell. The monster took a few unsteady steps and then fell to the ground. It twitched a little and then moved no more.

"Cool," said Jasmine.

"And now," said Kiyo, who was human again, "we also know how to deal with any vampires that come along."

Villagers began spilling out of the huts, hurrying to see the outcome of the monster that had been terrorizing them. I glanced over at Pagiel, who was visibly shaking. "You okay?" I asked.

He gave me a weak smile, but excitement glowed in his eyes. "Yes. I had no idea I could do that. I mean, I guess I didn't do it. You were doing a lot more."

"You weren't too shabby," I said. "You've got more strength than you know. Not sure I could've gotten it through him without you." Pagiel beamed.

Beside him, Jasmine scowled. "They're so ungrateful," she said, pointing to the villagers. They had now completely encircled the fallen monster, their backs to us. "Not even a thank-you."

"They're too busy," said Kiyo, squinting at them with his superior eyes.

"Doing what?" demanded Jasmine.

Kiyo grinned at her. "Butchering. That thing will feed them for weeks."

Chapter 15

The more we traveled, the more we learned something. Extreme cold and starvation weren't the only problems facing the Otherworld's residents. This world was full of all sorts of nightmarish creatures, most of which stayed away from the more civilized kingdoms. Creatures that were adapted to snowy climates also tended to live in obscurity since monarchs preferred to maintain pleasant conditions in their kingdoms.

Now, that had all changed. Monsters that had lived in ice and snow had just conveniently had their territory expanded exponentially, thanks to Varia. They began creeping out of their haunts, plaguing the bedraggled gentry. With so much infrastructure lost, monarchs were unable to muster much resistance to help their people fend off these threats. The Storm was only the first of many snow-loving adversaries we faced. Ice demons, albino trolls, more abominable knock-offs . . . the variety seemed endless the farther we traveled.

"Why haven't we seen these kinds of monsters in our kingdoms since the blight started?" I asked Dorian one day. It was midafternoon, and we rode our horses side by side. He didn't answer for a few seconds, and for the first time in a very long time, there was a weary—though not *quite* defeated—air about him. We'd been on the road for a week, and it was taking its toll on all of us.

"A couple reasons, I'd imagine," he said at last. "One is a matter of logistics. These creatures tend to live on the outskirts of our world. It's simply taken them time to discover the feast the blight has created for them, and then of course, they'd actually have to put in the time to spread out and make the journey. They may simply not have reached our lands yet."

That was a disheartening answer, its severity driven home by his sober look. "What's the other reason we haven't seen them yet?"

"We were living in a state of war before this disaster struck. Our armies were built up, our lands regularly patrolled. Much of that has stayed in place, even though our forces have taken heavy hits from the blight. But other kingdoms? Like the Palm Land? They were living an idyllic, peaceful existence. Their armies were minimal, so they had less to work with when the blight fell—and next to nothing now that the monsters are coming out of hiding."

"Will ours be enough?" I asked. "Will our forces be able to protect our people?"

He studied me for a few moments, and I got the impression he was debating whether to answer with truth or comfort. He opted for the former. "I don't know. We're in better shape than most, and it's a rule of nature that predators prefer easy prey. I don't wish harm on any of these lands, but they're probably more appealing to snow monsters than lands that fight back."

His point was proved by the fact that many of the creatures we encountered tried to back off once they discovered the kind of fight we could put up. The smart thing on our part would have been to let them run . . . but we, foolish or not, often pursued and took them out. It was hard not to when we kept passing more devastated villages. Leaving those people unguarded would have been cruel. It didn't matter if they were our kingdoms or not. We were all victims of Varia.

The occasional fight also broke the monotony of travel. Volusian and our own intelligence assured us we were on the right path, but our days were long and dreary. We weren't entirely sure how much farther we had to travel, and our rations were running low. I'd overheard Rurik and the soldiers debating whether or not they should impose new food restrictions to ensure our supplies would last. They'd decided against it at the time—we were already weak from hunger—but I'd gotten the impression that things might change very soon. I didn't like that, but I disliked the thought of running out of food altogether even more.

Kiyo continued to be a constant stress to me. Whenever he had me alone, he'd attempt his absurd "reasonable" arguments about why Isaac was such a threat. Fortunately, Kiyo rarely got me alone, since almost everyone else went out of their way to interrupt his attempts. When Dorian did it, he would always act as though he had something really important to ask me, which almost always turned out to be ridiculous—like whether the purple in his cloak clashed with his tan horse. Others, like Rurik, made no such pretenses. He would simply force himself into the conversation and glare until Kiyo backed off.

Despite his nagging, Kiyo otherwise seemed to go to great pains to act like we were all civilized and friendly. I supposed this was better than him being aggressive or homicidal, but it seemed ridiculous after what he'd done to me. I couldn't really believe he expected me to forgive and forget.

He scouted throughout most of the daylight hours, giving me some peace. One afternoon, he came tearing back toward us in fox form, with a sense of urgency that was obvious even as an animal. Immediately, we stopped and drew weapons, ready for an army of abominable snow-men around the bend. Kiyo reached us and turned human.

"What's going on?" I demanded. I was tired and sport-ing a headache (probably from lack of food) but was ready to fight if need be.

Kiyo was panting, meaning he'd run back to us at a pretty serious pace. His fox form was normally pretty hardy. "You . . . you have to see this. You won't believe it." Recovering himself, he glanced around and seemed to notice our tension. "And you don't need your weapons."

"What is it then?" asked Rurik, who showed no signs of putting his sword away.

"You just have to see it," said Kiyo wonderingly. "It's amazing." He shape-shifted back to a fox and began trot-ting away. He paused after a few steps and glanced back to ascertain we were following. We set out at a cautious pace, none of us disarming.

"The kitsune's gone insane," said Dorian with mock sadness. "I knew it would happen sooner or later. If cold or starvation didn't do it, I figured his own nature would bring it about. You can see these things coming, you know. I spot-ted it long ago, not that anyone bothered listening to me."

I smiled in spite of my apprehension. "Right. You're a regular—"

I gasped. The land had shifted around us, as it did a few times each day. Only this time . . . we weren't in a blighted kingdom.

Brilliant sunlight and a blue, blue sky nearly made me wince after spending so much time in the stark landscape of the blight. Chilling silence had been replaced by bird-song and the chatter of other animals. Trees—with *leaves*—spread out as far as we could see, radiantly green and alive. And the temperature . . . that was the most amaz-ing thing of all. Probably, it was only around seventy, but after being in the blight, we might as well have stepped into the tropics.

"There's no blight here," exclaimed Jasmine, her gray eyes wide. "It's like—plums! Holy shit! Plums!"

She was off her horse in a flash, running toward the nearest tree. With dexterity I hadn't known she possessed, she scurried up the trunk and began picking purple and gold fruit as soon as she could reach the branches. She tossed several of the plums to the ground and then hopped down holding a huge one for herself. She bit into it, juice running down her chin, and looked as though she would faint in ecstasy.

The rest of us wasted no time. We dismounted too and joined in the plum feast. The crazy thing was, I don't even like plums, but in that moment, they were the most delicious things I'd ever tasted. Our rations had consisted mostly of dried, salty goods that would travel well. Eating something so sweet and so fresh was exquisite. Plus, there were no limits here. We could eat as much as we wanted—and we did. I didn't doubt I'd regret it later, but for now, it was glorious to have a full stomach. I stretched out in the grass when I was finished, marveling in the warmth. Others joined me, also basking in the moment. It took Dorian to point out the obvious.

"You realize, of course, why there's no blight here?" he asked. No one responded. "This is one of Varia's subject kingdoms. If not the Yew Land itself."

That revelation certainly dampened the mood. I summoned Volusian, though it seemed like a shame on such a beautiful day. The only positive part was that this sort of cheery, bright location obviously bothered him.

"My mistress calls."

"Where are we?" I asked. "We're not in the Yew Land already, are we?"

"No, mistress. We are in the Beech Land."

"Are you sure?" asked Jasmine with a mouthful of fruit. "Seems like the Plum Land to me."

Volusian regarded her with narrowed eyes. "I am quite sure. This kingdom lies near the Yew Land, however."

"You were right," I said to Dorian. "One of Varia's subjects."

Dorian was sprawled on the grass, eyes closed and face tilted toward the sun. "Of course I was right."

Kiyo tossed aside a plum pit. "I checked where the road led. It crosses back to the blight in a few miles, then back to this land. Not sure after that."

"Still," I said. "It's a good sign that we're on the right track. We should stay here for a little while. Stock up, wash up . . ."

A number of us had begun peeling off our layered clothing, and the effects of not having bathed in a while were kind of obvious.

Jasmine sat up and peered around us. She pointed off to her right. "There's a body of fresh water over—"

The sound of hooves on the road startled all of us. The impromptu plum picnic had made me feel lazy and content, but we'd spent too much time on edge recently to go totally lax. We were all on our feet as a group of riders came into view. Just like the scenery, these gentry were a sharp contrast to those we'd seen in the blight. This group was clean, well dressed, and obviously eating well. They looked strong and healthy—and had weapons drawn. We followed suit, though I hoped an altercation wouldn't be necessary.

I also figured this probably wasn't the most ideal situation for Rurik to negotiate, so I stepped forward before he could attempt to take control. Dorian joined me, and I tried to look pleasant and nonthreatening as I faced the riders.

"We don't want any trouble," I called. "We just want to pass through peacefully."

"We can pay for the plums, if that's the problem," added Dorian helpfully.

"We know who you are," snapped one of the riders. She was a woman with graying, curly hair and bore the air and authority of a leader. "And we know why you're here."

That caught me by surprise, and I wondered what had given us away. Had someone leaked our plan to Varia? Had our descriptions been spread around? Did she have all of her kingdoms on high alert?

"So just turn back now," the rider continued. "We don't want your kind here."

I blinked in confusion. If Varia was on alert for us to attempt some ploy, she would hardly have her people simply send us away. "I . . . I don't understand," I said.

"You're like all the others," she said in disgust. "Dragging yourselves in from your wretched lands, trying to steal our food. Go back to where you came from and reap what you've sown for not acknowledging our queen as your mistress."

Dorian immediately figured out what was going on. "Do we look like refugees simply here to steal food?" That might not have been the best question since we had just stolen food and looked kind of tattered. Still, there was a big difference between us and the other gentry we'd passed on this journey. "The reason we're here *is* to fall upon your queen's mercy. Our king sent us here to plead with her."

The riders exchanged questioning looks with each other. "It's true. . . . You don't look like the usual rabble," admitted the spokeswoman. It was a sign of our worn state that we didn't look like royalty either. We certainly looked more like servants than masters. "What kingdom do you come from?"

"The Lilac Land," said Dorian quickly. This was met with blank looks, largely because said kingdom didn't exist, to my knowledge. "It's very far away. We've been traveling a long time and simply want to free our land from the curse."

The riders had a quiet conference with each other and finally came to a decision. "We'll escort you to our borders," said the gray-haired woman. "Just to be certain. Once you cross into the next loyal kingdom, however . . . be warned. You may not find such a warm reception. The Mimosa Land and its residents are not nearly so accommodating."

This was warm and accommodating? That didn't bode well for the next kingdom. I also found it sad that a place called the Mimosa Land was unfriendly. It sounded like a party waiting to happen.

"Thank you," said Dorian, in the humblest voice I'd ever heard him use. "May we rest here briefly? We promise not to take long. We wouldn't want to waste your valuable time, fair lady." He then diminished some of his meekness by flashing her one of his charming, come-hither smiles. To my astonishment, she actually blushed. Unbelievable.

We were granted our break, but it was hardly the long bath I'd hoped for. I mostly managed to get the worst of the travel grime off and chose to stay in the clothes I'd been wearing. By Kiyo's report, we weren't entirely free of the blight yet, so there was no point in getting rid of the warm clothing yet. In fact, our party had to manage some tricky maneuvers to get it on and off quickly once our journey resumed. The layers were too heavy for the Beech Land but instantly needed when the road took us across the blight. After about three crossings, we stepped from the Beech Land into a new kingdom. It was evening now, and I couldn't make out much in the darkness. The heat and humidity were immediately discernible, though. It kind of reminded me of Ohio.

"This is the Mimosa Land," declared the Beech woman. We had never learned her name, though Dorian had certainly tried to woo it out of her with his shameless flirtation. "And here we depart. If the road maintains the pattern it has recently, you won't cross the blight anymore."

"Thank you," said Dorian, sweeping her a bow. "Your kindness will not be forgotten. Nor will your beauty. My dreams will be haunted by your starry eyes and glossy hair."

She merely grunted at that, but as the riders turned around, I caught sight of her smoothing back her hair in some weak attempt at styling. "That was ridiculous," I told Dorian, once she'd left. "She's not the kind of person to fall for your flirting." ·

"On the contrary," said Dorian. "She's exactly the kind of person to fall for it. I understand these warrior maids, you know. They live such harsh, cold lives, always trying to keep up with the men . . . when really, they just need someone to make them feel like a woman. And that, of course, is an area in which I excel. Why, if I'd had ten minutes alone with her—"

I groaned but couldn't help laughing too. "Just stop," I said. "I don't want to hear it." Dorian grinned back at me, supremely pleased with himself.

"We need to make camp," said Kiyo harshly, not looking amused at all. In fact, he looked downright disapproving. "And post watches, if what she said was true about this being a hostile land."

The levity vanished, and we were back to business again. The blight itself was more than enough proof that Varia and her allies weren't people we wanted to underestimate. We doubled our usual night watch, and even those of us who weren't on duty had trouble sleeping. The tropical setting was full of night noises, and I tossed and turned over each one of them, certain every insect or rustle of leaves was a combatant sent by Varia.

And yet, morning came uneventfully. I didn't know if our presence had gone undetected or if the Mimosa residents really weren't as dangerous as the Beech captain had claimed. Since this land didn't seem to border any of the blighted ones, maybe there wasn't such a need to protect against refugees. Regardless, we deemed ourselves reasonably safe enough to finally take our full break and get in some serious bathing in a nearby lagoon. We took the baths in gender shifts—something most of the gentry found silly—while the other half of the group gathered food. The Mimosa Land didn't have fruit immediately growing on the road, but in this climate, one didn't have to search far for sustenance.

Once I was stripped and in the water, I was able to get the first good look at my body that I'd had in a while. All of my residual pregnancy weight was gone. Unfortunately, this was largely because of the stringent diet I'd been on these last couple weeks. I wasn't showing quite as many ribs as the others, but it was clear gym time would have been a much healthier way to get my figure back than near-starvation. Still, provided we survived this adventure, I could hope for nutrition soon and some return to my former state. The scar from my C-section was still obvious, but that would be the case for the rest of my life. For now, it was enough to have a moment's peace and the luxury of submerging myself in water.

"Eugenie."

There was an odd note to Jasmine's voice as I emerged from underwater and tossed my soaking hair back. Blinking, I glanced over at her and saw that she and Keeli were focused on something off on the shore. I followed their gazes and saw nothing at first. Then, a slight movement revealed a lithe, female figure. I hadn't noticed her because she literally blended into her surroundings.

Ostensibly, she had the same features as any pretty gentry or human woman. It was her coloring that was re- markable. Her hair and eyes were a vivid emerald green, her skin tanned to a shade of nut brown. Her only garment was a short dress made of leaves and flowers. She watched us nervously, like a doe ready to flee.

"Dryad," said Keeli matter-of-factly. "Usually harmless."

Dryads were rare in the human world, though some- times they made it over. I'd never encountered one myself but knew "usually harmless" was an accurate statement. Dryads were tree nymphs who preferred to be left alone in their woods. When threatened, they could get aggressive. Otherwise, they tended to be shy and were often in more danger from passing men who were attracted by that Oth- erworldly beauty. Dryads allegedly didn't welcome those advances and could be quite hostile to the opposite sex.

"I wonder if she could give us information about this place," Jasmine remarked. I raised an eyebrow. It was a good idea and a surprising one from Jasmine, who tended to run to extremes.

"She probably won't know much. It's unlikely she'd have any loyalty to Varia," added Keeli. "Dryads usually stay out of our affairs."

We were using "usually" a lot here, but it was worth a try. I attempted what I hoped was a friendly smile at the dryad as I took a few steps toward the shore. "Hi there," I said. "We aren't going to hurt you. We're just passing through."

Jasmine decided to help as well. "Nice, um, trees you've got around here."

The dryad regarded us thoughtfully with her long-lashed eyes. "You're human," she said in a voice that put one in mind of babbling brooks. She tilted her head. "Somewhat."

I gestured to Jasmine and me. "Half human."

"I've never met any human at all," said the dryad.

"We're harmless. I promise. What's your name? I'm Eugenie. This is Jasmine and Keeli."

Again, the dryad considered her words. "Astakana." It was a big name for someone so delicate, but at the same time, it suited her.

"Leave her be," murmured Keeli. "She'll come to us on her own. Or won't."

So, with a few more friendly smiles, we returned to our swim and ignored Astakana. Travel in the Otherworld had prepared me to carry a few essential toiletries, and once I was sufficiently scrubbed clean, I sat on a rock and began untangling my hair with a plastic comb. I felt rather mermaidlike. Also, considering I was sitting here naked with three other women around, I also kind of felt like something from a *Penthouse* letter.

"You have lovely hair."

I'd been so intent on playing casual that I had almost forgotten the dryad's presence. Glancing up, I was surprised to see she'd come closer to me. I hadn't noticed her moving. Keeli hadn't either, and even if she thought Astakana was "usually harmless," the guardswoman still swam over to stay near me. Jasmine soon followed.

"Uh, thanks," I said. "So do you."

"Can I braid it?" asked Astakana.

I glanced around at the others. They shrugged. Braiding? That was unexpected. I guessed we were now moving into slumber-party territory. Still, the dryad looked so hopeful that I held out the comb. "Knock yourself out."

She shook her head and sat behind me. "I can't touch that. And I don't need it anyway."

Sure enough. Her deft fingers began sorting and arranging my hair, working out any residual tangles with touch alone. Jasmine and Keeli moved in closer, enthralled.

"That's cool," said Jasmine, cocking her head to get a better view. "Can you do mine next?"

"Of course," said the dryad sweetly.

Astakana didn't massage me or anything like that, but her workmanship had the same soothing quality as she began braiding small sections of my hair. I sighed contentedly, feeling more relaxed than I had in months, and it was only halfway through that I remembered I was supposed to be getting information out of her.

"Have you lived in the Mimosa Land for long?" I asked.

"All of my life," she said.

"Seems like a nice place."

"It is," she assured me.

"Much better than other places," I added. "Lots of other lands are having a terrible winter right now."

"I've never seen any other lands," she said simply. "I've never left this glade."

I stifled a yawn, feeling mildly disappointed. If she'd never been outside this parcel of land, it seemed unlikely she'd know much about the world around her.

"Do you know anything about Varia?" I asked.

"Varia." Astakana said the name with a slightly puzzled tone. "She rules the shining ones of a neighboring kingdom."

"And this kingdom, from what I hear."

"Perhaps that is what the shining ones say. My people keep free of their affairs."

I looked over at Keeli and Jasmine to see if they had anything to add that might provide more information. So far, Astakana didn't seem to have much to offer. But my two companions looked as though they weren't even listening. They were too fixated by Astakana's braiding skills and bore a dreamy, languid look. When the dryad finally finished with me, I discovered I had long since dried from the bath. She moved on to Jasmine while I sought clean clothes. After so much time bundled up, it was nice to just put on jeans and a T-shirt. When I returned to the others, I watched Astakana's clever hands work and found myself just as fascinated as the others.

Jasmine's hair was longer than mine, so it took Astakana a while to arrange it. When Keeli's turn came, the dryad still took great pains with her hair, even though it was only chin-length. I sighed happily, watching the strands of hair go in and out, up and down. It was hypnotic. My eyelids felt heavy, and the afternoon heat and humidity were making me sleepy.

Afternoon?

I blinked myself awake and squinted up at the blue, blue sky. The sun was at its peak, and for a moment, I thought I was imagining things. We'd come here early this morning, and even with a "leisurely bath," we'd only intended to spend about an hour.

"How . . . how long have we been here?" I asked. A seed of panic was rising in me over the fact that I even had to ask a question like that. I honestly wasn't sure.

"Dunno," said Jasmine, not taking her eyes off of Astakana's hands in Keeli's hair.

I stood up and began pacing, trying to get my thoughts in order. "Why haven't any of the guys come looking for us?"

"They probably didn't want to bother us," said Keeli. "They know how you feel about male and female nudity."

"But after, what, four hours? I think they would've risked it." The more I walked around, the more I returned to myself. Keeli and Jasmine seemed lost in their own worlds, though. "You guys? What's the matter with you?"

Astakana glanced up from her work and gave me a pretty frown. "Why are you so agitated? Come back and join us. Once I finish her, I'll find some flowers to put in your hair."

"We don't have time for that!" I exclaimed. "We don't have time for this. You guys . . . we need to go."

Neither of my companions moved. I hurried back over and jerked Jasmine to her feet, dragging her away from the dryad. "Hey!" exclaimed Jasmine, with the first spark of energy I'd seen all day. "Why'd you do that?"

"You need to snap out of this. We need to get back to the camp. We've been here half the day!"

At first, Jasmine looked disbelieving. Then, glancing up, she deduced what I had about the time. She frowned, and I could see clarity returning to her eyes. "What the hell?"

I tossed Jasmine her satchel. "Keeli," I called. "Keeli, we need to go."

Keeli didn't respond, and I strode toward the dryad, grabbing my silver athame along the way. "What have you done to her? What have you done to us?" I demanded.

"Nothing," replied Astakana with another sweet smile. She finished the last of Keeli's braids and stood up. "Nothing but spend a pleasant morning with you. It's what we do. We bring peace and joy and leave happy memories—at least for women. With men, we leave nothing at all."

The men. "What's happened to them?" I suddenly felt cold all over. "Why were you distracting us? Never mind. Just get the hell away from her."

I advanced with the athame, but Astakana moved with all the speed of the doe I'd likened her to earlier. She sprinted away, laughing merrily.

"We've done you a favor," she called. "You don't need those men. Men cause war. Now you can pass through our land serenely and maintain Varia's great peace."

Before I could attempt to figure out what that meant, Astakana bounded off into the woods and melted away. It was unclear if she simply slipped into the trees or became one, but I had no more time to care. She was gone, and I turned back to my friends. Jasmine was dressed, and Keeli was staggering to her feet.

"We have to get back," I told them. Assuming they'd follow, I set off at a hard run back to where we'd left the guys.

If our experience had resembled a slumber party, the men's was about two steps away from an orgy. I found the five of them exactly where I'd left them—only, they weren't alone. Half a dozen dryads were there, performing the same kind of spa treatment Astakana had been giving us. Kiyo sat shirtless while a dryad rubbed some kind of flower oil into his back. Another dryad twined flowers into Danil's hair. Still another held Dorian's head on her lap and crooned to him as one of her cohorts rubbed his feet. All the men had the same dreamy, glazed-eyed looks we'd had at the lagoon.

I hurried forward with the athame, not entirely sure of my strategy, save that it would likely end in some dryad ass kicking. "Get away from them!" I yelled, hoping either silver or a pissed-off woman would scare them. "Leave them alone!"

The dryads scattered like a flock of birds, offering no resistance and disappearing into the trees with more merry laughter. After what Astakana had insinuated about men, I had thought there might be a fight ahead of us, as though the dryads would be busy slitting throats. All the men seemed to be alive, though, and I breathed a sigh of relief. We'd made it in time. Jasmine and Keeli soon joined me, also looking relieved.

"Well, that could have been a lot worse," I said, putting the athame away. "I didn't realize this would be the danger we'd face from the Mimosa residents."

None of the men responded. None of them even looked my way. I'd assumed that, like us, they would come back to themselves once the dryads' druglike presence was gone.

Yet, all of the guys were staring off into space with dopey looks on their faces, oblivious to us and the world.

"What's wrong with them?" asked Jasmine.

"Not sure," I said. I hurried over to Rurik and shook his shoulder. "Hey. Wake up. Walk it off, okay?" He said and did nothing. Frustrated, I attempted to rouse the others and received similar results. Astakana's words came back to me: *We bring peace and joy and leave happy memories— at least for women. With men, we leave nothing at all.*

I stared around in disbelief, clueless what to do. The men were still alive, but for all intents and purposes right now, they were dead to the world.

Chapter 16

"This is stupid," said Jasmine. Her usual condescension was tinged with a hint of uncertainty. "You're just not trying hard enough." She stormed over to Pagiel. A dryad had been giving him a shirtless massage, and he lay sprawled where she'd left him. Jasmine grabbed his arm and pulled him to a sitting position. She leaned close to his ear. "Hey! Wake up!" After a little awkward struggling, she actually managed to get him to his feet. To my astonishment, he not only remained standing but also took a few steps forward.

I gaped. Jasmine had been right. I *hadn't* tried hard enough. Except, Pagiel soon came to a stop. He stood where he was, still gazing off with that blank expression that saw nothing of the world. He was like a sleepwalker. Jasmine's brief grin of triumph crumpled, and she looked at me beseechingly.

"Eugenie?"

There it was again, the idea I could fix anything. I sighed and studied our men, searching for some clue that might undo this. Noting the flowers and flower oil, I momentarily hoped removing them would do the trick. But not everyone had flower exposure. There was just something intoxicating and deadly about the dryads' presence that created this enchantment. I'd certainly experienced it.

Out of answers, I summoned Volusian. He appeared in the shade of a magnolia tree and took in the scene at a glance.

"My mistress has been visited by dryads."

I nearly sagged in relief. Identification had to be a good sign. "Do you know how to fix this? Can we bring them back?"

"I would think my mistress would appreciate the peace and quiet," he said.

"Volusian! Answer the damned questions!"

His eyes narrowed—in thought or irritation, I couldn't say. "I don't know, mistress. Many men don't recover from dryad magic. There are ways to combat it, but they don't always work. Dryad victims usually starve to death or wander off of cliffs."

"Geez," said Jasmine. "They must *really* hate men."

"What do we have to do?" I asked Volusian.

"You can start by placing mistletoe berries under their tongues. A single one will do," he said.

I frowned. "I'm sketchy on my botany . . . but isn't mistletoe poisonous?"

"Not always fatally so," Volusian replied. "Especially in such a minute amount. At most, they will get fantastically ill, but that hardly seems worse than their present condition."

"'Fantastically ill.' What a great image," I said. "Then what? They're cured?"

"No. Mistletoe simply weakens the dryads' magic— but it cannot break it. To fully pull them out of the spell, you must give them a reason to come back. The dryads weave an enchantment of perfect contentment. Most don't want to leave that."

I thought back to our waterside slumber party. I wouldn't

exactly say I'd been perfectly content, but I had been charmed enough by simple hairstyling to obliviously waste part of the day. If we'd felt that way from just a brush of dryad magic, what would the full force of it do?

"So . . . when you say give them a reason, do you mean talk to them? Can they even hear us?" I glanced at the blank gazes around me. "It sure doesn't seem that way."

"If what you have to say is meaningful enough to them, they will hear it. That and the mistletoe may be able to free them of the enchantment. Much depends on the individual's will. The weak rarely escape."

I didn't like the implications. "Well, this is a pretty strong group. If anyone can break free, they can. So . . . we need mistletoe and a pep talk."

Keeli stepped toward Volusian and crossed her arms. "Spirit, what kind of mistletoe is required? White?"

"That would work best," he confirmed.

Whoa. I hadn't even known there were multiple types. I only knew about the kind you kissed under at Christmas, which was usually plastic in my experience. "You know plants?" I asked Keeli.

"Enough to get by," she said. "And enough to know that we're not likely to find white mistletoe in this climate."

"It grows in the Yew Land," said Volusian. "And we are very close."

"How close?" I asked, a bit startled by this news.

"Five miles down the road perhaps. At least, that's what I observed earlier. The road may have shifted."

"Your Majesty," said Keeli eagerly. "Allow me to ride on ahead and find the mistletoe. I know what it looks like."

I shook my head. "You can't ride into enemy territory alone."

"Yet we can't leave them alone either." She gestured to our slack-jawed men. "I won't raise notice if I slip in alone."

I considered. We needed to get the mistletoe, but she

was right that we couldn't leave the men alone. Who knew what else might come along in this land? I weighed everyone's abilities and then came up with the best division of labor I could.

"Jasmine will go with you," I said. "Volusian and I will stay here with the guys and try to talk some sense into them." No matter her brave words, I couldn't send Keeli alone, nor could I leave Jasmine alone on defense. This seemed the best option. "But I, uh, might need your help first to move them."

Much like Pagiel, the rest of the men could be coaxed to their feet and made to walk, so long as someone was there every step of the way. We ended up taking them back to the lagoon since it was relatively sheltered and not near the road. We brought the horses and supplies next, and I was surprised to find myself sweating when all was done, thanks to the heat. It was a welcome change after the blight. Keeli and Jasmine mounted their horses and prepared to go.

"Be careful," I warned.

"We will," said Jasmine. She eyed the men, whom we had sat down in an almost artful arrangement near the water's edge. "You know, this would be the perfect time to kill Kiyo."

"What?" I exclaimed.

She shrugged. "Just throwing it out there. You know he's going to keep being a pain in the ass. Toss him in the lake and claim he wandered in there and drowned. No one would know, and we wouldn't tell." Keeli nodded emphatically.

"Sorry," I said. It was a bit alarming that I could understand their reasoning—but there was no way I could go there. "Believe me, I wish I could get rid of him. But doing it to him in this state would be as bad as what he tried to do to me."

The two of them rode off, leaving me and Volusian behind. I gave him orders to patrol the area and let me know immediately if he heard or saw something concerning. Of course, it was hard to imagine anything much more concerning than my present situation. Despite all the life and noise of the forest around us, there was an eerie silence at the lagoon. It just didn't feel right to be sitting with five other people and have none of them make a sound. Those freaky, glassy-eyed stares also creeped me out.

Still, I had a job now. Volusian had said I needed to give them all a reason to come back. That sounded more like a job for my mom the therapist. I wasn't a prickly person, not exactly, but I hardly had that easy bedside manner for exploring feelings and making others feel better. The guys had apparently had a chance to gather food before the dryads came, and I'd helped carry their haul when we transferred everything to the lagoon. Most of it was fruit, but the blight was still too fresh in mind for me to even think about eating any more dried meat. Finding a banana, I sat crosslegged and studied each guy in turn, trying to think what would appeal to him.

When I finished eating, I decided to start my therapy with Rurik. I sat down beside him, feeling a little foolish at first, but knew I just had to jump right into it.

"Rurik, I know those dryads didn't really enthrall you. You're too crazy about Shaya to let those tree strumpets have any effect. If Shaya was here, I bet she could've kicked all their asses. I mean, she controls plants . . . so maybe her magic would've done something to them since they're into trees. Or maybe she would've just walked up and punched them. That's what I'd probably do. Wipe those smirks off their little nymph faces. You have to get better

so you can go back to her, you know. I'm still not sure
what you did to win her over, but it must have been a lot
of work. You can't let that all go to waste, and no matter
how 'frivolous' she thinks it is, I still think you guys need
a honeymoon. I'm going to order it once we're all home
and this blight is put to rest. I can do that because, you
know, I'm queen. So, if she's not reason enough to snap out
of this, I don't know what it is. I mean, I suppose I'd miss
you too if you die here. You don't always have the most
respectful attitude, but you do get things done. I hate to
admit it, but I'd have a hard time replacing you. I guess I'd
have to appoint Davin in your place."

I stopped talking, suddenly wondering if I wasn't doing
more harm than good. While Rurik was unquestionably the
leader of my forces, Davin was another soldier and kind of
Rurik's rival. I'd inherited Davin with the Rowan Land, and
he'd proved remarkably loyal and competent—and made it
abundantly clear that he thought he'd do a better job than
Rurik. It didn't help matters that they were polar opposites.
Rurik was a soldier to the heart, rough and efficient. Davin
served well but also had a great appreciation for the finer
things that Rurik scoffed at. Studying Rurik, who had had
no reaction since I began talking, I reconsidered my doubts.
Rurik was just contrary enough that maybe a little tough
love was the real tactic here.

"Of course," I continued, "maybe that'd be easier for
you in the long run. I know how much you hate it when
your job makes you dress up and go to diplomatic functions. Davin doesn't mind that stuff, though. Have you ever
seen his wardrobe? It's pretty amazing. I think he spends
more time on his hair than I do. Even if you do get out of
this enchantment, I might just have him start doing that
high-level stuff anyway. It'd be a favor to you, really, since
you're not that good at it. Plus, I know how much you hate
going to some of those balls and parties with Shaya. I'm

sure Davin wouldn't mind escorting her. He'd probably even coordinate his clothes to match hers. That way, you could just stay home or go hunting or whatever."

Still no reaction. Volusian had given me the impression that even if the guys heard me, they might not show it. Furthermore, it still might not be enough without the mistletoe to counteract some of the magic. I decided to give Rurik a rest and move on to the others. I'd keep making the rounds, and maybe, bit by bit, I'd chink away at the dryads' enthrallment.

Danil was next. I didn't attempt the cruel reverse psychology I had on Rurik, but I did put the same emphasis on his loved ones. Danil had been with me since I took over the Thorn Land, so I knew something about his life, like that he'd been married for a year and just had a baby. I talked to him about his family, pointing out how happy they'd be to see him. I even briefly mentioned Isaac and Ivy, saying that it'd be great if our children could play together someday.

I nearly skipped Alistir. He was Dorian's man, and I didn't know much about him. Still, I took the time to chat about what I did know, like how much Dorian valued him and how we needed Alistir to save our kingdoms. Hopefully, Keeli would know something more after having talked so much to him on this trip. Or, Dorian himself might help once he was restored.

Kiyo was difficult, and I nearly skipped him for an entirely different set of reasons. Jasmine's parting words really didn't help because they were all I kept thinking about as I sat next to Kiyo. Maybe he was our ally now, but he'd made it clear he wasn't about to let the prophecy go. Even if our blight quest had a happy ending, what then? There'd be no peace for me. Far easier to get rid of him now when Dorian couldn't come to his defense.

But as I'd told Jasmine, taking advantage of Kiyo's situation would be as despicable as what he'd done to me. I wouldn't stoop to that level, and even though I intended them to grow up without him, he *was* still the father of my children.

"I'm sure Maiwenn will want to see you again," I began awkwardly. Were they romantically involved? Those two were always on and off again, but I wasn't up on the latest gossip. Talking about her wasn't my favorite topic, but Kiyo's young daughter with her was a bit easier. "And I know Marta will too. She must be so big now. Does she walk and talk? Maybe I'll see her someday. Regardless, you have to break this spell so you can get back to her. Even being on this journey must be hard. You're probably missing all kinds of neat things she's doing. I know how you feel. I keep thinking about Isaac and Ivy and how every day keeps me from something amazing. So hurry up and come back to us so we can get you back to the Willow Land."

Some cynical part of me noted that I could probably inspire him if I started reminding him that he had to break the enchantment and keep hunting me and my children. It might very well work, but there was no way I could hint at him harming my children—even if it might save his life. I'd refused Jasmine's offer to kill him outright, but I'd gladly let him die from the dryads' magic before giving any acknowledgment to his crazy attitude about the prophecy.

So I stuck to Marta and Maiwenn and how Kiyo had to help us defeat Varia. I even mentioned the menagerie of pets he had back in Arizona. When I felt I'd made a decent effort, I moved on to Pagiel, who was a bit easier. I praised his bravery and loyalty and talked about his family, even saying kind words about Ysabel and Edria. After Kiyo, those two women no longer ranked so high on my list of despised people.

That left Dorian. It was weird because I probably knew him the best, and yet . . . I really wasn't sure exactly which words would get through to him. As it was, I had a hard enough time making myself say anything. It was too weird seeing him so lifeless. Dorian was always in motion. Even when he was deceptively calm, there was an energy that crackled within him. He was always thinking something, always planning ahead. But now? This wasn't right. This wasn't how he was supposed to be. How many times had that little smirk of his infuriated me? I'd give anything now to see it replace this listlessness.

I stared at him for a long time. Panic seized me, mostly because I was suddenly afraid I would fail. There was so much between us that I'd been putting off. Had I lost my chance forever? It took me three tries to finally talk to him because I kept choking up.

"We can't do this without you," I managed at last. "Everyone talks about my powers, but you're the badass here. We need you to pull this off—and for more than just your magic. Who else is going to be smart enough to get us to those gifts? Even Volusian's not sure where they're at. We need you for the planning—and I know you're sure as hell not going to let that Varia bitch get the best of you. The Oak Land means too much to you. It's everything to you."

I exhausted those topics as much as I could, praising his strength and cleverness. I knew there were deeper topics to address but couldn't quite get myself to go there. I was about to start the rounds again with the other guys when I heard someone coming through the woods. I turned, silently cursing Volusian for not warning me, and then saw it was Jasmine and Keeli. They and their horses looked as if they'd been traveling at breakneck speeds. Keeli climbed down practically before her horse even came to a halt and proudly showed me several vines of mistletoe.

"More than enough," I said in approval. "Any trouble? Were you spotted?"

"Never saw anyone," said Jasmine, joining Keeli. "We

were lucky enough to find some oaks not far from the border that had this stuff growing."

I took one of the vines. "Okay, then. Let's try this. Remember—just one berry. We want 'fantastically ill,' not dead."

We went around and carefully placed a berry under each man's tongue. It was a little gross but not much weirder than half the things I did on a daily basis. Part of me had kind of hoped for a miraculous transformation the instant the mistletoe was placed, but it was obvious this enchantment was still a ways from being broken.

"We should keep talking to them," I told Jasmine and Keeli. "Do either of you know anything about Alistir? Like his personal life?"

"He's in love," said Keeli, expression softening. "With a girl back in the Oak Land. She loves him too, but her father doesn't approve. That's why he joined the king's guard—to prove himself."

"Movie quality," I murmured. "Can you go talk to him? Remind him of all he's got?"

She did, and Jasmine went on to Pagiel. I decided to repeat my pattern and start with Rurik again, hoping that Shaya and Davin would have more impact with the mistletoe. The other women and I rotated through the men, each hoping we might think of something that would be the key to unlocking this spell. Neither Keeli nor Jasmine would talk to Kiyo, however. That was all on me.

The sky was turning red when we finally called a dinner break. The three of us were exhausted mentally and physically. We'd lost a day here in the Mimosa Land, but that was nothing compared to the fact that none of our efforts had yielded any results. The men sat there, unchanged. There'd been no time to search for other food, so dinner was simply more fruit.

"I'll call Volusian soon and see what else we should do,"

I said, biting into a papaya. "Maybe we have to replenish the mistletoe or something." It sounded lame, even to me, but I didn't know what other options we had.

"I hope those dryads come back," growled Jasmine. "After I make them fix all of this, I'm going to rip their hair out and wreck their pretty little bitch faces." Jasmine had even gone as far to unravel some of her braids while riding to and from the Yew Land. They'd been bound tightly, though, and her haphazard efforts had left her hair looking pretty ratty. I appreciated the zealous initiative, though. Both Keeli and I had been too busy to bother with our hair.

"I doubt they'll be back," I said. "They did what they intended. Got revenge on men and took out strangers to their land at the same time."

This was merely met with nods. We were all too disheartened to make much conversation and simply ate in silence as night fell. The hum of the forest made a background of white noise I hardly even noticed anymore, which was why it was so startling when a voice spoke out of the shadows.

"You are *not* going to replace me with that pretty boy Davin."

I nearly choked on my berries. Hastily swallowing, I spun around to look at Rurik. He was still sitting but no longer in a frozen, blank way. He was shifting, working the kinks out of his arms as he blinked the world into focus.

"Rurik!" I ran over and knelt before him, Keeli and Jasmine right behind me. "Rurik, are you okay?"

He started to speak, and then a grimace came over his face. Turning, he spat onto the ground. "What was in my mouth?"

"A necessary evil," I said, grinning like a fool. "Oh my God. You have no idea how happy I am to see you."

"I hear that a lot from women," he said, wincing as he shrugged his undoubtedly stiff shoulders.

224 of Richelle Mead

"Do you remember anything?" asked Jasmine. "From this morning?"

"I remember . . ." He frowned and suddenly looked confused. "Those women . . . the green-haired women. I remember them coming to us, and then . . . I don't know. It was like I was in a tunnel, and there were voices coming to me from a long ways away." He glanced at the three of us. "Your voices."

I was so happy that I didn't know whether to laugh or cry. "This is the best news ever. Now that we know the enchantment can be broken, we can get the others out of it too."

"The others . . ." Rurik looked around him and noticed his fellow men. The sun was nearly gone, but our campfire clearly illuminated the statuelike quality of the others. Rurik jumped to his feet with amazing speed for someone who'd been catatonic all day. "What the—? My lord! My lord, what's wrong?"

He flew to Dorian's side with a devotion that almost brought tears to my eyes. Much as we'd first tried, Rurik began shaking Dorian in an effort to wake him up.

"It won't work," I said.

Rurik turned to me, and I think it was the most scared I'd ever seen him. "What's wrong with him? With them?"

We explained, and Rurik wanted to waste no time in helping. I urged him to take a moment to recover from his ordeal, but he'd hear nothing of it. His energy and awakening inspired the rest of us, and we continued our efforts with new vigor.

And miraculously, over the next couple hours, the men began to wake up one by one. Blessedly, only Danil got sick from the mistletoe, and it was hardly "fantastically ill." Like Rurik, all the men were eager to help, and before long,

we had everyone restored to their original states—except
Dorian.

"Why won't he wake up?" I asked. The flickering fire-
light cast weird shadows on his face. "Volusian said it was
tied to strength and will. Dorian's probably the strongest
person I know."

Alistir frowned as he sipped water from a skin. "I seem
to recall . . . I feel like there were two of those dryads with
him?" There was uncertainty in his words, but they sparked
a memory.

"You're right," I said. "There were two with him when
we approached. Would that do it? Two dryads—double the
power?"

"Makes sense," said Keeli. "Especially if they tagged
him as the strongest."

"Then we'll have to work twice as hard," said Rurik,
feeling no shame at just having been declared second best.
He finished off a banana. All of the men had been starving and thirsty. "I'll talk to him now."

Rurik jumped to it with zeal, and others followed in
shifts. As midnight came around, the effort faded a little,
mostly from exhaustion. Watches were set, and the rest
of my companions began settling down for sleep. Keeli
and Jasmine had offered to take the first watch. They were
tired but still felt the men needed some true rest. Kiyo
stopped me when I passed where he'd spread out his blanket.

"If he's not better by morning, we're going to have to
make some hard decisions." Kiyo nodded toward where
Dorian sat straight and still.

It took me a moment to follow. "What? No. We're not
leaving until he's better."

"But what if he's not? You've been trying all day."

"He was hit twice as much as the rest of you! He just
needs longer to recover," I said, working hard not to shout.

"Or, he may not recover at all," said Kiyo ominously. "Depending on how strong the magic is. What then? How long do we wait here?"

"As long as it takes! We have plenty of food."

Kiyo sighed. "But again—what if he simply isn't going to wake up? How much time do we waste? Every day means others suffer in the blight."

"We can't leave him," I said stubbornly. "I know you don't like him, but this isn't negotiable."

Irritation crossed Kiyo's features. "My personal feelings have nothing to do with this! He's a huge asset on this trip. I don't want to go to the Yew Land without him. But I don't want to waste valuable time either." Kiyo rested a hand on my arm. "Eugenie, please. Just think reasonably."

I jerked away. Whenever he talked about me being reasonable, it usually involved harm to my children.

"Dorian's going to get better," I said. "Just wait until morning. You'll see."

"Yes," Kiyo said grimly. "I will."

I stormed off to where Dorian sat and managed to get him upright. I walked him a little ways from where the others were sleeping and tried to ignore that he moved much more stiffly than he had earlier. Once I was satisfied we were still within safety but wouldn't interrupt anyone's sleep with talking, I settled him back down in the grass. After a moment's thought, I laid him down and curled up by his side. His green eyes looked dark in the poor lighting and stared up at the stars without seeing them.

"Don't leave me with him," I whispered fiercely. "Don't leave me alone. You're the only one who really understands me in all of this, and I know Kiyo's wrong. You're going to get better. We need you too much. *I* need you."

I nearly started in on the same spiel I had before, about how we couldn't pull this mission off without Dorian's skills. Then, I reconsidered. I'd been going on with that song and dance all day—and it had had no effect. *You must give them a reason to come back.*

"I'm sorry," I said, still keeping my voice low so that only Dorian could hear. And I was certain he could. He *had* to. "I'm sorry I haven't been very nice to you . . . for a while. You've done a lot for me—probably more than anyone else—and I threw a lot of it back at you. That was wrong. I mean, I don't agree with the philosophy of the Iron Crown—you know I don't—but I understand why you did it. And I know it wasn't done to be manipulative. Not intentionally, anyway. I know how you are. You need to get things accomplished, and when you see the most efficient way, you do it. It's why you're such a great leader. It's why people will follow you anywhere."

No response, of course. I felt tears spill out of my eyes and was again overcome with the *wrongness* of this. Things like this didn't happen to Dorian. Others, maybe. But not him.

I rested my cheek against his arm. "You're the only one who asked, you know. About the twins. And leaving them. I miss them, Dorian. I miss them so much. All the time we've spent trudging down this miserable road, lying out in the cold . . . they're always on my mind. What are they doing? Are they okay? I keep wondering if they're out of the NICU. I hope so—and it's not just because it means they're better. I don't want them spending any more time than they have to with machines. They need people and love. And the people I left them with? They're wonderful. They'll be good to Isaac and Ivy, but still . . . I wish *I* could be there with them."

It occurred to me I was doing therapy more for myself than him. Yawning, I tried to get back on track. "I want you to meet them. I don't know if I can ever bring them to the Otherworld, but maybe we can find a way to get you to them. We both know their father's useless, but I want them to have men in their lives who are good and strong. You and Roland are probably the greatest men I know, and I want you both around to help Isaac and Ivy—especially Isaac. He'll need good role models."

I nearly added that Isaac needed guidance to protect him from the prophecy, but that wasn't a good idea for Dorian. "Anyway, you have to come back to me. There's too much I need you for. Too much we still have to do. Not just the blight. You said you wanted to fix things between us and bring back the trust. I want that too—but I can't do it without you."

In a movie, this would've been the optimal moment for him to come back to life a la Prince Charming. No such luck. He stayed exactly as he was. Feeling defeated, I wiped away my traitorous tears. The day's weariness was taking its toll, and I couldn't muster any more encouraging words. Nonetheless, I refused to leave his side. Maybe I was too tired for pleading, but I wanted him to know I was there. I snuggled in closer, keeping my face close to his sleeve in case any more tears broke free.

Sleep found me in spite of my sorrow. The body always knows best, even if the mind doesn't. I slept heavily, and no one woke me for my watch—which they really should have. I stirred in the morning, when I felt the sun's first rays warming my skin.

Something brushed my face, and I opened my eyes, thinking a butterfly had landed on me. Instead, I found Dorian's fingertips touching my cheek and his eyes regarding me fondly. They were green and gold—and full of all the life and cunning I remembered.

"Dorian?" I whispered, barely daring to believe it. A happiness and wonder I hadn't even known I was capable of spread through me.

"The same," he said, just before pressing a kiss to my forehead. "Did you miss me?"

"Maybe a little."

"A little?"

"Okay. Maybe a lot."

A smile lit his features, more glorious than the sunrise around us. There was a joyous shout from the other side of the clearing. Someone had noticed he was awake. Dorian's smile turned rueful.

"Never a moment's peace, is there? Well, then." He shifted himself up, wincing a little from being inactive for so long. "Let's go do great things, shall we?"

Chapter 17

None of the men seemed to show any serious after-effects from the dryad magic, aside from dehydration and distaste for mistletoe. I watched them all with concern, especially Dorian. I thought I was managing it covertly—but apparently not.

"I'm not going to break, you know," he told me. We were getting ready to set out, and I was packing up my bag near him. "You can let me out of your sight once in a while—not that I mind the touching show of concern. It's almost like you care."

I flushed and focused on my packing. "Of course I care. I mean, you know, because you're my friend. And we need you. And you were hit the hardest by the dryad magic. It's perfectly normal to be worried about you."

"Perfectly normal," he agreed. His face was the picture of innocence, but I caught the amusement in his voice. There was no mention of that brief, golden moment when I'd woken up with him, but the warmth of it stayed with me for the rest of the day.

Based on Keeli and Jasmine's mistletoe run, we knew we could expect to cross into the Yew Land today, which sent a whole new sort of tension through us. Thus far, our journey had concentrated on the specific stages we needed to accomplish at the time—first crossing the blight, then Varia's subjugated kingdoms. Those were big enough obstacles, and there'd been little time to talk about anything more. Now we had decisions to make.

"No idea yet if you can cross the border?" I asked Volusian.

"No, mistress." The rest of our party was gathered in a circle, but he stood slightly apart. "At least, I don't know yet if I can cross with you. I know I can't alone."

"And so now we figure out where we actually have to go," mused Kiyo. "What's your best guess about where Varia would be keeping the talismans?"

Volusian eyed him with disdain. "I do not guess. I make logical assumptions based on my considerable knowledge and experience."

I hid a smile. "Then what's your logical assumption about this?"

"That there are two options, mistress—straightforward ones that even most of you could deduce. Varia will either keep the objects as close to her as possible so that she can rest assured of their safety—or she will hide them in the most remote spot possible."

"There's straightforward," I pointed out. "And then there's stating the obvious. You're dangerously close to the latter. Is it really split that evenly? I mean, should we just flip a coin about where they might be?"

Volusian considered. "I would recommend you assume they're near her. Likely she's in her capital or some other well-situated place, which will give you a more concrete goal to search. It also seems likely she'd need the objects somewhat accessible to her magic users—which would be more convenient for them in a place that didn't require a considerable or difficult journey."

"So we go to the capital then," said Pagiel eagerly. The

long journey had made him restless, and he was ready for action. "You can lead us, right?"

Volusian usually came off straight-faced, but I could often pick up on certain nuances now and then that indicated his true feelings. I got a distinct you're-wasting-my-time vibe as he answered Pagiel: "Of course I could lead you—were I certain I can go into the Yew Land. Which I am not. As I just stated moments ago."

Pagiel scowled, and I quickly spoke before he tried to pick a fight with Volusian. "Then we're going to need you to give us directions or a map or something to help us once we cross, just in case we lose you. I'm sure the layout's changed since your day, but a few guidelines will help—and I can't imagine the capital's exactly inconspicuous."

"It isn't," Volusian agreed. "And it's called Withywele."

"With-a-what?" asked Jasmine.

It seemed kind of a lighthearted name for the lair of someone so conniving. Volusian gave us what info he could, and before long, we were finally ready to head out for real. Between this planning and yesterday's "incident," we'd lost almost a day and a half of travel time. Having food and warmth made the delay easier to cope with, but we were always aware that a day had much more impact on those still suffering in the blight.

About five miles down the road, we crossed into the Yew Land and paused to look around. The climate was temperate, a hair cooler than the Rowan Land (when not blighted), with big deciduous trees that reminded me of the Pacific Northwest. The forest had its own set of chattering insects and animals and gave off the same rich vibe of life and fertility that the Mimosa Land had had. Both were miraculous after the snowy kingdoms we'd left behind. I was so entranced that I didn't notice the obvious until Kiyo pointed it out.

"Volusian's gone."

I glanced to my side, where Volusian had been hovering along earlier. Sure enough, he'd vanished at the border. "No need to panic yet," I said. "He seemed to think that would happen. I can re-summon him."

I spoke the words and waited. I felt the magic stir within me and then spread out when I called for him. As I did, I had the impression the magic was breaking apart and scattering, like dandelion seeds on the wind. Usually, that magic was like an arrow heading straight for him and bringing him back to me. Frowning, I took out my wand and attempted it again. I'd grown so strong in the last year that I'd no longer had to use the wand for summoning him. Now, its extra power might help.

The magic spread out from me again, this time feeling more cohesive and stabilized . . . at first. Then, after several moments, I felt it start to fracture again. No Volusian. The fact that I'd felt a change at all inspired me, and I refused to give up. Tightening my grip on the wand, I made a third attempt, using a focus and harnessing of power I hadn't needed with him in ages. The effort made me tense all my muscles and begin to sweat, but I felt the magic hold. At long last, Volusian appeared, but he was a shadow of his former self. Often, spirits looked different between the human world and Otherworld, with a more solid form in the latter. Volusian was so strong that he appeared the same in both worlds—usually. Now, although his features were the same, he was translucent and wavering, like I'd expect to see from a weak spirit in the human world.

"It seems my mistress's bonds have overridden those of the Yew Land," he said. I wouldn't go so far as to say he sounded impressed, but he definitely seemed a little less scathing than usual.

"Yeah, but not without a lot of effort," I pointed out. Although I didn't constantly have to pump magic through the bond to hold me, I had a feeling that slipping up even a little would cause me to lose him again.

"Too much effort," he replied. "I would recommend my mistress not call me until absolutely needed. If you exert this kind of power continuously, you may weaken yourself for Varia or not be able to command me anymore."

"Fair enough," I said. I didn't feel as though he was close to breaking his servitude, but there seemed no point exerting unnecessary effort. "And now we at least know it works. You can go." He vanished, and I breathed a little easier.

We continued on, all of us on high alert as we watched the forest for any sign of trouble. Dorian brought his horse up beside mine and said in a low voice, "Was I the only one who noticed Volusian actually advised you of a strategy that would keep you bound to him? Unless things have changed, I'm fairly certain he loathes and wants to destroy you."

I nodded, thinking back to Volusian's words. "Oh, that hasn't changed. But as hard as it is to believe, I think he hates the Yew Land more."

"That *is* hard to believe."

I smiled. "If I did keep him with me nonstop here, it's possible I would grow too weak to bind him as my servant anymore. True, he'd be able to kill me then—but not while I was in the Yew Land. Because as soon as he broke free, there'd be nothing to pull him back. He'd be banished once again. I think he wants to be here, and I'm the only way to make that happen."

"Do you think he wants revenge?" asked Dorian.

I recalled Volusian's animosity when he'd first seen the ambassador's statues. "Absolutely. Although . . . I'm not sure on whom since everyone from that era is dead."

"Still, you might be courting trouble in allowing him to

be here. He might act out on his own—and you might not
be able to keep him in check."

"I know," I said, wondering what Volusian on a rampage would look like. Not something I wanted to ponder
too much. "But he's still useful to us, which is something I don't think we can put aside. Besides, this sounds
terrible . . . but all of us have the same end goals, even
him. None of us like the Yew Land."

"Correction. Volusian doesn't like the Yew Land. We
don't like Varia."

"True. Does that mean you think I'm making a mistake
in keeping him around?"

"No," said Dorian, shaking his head. "He's an asset. And
I know how much those mean to you. You certainly told me
that enough when I was entranced."

I groaned and looked away. "I'd been wondering how
much you'd remember."

"Probably more than you'd like," he said, sounding far
too cheerful. "But I found it quite delightful. In fact, I'm
very pleased to be invited to train up little Ivy and Thundro. That was most kind of you."

"Hey!" I turned back to him and was treated to a full-on
Dorian smirk. "That is *not* what I said. Not exactly."

"But it's very reasonable," he teased. "I have skills no
one else can teach your children. And it'd be a shame not
to pass my legendary charm and charisma on to the next
generation. A tragedy, even."

"Legendary, huh? That might be an exaggeration."

"It's truth, my dear. And I'm willing to put it all at your
disposal—I'm willing to put anything at your disposal—if
it'll help you and yours. As I keep saying: What wouldn't I
do for you?"

I met his eyes, expecting to see some Dorian sarcasm,
but he was utterly serious. I was uncomfortably reminded
of this morning, when I'd woken up and seen him alive and

well. Something inside of me had opened and felt more joyous than I'd been in a while. I was starting to feel that way now, and it frightened me.

We kept our conversation to ourselves, but our growing rapport was noticeable to others. Kiyo had a lot to say about it.

"So," he said to me as we took a midday break, "I see you and Dorian are allies again."

I took a long drink from a water jug as I contemplated my answer. We'd just crossed into another kingdom, as was typical when traveling. It was always a little disconcerting to leave the place you were going to, but Volusian had assured us we'd be back in the Yew Land before long.

"Dorian and I have always been allies."

"Not the way I remember it," said Kiyo darkly. "Didn't he lie and trick you into winning the Iron Crown?"

"He did," I agreed. "I don't like it, but I've become more understanding of why he did it. It was for the greater good."

"It was for his own selfish ambition!" Kiyo cast a glance over his shoulder to see if anyone was listening. "You know that. You know how he is. He wants to use you for his own ends."

"Maybe," I said, thinking back on recent conversations with Dorian. "But I also think he wants what's best for me and my children."

"He wants what *he* thinks is best for you."

I narrowed my eyes. "Well, considering that involves my children staying alive, I'll gladly take that over you advising on what *you* think is best. You really have no business preaching to me about this, especially after I was the only one yesterday who even bothered to—"

A shout from Rurik immediately turned me from Kiyo. The others in my party were already looking in the direction we'd just come from, and I quickly spotted what they had. I leapt to my feet and drew my weapons as a group of people on horseback emerged around a bend in the road. Seeing us, they came to an abrupt halt and drew weapons of their own.

"Stay right where you are," warned one of the men in the strange group. He had a curly blond beard and wielded a worn but effective-looking copper sword. "Attack us, and you'll regret it."

Rurik grinned at him, but there was no genuine humor to it. "If you don't lower *your* weapons, you'll regret it. Set them on the ground now before we have to take them from you."

All this did was make the strangers tense and brace for battle. My group did the same, myself included. Yet, as I did, I took the opportunity to study our combatants more closely. They were all gentry, all armed, but their weapons didn't have the uniformity or maintenance of the Beech soldiers'. This group wore nothing resembling uniforms either. Their clothing was worn and, in some cases, mismatched. Cloaks and furs were draped in front of them on their horses, like they'd been hastily pulled off when the climate had changed. Some of their faces were smudged, and all looked like they hadn't been eating well.

"Wait," I said, hurrying forward.

"I wouldn't advise it," said Rurik, gaze fixed on the strangers. "Stay back for your own safety."

I halted in the middle of our two groups. "Who are you? Where are you from?"

The new group eyed me suspiciously. "Who are *you*?" asked the blond-bearded man.

"You're from one of the blighted lands, aren't you?" I asked, positive I was right.

Nobody changed their stance, but the bearded guy regarded me with new interest. "What of it?"

"So are we," I said. "We're from . . ." What was that absurd name Dorian had come up with the other day?

". . . the Lilac Land," he said, coming to stand beside me. He held his sword still, but his posture was more relaxed. I think he'd come to the same conclusion I had about these people.

"Never heard of it," said a woman from the newcomers. A spotted falcon sat upon her shoulder and watched us with equal suspicion.

"Most haven't," said Dorian, deadpan. "It's very far away." He glanced between her and the blond man and must have decided she was a better bet. Dorian gave her one of his charming smiles. "What's *your* kingdom called?"

There was a moment's hesitation, and then she said, "The Hemlock Land."

"You've suffered considerably," said Dorian. "Just as we have."

My next leap was drastic, but again, I felt pretty confident of my instincts. "You're going to surrender to Varia, aren't you?" It seemed logical. They weren't a big enough force to stage a rebellion, but underneath the wear and tear, something about this group said they weren't commoners. I was certain they were here to negotiate. "So are we."

Some of them shifted uncomfortably. "It's the best thing for our people," the woman said, almost defensively. "That's what matters."

"It is," I agreed, hoping I sounded compassionate. "There's no need to be ashamed."

"We never said we were," she said. Clearly this was a sensitive topic, which I understood perfectly.

The blond man lowered his sword, which I took as an excellent sign. "Are you going to Withywele?"

"Yes," said Dorian quickly, before anyone could mess up the story. He lowered his sword too. "We assumed that would be the place to find the queen. A guide gave us directions."

"You've never been there?"

"No."

The spokesman turned and murmured a few words to his group. Most of them nodded, though a couple—like the woman—shook their heads emphatically. At last, the blond man turned his attention back to us. "We know the way. If you wish, you may travel with us. It will certainly help to have more of us to face the peacekeepers."

I glanced at Dorian and was met with a puzzled shake of the head. "What are the peacekeepers?"

"A jest of a term," said the Hemlock woman, scowling. "Queen Varia leaves certain enchantments and obstacles in her subservient kingdoms to keep them in line. The residents are given ways to avoid them and be safe . . . unless they displease her. The peacekeepers also discourage outsiders."

Kiyo spoke up. "Would you consider a group of dryads part of this, uh, peacekeeping?"

The woman nodded gravely. "Most certainly. They're an excellent force to be used against strangers—but can be coaxed to leave natives alone."

"Give us a second," I said.

Hoping I wouldn't be attacked in the back, I turned and walked back to the group with Dorian. "I don't trust them," said Rurik promptly.

"Nor should we," said Dorian. "Not entirely. Though, they may be useful if they know the Yew Land—and about these 'peacekeepers.' That certainly would've been helpful information earlier when we met those wenches."

"Volusian couldn't have known," I said, barely believing I was defending my minion.

Kiyo sighed. "I don't like the idea of traveling with strangers, but we certainly need all the intel we can get."

"They don't look any happier about traveling with us than we do with them," said Pagiel. It was a remarkably observant statement. "We could probably pretty much keep to ourselves until we got to Withywele. Even there, they might be able to help us with the city."

"Are we agreed then?" I asked, looking at each of my friends' faces. Seeing Rurik's scowl, I added, "Don't worry. You can keep your weapons handy. And we'll double the watches."

That mollified him slightly, and when we told the Hemlock leader—whose name turned out to be Orj—our decision, I got the impression their group had also been having a similar conference for traveling procedure and defense. So, we all set off together, the air heavy with wariness but also with a sense of solidarity. There was comfort in numbers.

We spoke little to our new companions at first. When we settled down to camp for the night, a bit of the tension lifted. Each group offered up food, and there's something about a shared meal that encourages friendliness, particularly among the gentry with their strong ideas about hospitality. The soldiers in our group—though always on guard—had the easiest time bonding. When your life involves constantly being shuffled to new situations and fighting with those you don't know, I think it becomes easier to make friends where you can.

Unsurprisingly, each party contributed its own people to the watches. Mine was later in the night, and as I spread out my blanket near the campfire, Alea—the woman with the falcon—came and sat beside me. The bird sat on her shoulder.

"Spots is surprised you aren't sleeping with him," she said.

It took me a few seconds to dissect that statement. First, I realized Spots must be the falcon's name. Then, I thought she meant the bird wanted to sleep with me—until I saw her gaze on Dorian.

"Ah," I said in understanding, staring at the opposite side of the fire. Dorian caught my eye and smiled. I quickly looked back at Alea. "No."

"Isn't he your man?" she asked curiously. "It seemed like it from what I observed today."

I didn't recall Dorian and I doing much more than our usual chatting while traveling, but maybe others saw things I couldn't. "He used to be," I admitted. "But not anymore."

She arched an eyebrow. "Why ever not? He's very attractive."

"He is," I said, a bit more wistfully than I intended. "And smart and powerful and resourceful." I thought about it a moment more. "And kind."

The bird made a couple of clicking sounds. Alea tilted her head to listen and then nodded. "Spots says he sounds like an ideal mate and can't understand what your problem is."

I laughed. "It sounds like Spots has a lot to say about romance."

She shrugged. "He sees things we sometimes miss. Often, his view of the world is much simpler than ours. That's why he has trouble understanding your comments." She murmured something to him that sounded like squawks, and the falcon flew off into the night.

"I guess because it's not simple," I said, trying not to look at Dorian again. "We had some disagreements."

"Everyone has disagreements," she said dismissively. "Only fools think otherwise. And only fools allow their pride to hinder reconciliation, especially in these times."

The bitter note in her voice wasn't lost on me. "Has your kingdom suffered a lot?"

"Yes. It's the only thing that would drive us to this course of action." She stared off into the night, face filled with anger and frustration. "I've been to war, you know. And nothing I saw there matched the horror of children starving and freezing to death. Or of entire villages being slaughtered by monsters from the frozen reaches."

I shuddered. "We've seen that too."

She sighed. "I don't like bending the knee to Varia. But I like seeing my people and king suffer less. So. Here we are. As I said, only fools refuse to put their pride aside."

I said nothing right away. Even without talking to Orj or the others in the Hemlock party, I'd picked up on this same angry vibe—people pushed into a corner and out of options. Traveling with them was good for us because it ensured we'd get straight to Varia's capital. Yet, I also wondered if some other good might come out of it. I'd have to tread cautiously, though.

"Have you ever thought of any other options?" I asked. "Like not giving into her?"

Alea glanced back, irritation in her dark eyes. "I already told you. It's not worth my kingdom's suffering."

"No—I don't mean bravely refusing and letting the blight go on. Have you ever thought about openly opposing her? Rebelling? Attacking?"

She didn't answer, and I couldn't read her thoughts. "Have *you*?" she asked at last. "It doesn't seem possible."

I was careful not to directly answer the question. "Maybe it is. Maybe it isn't. Maybe it would depend on how many people were willing to work together against her."

Various emotions played across Alea's face, as though this was a debate she'd had with herself many times. A resigned expression fell over her, and I suspected she'd reached the same conclusion she had countless times before, the one that had led to this path.

"No. The stakes are too great." She rose abruptly to her feet. "Forgive me. I've delayed your sleep too long."

She stalked off to her own blanket without another word. I curled up in my own, more exhausted than I realized. Just before I fell asleep, I opened my eyes and caught sight of Alea. She sat on her blanket, staring at the fire, pain and indecision all over her.

Chapter 18

When the Hemlock group had first described "peace-keepers," the dryads had become the model in my mind. I figured we could expect to see more of the same type of obstacle: creatures or monsters that had to be overcome by magic or brute force. In some ways, the various arctic creatures we'd encountered in the blight met this description. They preyed on those who weren't Varia's cronies. So, I was on the lookout for living foes, not inanimate ones, which made it that much more of a surprise when the road turned into a lake the next morning.

We had just crossed into a subjugated kingdom, but such crossings were growing fewer and fewer as we approached the heart of the Yew Land. Most of our travels were now strictly in the Yew Land. Our new companions had told us that we could expect to find a road branching off this one soon that would lead toward the capital. Volusian's rough directions matched this, so I was optimistic about finding it the next time we were back in the Yew kingdom.

Like many things in the Otherworld, the lake appeared out of nowhere. One moment we were trotting down the road, the next there was water as far as the eye could see.

My horse shied and came to a halt, and I shared its unease. The water was unnaturally smooth and still, like a sheet of glass spread out before us. I couldn't see its end.

"That's an optical illusion, right?" I asked, gesturing vaguely forward. "The water can't go on forever. It's like when a kingdom seems to extend ahead, and two steps later, you walk into another one."

"Yes and no," said Dorian. "The water most certainly doesn't go on forever. What's wrong here is that the main roads of this world don't naturally have these kinds of obstacles and impediments. Think about how even in the blighted lands, the roads stayed semi-clear. That's their magic. They cross the Otherworld unbound. For this lake to be here, someone went to a lot of trouble to put it here."

"Like Varia," guessed Rurik.

Orj nodded as he dismounted and walked to the water's edge with a sneer. "This is a peacekeeper. Most likely there's a word or charm that the residents here use to bypass this or make it clear up. The rest of us . . . we either have to turn around or find a way through."

Pagiel tilted his head. "Is it really even that deep? Maybe we can just ford it with horses."

Jasmine spoke before I could. "It's deep. It gets deep really fast, actually . . . but it doesn't go as far as it looks." She glanced at me. "Can you feel it?"

I opened up my magical senses and called to the water, trying to feel what she had. Sure enough, my illusion suspicion was correct. The water didn't extend "forever," but it was very deep and still enough of a distance across that it would delay us.

"Too much for me to move," added Jasmine.

"Me too," I agreed quickly.

Her eyebrows rose. "No way. You could wipe this whole thing out if you wanted."

"No," I said firmly, hoping she caught my tone. "I can't."

Jasmine bit her lip and said no more. The truth was, I had a feeling I could have parted this water in classic Bible style. It would take a lot of power . . . but I had it. The problem was, I didn't want to do it in front of the Hemlock people. Maybe they weren't our enemies, but there was only a handful of people who could work magic like that with water, and I wasn't ready to reveal my identity. We'd even given false names.

Dorian had dismounted and was pacing around. To my surprise, he'd stopped paying attention to the lake and was instead checking out the terrain we'd just come through. The kingdom—none of us were sure which one it was—had a stony landscape, with a heavy, silt soil. Vegetation was sparse, and off in the distance, rocky foothills rose from the land and eventually gave way to far off mountains. Dorian seemed to be murmuring something to himself and then gave a satisfied nod. He turned to one of the Hemlock people, a young man who looked to be a little younger than Pagiel.

"You," said Dorian. "You have some sort of earth magic, correct?"

The boy blinked in surprise. "Er, yes. I'm able to manipulate stones and rocks. I—I sculpt them sometimes."

"Well," said Dorian. "You may have to lower yourself to something a little less refined, but hopefully your skills will be adequate."

"What do you have in mind?" asked Kiyo. He made no attempt to hide the mistrust in his voice. Maybe he felt Dorian had a lot to offer on this quest, but Kiyo wasn't about to accept Dorian's decisions blindly.

"We're going to build our own road," explained Dorian. "My young friend here and I—what's your name again?"

"Kellum," squeaked the boy.

"Kellum," repeated Dorian. "Right. Kellum and I are going to use dirt and rocks to create a road across. Or, well,

I'll use dirt and rocks. He'll assist with the rocks. There's plenty of raw material out here to work with."

I shook my head. "Not to reach the bottom. It's too deep."

"We'll build it on the surface then," said Dorian. "A floating bridge of sorts. Keeping the materials suspended there is well within my powers. Once everyone begins walking across it, however, it would be nice if, say, we could get a little support from the water." He looked meaningfully at Jasmine and me.

"We can do that," I said. Dorian and Kellum would suspend the earth and stones over the water, and Jasmine and I would control the water to keep the "bridge" from sinking. Between the four of us, it was doable, and it didn't give away the full extent of my power.

Dorian conferred for a few minutes with Kellum, and then they set to their task. Despite how powerful he was, I hardly ever saw Dorian wield his magic. He rarely needed to since his subjects were well aware of its strength. When he went into battle, he stuck to his sword, and although his earth magic enhanced the copper blade, that was a very different act from what I was observing now. There was an art to what Dorian did. Just as my senses sang out to water and air, he could call to all the elements within the earth and make them obey him. I'd once seen him use that power to rain destruction on enemies, and it had been terrifying. This act of creation, on the other hand, was mesmerizing.

The two of them summoned rocks and stones to lay across the water, effortlessly arranging the various sizes so that they fit together like a game of Tetris. Once a section of rock was laid across the water, Dorian would then call up the dirt. It floated up from the ground in chunks, almost like a storm cloud, and then spread itself neatly over the stone foundation in layers to create a smooth surface. Dorian and Kellum did this for about a half hour, and although Dorian did it with his usual smirk and quips, I could see the lines of tension on his face and sweat along his hairline. This was a huge feat of magic, much greater than I'd realized when the plan was initially proposed.

At one point, Dorian told Kellum to stop and glanced at the rest of us. "I need a volunteer to try it out."

"To see if it'll sink?" asked Kiyo dryly.

Dorian smiled. "To see how far it's needed. My guess is that after walking on it a bit, there'll be a land shift and we won't need to build this out as far as we think." He gave Kiyo a once-over. "You'd be an excellent volunteer, seeing as in a pinch, your fox form would be light enough to scurry out of there or be lifted with Pagiel's air power." Pagiel's expression told me there was a good possibility he'd let Kiyo sink.

"You can't be a volunteer when someone suggests you," said Kiyo.

I sighed. "Stop being contrary and just do it, please? I'll be guiding the water, so you don't need to worry."

Alea seemed impatient with our delay. "While you debate, I'm going to send Spots ahead to scout." She crooned more nonsensical words to the bird and then set him free. He took off, powerful wings carrying him over the water. He flew in a straight line over Dorian's bridge, cleared it, and then soon vanished out of view.

"There you are," said Dorian. "That's where the land shifts. We're almost there already. Wait just a moment, volunteer."

Kiyo rolled his eyes. Dorian and Kellum resumed their bridge-building, stopping when they reached a point that was just past where Spots had disappeared. To our eyes, the bridge ended abruptly in the lake, but those on it would cross into the next kingdom before reaching the water.

Dorian admired his work and then nodded to Kiyo. "Well, then, go ahead. Try it out."

Kiyo hesitated only a moment, as though trying to decide for sure if Dorian had done all of this as part of some elaborate ruse to drown him. Finally, deciding this was a necessary part of the mission, Kiyo set out and stepped onto the bridge. Jasmine and I both were connected to the water and were using our combined strength to make sure the bridge didn't sink. Between us and the earth wielders, the bridge didn't budge. Kiyo relaxed slightly and walked out the rest of the bridge's length. Just before he reached the water, he vanished. A couple seconds later, he reemerged.

"It worked," he said.

"Well, of course it did. No need to sound so astonished," chastised Dorian.

"The Yew Land's on the other side," said Kiyo. "You can't even see the water from there."

"Go there and wait for us," I said. Kiyo gave me an incredulous look. "There's nothing you can do here! And we can't have extra weight on the bridge."

Reluctantly, he agreed and vanished once more. Slowly, single file, the others began to cross as well. I was a little nervous when the horses stepped out, but those of us who were working magic here were strong enough to keep everything steady. In fact, before long, the four of us were the only ones who remained since we were needed to maintain the bridge's integrity.

"Go on," Dorian told Jasmine and Kellum. "We can hold it without you, enough to cross right after."

Jasmine looked reluctant to go, but Kellum didn't have to be told twice. He seemed nervous at being left alone with us. The two of them hurried over and disappeared into thin air, just as the others had done. Dorian held out his hand.

"Shall we, my dear?"

I smiled. "It's too narrow for that. We have to go single file."

"Mmm," he said, with a small frown. "Oversight on my part. I'll have to work on that the next time I build an amazingly brilliant impromptu bridge to save us all."

"Next time," I agreed.

Ever the gentleman, he let me walk first. Our horses had already gone on ahead, so we didn't put much weight on the structure. Plus, he was right that our magic was more than enough to keep the bridge in its suspended state. Unfortunately, there wasn't much we could do when a huge green-and-red-scaled serpent emerged from the lake's surface and roared a challenge to us. Along with the tacky Christmas-color scheme, it had pointed gills radiating out from its body. Its mouth was full of sharp teeth and was more than big enough to swallow one of us whole.

"Really?" I asked with dismay. "We couldn't have gotten a break just once?"

"Go!" said Dorian, with no trace of his earlier levity. "We're nearly there."

It was true. We were over two-thirds of the way across. Still remembering to keep the water in check, I sprinted forward. I could see the bridge's end and knew I was about to reach the other side when the serpent roared again—practically right behind me. I turned and was just in time to see it make a lunge for Dorian. He dodged the attempt and dropped to the ground. Unfortunately, doing so broke his concentration on keeping the bridge up. I had enough presence of mind to continue making the water reject the earth but only where we stood. Behind us, all that rock and dirt crumbled away into the water.

I held out my hand to Dorian. "Come on."

Dorian started to rise, and then, with speed that seemed too great for its size, the serpent struck out again and knocked Dorian back to the ground. One of its pointed gills or fins or whatever it was called made contact with Dorian's forehead, and I saw blood appear. More pieces of the bridge started to fall, and I adamantly ordered the water not to accept them. Still, as I watched the serpent come back for another strike, I knew maintaining the bridge wouldn't be enough. I acted quickly, doing the first thing that came to mind.

I removed all the water around the serpent.

One instant the water was there, the next it wasn't. Part of the water I simply pushed aside with magic, creating the Red Sea effect I'd speculated about earlier. For the rest of it, I simply caused evaporation. It created a considerable amount of steam, but I could still clearly see the results. The serpent had nothing to swim in, and as Jasmine and I had noted, the lake ran deep. With said lake no longer there to support the serpent, the creature immediately dropped into the chasm created by the water's absence.

"Impressive," Dorian managed as he staggered to his feet with my help. I wanted to check his head wound, but there was no time. I couldn't both hold the bridge and keep the water away for long.

"I'm just glad everyone else was gone so there were no witnesses to that," I remarked as we scurried across the last few feet of the disintegrating bridge. We were single file, but I still managed to keep hold of his hand nonetheless.

The land shifted, and suddenly, we were both on solid— very solid—ground. The tall evergreens of the Yew Land surrounded us, and the Otherworld's familiar road was beneath us. I laughed with relief. A smile started to break out over Dorian's face too, but then his expression shifted to one of horror. Spinning around, I looked for what he'd seen.

Two dozen uniformed soldiers stood ahead of us on the road. Standing with them, tied up and restrained, were our friends. Notably not bound were those from the Hemlock Land. They stood off to the side, weapons drawn—against us.

One of the soldiers stepped forward and gave us an icy smile, along with a mock bow. "Queen Eugenie, King Dorian. Allow me to introduce myself. I'm Gallus, general of Her Majesty Queen Varia of the Yew Land's forces. We've come to escort you to her."

Chapter 19

I was dumbfounded for only a moment until I pieced together what had happened.

I glared at Orj and his companions. "That'll teach me to give people the benefit of the doubt."

Gallus chuckled. "If it makes you feel better, you were identified as soon as you crossed into the Beech Land." So much for Dorian charming the Beech squadron's leader. "Even if this lot hadn't helped us, we would have seized you through other means before you reached Withywele. They simply reported on your magic and descriptions to help us further verify who you are."

I glanced over at Alea, whose spotted falcon now rested on her shoulder again. I'd paid little attention each time she sent him off ahead and only now thought about how he'd never returned this last time when he was allegedly only scouting a short distance. It had been sloppy of me—as was my confidence that not working any great feats of magic would protect my identity. If they already had us flagged because of our physical descriptions, any use of water or air—even if it wasn't monumental—would tip them off. I'd also been so arrogantly concerned about my own prowess that I hadn't realized Dorian's remarkable bridge-building would also be telling.

One of Gallus's men stepped forward holding silver chains laced with sporadic iron links. "I know these won't truly restrain you," Gallus told me. "But I trust you'll be accommodating about them, in light of this . . . situation." He nodded toward my captive friends, and I saw that aside from being tied up, Keeli and Danil also had copper blades at their throats. Binding gentry with even a little iron was usually enough to stunt their magic, but my human blood protected me. Even chained, I could call on my magic and summon a storm that would wipe out half this group. But I didn't know if I could do it before Keeli and Danil had their throats slit.

Accepting this momentary defeat, I nodded with a grimace and extended my arms. Dorian held his out as well. The iron would bind him, as it would the rest of my party—even Jasmine. I was the only one capable of magic, but it would do no good until we reached our destination. No—that wasn't entirely true, I realized moments later. Kiyo would be unaffected by the iron too. His only magic was shape-shifting, and the gentry aversion to iron wouldn't stop that. I wondered if Varia's people knew that. Still, like me, Kiyo risked getting someone killed if he acted. We would both have to bide our time.

The Yew soldiers confiscated our horses and weapons, forcing us prisoners to travel on foot. We walked along sullenly, and I knew that each one of us was trying to figure out an escape plan. The only bright side, I supposed, was that now we knew we were getting a direct ticket to Varia. One of the prevailing theories was that if the gifts were indeed in Withywele, they'd be kept in Varia's own palace—which was likely to be heavily guarded. Now, I thought bitterly, we didn't have to break in.

At one point in the trip, Alea passed near me. I glared up

at her and Spots. "You guys make convincing refugees."
Along with everything else, it irked me that I could have so
misjudged them. Their appearances and frustration had
seemed genuine.

"We are refugees," she snapped. "You have no idea the
things our people have suffered."

"I wouldn't be so sure about that."

She stared stonily ahead. "What we've done here has
bought us favor with Varia and will lift the blight from
our land."

"If you hadn't betrayed us, we could have worked together to lift the blight *and* keep your self-respect."

With a scowl, she left me and rode on ahead.

Withywele was impressive when it came into sight. The
Otherworld had few cities, and while they were hardly
strewn with concrete or skyscrapers, there was still an
urban feel to them. Stone and wood buildings were built
closely together and had multiple floors, something rarely
seen outside of castles. The cobblestone streets were busy
with horses and people. Vendors were everywhere, hock-
ing their goods. A few buildings were true works of art,
with marble and fanciful architecture. Nobody paid much
attention to us captives as we went by, though the crowds
quickly made way for the guards to pass. Maybe prisoner
transport was a common thing around here.

Varia's palace was one of the pretty buildings. It had
rounded domes adorned with that white and green stone
the Yew people seemed to like. Damarian jade, that was it.
The palace spread out over extensive gardens, which were
adorned with statues and fountains. As we passed them, I
occasionally caught glimpses of name placards. One statue,
of a sharp-faced woman with a beehive hairdo, was labeled
Ganene the Great.

Ganene. The name was familiar, and I rifled through my
memories to try and figure out where I'd heard it. Soon, it

came to me. When Volusian had first seen the ambassador's statues, I'd mentioned they were from Varia. *She must be Ganene's daughter*, he'd said.

Volusian!

Volusian might be my ace in the hole here. Of course, there was one slight problem. I couldn't summon him in this kingdom without the help of my wand, and the guards had taken that from me.

Inside the palace walls, our party dispersed. The Hemlock people were escorted to "guest quarters" to rest before making some appeal to Queen Varia. As they left, I saw Alea giving me one last look, which turned to a glare when she realized I'd noticed her. I figured the rest of us would be taken to prison cells. What I didn't expect was that we'd be taken to different ones. Dorian and I were led one way, the rest of our party another.

"Hey, wait," I protested, coming to a halt despite my escort's attempts to move me forward. "Where are you taking them?"

"To the dungeon, of course," said Gallus.

I frowned. "Then . . . where are you taking *us*?"

"To confinement more suited to your stations," he replied. "We're not complete savages, you know. We want you to be comfortable so that you're in good shape when you surrender your lands to Her Majesty."

"That," I said, "is not going to happen."

Gallus shrugged and gestured toward those going to the dungeon. "Protest all you want, but never forget we have them in our grasp. Step out of line, and they die."

"Forget us," growled Rurik. "Summon a storm that'll blast this place to pieces. We'd gladly die to see that bitch ripped apart."

One of the guards slammed the hilt of his sword into Rurik's head. "Do *not* talk about Her Majesty that way."

"Be patient," I told Rurik. I didn't want him killed for

any reason, certainly not through guard brutality. I spoke my words confidently, like I had a plan, and I hoped it would give him faith. I also hoped it would give me an idea or two.

Dorian and I were taken to the palace's third floor, to a forlorn-looking hallway. There, we split again and were led in opposite directions. Even if we were going to royal accommodations, I supposed they wouldn't want us too near each other, lest we carve holes in the wall to talk. He met my eyes before he was led away, giving me a fleeting smile. It gave me hope because I knew he would never stop planning a way out of this. It also inspired me to keep up my own courage and be a worthy match to his dedication.

But being separated from him made me feel terribly alone, especially when I saw my "royal" cell. If this was one of their nicer lodgings, I couldn't imagine what the rest of our friends were in. The cell was cramped, with dreary gray stone walls and a tiny, high window that barely let in light through its bars. A straw-filled mattress lay on one side of the room, while a few other "niceties"—like water and a rickety wooden chair—sat on the other.

"Make yourself presentable," one of the guards told me, after he'd undone the chains. He tossed my travel satchel, which had been stripped of weapons, to the floor. "We will come for you when the queen calls you into her exalted presence. And remember—don't get any foolish ideas. We have magic users out here too who will sense if you act."

They shut the door, and I heard a heavy lock slide into place. I gave the door a good solid kick, mostly to ease my frustration. It didn't work. It was maddening because I was in full possession of my gentry magic and could do nothing with it so long as they held the others hostage. I stared at my satchel. At first, I had no intention of becoming "presentable." I had no desire to impress that bitch. After a little thought, though, I decided it was less about impressing

her and more about presenting myself as more than a
bedraggled prisoner. I was a queen of two lands, lands I'd
earned—unlike her and her blackmail.

Not that I could do much preparation with such limited
means. My recent bath had gone a long way to help, and
the water in here let me clean up any smudges I'd since
acquired. I combed my hair into a semi-neat ponytail and
changed into my last clean sweater, which was green with
snowflakes on it. Honestly, did all sweaters have to contain
holiday decorations? At least I still had all my jewelry,
which gave me some air of regality.

Jewelry . . .

A strange, slightly crazy idea came to me. Quickly, I
stripped off my rings, bracelets, and necklace and spread
them out on the bed. I took an assessment of the jewels I
had. Moonstone, amethyst, citrine, quartz, obsidian, and a
few others. Worn as jewelry, their powers were passive,
mostly offering protection and occasional clarity for focusing shamanic magic. I separated out the ones that could
be manipulated into objects of power and put the remain-
ing jewelry back on. Then began the arduous task of prying
out the jewels I'd set aside. Stripped of all truly useful tools,
I had to rely on the hard plastic edges of my toothbrush
and comb. Amazingly, I was able to make it work, but the
process wasn't graceful.

Next, I went to the pathetic chair and attempted to break
off one of the legs. The wood looked so old and rotten that
I was certain I could do it with my bare hands. Nope. I
couldn't. So, I gave it a few thwacks against the wall—
hoping no one outside overheard—that successfully weakened the wood, allowing me to finally pull off a leg.

Returning to my bag, I found a long knee sock (a dirty
one, unfortunately) and stuffed all the jewels inside it. I
then wrapped the sock around the chair leg, knotting it so

that the bundle stayed affixed to the wood without any of the jewels escaping. Satisfied, I stared at my creation.

I had just made the tackiest, most pathetic wand in history.

It would in no way match my confiscated one, but a lot of the principles remained the same. The wood would allow me to focus my magic through the jewels, drawing on their inherent properties. It would've been better if the jewels had been properly charmed, but then, there were a lot of things about this wand that could be better.

Casting a wary glance at the door, I stood and held the wand straight out. This magic was shamanic and human. It should be undetectable to the gentry outside. I spoke Volusian's summoning words and felt the magic falter as it went through the wand. Still, it was stronger than if I'd summoned him unaided. Remembering the effort I'd needed before, I channeled every bit of focus I could into the magic, trying to break through the land's enchantment blocking his bond to me.

Against all reason, just when I thought I'd failed, Volusian appeared in the cell. He had that flickering appearance again but didn't look like he was going anywhere. The bond between us had been hard to summon, but I didn't feel it was going anywhere either. His red eyes took in the scene and then came to rest on my "wand."

"My mistress summoned me with . . . that?"

"My options were kind of limited," I said, sitting on the mattress.

"I would feel insulted," he said, "save that it's a greater slight to those who cursed me that their wards could be overcome so easily."

I smiled. "Well, don't get too cocky because we're still in kind of a mess. Varia's people have us all prisoner here in her palace."

"You are still in possession of your magic."

"If I use it, there's a good chance they'll kill off my friends before I can actually accomplish anything."

Volusian said nothing but gave me a look that clearly stated he didn't see what the problem was.

"Is there any way you can free them?" I asked. "That would take a lot of stress off me."

"It seems to me, mistress, it would remove a lot of stress if I freed *you*."

I shrugged. "I'm sure I can free myself. Well, maybe. I mean, I'm not the one with a handicap here. The rest of them are bound and blocked off from their magic. I'm not because Varia knows I won't risk their lives. Once they're out of trouble, though, I can start doing some serious damage."

"That plan is ill-conceived and ill-advised, mistress. Fortunately for you, I am unable to comply. I can't stray vary far from you in this land." It was kind of what Dorian and I had talked about, how Volusian needed me and our bond to overcome the magic that would normally bar him from the Yew Land.

"Can you go to Dorian?" I asked. "I think he's down the hall."

Volusian tilted his head as though listening to something. "Yes. I can probably reach the Oak King. Do you want me to go now?"

"No, not until I have a plan to—"

There was a click outside my door as the lock was undone. I hissed for Volusian to disappear as I shoved my half-ass wand into my satchel. I'd placed the broken chair as far as it would go into a corner earlier and hoped no guards would notice it.

They didn't. Their concern was getting my chains back on. Maybe Varia didn't think I'd do anything drastic with my friends' lives on the line, but that didn't mean I could walk around her palace free and unencumbered. My guards escorted me back to the main floor and then into what could only be called a throne room.

I didn't have a throne room. My predecessors might have, but I'd ordered my people to strip down the rooms in my castles and make them utilitarian. When I had official visits, it was usually in cozy sitting rooms with little pretension. Dorian didn't technically have a throne room either, though he did have a raised throne sitting high in his dining hall, which he would sometimes sit in when he wanted to look impressive.

But this . . . this was another story. The room was huge and could have doubled as a ballroom. Larger-than-life portraits of past monarchs lined the walls. The wide, smooth floor was made of more damarian jade, and pillars lined the room in a way that drew the eye toward the front. There Varia's throne sat, even higher than Dorian's dining room throne. The chair itself was fantastically huge, its back made of elaborate gold filigree and bedecked with gems. Despite the room's enormity, that throne was the only furniture in the entire place. It again made sure all attention went to the front—and that those who came to see the queen were uncomfortable.

I had a feeling this room probably filled up regularly with petitioners and courtiers. Today, it was just me and my guards. Our footsteps echoed around the room as we approached the stairs leading up to the throne. I refused to be awed by the throne and instead studied the paintings on the walls. The names were meaningless until I saw Ganene again. Only, she wasn't alone in her portrait. An inscription read *Queen Onya and Her Daughters, Ganene and Nissa.* Queen Onya was a stern-looking figure with a giant crown, providing a contrast to the woman on her left. That one was young and delicate-looking, very beautiful with a nervous expression. The woman on Onya's right had a hard look to her and a very strong resemblance to the woman sitting before me.

That would be Varia. She was seated grandly on her throne, wearing a dress of ruby red velvet with a skirt far too big for practical movement. I suspected servants had spread it out and draped it over the throne in an artful way. She had brown eyes and brown hair arranged in another of those high hairstyles I kept seeing among Yew women. Her age was difficult to guess, but she was certainly older than me. Jewels adorned almost every free spot: fingers, wrists, neck, ears, and hair. It was a dazzling display that walked a very, very fine line between regal and gaudy. On her lap were two tiny, furry little dogs that looked suspiciously like the annoying yappy kind I despised.

"Kneel," one of the guards said. He started to shove me down, but Varia made a small, delicate motion with her hand, and he immediately stopped.

"No need for that," said Varia, stroking one of the dogs. She pitched her voice in a way that was well received by the room's acoustics, something she'd probably practiced quite a bit. "Queen Eugenie here is a fellow sovereign. We don't kneel to each other."

"Do we often take each other prisoner?" I demanded.

She smiled sweetly. "Well, now, that depends on whether or not we are staging coups into each other's lands. You can hardly expect me to take no action when you and your cohorts come with plans to assassinate me in some feeble attempt to end the Winter Enchantment."

"We call it the blight," I said. "'Winter Enchantment' sounds like some kind of ice-skating show." I didn't really expect her to catch the reference. What had seized my attention was her accusation that we'd been coming to take her out personally. She didn't know about our actual plans. She didn't know about Volusian's help and the deductions we'd made about the gifts she was holding.

"It makes no difference what you call it," she declared. "And don't flatter yourself by thinking you're the first monarch who has tried to take matters into her own hands. The watchers I keep in my lands have descriptions of most of the kingdoms' royalty. That's the charming thing, you see. Monarchs who plan to surrender send emissaries. Monarchs with grand plans of rebellion come in person. Some delusion of personal greatness, I suppose."

"Or," I said bitterly, "maybe it's because those monarchs care about their people and are willing to risk themselves." I was guessing Varia and her dogs rarely dirtied their hands.

Varia shrugged. "Perhaps. Whatever the reason, it's foolish. Far smarter to join my united kingdoms. I was quite disappointed when I heard reports that you and King Dorian had entered my lands with your nefarious plots. You're both quite conspicuous, you know. I'd hoped you two—particularly you—would come to your senses and join me. Especially after the kind offer my ambassador made you."

"To run away from my problems and hide out here?" I scoffed. "No thanks."

"From what I hear, that's exactly what you did do, however. You just picked a different venue and were probably on guard the entire time." She gestured around her. "Had you been here, you could have relaxed and enjoyed the final months of your pregnancy. Perhaps if you hadn't been so stressed and afraid, your children wouldn't have been born early and in danger."

I stiffened, not liking the implication that my actions were responsible for the twins' risky delivery. "That's *not* why they came early. It just happens with twins sometimes."

"So you say. I'm a mother too, so I can relate to these niceties we try to convince ourselves of. And as a mother, I was quite sincere in my invitation to protect you. I think it's appalling what the Willow Queen and others tried to do to you. Appalling and cowardly. I would've helped you on principle alone. That, and I have so wanted a friend I can talk to and be on equal terms with."

"Ilania mentioned that too," I said, not really buying it. "Some kind of female-solidarity thing?"

"I need to talk to someone, don't I? Aside from my little darlings here." She paused to scratch the dogs' chins. Both had jeweled collars and little bows on their heads. "And men have proved far too disappointing. I gave up on them years ago, except for the necessary pleasures, of course. Mostly, they bore or irritate me. I would greatly welcome smart female companionship. It's lonely having all this power." There was a wistful, melodramatic way to her delivery of that last line that made me want to punch her.

"Sorry if I don't feel bad for you. It's hard for me to muster a lot of empathy for someone who's been responsible for so much innocent death and destruction."

Varia laughed merrily. "Innocent? There are few who can really claim that. And what would you think if I told you that I can focus the Winter Enchantment more harshly on specific kingdoms? You find me cruel, but the enchantment as it currently stands still allows life to go on in your kingdoms." The laughter died, and she leaned slightly forward. "I have the means to focus the spell and increase its intensity. If you liked, I could focus on the Willow Land and completely destroy it."

I gaped. "You'd completely destroy a kingdom full of innocent people?"

"Including Queen Maiwenn," she pointed out. "That would be terribly convenient for you. And a nice bit of revenge after all she's done to you—she certainly hasn't balked at hurting innocents. Why not return the favor?"

I didn't have a great opinion of the person who'd created the blight, but this conversation was making her credibility deteriorate even more rapidly.

"There's revenge . . . and then there's madness and cruelty," I said. "And I would never kill off her entire kingdom for what she's done."

"Easy to say with your children alive and well. Still, I hope it emphasizes what a great friend I could be to you. Believe me, I really do prefer it that way. This situation only has a couple of possible outcomes for you, and you willingly signing on as my ally would be preferable to all of us."

"Oh, I'm sure," I said, not bothering to hide my sarcasm. "And all you'd ask in return for these friendly feats of destruction is us being pals and having a little girl time now and then."

Varia's lips quirked. "Well, as an important ally, I have no doubt you'd want to help me out now and then."

Gentry wheeling and dealing. At least it was familiar territory.

"Here we go," I said. "Let me guess. You want to help lead my son's armies when we conquer the human world?"

"*Human* world?" She shook her head in amazement and looked as though she was ready to burst into laughter again. She lifted one of the dogs and peered into its face. "Did you hear that, Lady Snowington? How silly." She returned the dog to her lap and looked back at me. "Why on earth would I care about humans when there's plenty to entertain me here in this world? This is the world I want. The problem is, it's such a nuisance keeping my subject kingdoms in line. Even though they surrender and allow my forces within their borders, I'm constantly having to reassert my power with dramatic shows of force. It's very tiring."

"How terrible for you."

She continued, either not noticing or no longer caring about my sarcasm. "That's the nature of the game, however . . . unless I had a more permanent way to bond to all of these lands, one that would give me unbreakable authority without the constant maintenance."

I gave a harsh laugh. "Sounds pretty easy then. Just kill off all the monarchs and take the lands' bonds and—" My smile faded, as a terrible, sinking realization hit me. "That's it. That's why you want to be my 'friend.' You want the Iron Crown."

Varia didn't deny it. "It makes things so much simpler."

What made the Iron Crown so deadly was that it broke the bond between a monarch and his or her land. As I was constantly reminded, that bond ran deep. It was tied into my life and being, and short of death or a monarch inexplicably losing power, there was no way to end that bond or pass it on. If there had been, I likely would've given the Thorn Land away when I first won it. Then, the discovery of the Iron Crown had changed everything. With the Iron Crown, I'd ripped away Katrice's connection to the Rowan Land. Left unclaimed, the land had then been ripe for me to bond with it and take control.

My earlier joke had been right to a certain extent: Varia could just kill off all those monarchs. But that wasn't easy, seeing as monarchs, by their nature, were usually among the most powerful magic users in their kingdoms. It would make for long, taxing battles, and no matter how badass Varia wanted to seem, I knew she wasn't all-powerful. Magic for magic, whatever hers was, I doubted she was stronger than me. What made her remarkable was that she had a league of magic users to work with, creating the kind of power that had led to the blight. Organizing a group for a passive enchantment was one thing. Getting them all together to go hunt down monarchs in outside kingdoms was an entirely different matter.

"No. There is nothing you can do that would get me to give you the Iron Crown—not that I could if I wanted to," I added. "It can only be used by the person who won it."

"So I hear," she said. "But that's fine. I'd only need you to shatter the bonds. I'd take care of the rest."

I thought about all the kingdoms near me and the many I'd heard about under her control. "You can't bond with that many. It's not possible. No one's that strong, not even you. Two is taxing enough."

Varia looked at me like I was crazy, which was saying something. "Well, of course I wouldn't bond them all! That's absurd. I'd simply make sure they were claimed by those I could trust. My daughters, for example, would make excellent queens. If you stayed on my good side— and I must admit, you aren't endearing yourself very much right now—I might give you a couple."

"No," I repeated. "I'm not using it on your behalf. I'm never using it again, and I'm not telling you where it's at. You want it? Kill me off so it'll return to its resting place. Then you can go get it and do whatever you want."

"That's hardly practical, and you know it." The Iron Crown's resting place was in a land packed with so much iron that most gentry couldn't set foot in it.

"Well, then, we're at an impasse," I said triumphantly. "I have something you want, and there's no way I'm giving it to you. End of story."

"No, child," she said, shaking her head with mock sympathy. "That's where you're mistaken. Really, you have nothing at all—and I have everything." She paused for dramatic effect. "Like your friends in my dungeon."

I went perfectly still. "What are you saying? That you'll kill them if I don't use the crown for you?"

"It's certainly an option. The fact that you have yet to attempt any magic to fight me has already given away how much they mean to you."

"Yes," I said, my heart sinking. "But they would all willingly die to prevent the enslavement of countless other kingdoms or abuse of the Iron Crown." I knew the words were true as I said them, but they still hurt. I'd held back on using magic, not just because my friends' lives were on the line, but also because I didn't have an entirely clear plan on what to do with my magic. But something like this? Varia's world domination? No question. None of my companions would be able to live with themselves knowing the scope of what their freedom had cost others.

"At some point, you have to decide what number of lives tips the scale. So, you're saying these, what, six or seven individuals aren't worth the crown's cost? What about your kingdom? *Kingdoms?* What I offered to do to the Willow Land—by focusing the enchantment—can be done to yours instead." Her smile grew particularly cunning. "Or maybe it's less about quantity than quality. Your children are out there somewhere. Do you think they can stay hidden forever? Even in the human world, I can find them. I have many subjects, and you and your sister aren't the only ones who can pass through with ease."

The room threatened to spin around me, and I had to focus myself to stay calm and not give away how hard her words had hit. "Are you really so heartless?" I demanded. "Listen to yourself! You're threatening to wipe out two entire kingdoms and hunt down my children!" Seeing her smirk, I had to restrain from clenching my fists. "Do you enjoy this? Do you get some kind of sick thrill from these kinds of psycho threats?"

"No," she told me, still smiling and petting the dogs. "I simply take satisfaction out of pointing out the obvious, and it's exactly as I already said: you hold nothing here, and I hold everything."

Chapter 20

Then, much as though I were a naughty child, Varia told me she was sending me back to my cell to "think about what I had to do." Before I left, she added, "And lest you think me too lenient, let me emphasize to you that I'm most anxious to have this friendship of ours settled. I don't like loose ends. Besides, some of these kingdoms are becoming an absolute nuisance. Much tidier for all of us if we can take care of this soon."

"Noted," I muttered as the guards grabbed my arms to lead me away.

"And so," she continued, "when I say I'm going to emphasize the point to you, I mean that I will soon start taking action to encourage you to do the right thing. Starting with the elimination of your lesser companions. Then moving on to your kingdoms. Then your children."

"My friends haven't done anything to you," I said, panic seizing me over how quickly the threat had escalated. "They're potential subjects."

Varia shrugged. "I have plenty of those."

"Can I at least talk to them?" I asked. "Make sure they're okay so I know you haven't killed them already?"

She gave me a tight, knowing smile. "My dear, how foolish do you think I am?"

And with that, I was led out of the throne room. At the door, we ran into a slight traffic jam. A number of petitioners were lined up to see Varia, but a sentry held them all back and explained why they couldn't be allowed entrance.

"Her Majesty has a meeting with the Oak King," the guard said. "That takes priority. She will see no one else until after that—and that's if she feels up for it. She's had a very taxing day, so you may have to wait until tomorrow."

The Oak King. I would've killed to be a fly on the wall for that audience and wondered if Dorian would opt for charm or mockery. Sometimes with him, there was a fine line between the two. I was also skeptical of just how "taxing" Varia's day had been. Considering the impracticality of that dress, it didn't seem like she could even walk without assistance. I really wouldn't have been surprised to learn she and her dogs were carried around in a sedan chair.

Among the disgruntled petitioners were my "pals" from the Hemlock Land. They appeared as though they too had done a bit of hasty cleanup but otherwise possessed the same worn appearance they'd had on the road. Orj's face hardened at the sentry's words but nonetheless managed stiff politeness.

"We were told that if we assisted Her Majesty in her task . . ." His eyes flicked nervously to me and then back to the guard. "We were told she'd release our king and allow him to return to our land. We did all she asked."

The guard looked unconcerned. "Then you'll get him tomorrow. Or the next day."

Alea stepped up beside Orj. "But he's been imprisoned for two months! He and the land are both suffering from being apart. What good is it being freed of the curse if our land is simply going to die off this way?"

"If it makes no difference then," said the guard, "I'm sure Her Majesty would be happy to return the Winter Enchantment to you."

I heard no more because my guards finally managed to push me through the bottleneck. I was taken without incident to my cell, but as the guards unlocked it, I glanced at the other closed doors in the hallway. I knew Dorian was there somewhere. Was the Hemlock King as well? These were the "nicer" chambers, after all. How many monarchs were imprisoned around me? It may have been egotistical presuming all these guards and magic users were just for me. Varia couldn't maintain her subjugated kingdoms without the monarchs occasionally bonding with the land, but keeping them apart for great lengths of time certainly created a new element of vulnerability that she could manipulate. She also now had a hostage system that probably worked well to keep the conquered kingdoms in line. Most gentry loved their rulers with fierce devotion and, as Orj had shown, would go to considerable lengths for them.

As soon as I was locked up and alone again, I summoned Volusian with the makeshift wand.

"Are there other monarchs locked up in this corridor?" I demanded. "Aside from me and Dorian?"

"There are other shining ones here, yes," Volusian said. "Ones I can sense considerable power from, though they are forced to wear their iron, even when locked up. They apparently don't have the luxuries you do."

I sighed and sat down on the cot. "I might as well be in iron for all the good I can do! That bitch was right. She has everything, and I have nothing. And now she's threatening to destroy my friends, my kingdoms, Isaac and Ivy. . . ."

My heart lurched at that last one. I valued my own life, certainly, but I never went into any of these crazy Otherworldly missions without the understanding that I might not come back. It was something I'd had to come to terms with a long time ago. I didn't relish the thought of my traveling companions dying—especially Jasmine and Pagiel—but I knew they too had accepted certain dangers.

The twins? They were a different matter. They were innocents. They had nothing to do with any of this, and just thinking about Varia hurting them filled me with a mix of rage and fear. With the prophecy taking backseat to the blight, I'd thought Isaac and Ivy were out of danger, but it seemed, once again, someone wanted to use them against me.

"There are guards and magic users out there," I murmured, thinking aloud. "Obviously enough to subdue an escape—or so Varia thinks. But she can't be thinking past a single person trying to break out. What about *all* of us? If we managed to free the other monarchs here, we'd have a force of some of the most powerful gentry in this world. The guards here couldn't stand against that. This palace couldn't stand against that. Plus, there'd be such a commotion that my friends in the dungeon would probably be low priority."

I thought I detected an eager glint in Volusian's eyes, though his face otherwise remained typically smooth. "As much as I would love nothing more than to start laying waste to this place, I must point out that if my mistress truly wishes to lift the blight, you should probably first make sure you know where the talismans are. Your conquest of Varia will be more effective if you can strip her of those."

"I agree. Except, we have no way of finding out. I mean, they're probably in this palace, but it's huge! Damn. I wish you could wander freely. We need someone to scope out this facility." My breath caught as an idea came to me. I straightened up. "Volusian! Go to Dorian's cell right now. You have to give him this message. . . ."

I quickly relayed it, and Volusian vanished. I bit my lip

the entire time he was gone, praying Dorian hadn't been taken to Varia yet. Why hadn't I thought of this sooner? If I'd missed my chance, I didn't know what we would do. I just hoped Varia had to take a bonbon break or have her dogs' hair restyled between sessions. Even if Volusian did make it in time, this idea was still pretty shaky.

I jumped up when Volusian reappeared. "Was he still there?"

"Yes, mistress. I relayed your message. The Oak King said he would try what you asked and idiotically asked what he wouldn't do for you." A distinct look of distaste crossed his features. "He also said to tell you . . . that he isn't surprised at all that you're planning a way out. He says he has never once doubted you and has the utmost faith in whatever you do."

I almost smiled. "Boy, relaying something that sentimental was pretty terrible for you, wasn't it?"

Volusian didn't respond.

The truth was, Dorian's warm words had unsettled me too—but probably for very different reasons from Volusian. Still wanting to conserve the power it took to keep him within the Yew Land, I sent Volusian away and then stretched out on my cot to wait. I didn't know how long it would take to get results from my plan—if I'd even get them. I was also worried about Varia acting on her threats to start killing off my companions in the dungeon. I could only hope that like any good super villain, she'd give me fair warning and try to kill them in front of me in order to force my hand. That wasn't a fate I wanted, but at least I could be reasonably confident they weren't dead already.

Hours passed. The guards brought me a meager meal, again making me wonder what those in lesser accommodations had. I didn't think Varia had reason to poison me, but I still summoned Volusian briefly to see if he detected anything magical about the food. He didn't, so I took the risk of eating in order to keep my strength up.

I was just finishing the food up when something caught my eye in the tiny window near the ceiling. Spots, Alea's falcon, had just landed. With a bit of maneuvering, he worked his way through the bars so that he could look down at me but otherwise didn't leave the sill.

"Well, I'll be damned," I breathed. "You actually made it."

My gamble had been that the Hemlock people would still be hanging around the throne room, hoping for an audience with Varia. In the message I'd sent with Volusian, I'd told Dorian to see if he could manage any private words with Alea when he went to see the queen. There were guards everywhere, but if ever there was someone who could cause distraction and misdirection, it was Dorian. If he pulled it off, I'd asked that he tell Alea to send her falcon to me. The only directions I had were to look for a small window on the third floor, but I figured Spots could fly from window to window in search of me—provided there were no enchantments on the windows. The entire plan had been tenuous, and yet, here I was, with a semi-intelligent falcon watching me expectantly.

"So, um, thanks for coming," I said to Spots. He blinked and said nothing, not that I really could have expected otherwise. "Anyway. I know you have some connection to Alea. I don't know if you relay messages through bird language or if she sees through your eyes, but I need you to convey something to her. Can you do that? Is there some sign you can give me?"

If staring without a sound was the way birds said, "Yes," then Spots gave me a resoundingly affirmative answer.

"Okay." I was starting to feel stupid. "I'll just talk and hope this gets to her. Tell Alea that I have the means to free her king. I also know how to break Varia's hold on all of us, but I need help. I know Alea and her people are willing to give in to Varia to keep their land safe, but if they work with me, I really believe we can overpower Varia and be free of her tyranny. Here's the thing. Somewhere in this palace, there is a very heavily guarded room. I mean, there's probably a bunch of rooms like that. The dungeons, Varia's bedroom, her dogs' kennel, whatever. But I feel like this is going to be *really* guarded. I don't expect Alea to get anywhere near it, since I'm guessing subjects' access only goes so far. That's the thing. Alea probably won't even see the masses of guards because this room is going to have a huge perimeter around it. That's probably one clue. The other is that it won't be obvious why it's so guarded. Dungeons make sense. This won't. So, if there's any way she can figure out where this is at and let me know, that would be huge."

I paused then, wondering about that last part. I was banking on the bird magically communicating my words to Alea. How hers would get back to me was less obvious. Well. That was a problem for later, and we had plenty of others before we reached that point.

"Having some idea of that place's location will make a big difference when I bust out her king. And I will, by the way. Him and all the other captive monarchs. So, if she knows any other disgruntled emissaries from other lands, tell them to be ready for a huge coup in the next day or so." Until that moment, I hadn't realized I was truly going to stage one . . . but, well, why else had I come here? "But again, the key is figuring out this stronghold of Varia's. We can still stage a nasty rebellion, but the threat of the blight isn't going to go away until we get to what she's hiding."

Spots groomed his foot. I wasn't sure if he was simply listening and multitasking or had grown bored.

"Can you tell her that?"

For a moment, I thought nothing would happen, and then Spots made some kind of chirping noise. He worked his way back out through the bars and flew off.

"Well," I remarked. "Not the weirdest thing I've ever done by far . . . but it's up there." I then realized I was talking to myself and wondered if that was better or worse than speaking to a bird.

It was hard for me to sit still and wait. My nature usually required that I do something; it was why I'd had such a difficult time in Alabama. At least while there, I'd known my patience would pay off for the twins' safety. Here, I was constantly pressed with the knowledge that every day meant more of Varia's reign, more suffering in the blight, and more dangers for my friends.

As evening fell and my cell darkened, I summoned Volusian back. Maybe it was a trick of the lighting, but his appearance seemed more substantial now. "You can move around this hallway. I want you to go and talk to each of the monarchs and give them a heads-up on what's going on. Tell them there may be a commotion soon and that we'll be freeing them from their chains to go take on Varia and the blight once and for all. Let them know I'll have more details when the time comes." God, I hoped that was actually true. "Give them my description so they know I'm the one with instructions. And Dorian. Give them his description too. In fact, go to Dorian first and catch him up on everything. He may not know about our fellow cellmates. And tell him I talked to the bird."

Volusian gave me a long-suffering look. "This may be a new low for me, mistress."

"Hey, it's necessary for the bigger plan. Besides, I figured you'd be all about getting closer to our endgame with Varia. I thought you wanted to prove something to these Yew people."

His eyes narrowed. "Mistress, you have no idea just how much I want that."

He vanished, and I was left alone again. I didn't know how many monarchs were in the hall exactly, but it took a while for Volusian to make the rounds to them and Dorian. I had actually dozed off when my minion returned. Waking up to those red eyes in a dark room is not a fate I'd wish on anyone, not that I let him know how much it freaked me out.

"And?" I asked. "How'd it go? Did you talk to everyone?"

"Yes, mistress."

"How many others are there besides Dorian and me?"

"There are five."

Five. Somehow, I'd been hoping for a dozen or so. Still, five gentry with magic on par with Dorian and me were nothing to scoff at. We could do some serious damage to this place. "Did they say they'll help?"

"Three were quite zealous. I believe they would have attempted an escape right then, with or without a plan. The other two have been here a considerable time. Their spirits are broken. They were listless in responses, seeming to have little hope that we could actually accomplish anything."

An uneasy thought occurred to me. "They aren't so desperate that they'll report on me in some attempt to buy favor, are they?"

"I do not believe so, mistress. I believe they have simply given up altogether. Should the opportunity for revenge and escape arise, it's possible they may regain their momentum."

"Let's hope so," I muttered. We'd gone from five to three allies. I still thought those were good odds, but I preferred "overwhelming" to "good."

"Also," added Volusian, with what I was certain was a note of displeasure, "I have a message from the Oak King."

"What'd he say?"

"He says that in addition to finding the talismans' location, you should also consider that they will have some sort of magical protection on them. Finding them and defeating their guards may not be enough if there is a shield or enchantment in place that you don't know how to defeat."

"Excellent point—not that I should expect less from Dorian. Do you think that's likely?"

"Almost certainly."

"No spell's permanent, of course. Someone powerful enough could blast through it—or several someones. And that's the thing. She probably had multiple people helping set up these defenses, just like with the blight. This thing's going to be a bitch to crack."

Volusian considered. "Yes, but there is probably a trick or simpler way of undoing any protective magic around the gifts. No one wants to be locked out of their own spell, and she must get through her defenses occasionally to move new objects in."

My head was hurting from all the growing complications. "So, there's something else we have to figure out. Unless we can just make it work with brute magical force."

"That is still an option," he agreed.

"Thanks. You can go."

I sighed and stretched back out on the bed, trying to figure out how I was going to stage a master escape plan when my allies consisted of a bunch of restrained prisoners, a spirit confined to a hallway, and a bird that may or may not understand me. Glancing over, I saw that Volusian was still standing there and watching me.

"What?" I asked. "Is there something else?"

"The Oak King had another message for you."

"Oh? What was it?"

"He said . . ." I again got that vibe of distaste from Volusian. "He said to tell you he misses you and takes comfort in knowing your room is close to his—though it's still not nearly close enough. He says he will lie in bed tonight and imagine the distance between you is gone and that you are there with him."

"My God," I said, nearly bursting out laughing. "I thought it was bad for you before."

Volusian made no response. I tried to adopt some seriousness but knew I was grinning.

"Tell him that's very sweet but awfully presumptuous, in light of our history."

Volusian disappeared and returned about a minute later. "The Oak King says that in light of the current situation, he imagines you might be more open to such suggestions. He said—and I quote—'Daring escapes do wonders for passion. What would ordinarily be deemed presumptuous might actually seem quite reasonable in troubled times. Perhaps the blight wouldn't have been so cold, had we come to that conclusion sooner.'"

I scoffed. "Well, tell him that remains to be seen, seeing as we haven't pulled off any daring escape yet."

Volusian hesitated. "Mistress, I have never asked anything of you in my servitude. But now, I beg you this: do not make me keep passing these adolescent sentiments back and forth all night."

"Fair enough," I said, feeling a smile start to return. "Go ahead and tell Dorian that too. This is the last note you pass tonight. I need some sleep, and it takes too much power to keep you here."

Volusian didn't thank me—that would be asking too much—but he did look relieved. He vanished into the darkness and didn't come back that night.

I tried to sleep in earnest, knowing I'd need my strength for whatever wacky mishaps were to come. That's easier said than done in enemy hands—especially for an insomniac like me—and I tossed and turned a fair amount. Sleep did finally come after a couple of hours, mercifully free of dreams. I didn't wake until something pulled at my hair. At first, I shrugged it off in my sleepy state. Then, it happened again, a tug so painful I yelped and opened my eyes.

And found Spots the falcon staring at me, about two inches from my face.

"Jesus Christ!" I jumped up, certain my eyes were about to be pecked out. "Couldn't you just squawk from the window? Or tap the wall with your beak?"

Spots made no reply, save to preen his wing.

"I assume you're here for a reason," I said. "But you probably can't tell me."

He looked back up at me and extended a leg. Peering closely, I saw a teeny-tiny roll of paper tied there. Carefully, unsure if he'd decide to gouge me with his claws, I removed the miniature scroll from his leg. The paper was very fine and delicate, and I was half afraid it would tear before I could unroll it. When I finally got a good look at it, I could see a handful of words scrawled in tiny writing:

ROOM IS UNDERGROUND. SCOUT IS INVESTIGATING.

Cryptic but promising overall, I decided. I was about to give the bird a return message when I suddenly heard the lock being opened on my door.

"Get out of here!" I told Spots. "Come back . . . er, later."

He was already up in the window before I could finish talking and wiggled his way out through the bars just as some guards entered. Their faces were grim. One jerked my hands forward while another bound them with chains.

"Her Majesty wants you. Now."

For a moment, I thought the time I'd been dreading had come. Varia was going to give me some terrible ultimatum. Yet, something about her and her flair for the dramatic told me there would have been a lot of setup and fanfare. This had a hurried feel. An urgency, like something was wrong.

The feeling further intensified when I wasn't marched to the throne room. Instead, I was taken to Varia's own chambers, shoved roughly inside a posh sitting room done entirely in periwinkle velvet. Varia was there, lounging on a divan, looking as though she'd gotten out of bed in the last hour. She wore a robe that matched the room, as well as some furry slippers. Her brown hair was worn down but didn't look like it had been brushed. She stayed in that reclined position, as though trying to present an unconcerned air, but the anger in her voice betrayed her when she saw me.

"Where are they?" she demanded. The dogs were at her feet and began yipping. She silenced them with some treats.

I glanced around, looking for some kind of assistance or context for her question. "Um, where are what?"

"The people you traveled here with." She sat up and fixed me with a glare so icy that it was easy to see her as the blight's creator. "Where are they, and how in the world did you break them out?"

Chapter 21

I said the first thing that came to mind.

"Sooo . . . you lost them?"

Varia glared, not nearly as serene and commanding as she'd been yesterday. "This is not a game! Tell me how you accomplished it. You are still in possession of your powers. How did you escape and set them free?"

I put my hands on my hips. "I may still have my powers, but I'm also being kept in a locked room surrounded by guards and magic users! The kind of magic I'd need to escape would involve me blowing out the door, and I think someone would've probably noticed that. Besides, why the hell would I then go back to my cell? I would've walked out with my friends."

"I don't believe you," said Varia. "No one can escape those dungeons. They must have had assistance." The dogs started their racket again. More treats.

I shrugged and tried not to look too smug. "My friends are pretty resourceful. Maybe your security's not as good as you think."

Inside, I was jubilant. Jasmine and the others had gotten away! At a basic level, I was simply happy they were safe. In the greater scheme of things, it also meant my hands were no longer tied. I could summon a storm right now and have no fears of retribution. Of course, that would be pre-emptive since the rest of my plan wasn't yet fully developed. The more I studied Varia, though, the more it became obvious I wasn't the only one who'd reached this conclusion about my new freedom.

"I wouldn't be so arrogant if I were you," she said. "As I said before, I hold a lot more game pieces than you do and control a lot that's dear to you."

I kept my face neutral, but inside, my heart was racing. I remembered her previous lists of threats. Right now, my friends were off the table, and I sincerely doubted she'd found Isaac and Ivy. What did that leave? My kingdoms. She was pissed off enough about the escape to do something drastic, and nightmare scenarios ran through my mind. What if she blasted one kingdom to show me she was serious about the other? There was a staggering amount of innocent lives in my hands, and if she did attempt to hurt them, I really would blow her apart now, storm or no storm.

Varia smiled cruelly. "Soon you'll see just how much I control when—oh, for the gods' sake! Get them out of here!"

Her moment of drama had been derailed when those wretched little dogs began barking again. A servant quickly scooped them up and scurried out of the room. She swore when one of them bit her.

"Now then." Varia nodded toward a guard. "Bring him in."

The guard gave a curt salute and hurried out the door. He returned a moment later with a prisoner—Dorian.

Apparently, I wasn't the only one who'd gotten an early wake-up call. Dorian looked a little worn around the edges but otherwise showed no signs of injury or distress. Indeed, he wore his typically indolent look, as though he'd wanted to come here in chains and Varia had been kind enough to oblige him. His eyes flicked briefly to me before focusing on Varia. He gave her one of his charming smiles.

"Your Majesty. How nice of you to call me to breakfast. And I must say, you look very fetching this morning. I'm always saying women don't go to enough trouble to match their décor. I also always say that brushes are overrated. Right, Eugenie?"

I didn't answer, mostly because I was too preoccupied with what Varia's next move was going to be. I didn't think Dorian's presence here was a good sign. She studied him for several long moments and then turned her attention back to me.

"I should not have given you the night to think things over," she said crisply. "That was an indulgence on my part, one I won't repeat. I want your fealty. I want the Iron Crown. If I don't get them, I will execute the Oak King as part of my dinner entertainment later."

I laughed in spite of myself. "You can't kill him. You need him. You want him to sign his kingdom over to you." I didn't know the exact details of yesterday's conversation, but I had to assume she'd given him the same ultimatum about surrendering his kingdom to her. I also assumed he'd refused.

"True, it's simpler when I have a land's monarch on hand, but his is only one kingdom. His death will serve me better than his surrender. Someone else will simply claim the land, and although it may take longer this way, the Oak Land will become mine once that new king or queen swears allegiance."

Dorian was still smiling, though there was a tightness in his features that hadn't been there earlier. He narrowed his eyes. "Say what you want, but even if the lowest scullery maid in my castle seizes control of the land, she still won't surrender to you. And Eugenie certainly isn't going to yield the Iron Crown to your control simply for my sake. She doesn't like me nearly that much. This is an absurd waste of time. Why don't we all just sit down for a delightful morning meal of tea and pastries and put this absurdity behind us? Where are your charming pets, by the way?"

There was some truth to his words. I wasn't going to give up the Iron Crown, even to save his life—but that decision wasn't nearly as carefree as he made it sound. It was a head-over-heart choice, one that I knew accomplished the most good but which would probably kill me in the application.

"This is no joke. The Oak King will die if my request is denied. And," Varia continued to me, "as I said, I'm not going to let you debate in luxury."

Was my cell considered luxury? I *really* had to see what passed for dismal lodging around this place. Before I could question her further, a slight gesture from her brought a guard striding toward Dorian. In one smooth motion, he halted before Dorian and punched him hard in the stomach. Dorian doubled over, and a spasm of pain crossed his face, but he otherwise made no sound. Me, on the other hand . . . well, I had a few things to say.

"You fucking bitch!" I exclaimed, straining forward. Guards were already in place to restrain my arms, probably having anticipated my reaction. "I am going to *kill* you!" Without further thought, I had drawn the magic of air and water around me. The room grew thick with humidity and tension. All I needed was a source to blast it into.

"Eugenie," said Dorian sharply. All mirth was gone. "Do *not* do anything rash. You have a lot to think over."

I met his eyes, which were greener than ever in the morning light streaming through Varia's windows. I caught the subtext. If I unleashed my magic now, it would be without a well-formed plan. Again, I had a head vs. heart

decision here, and my head's argument didn't seem so
compelling just then. Still, after a deep breath, I dropped
my magic and fixed a glare on Varia.

"Perhaps the Oak King is more reasonable than I suspected," she mused. She nodded toward the same guard
again. He stepped forward and punched Dorian in the face,
hard enough that I heard a *thwack*.

"Ow," moaned Dorian, wincing from the pain. "My
greatest asset."

I bit my lip so hard that I tasted blood. But I had to do
something to stop myself from striking Varia down with
lightning. "What is the point of this?" I asked Varia, once I
had some semblance of control. "To convince me what a
badass you are? That you can bully a chained-up man? Or
is it just so I'll believe you really will kill him?"

"Oh," she said. "You can rest assured that I *will* kill him.
Mostly this is to emphasize what I said before: no more
time to lounge around and decide with no consequences.
For every moment you waste deliberating today, the Oak
King will be in the hands of my torturers, experiencing the
most excruciating pain. Your delay extends that agony."

"Oh, irony," murmured Dorian.

I stiffened. This was not good news, first because I
simply didn't want Dorian suffering. What also sucked was
that I was certain the torturers were not on the same floor
as my cell, meaning I wouldn't have Dorian on hand when
I attempted my great coup. Jasmine and the others' escape
had given me one less variable to worry about inside the
palace. Dorian being taken out of my sight was a brand-
new complication.

Varia continued. "And believe me when I say that my
professionals make Garik's attempts here seem quite child-
ish. No offense, Garik." The punching guard gave a bow
of acknowledgment to his queen. "Fortunately for the

Oak King, his pain will be short-lived—either because you'll make the right decision or I'll be forced to kill him at suppertime."

"Remember—nothing rash, Eugenie," said Dorian, far too cheerful for someone whose face was swelling rapidly. "I can take as much pain as I can dole out—and you certainly know how much I can dole out. Don't worry about me."

Again, I caught the message to carry out the other plans with caution. There was also, I suspected, a joke in there about some of Dorian's sexual preferences, which tended to run toward BDSM. I had little appreciation for the weak attempt at humor just now, however. It took every ounce of strength I had to remain hard and impassive to Varia. Otherwise, there was a good chance I'd fall to my knees and beg for Dorian's release.

"I'm not swearing any loyalty to you," I told her. "And I'm not going to use the Iron Crown on your behalf. That answer's not going to change."

"Suit yourself," she said. "We'll see what you say later today." She gave us a wave of dismissal. "Take them to their respective locations."

I wasn't able to exchange another word with Dorian because we were both hurried out too quickly. The urge to unleash a storm surged within me one last time, and I again fought it back. I would do this right. So, I allowed my escort to take me back to my cell on the third floor. They again gave me the faux courtesy of removing my chains before locking the door. Glancing around, I saw that someone had left a covered meal tray on my palette. I lifted the lid and found a piece of bread and some water—and a rat that quickly darted off the tray. Talk about adding insult to injury.

"Oh," I said. "That's just lovely."

Yet, before I finished speaking, I noticed something weird about the rat—mainly, that it wasn't actually a rat. Instead, it was a rat-sized miniature red fox. I caught my breath.

"No way. Kiyo?"

The rat-fox scurried to the center of my cell. Within moments, he transformed, and I had a full-sized Kiyo standing before me. I cast a wary look behind me, half expecting guards to come busting in. Then, I had to remind myself that his kitsune magic would not be readily detectable to gentry.

"How'd you do that?" I asked Kiyo. "Did a mad scientist give you a shrink ray?"

He smiled, but his eyes looked tired. "Afraid not. It's just another variation on the shape-shifting, just like I can turn into a super-sized fox. I've just never had much reason for the small size. Turns out it's terribly convenient for poking around a palace."

"I thought you were a rat," I admitted.

"So did one of the cooks in the kitchen. I have a new respect for brooms."

"Is that how you guys escaped? Where's everyone else? Are they okay?"

He leaned against the wall and ran a hand through his dark hair. "The chains couldn't stop me, especially once I shape-shifted. Once I had a moment to free myself, I got the chains off everyone else, and then we just kind of busted our way out in the night. Why haven't you done that?"

"Would if I could," I muttered. "Varia's keeping me in check with a few things. First, it was you guys. Then she tacked on the destruction of my kingdoms and finding Isaac and Ivy for good measure. Now she's got Dorian with torturers and his execution penciled in." I gave him a brief recap of my morning meeting.

"You were smart not to act then," said Kiyo, when I was finished. "Dorian's strong. He'll hold out."

I wondered if Kiyo meant that or if he just didn't really care about Dorian suffering. "You never told me where the others are."

"Hidden in the city," Kiyo said. "Your Hemlock friends helped us find a safe place."

"Hemlock . . ." A light went off. "You're Alea's scout, aren't you? You've been looking for the room with the talismans."

"Found it," he said, in a manner far too casual for the importance of those words. "Like I said, you can get to a lot when you're rat-sized."

"Is it in the basement, like Alea said?"

"Well, yes, but there are a bunch of basements here. This place goes as far underground as it does above. The room's about four floors down and has lots of guards. The objects are inside, in two collections, surrounded by some magic I can't really figure out. But then, gentry magic isn't my specialty."

"Two collections . . . let me guess. One for the lands actually in the blight and one for those who've sworn allegiance. But obviously, she'd still keep their tokens around as leverage."

Kiyo nodded. "That's what I thought too. Not sure if this makes you feel better or worse, but the blighted pile was much larger. More are resisting than giving in."

"How do you know it was the blighted pile? Did you recognize Maiwenn's gift?"

"No, but there was a marble bust of Dorian in there, which I figured must have been his kingdom's 'humble' gift."

That normally would've brought a smile to my face, but thinking of Dorian only served to remind me of the trouble he was in because of me. The image of him being punched in the face was etched in my mind.

"We have to expedite things and get out of here," I said. If Kiyo had talked to Alea, she probably would've mentioned me telling Spots that I would free her king. But, obviously, there was a lot more to the plan that Kiyo needed to be caught up on. I quickly explained about the other captive monarchs and how Volusian had been in contact with them. Kiyo's eyes were aglow as he listened.

"That's brilliant," he said. "So long as they haven't been badly treated, they'll be a huge force to have on our side."

I nodded. "Volusian didn't give me the impression that they'd been physically harmed . . . just that some were kind of defeated mentally."

"Understandable," said Kiyo. "But if they can fight, we may not need to figure out the key to the enchantment around the objects. You guys can just overpower it."

"We talked about that too. It's an option. Still, if there's any edge we can get, I want it. I don't want to go down there with my little posse of six or so, only to find out Varia used six hundred to cast her spell and that we can't even come close to matching that."

"I can ask Orj and the rest of the Hemlock group about it. Along with some dissidents from other kingdoms, it seems Varia has a number of malcontents within her own borders."

That was a surprise. "Everyone I've met sure seems devoted, though. She's massively powerful and controls lots of other kingdoms. Seems like her subjects would be happy about that."

"They're devoted because they're afraid of her," Kiyo pointed out. "And from what I've been hearing, the people in her own kingdom don't always fare much better than those she subjugates."

That also surprised me, since I regarded protecting my

subjects as my main job as queen. Of course, Varia and I were coming from very different points of view, seeing as I also didn't really feel the need to blackmail the innocents of other kingdoms with death and suffering in order to expand my empire. So, it was reasonable she and I would have different ruling styles in general.

"Well, find out what you can," I told him. "One thing I know for sure—we need to get Dorian out before we launch our master attack."

Kiyo shifted uncomfortably. "We might not have time for that. We can get him once everything else is taken care of."

"We may not have the chance! The whole reason she's holding him is to ensure my good behavior. If we start some commotion up here, he could end up dead before we get back to him."

I admit, part of me had been a little amazed this whole time that Kiyo and I had been having such a civil conversation. It was almost—*almost*—like we didn't have this history of blood and betrayal between us. Nonetheless, I think I'd been subconsciously waiting for something to pick a fight over, some reason for our tenuous alliance to fall apart. Kiyo, to his credit, seemed to take his time in forming a civil response.

"If you go after Dorian beforehand and something goes wrong, *you* could end up dead before you ever get a chance to free the hostage monarchs and go after the objects. Or, even if you bring the monarchs with you, there's still the chance something could go amiss." He gave me a wry look. "You aren't all-powerful, Eugenie. You keep talking like all you really need to do is walk out of here, and everything will be taken care of. You're a badass, but this place is packed full of magic users and soldiers. That can wear even you down."

He was annoying because he was right. It was entirely

possible we could achieve everything—destroying the talismans and freeing Dorian—but the former had to take first priority. We couldn't risk losing our shot at that. It's what Dorian would want. And yet . . .

"I just can't abandon him," I said in a small voice.

Kiyo studied me for a long time before responding. "I'll rescue him."

I looked up sharply. "What?"

"I'll rescue him. You don't need me for when you break this group out, and really, you don't need me when you go after the objects. You need magic users for that, not a fighter. In fact, if I go after Dorian when your breakout starts, it might pose a neat distraction to take the heat off you. I can even probably recruit some of the rest of the gang to help me—though you'd probably be better off if Jasmine and Pagiel were with you."

I stared at him in amazement. "You could be killed."

Kiyo gave me a dry smile. "I knew that when I set out from the Willow Land."

"Yeah, but it'd be on Dorian's behalf. I can't really say I saw that coming."

"My priority's always been the mission. There's nothing personal about Dorian—that's what I tried to tell you when he was in the dryads' trance. If I can save him and help us achieve our goal at the same time . . . well, then. So much the better."

"Thank you," I said. "That . . . that really means a lot."

Kiyo arched an eyebrow. "You care about him a lot, eh?"

"I always have," I said, not meeting his eyes. "Even when we were mad at each other over something, we've always been there for each other."

Until those words left my mouth, I hadn't realized how powerful they were. When Kiyo and I had disagreed on things, it had almost always resulted in a breakup—hence the on-and-off-again nature of our relationship, and its eventual degradation into *way off*. I'd noted in Alabama how idyllic things were with Evan . . . how peaceful and easy. And they were—because we never disagreed. He never contradicted me or told me what to do. Some might argue that's a good thing, but I wasn't sure it was a realistic thing. Of course it's easy to like someone who always agrees with you. The trick is still standing united with someone who will tell you things you don't want to hear. That's how Dorian and I had always been. With very few exceptions, we'd always worked as a strong team, even when totally pissed off at each other.

If Kiyo knew the thoughts churning within me, he didn't let on. He switched back to strategy. "The trick's got to be in the timing. We need to sync up rescuing him and the other monarchs—but still allow enough time to see if we can figure out the key to the enchantment."

"Not *too* much time, though," I warned. "That bitch wants to execute him for her dinner entertainment."

"No watches or clocks to go by either." Kiyo glanced at the small window. "And you don't have much of a sense of the sun here either. That window's really not good for— wait. The falcon. We'll send Alea's falcon."

"Spots?" I asked.

"That's his name?" Kiyo asked incredulously.

"You have cats named after the Four Horsemen. What's wrong with Spots?"

Kiyo shook his head, having no time for such debates. "I have to see the Hemlock gang anyway. I'll make arrangements for Alea to send, uh, Spots here when we go in to rescue Dorian. So, when the falcon arrives . . . wait, oh, ten minutes and then go for it."

It was as good as we were going to get with our limited options. Kiyo and I hashed out as many other details as we could in our time together, including very specific directions on how to get to the palace's lower levels from here. We talked until we finally heard my door unlock. Quickly, he transformed into the rat-fox again and crawled onto the plate, just in time for me to put the lid down and hand the covered tray to the servant doing cleanup. Kiyo had seemed pretty confident that he'd have no trouble getting out of the kitchens, so I had to trust him from there.

The servant swapped the tray for a new one, which I realized was for my midday meal already. Time went a lot faster when you had company and weren't staring at the walls. Once I was alone again, though, I recalled Varia's comment that every minute I delayed meant more time for Dorian in the hands of the torturers. A good part of the day had gone by, and as more of it passed, I grew restless wondering if she'd be calling me for her deadly ultimatum.

Time passed, though, with no word from her. Maybe she had changed her mind. After three hours, I was actually starting to get worried for a whole other set of reasons. The light coming in my window still told me we had plenty of day left, but if Kiyo was going to make good on his word to rescue Dorian, he needed to act soon before the "dinner show."

A flutter of wings in the window made me jump. Spots wiggled his way in and hopped down right next to me on the cot. Adrenaline surged through me. After a day of waiting on any action to happen, things were finally about to get moving.

"Showtime, huh?" I asked Spots.

His answer was to extend his leg, which again had a tiny scroll affixed to it. I removed the scroll and found when I unrolled it that it had a lot more writing than the last message. As such, it was nearly impossible to read since microscopic writing had been required to contain it all. After much squinting, I deduced the two main points of the message. One was that all was in place, and I could commence with the plan. The other was that the objects' protective enchantment could be weakened by an incantation spoken by someone wielding a considerable amount of power. The incantation, which wasn't long, was also listed.

"Seems awfully easy," I muttered. "Too easy." Conscious of the time, I retrieved my half-ass wand and summoned Volusian. I quickly got him up to speed on the latest developments and showed him the incantation.

"It does seem easy," he agreed.

"Could my friends have been misled? Maybe their so-called Yew dissidents lied."

"This is the language of a Yew spell," said Volusian. "So that much is accurate, mistress. What I wonder is if part of it is missing."

"Well, that's a problem for later," I said. That seemed to be my operating procedure here. I put the scroll in my pocket and tried not to let his words bring me too down. "For now, we've got to get moving. The clock's ticking and—"

Again, I heard the sound of the door unlocking. "Go," I told Volusian as I hid the wand under my shirt. "It's probably for the tray. You go too, Spots. Tell your mistress things are about to get going."

But when the door opened, it wasn't the servant who entered. It was my usual escort of guards. "Her Majesty has summoned you," said one of them. "Let's go."

What? I was being ordered to Varia *now*, seconds before I staged my great escape? I stood where I was.

"What for? I thought I didn't have to make any decisions until dinnertime," I said, crossing my arms. Much of the day had passed, but I was pretty sure it wasn't *quite* that late in the evening.

"Her Majesty wishes you to see the Oak King," explained the guard.

Irony strikes again. I'd wanted nothing more than to go bust Dorian out myself, and Kiyo had volunteered to free me up for the monarchs. Here were the guards, offering to take me straight to Dorian—but I needed to dodge it. I was needed up here.

"Sorry," I said haughtily. "I'm not going anywhere. I'm not going to play her game and let her try to psych me out with her ability to inflict pain. That's not how I work." Even as I spoke, it occurred to me I would just have to start my breakout now. What was the difference if the guards were in or out of my cell? I'd have to contend with them one way or another. I was on the verge of summoning my magic when the guard's next words drew me up short.

"Suit yourself," he said with a shrug. "I'm not even sure the Oak King's still alive."

Chapter 22

My heart stopped.

"What the hell are you talking about?" I demanded.

The guard remained blasé. "Some of the torturers were a little too zealous in their art, it seems. When Her Majesty discovered this, she graciously decided to allow you the opportunity to visit before the Oak King passes. I don't know his current status. It's not really my job."

"There's nothing gracious about that!" I exclaimed. "And that wasn't part of the plan. Varia told me he was going to be executed later."

"Our lady doesn't answer to you, nor is she required to keep her word to her inferiors. She may do whatever she likes."

My heart was working again, only to start beating in double-time. In deviating from her plan, Varia was ruining mine. Dorian . . . dead? I'd known he was in danger, but in the back of my mind, that danger had always been "later." And, with the way I normally operated, "later" always meant I had a chance to intervene. An internal voice kept saying *Stick to the plan, stick to the plan*. If Dorian was dead, there was nothing I could do. If he was still alive, then Kiyo and the others could rescue him.

And yet . . .

"I'll go," I said.

It went against every kind of logic. It played into Varia's hands. And yet, there was no way I could abandon Dorian if he was near his last breath.

They took me to the torturers' chamber, which was every bit as terrible as one might imagine. Wicked-looking weapons—most of which seemed to favor spikes—lined the walls. But when they took me to Dorian, I didn't see a single mark on him—aside from the ones inflicted earlier—making me think gentry forms of torture were far more insidious than I knew. He lay on his back, on a long stone table, like a corpse in a morgue. I hurried to his side, and even without any ostensible signs of injury, it was obvious he wasn't in good shape.

Dorian had always been pale, but it was the natural marble complexion that came with red hair and caution with the sun. This . . . this was something different altogether. It was the unhealthy white of near death. His skin was clammy, and his breathing was shallow. Still, that last one filled me with hope. *He was breathing.* I rested a couple fingers on the side of his neck and felt a faint pulse. That was about the extent of my medical knowledge, but again, the fact that there was a pulse had to be a good sign.

I glared around at the others in the room, unsure of whom I should direct my righteous fury to since Varia apparently couldn't be troubled to come see me. Probably it was the dogs' bath time. My contingent of guards had received reinforcements, but they were mostly there as precautions to keep me in line. The real culprits, I assumed, were two gentry standing in long brown robes with gold embroidery, watching me in silence. One was a man, one was a woman.

"What did you do to him?" I asked.

The male torturer spread his hands out in an absurdly

serene way. "What our queen asked of us. She wished to make a point."

"What, that she's a raging psychopathic bitch? She made that point a long time ago when she started exploiting other kingdoms."

A few of the guards frowned at my language, but no one came forward to stop me. "She wished merely to show her power," said the female torturer. "And encourage you to choose a wise course of action."

"I am *not* helping her with her insane plans," I said. "And she damned well knows it. Where is she anyway?"

"At afternoon tea," said one of the guards. "We are to relay your message to her."

"You can tell her to go fuck herself," I replied. I turned back to Dorian and gently brushed hair away from his face. "Stay with me," I murmured. "It was bad enough with the dryads. You can't keep doing this to me."

"If that is your 'answer,'" said another of the guards coldly, "then we are to return you to your cell."

"Fine," I said, still not looking at any of them. "What about Dorian?"

"He stays with us," said the female torturer.

My head jerked up. "What? He needs a healer! You've already pushed him to the edge. He'll die if you keep at it."

"I believe that is the point," said the male torturer. He arched an eyebrow. "What exactly did you expect? That you could refuse and Her Majesty would free him? If you want him healed, comply with her requests. Those are your only choices."

No, I actually had a couple of other choices. One was to fake them out and claim I would give in to Varia. After all, that was hardly the kind of decision I had to immediately act on. I didn't have the Iron Crown with me. It was hidden far away in my own lands. If I claimed I would give it to her, I had plenty of time to figure out the rest of this before I actually had to produce said crown.

Just then, Dorian started coughing. No, not coughing. Gasping. Like he couldn't get enough air. His eyes fluttered open, a frantic and desperate look in them as he fought to breathe.

"Dorian!" I cried, grabbing hold of him. "Dorian, breathe! Relax. You can do it."

Yet, it was clear he couldn't hear me or see me. He was somewhere else, somewhere locked in pain that had done so much damage, it was now about to finish him off. I looked up at all the gathered people in the room, unable to believe they were all just standing around.

"Ah," remarked one of the torturers. "I wondered when his lungs would give out."

"Do something!" I yelled. "Help him."

Dorian suddenly stilled, a look of horror on his face. I shared his feelings because I realized he was no longer breathing. A new sort of panic shot through me, as well as frustration and a terrible aching sadness. I possessed a power that could bring many to their knees, a power that was widely envied. What good was it, I wondered angrily, when it left me completely helpless to defend those I cared about?

"We do nothing until you make your choice," replied the male torturer.

Choice? Yeah. I was going to make my choice—and it wasn't going to be giving in to Varia. It wouldn't even be faking her out. It was going to be the choice I'd wanted to make from the very beginning.

I was going to blow this room apart and get Dorian out of here.

Magic surged within me, the power of water and air that surrounded all living things. The room grew thick with humidity as the air swelled and tensed, just as it had in my morning meeting with Varia. Now, I went further. The scent of ozone spread around us, and I felt the hairs on the back of my neck stand up from the electrical charges in the air. Some of those gathered sensed me pulling on my magic. Everyone else simply felt the obvious signs of a storm about to break loose. People tensed, weapons were drawn. *Good luck with that*, I thought.

A huge burst of air, reaching a breaking point, suddenly exploded and took out one of the room's walls. Stone and debris flew everywhere, and I barely had the presence of mind to lean over and shield Dorian with my body. My own injury didn't matter. Others in the room didn't have such protection.

The funny thing was, though, I wasn't the one who'd blown the wall apart.

From a now-visible room next door, Kiyo and Rurik surged in, the rest of our soldiers right behind them, along with some Hemlock fighters. And behind them were Jasmine and Pagiel, tipping me off about what had happened to the wall. Immediately, the Yew soldiers jumped forward to engage this new threat, forgetting all about me.

"Alistir!" I yelled, somehow making my voice heard above the fray.

Dorian's soldier jerked his head toward me. I beckoned him over. He gave a curt nod, after first dispatching a Yew warrior. Dodging a few others, Alistir soon made his way to me. I gestured frantically to Dorian.

"Help him. He hasn't been breathing for almost a minute."

Alistir blanched. Quickly he put his hands on Dorian. I couldn't sense his healing magic, but from the look on Alistir's face, he had a struggle ahead of him. I didn't doubt Alistir was gifted, but I also wished just then that we had brought a sure healer like Shaya after all.

"Eugenie!" Kiyo's voice drew me from the healing

drama. He punched a Yew soldier and then gave me an incredulous look. "What the hell are you doing here? Get out! You know what you have to do!"

Feeling conflicted, I cast an anxious look at Dorian. How could I leave him? I couldn't tell what Alistir was doing or if Dorian was even breathing again.

"Go!" screamed Kiyo.

"There's nothing you can do, Your Majesty," said Alistir through clenched teeth. "Go. Leave him to me."

I knew he was right, and again, that frustration filled me, the sense of being superpowerful and yet completely devoid of power. I could do nothing here, but there was a lot I could do upstairs.

The entrance I'd come in through was completely congested with fighting, so I hurried over to the impromptu door Pagiel had made in the wall. Someone fell in step beside me, and I braced myself for a fight until I realized it was Jasmine.

"I'm coming with you," she said before I could utter a word. "They've got that under control. What are you doing here anyway? Aren't you supposed to be leading a revolution?"

"I got sidetracked," I muttered.

Making our way back to the third floor was easier than I thought. A lot of guards ran right past us, only knowing there was a fight in the basement they had to get to. It never occurred to them that they were going right by their star prisoner. Those who did challenge us were easily knocked aside with our combined magic, falling over like dominos as we cleared them out of our way.

Back in the royal holding hall, I saw the number of guards had lessened, probably because they'd been dispatched downstairs. Most of the magic users were still there, giving

Jasmine and I quite the fight. One of the first soldiers I took out was someone I recognized as the chief jailer.

"Get his keys and start freeing the others," I told Jasmine. "I'll handle this group."

She didn't hesitate, and I made sure to make such a spectacle that I drew all the attention. The magic users who'd been left on duty ran a wide gamut of powers. Some I was able to toss around with wind before they even struck. One sent a wave of fire at me, inadvertently singeing one of his colleagues. As the fire raced toward me, I called on the moisture around me. The air around us went bone dry, but a wall of water materialized to stop the fire. I followed it up with a gust of wind to ensure he didn't repeat the act.

The hall's space limited me in some ways. Normally, I would've kept hurricane-worthy winds churning nonstop, in an effort to stop my adversaries from even standing. I couldn't do that easily without affecting Jasmine, however. Likewise, I was hesitant to use lightning in such a confined space. I was pretty good at controlling it—and it was an excellent weapon—but it had the potential to get out of control. Again, I had to consider Jasmine and the prisoners' safety.

So, I stuck to wind and water, which were effective but took a little more time in these quarters since those powers had to be wielded carefully. I'd gotten down to just one magic user when something hard, big, and solid slammed into me from the side. One of the doors of the cells had been ripped off its hinges and thrown at me. I stumbled to the ground. Judging from the satisfied look of the gentry advancing on me, that had been her doing. She must have some affinity to trees or wood in general. I would've sensed air magic and had warning.

I scrambled to my feet and reached for my power. Before I could do anything, what looked like a net of blue light flew out and wrapped her up like a cocoon. She screamed in pain as the net contracted tighter and tighter around her. It enveloped her torso—as well as her neck. Soon her screams quieted as her oxygen was cut off. She fell to the ground, dead or unconscious I couldn't say. I was reminded uncomfortably of Dorian.

Looking around, I saw a tall man with shoulder-length black hair and a pointed beard standing in the doorway to one of the cells. He made a small motion with his hand, and the net of light disappeared. He surveyed his victim for a few moments and seemed satisfied with what he found. He then glanced up and gave me a nod of acknowledgment.

"Thanks," I said.

"You're Eugenie?"

"Yes."

"Then I'm indebted to you," he said gravely. "I'm Hadic, King of the Hemlock Land."

"Oh man," I said. "I know some people that are going to be glad to see you."

We were soon joined by Jasmine and the rest of the monarchs. There was no time for extensive introductions, but I quickly understood what Volusian had meant about the variety of attitudes. A few, like Hadic, looked ready to take on Varia singlehandedly. The others seemed dazed, like they had just woken from a dream. Still, as they took in their surroundings, I saw sparks of life in their eyes that I hoped would grow. All looked thin and worn, no doubt the result of a long time of eating prisoner rations and being deprived of their lands.

"Come on," I said, not waiting to see if they would all follow. "We've got to defeat Varia and get rid of this blight once and for all."

I'd memorized Kiyo's directions and found running downstairs was much like the journey up—a mixture of obliviousness and challenges on the parts of the soldiers.

One thing that had changed was that the situation had grown increasingly chaotic. Guards and civilians alike were in a panic. I guess when you were ruled by a powerful despot like Varia, you just didn't expect many challenges to the status quo.

The torture chamber had been one floor down. There was a big temptation to go check on the situation there, but I'd already deviated from the plan once today. So, I kept going down the stairs, down to the fourth subterranean level. We met little resistance on the stairs but were swarmed with guards as soon as we headed down the corridor toward the room holding the gifts. It was closed with double doors, just as Kiyo had described to me. Hadic's hands blazed with blue light.

"You know how to stop the blight?" he asked me.

"I think so."

"Then do it. We'll hold them off."

All five monarchs seemed to be on board now, much to my relief. I had to assume their powers, even a little weakened, were more or less comparable to mine and Dorian's. Could the two of us have taken on this force of soldiers? Probably. Or at least made a damned good showing. That seemed to favor the odds of this group handling everything.

"The room's at the end of the hall," I said. "Come to us when you can." If the incantation didn't work, I was going to have to try the brute-force method to shatter the enchantment.

Jasmine and I had to squeeze our way past the mob of guards and magic users, but fortunately, the monarchs did a good job covering us. Once we reached the double doors, we encountered a few more sentries, but the bulk of the forces were engaged elsewhere. Jasmine and I easily took this handful out and tried to open the doors. Unsurprisingly, they were locked. Rather than search for keys on the guards, I simply blasted the doors open. It was kind of therapeutic after my recent frustrations.

We hurried inside and came to a halt. It was exactly as Kiyo had described. A wide vault of a room with high ceilings. Two piles of objects sat before us, ranging from statues to jewels to cloth. One collection was quite small, the other sickeningly large. Each of those objects represented a kingdom held in thrall by the blight, every single one of those kingdoms suffering as badly as my own.

Jasmine darted toward them, the desire for destruction written all over her features. "Wait—" I called.

Too late. She hit one of the invisible walls protecting the stash and bounced off it, stumbling back and hitting the floor. Flushing, she got back on her feet and glared.

"It's really there, huh?"

"Yup." My ability to sense various types of gentry magic was erratic, but I could feel this, even though I couldn't see it. It was strong—very strong. I wondered again how many it would've taken to build it.

Reaching for the scroll in my pocket, I cleared my throat. "Let's hope this knocks it down for us." I had to squint again to read the incantation, most of which was nonsensical syllables in an ancient language of magic. When I finished, I looked up at the objects. Nothing had changed, to my senses. That powerful magic was still in place.

"Shit," I said.

"Maybe you didn't pronounce it correctly," said Jasmine.

"Maybe," I said skeptically. It was written pretty much like it sounded, and Volusian had listened to my recitation in my cell, correcting me when needed.

"It's because you weren't born in the Yew Land," said a voice behind me.

I spun around, instinctively reaching for the only weapon I had—which was the crappy wand. Varia stood in the doorway, wearing a sensible dress for a change, as she regarded us with that annoyingly condescending expression she excelled at. So help me, those ridiculous dogs were at her feet, wearing their bows, barking at us.

"Whatever spy got you that charm did an excellent job," she continued. "I don't know whether to be impressed or annoyed. It's perfect, word for word. Unfortunately, what he or she failed to discover is that it must be performed by a magic user of significant strength—one who is from the Yew Land. You don't really think I would have gone to all this trouble so that anyone could come along and destroy it with a little chant? Everything you see, everything having to do with the Winter Enchantment has been the result of *years* of preparation."

"Fuck," I said, realizing this needed an upgrade in profanity.

There was nothing to be done now but hope the monarchs and I could simply blast our way through the shield. Well, that and I could also take out Varia while I was killing time. She certainly wasn't going to stand by when the rest of us attempted to destroy the gifts. Besides, after everything she'd put me through, I was kind of—

My thoughts grew disoriented as a wave of dizziness hit me. I shook my head to clear it and readjusted my stance. Too much exertion today, I supposed. I focused back on Varia, who was watching me with an amused curl of her lips. Beside me, I heard a surprised cry from Jasmine. She took a few steps forward and suddenly fell to her knees. She clasped her hands to her head and winced, as though she was being subjected to some terrible noise.

As for me, the disorientation returned, again messing with my sense of balance. I nearly joined Jasmine on the floor but just barely managed to stay upright. I didn't do so gracefully, however, and probably looked like some kind of drunken ballet dancer. With only Varia for an audience, I didn't really care.

"What . . . are you doing?" I asked through clenched teeth, still fighting to keep control.

"What I do naturally," Varia replied. "Come now. Did you think that I had no power of my own? That I only organized others into doing my errands?"

To be honest, I hadn't thought much about it. We'd talked a lot about the complex group spells worked in the Yew Land. The fact that she ruled a kingdom implied she possessed considerable magic, but the specifics had been less important in the face of the blight's greater threat. Now, as a grating buzzing filled my ears, I realized Varia must have some ability to affect a person's equilibrium and neurological functions. In less scientific gentry terms, she could "mess with your head."

It was astonishing and frustrating how crippling this was. In some ways, it was a lot like my helplessness with healing. Gentry magic expressed itself in a wide variety of forms, and mine was primarily a physical manifestation. If she'd started hurling fireballs at me, I could've answered her in kind with tangible elements. This kind of attack— invisible and almost psychic in nature—wasn't anything I could throw a lightning bolt at. I could throw a lightning bolt at *her*, but that was going to require me pushing back against this mind melt—and right now, that was pretty damned difficult. The best I could hope for was that the others in the hall would show up before she killed us. Surely she couldn't exert this kind of control over a bunch of people, and maybe someone would be more resistant than—

I gasped as a revelation came to me. Mustering my strength, I tried to ignore her mental attack as best I could in order to extend my homemade wand. I managed to recite Volusian's summoning words, unsure if I could actually get him when I was in such a compromised state. Miraculously, he appeared.

"Volusian!" I exclaimed. "Help us."

Volusian didn't respond right away. He didn't even look at me, really. Despite his shifting, flickering form, his red eyes burned bright and steady as he fixed them on Varia.

"Varia, daughter of Ganene," he said, almost politely. "You resemble your mother."

Varia frowned, and I felt the slightest easing of the magic she was working on me. Apparently, she could only focus on a limited number of things, which boded well for when my reinforcements arrived. Which I hoped would be soon.

"Who are you?" Varia demanded. "*What* are you? There's something about you . . . familiar and not familiar."

"I should be familiar, as I still bear the brand of your mother and grandmother's magic."

Her eyes flicked to me, as though recalling my words when I'd called him. "Volusian? Surely not . . . not *that* Volusian. He died long ago."

"Dead and not dead," he said. "Per the terms of the curse."

While I was sure Volusian's life history was fascinating, we had no time for it. "Volusian, enough small talk! Do something to help us!"

"Gladly, mistress."

Volusian moved as though to attack but didn't get far when Varia shrieked, "No!" Her mental attack on me disappeared, and instead, I felt a ripple of invisible power go through the air and threaten to unravel the bonds that held me and Volusian together. His image flickered, and I could barely believe what was happening.

"Impossible," I murmured. "She's trying to banish him." Considering I couldn't even banish him alone, I at first thought this must mean Varia was far more formidable than

I'd suspected. Then, thinking about the conversation I'd just overheard, I reconsidered. If she had some sort of familial connection to Volusian's curse, she might also possess an inherent ability to shatter it and send him from this world. Volusian was a pain in the ass, but I couldn't risk losing an ally like him—especially now. I was in possession of my powers once more and used them to slam Varia into a wall with a blast of wind. At the impact, her grip on Volusian loosened, and my bonds to him reestablished themselves.

"I'm doing you a favor!" she hissed to me. "You want nothing to do with a black wizard like him! He's evil and traitorous!"

"You can thank your mother and grandmother for that," returned Volusian smoothly. "I would have been the most loyal of servants if they hadn't betrayed me. Had I been able to then, I would've made them pay. Instead, I had to wait all these centuries until I was bonded to someone strong enough to bring me back to this wretched land. I would rather take my revenge on Ganene and Onya than you, but I've long learned to make do with what I have."

I thought for sure that Volusian was going to rip her apart with his bare hands, just as he'd threatened to do to me on countless occasions. I wondered if I should stop him. Before he made any more advances, however, he paused and glanced at me.

"The cost of me being here, of course, is that I must still serve you, mistress. You asked me to help in some way. From what I can see, the enchantment on the talismans holds."

"The incantation didn't work," I said. "It has to be recited by a Yew magic user—"

Volusian was already chanting. I hadn't been aware that he'd memorized the incantation in my cell, but he knew it word for word. Power radiated out from him as he spoke. Varia let out a strangled cry and pushed forward against the wind I was still using to hold her in place. With more strength than I'd known she had, she sent another blast of that disorientation to Jasmine and me. We lost our balance again, and I dropped the magic. Varia didn't waste a moment once freed. As soon as she wasn't fighting my elements, she directed all her strength into banishing Volusian. Doing so meant she had to let up on Jasmine and me again, probably hoping her last attack would delay us from acting in the time it'd take us to recover.

She was right because it took me several moments to get back to my feet and clear my head. As I did, a couple of things happened. Volusian finished his incantation, and although there was no visible indication, I felt the power that had been shielding the objects vanish. Maybe there was some residual protective force left, but it was nothing that couldn't be broken. The other thing that happened was . . .

Varia banished Volusian.

"Be gone, you wretched traitor!" she cried. I felt her magic swell, and the bonds that held Volusian and I together disintegrated. "Go to the Underworld and never return."

"I shall see you there soon," said Volusian, undaunted as he began to fade. His gaze turned to me. "I have served you dutifully. Now help me. Destroy her. . . ."

He said no more because he disintegrated into sparkles, which soon faded into nothingness. Volusian was gone from this world forever.

She'd barely finished that banishing when she unleashed another brain blast at me and Jasmine, even stronger than previous ones. I cried out as that buzzing sound shifted to more of a screech. I felt like my ears would explode. Even through it, I could still hear Varia when she spoke.

"You really think you've accomplished anything? Just because your minion took down the shield? Once I gather my conclave, we can have it back up in an instant. Nothing

has changed. All of those objects—and your kingdoms—
are still in the thrall of the Winter Enchantment." She took
a few menacing steps toward us. "Not that it'll be your concern before long. Know this, before I make the blood in
your head burst: Your lands will suffer terribly for this
insult. It won't matter who succeeds after your death. I will
strip those lands of all life, they will freeze and suffer as no
other—ah!"

The buzzing and wailing in my ears stopped as one of
the objects from the piles came flying over and hit Varia
in the head. And when I say hit, it *nailed* her. There was an
audible crack, and she went down instantly, eyes staring
vacantly ahead. Her dogs—which had been yapping
nonstop—fell silent in astonishment.

I heard a sharp intake of breath and saw Jasmine struggling to shake off the lingering effects of the disorientation.
Blood ran from her ears, but she didn't look like she'd suffered any other ill effects. I caught her hand and helped her
up. Once on my feet again, I peered back at Varia's still
body and got a good look at what had hit her. It was the
marble bust of Dorian that had been the Oak Land's gift.

A tremor ran through the room, and I immediately
looked up at the ceiling, afraid some earthquake was about
to bring the whole place crashing down. Four floors underground was not a great place to be during seismic events.
The shaking stopped after a few seconds.

"It's just the land reacting to her death," said a pleasant
voice. "It's now unclaimed and seeking a new master or
mistress. You could add on to your empire, if you wanted."

"Dorian?" I asked incredulously.

Sure enough, he was leaning in the doorway, looking
as though that was all that was keeping him upright. He actually didn't look much better than when I last saw him,

fresh out of the torturers' hands. The only difference now, of course, was that he was breathing and conscious. Otherwise, he still looked sickly and broken.

He glanced down at Varia. "That was rather clumsy of me to hit her so hard, I suppose. And a very brutish tactic to boot. I didn't have much time to think and had to decide on the spot how best to stop her from hurting my two favorite sisters." He suddenly looked very pleased. "I did, however, manage to do it without hurting those dogs. Very considerate of me. Don't let it be said I'm not an animal lover—that wretched kitsune aside."

"Dorian!" It was all I could keep managing to say. Assured of my footing, I ran over to him and threw my arms around him. He returned the hug as best he could while still managing to support himself in the doorway.

"Why, Eugenie. Once again, I almost think you're happy to see me. Surely you didn't expect me to let you keep being the hero, did you? You've saved me far too many times. I needed to pull my share."

I was so happy he was alive and mostly well that I still struggled to say anything coherent. I carefully disentangled myself from him. "I don't know what to do," I laughed. "I feel like I should cry or slap you."

He grimaced. "Neither, please. If you like, I'll provide you with several other more acceptable alternatives for later. But first . . . I believe we have a blight to deal with."

Dorian stretched out his hand, and the marble bust floated to him, compelled by his power over stone and earth. He held the bust in his hands and gazed admiringly at himself. "Such a fetching likeness, isn't it?"

And with that, he hurled the bust to the tiled floor. The marble sculpture smashed into a hundred fragments and shards. Far away in the Otherworld, the Oak Land woke up.

Chapter 23

It didn't take long for the Yew Land to be claimed. The same magic users that had aided Varia with the blight were all quick to scramble and seize a piece of her former land. As a result, the kingdom ended up reshifting into three smaller kingdoms. I'd been told that was possible in the Otherworld, but I'd never seen it happen. The three kingdoms shaped themselves to their new masters, becoming the Cork Land, the Cottonwood Land, and the Hickory Land. The Yew Land was no more.

Despite their involvement in Varia's schemes, the new monarchs—two queens and one king—were quick to make pledges of peace and friendship to my party and the Hemlock contingent. These offers were legitimate, unlike Varia's absurd "friendly" offer. The new monarchs were concerned with consolidating their power and establishing a rule. Alliances were far more beneficial than conquests.

The new monarchs would've hosted us for a while, but my group was anxious to return to our own lands and begin the healing there. We declined all the offers, promising to send ambassadors soon to set up trade agreements and treaties. Considering it might take a while before food production was back up in my kingdoms, this was actually a pretty solid plan.

Before we left, however, I had a very interesting conversation with Magia, the newly crowned Hickory Queen. As someone born and raised in the Yew Land, she was well versed in its history and legends.

"Of course I know about Volusian, Slayer of Souls," she told me.

Dorian was with me, sitting with Magia in an inn that she'd made her headquarters until a castle could be built. I exchanged surprised glances with him.

"Slayer of Souls?" I asked.

"Definitely an impressive title," mused Dorian. "I might start calling myself that." He looked tired but had recovered by leaps and bounds, thanks to Alistir and a healer lent to us by Hadic of the Hemlock Land.

"I admit," Magia added, "that I thought most of it was legend. According to the stories, Volusian was one of Onya's most trusted advisers."

"Onya?" Moments later, I remembered the portrait I'd seen in the throne room, depicting a queen of the same name and her two daughters.

Magia nodded. "Onya the Magnificent. Ganene's mother. Varia's grandmother. One of the Yew Land's most powerful leaders. Their whole family was powerful. It was how they were able to keep passing the land down through the generations."

"Remarkable," Dorian agreed. I'd learned enough to know that lineage didn't affect who controlled Other-worldly kingdoms. Power did. Monarchs certainly wanted their children to inherit, but many times, those offspring simply weren't strong enough to claim the land.

"Onya had a younger daughter, Nissa the Fair." I remembered the pretty girl in the painting and wondered if this use of nicknames was a Yew custom or simply a product of that era. I wondered also if history would remember me as Eugenie the Badass. "Nissa didn't possess nearly the power of her sister and mother, but she was beautiful and kind and loved by many—including Volusian."

I stared in disbelief. "Volusian—*in love*?" I think that was more unbelievable to me than any of the crazy acts of magic I had witnessed in the Otherworld.

"He was alive back then," Dorian reminded me. "Not an undead creature forced to wander the worlds without peace. I imagine that would change a person."

"Nissa loved him too, even though he wasn't of the same rank," continued Magia. "Onya didn't approve, but she valued him and desperately needed his powers in a war she was waging with a neighboring kingdom. She and Ganene came up with a plan to convince the couple that they could marry after the war, once Volusian had helped lead Onya's forces to victory. It was all a lie, though, and while he was gone, Ganene and Onya forcibly made Nissa marry a king that they were hoping to secure as an ally. Shortly after the wedding, Nissa committed suicide."

I was totally hooked now and had nearly forgotten that Volusian—*my* Volusian—was the hero of this tale. It was rapidly taking on the status of a Shakespearean tragedy.

"Volusian returned to find not only that his betrothed had been given to another man but that she was dead. He was so enraged that he turned to the dark arts and ended up aiding Onya's enemies. They brought a level of horror and devastation to the Yew Land without compare."

Thinking of the blight, I questioned that. Of course, Volusian couldn't have earned the "Slayer of Souls" title without doing some pretty awful things.

Magia's eyes grew thoughtful. "It's almost certain the Yew Land would have been completely destroyed, but Onya and Ganene were finally able to trap and capture Volusian. They decided simple execution wasn't a great enough punishment for what he had done, and so he was killed and cursed into the state you found him. Without his assistance, the Yew Land's enemies backed off and made peace."

"Well," I said, still a bit stunned, "that certainly explains why he hated the Yew Land and Varia so much. I can't say I approve of his actions, but it is a little sad that in the end, Onya's line defeated him after all."

"I don't know about that. Varia met her end," Dorian pointed out. "Surely that will give him some peace in the Underworld." Dorian sighed. "That really was an inelegant way to kill her. That's what happens when you act in the heat of passion."

It may have been inelegant, but it had most certainly saved my life. I didn't know how long it would have taken him and the others to subdue Varia through other means, and the odds were good that she might have really made our heads explode. I was happy to be alive and have Dorian err on the side of crudeness in accomplishing the task.

In some ways, the journey home felt longer than the initial one. The conditions were much better—and actually made for faster travel—but we were all anxious and impatient to see how our kingdoms had recovered. Traveling through the blighted lands we'd passed before was actually pretty inspiring. Most had returned to their initial temperatures, facilitating the melting of snow. Of course, that offered another set of problems. Mud and floods became commonplace, and the food situation couldn't be remedied overnight. When we passed through the Palm Land, I looked at the giant trees with regret. The blight's end wouldn't bring them back to life.

"Those won't grow back anytime soon," I murmured regretfully.

"But they'll grow back faster than you think," said Kiyo. "Remember where you're at."

Around the eighth day of travel, the road shifted and brought us into the Rowan Land. The land sang to me, its energy radiating out to me in a palpable wave that brought me to a halt. I gasped, overwhelmed by that force and life pouring into me. I jumped off the horse and ran off the road, falling to my knees on the muddy ground. I sank my fingers into it, closing my eyes in ecstasy as I felt the land's welcome.

I breathed in the air around me, which was back to its typically mild temperature. There was an overwhelming scent of water and dirt, but as a light breeze ruffled my hair, I sensed something else . . . the promise of growth and new life. Opening my eyes, I saw little but a dark, muddy landscape, but I could tell the plants and trees were on the verge of making their comeback. Kiyo had been right. I had to remember which world I was in.

I got to my feet and found the rest of my companions watching me indulgently. Dorian even had a wistful look on his face, no doubt yearning for his own land. "It's recovering," I said. "Slowly but surely."

"What do you want to do?" asked Rurik. "Cut across country or follow the road?"

I understood what he was asking. In the Otherworld's bizarre layout, it would take us longer to turn off into the Rowan Land and reach my castle. The road would be shorter but would crisscross through other kingdoms. I admit, I just wanted to lose myself in this land but opted for practicality instead.

"We'll stick to the road," I said. "I want to see the Thorn Land if I can."

It was early evening, and we'd have to camp soon, even though all of us were eager to push forward. We traveled as long as the light allowed and finally made camp just over the border of the Oak Land, much to Dorian's delight. As was

the case with me, this wasn't an ideal spot from which to
go to his castle, so he was content to stay overnight with us.

Honestly, I think it was enough for him just to be home
again. I'd never seen him so entranced by something. Usually he was always watching the people around him, always
on top of whatever plots were developing. Now, he had
eyes only for the land. He paced around, examining the dirt
and touching the trees. Whenever he walked away, I saw
shoots and buds on the trees. He and I had taken to having
bedtime talks near the fire, but I left him alone tonight.

Kiyo sat beside me as I unfolded my bedroll. "I'll likely
be leaving tomorrow," he told me. "We should reach the
Willow Land."

"I'm kind of surprised you haven't tried to kill me, now
that we've ended the blight," I remarked lightly.

He sighed. "You're not the problem anymore, Eugenie.
You know that."

"Neither are my children."

The end of the blight had allowed me to hope I might be
seeing Isaac and Ivy soon. Nearly a month had passed,
which was huge for infants their age. So much could
change, and I yearned to hurry back before I missed much
more. After the way Kiyo and I had worked together in the
Yew Land, I'd kind of hoped things might improve between
us. I hadn't forgiven him, but it had seemed like we had
the potential to establish some sort of civility now. Apparently not.

"Is there anything at all that would change your mind?"
Kiyo asked. "Anything at all to convince you of the danger
he represents?"

"Is there anything that would convince *you* that your son
is a real person with the right to live and not some pawn
of destiny?" I returned.

He frowned and wouldn't meet my eyes. "We won't stop
looking for them, you know."

"You'll be looking forever," I said.

Kiyo said no more and left me. Thinking back to when he'd been ensnared by dryads, I couldn't help but again see Jasmine and Keeli's reasoning about letting him die. It really would've made things simpler. He was Maiwenn's main contact in the human world. Her search wouldn't get far without him.

The next day, he departed from our group, his fox form scurrying off across the muddy landscape of the Willow Land. All the recovering kingdoms had a similar appearance right now, but I knew they'd show their true natures soon.

Dorian and I split shortly thereafter in the Thorn Land. Even though the land's song burned within me, I was reluctant to leave him. I suspected he felt the same way, though it was hard to tell with his poker face and gallantries.

"Well, here we are," he declared. Alistir and Pagiel were by his side. "It's time for me to go get my subjects out of trouble, I suppose. Thank you as always for a lovely time. You always arrange the best soirees."

I smiled. "I try."

"And I'll try to come see you as soon as I can."

That was unexpected. "I figured you wouldn't want to leave your land for a while."

"Oh, I don't, but you and I still have a lot to discuss. Seeing as you'll have twice as much work on your hands, it'll be easier for me to come to you." I caught his eye and wondered what exactly he wanted to discuss. Maiwenn and the twins were the obvious topic, but I got a sense there might be more.

Pagiel and Jasmine were equally formal in their parting, but I saw them watch each other longingly. Ah, young love. So much simpler than grown-up love.

Although, when I saw Shaya and Rurik's reunion, I had to admit that was a pretty touching example of grown-up love. It had total movie-quality epicness, including them racing into each other's arms. I tried not to watch, but it was kind of hard not to. I even felt a little misty-eyed, and this time, I couldn't blame it on hormones since I was well over those.

Thinking of hormones again brought Isaac and Ivy to mind. I still wanted to go to them, but one look at the state of my kingdoms told me I'd be here for a while. At the very least, I wanted to let Roland know everything had worked out . . . but I had no means to, short of traveling to Tucson myself. I certainly didn't miss Volusian's biting personality or constant threats to kill me, but he'd had his uses in my service. After his story, I even felt slightly sympathetic. But only slightly. Ganene and Onya had wronged him, but he'd taken out his revenge on innocents. Why, I wondered, did this seem to be such a recurring theme among those I encountered?

One of the first things I did upon my return to my lands was start arranging those delegations to Varia's freed kingdoms. We needed food badly, and our copper supply gave us an unharmed currency other blighted kingdoms weren't lucky enough to have. After meeting the new monarchs, I knew there'd be no more price gouging either. Shaya excelled at organizing this sort of thing. She actually would've been a great choice to lead the groups, but I couldn't bring myself to part her and Rurik so soon. I trusted her judgment to find others who were capable.

Along with the food shortage, we simply had to deal with the aftermath of the blight's devastation. People were sick. Homes and other structures were damaged. And despite how much we could repair, nothing could make up for the loss of life. Both kingdoms' populations had suffered, meaning we had less help to rebuild. It was disheartening some days.

Along with the lands' natural magic, I also discovered I could speed along the healing and regrowth. Just as I'd seen

Dorian healing his oaks, I was able to coax the plants and trees of my kingdoms to grow again. Most of my efforts were focused on the Rowan Land, which contained more food-bearing plant life. In particular, I worked on the cherry trees since they were so plentiful. I sped them through their leaf and flowering phases, and after a few weeks, we began to see the first signs of fruit. Cherries weren't exactly the most filling food, but they were welcome to everyone after what we'd endured.

Even though the Thorn Land wasn't a priority for food production, I still worked to restore some of the plants and trees there. It brought hope to the land's residents, who had gotten used to their desert kingdom. Each flower that bloomed on a cactus was a sign that we were on our way to recovery, and the land radiated its gratitude to me.

Healing the vegetation wasn't easy or fast. I often had to spend a lot of alone time with one tree or plant, and then frequent visits were required to keep aiding each step in the process. One day, I was sitting in an orchard near the Rowan castle, painstakingly encouraging each tree to grow its fruit. The day was sunny, and the grass—which had returned quickly—was green and lush beneath me. There was less birdsong than there used to be, which was a little weird. The animals had been hit as hard as the people, but many assured me that within a year, we could expect our furry and feathered countrymen to replenish their numbers.

I rested my hand on the bark of a cherry tree, my eyes closed. I felt the pulse of the tree's life and tried to join it with both myself and the land so that we could lend the tree our strength. A *thump* in the grass beside me snapped me out of my trance, and I looked down to see a bright red apple in the grass beside me. I smiled and picked it up.

"This isn't one of mine," I said as a familiar shadow fell over me.

Dorian eased himself down beside me, sitting crosslegged. He carried an apple of his own and bit into it. He swallowed and smiled back at me. "Our second harvest. I would've brought you some from the first, but we needed them too badly."

"You should've kept these too." I bit into the apple. It was delicious. "Second, huh? I'm behind."

He glanced up at the cherry tree. "You seem to be doing just fine. Besides, you've also had to do twice as much work as me, remember? You're not overtiring yourself, are you?"

I leaned back in the grass and swallowed another bite of apple. "Nothing I can't handle. After that crazy journey to the Yew Land, hanging out here with trees all day feels downright lazy."

Dorian stretched out beside me so that our shoulders touched. "Do you have plans to go back to the human world? I know you must be burning to."

"I am," I admitted. "We're pushing two months. Two months, Dorian! Isaac and Ivy have to be out of the NICU now. I need them to know who I am. And I need Roland to know I'm okay too. I'm nearing a point where the lands will be okay without me, but then . . . well, I'm not sure of my next move. When I last saw Kiyo, he made it clear they weren't giving up on preventing the prophecy."

"I feel pretty confident that Maiwenn's preoccupied with exactly the same kinds of tasks we are in restoring our lands," he said.

"I don't doubt it. But I also wouldn't be surprised if Kiyo's out there watching and waiting. If I go to the twins, there's a good chance I'll compromise their location." I sighed. This had been something I'd had a lot of time to think about while tending my lands. "I'm in the same bind as before they were born."

"Not entirely," said Dorian. "Before, you were a moving target because you always had to be in multiple places.

Now? Your children don't have to move around. You keep them in one place, and you keep them safe. Go to them and bring them back with you. Put them in a stronghold somewhere."

"But will they ever have peace?" I asked sadly. "Even if they grow up surrounded in bodyguards, their identities will be known here. There'll always be people trying to kill them—or at least trying to kill Isaac."

Dorian was adamant. "I have no doubt they'll be powerful once they're older. They'll be able to look after themselves. And until then, I swear, I'll give you half my forces to keep them safe in whatever location you choose."

I turned to him, unable to hide a smile. "Half? Isn't that kind of extreme?"

His eyes, completely serious, studied me for several moments. "Not for you."

My smile faded, and I suddenly felt confused. My heart leapt in my chest. "Why would you do that for me?"

"What wouldn't I do for you?"

His voice was husky, and he propped himself up so that he could lean over me. I closed my eyes and felt his lips touch mine. It was a sweet kiss, a kiss as warm and lazy as the sunny day around us. It filled my body with a life and light not unlike what I felt from my kingdoms. There was a rightness to the feel of his body against mine, and I wrapped my arms around his neck, entwining my fingers in his hair and drawing him closer. His kiss picked up in intensity, and I welcomed it, parting my lips to taste more of him.

With as much caution as I'd ever seen Dorian exert in amorous affairs, his hand slid up my shirt and lightly grazed my breast. I gasped and arched my body toward his, giving him more than enough encouragement to grow bolder. He pushed my shirt up altogether and then brought his mouth down to my nipple. I gasped again, my own hands moving toward his pants. After unplanned pregnancy, childbirth, and near-starvation, I hadn't thought my body would ever feel like this. Now, it was as though none of those things had ever happened. My body was alive again. It wanted him.

The problem was, I wasn't sure if I did.

"No . . . wait . . ." With great reluctance, I gently pushed him up. He complied immediately, still hovering over me but halting in his advances. A regretful look came over his face.

"Too soon," he guessed.

"Eh, well, not exactly . . . I mean I have no problem doing *it*," I said. "I just don't know where we stand with . . . other stuff."

He considered this. "I assume we stand in a much better place than before."

I almost laughed. "Well, yes, but there are things we need to figure out."

Dorian stared at me and brushed hair from my face. "Not me. I already know everything I need to know."

I fell into that gaze and felt something start to open in my heart. I began to reach toward him, wanting to kiss him again when—

"Your Majesty!"

The perfect, golden moment shattered as I heard voices and running feet. Well, it shattered for me, at least. From the way I had to get out from under him, it was clear that Dorian could have continued kissing through a war zone. I sat up in the grass, dazzled by the sun and my pounding heart and the myriad feelings churning within me. I fixed my shirt and hoped I didn't look too disheveled. It took my soldiers a moment to find me, since I no longer traveled with a bodyguard at all times. They looked relieved to see me.

"Your Majesty," exclaimed the leader, giving me a quick bow. "You have a visitor. Roland Storm Slayer is—"

"Roland!"

He was walking out across the green toward us, in no haste to keep up with the guards who had heralded his arrival. I ran to him with my arms outstretched and heard Dorian say ruefully, "A man can never compete with a woman's father."

Roland lifted me up and spun me around as he returned the hug. His eyes shone, and I actually think he looked more relieved to see me now than he had in Alabama.

"Eugenie, you're alive," he said, once he'd set me down. He still kept his arms around me. "When so much time went by without any news, I thought . . . well, I thought the worst." He glanced around at the verdant landscape. "I take it you fixed the problem."

"We did," I said happily. "We've still got a lot of recovery to do, but things are on the mend. That's why I haven't been able to get back to you. Plus, Volusian's gone—banished—so I couldn't send a message."

That earned me raised eyebrows. "I wondered why I hadn't heard from him. Though I can't say I'm disappointed he's gone."

Dorian reached us then and gave Roland a nod of greeting. "I agree with you on that," Dorian said. "Though, as much as I hate acknowledging it, Volusian was the reason we were able to destroy the blight in the end."

"Well, then," said Roland. "I guess something positive came from that fiend. I knew something had happened here when I saw the boy, but I wasn't exactly sure if it was good or bad."

Roland's happy expression had dimmed a little, which I couldn't understand. I didn't know what his comment had meant either. "The boy?"

He nodded. "The one I met before. The one who was raiding Tucson and Phoenix."

I exchanged puzzled glances with Dorian. "You mean Pagiel?" I asked. "What about him?"

"He's back," said Roland. "And since I knew you took him with you on your quest, I figured either you'd succeeded and freed him up to come back or else failed and forced him to more of the same."

For a few moments, I was totally confused. When I was finally able to parse what Roland was saying, I nearly reeled. I was certain I'd misunderstood.

"You don't mean . . . you don't mean Pagiel's back in Arizona?"

Roland nodded. "Back with more people. Back for more raids."

Chapter 24

I immediately turned to Dorian.

"I know nothing," he said, quickly guessing my question. "This is the first time I've heard anything about this." He turned to Roland. "Forgive me for any doubts . . . but I have to ask: are you certain you saw him?" It was amazing how quickly Dorian had recovered from my romantic mixed signals to dealing with the task at hand. I was reminded of my discussion with Kiyo: no matter the problems between Dorian and me, we always put them aside to work as a team.

"Positive," said Roland. "I was on the scene at one of the raids. He's hard to miss with that hair. The others have made the news, and each time, the footage showed these crazy haboobs that just didn't look natural. That, and we don't generally get four of them in two weeks. The boy controls wind and air, right?"

"Right," I said with dismay.

Dorian arched an eyebrow. "Haboob? Isn't that slang for—"

"It's a kind of sandstorm," I interrupted. "They occur all over the world, and Arizona gets them every once in a while. The Thorn Land theoretically could, but I'm too in sync with its weather to let one happen."

"Shortly after our return from the Yew Land, Pagiel left to visit the village he'd grown up in, on the far edge of my kingdom," said Dorian thoughtfully. "You knew he lived out there before Ysabel dragged him to my court, right? He was worried that those villagers hadn't fared as well as the people in my castle during the blight and wanted to help them rebuild. I haven't heard from him since and just assumed he was preoccupied with the rebuilding."

My guards were still hovering around, waiting for orders. I gestured to one of them. "Go find the Lady Jasmine and bring her here." When he was gone, I turned back to Roland and Dorian. "There must be some mistake. Pagiel wouldn't do this."

"He did it before," pointed out Roland.

"Yeah, when the land was blighted and his people were starving," I countered. "Everything's fixed now."

"Well," said Dorian reasonably, "not everything. None of us are in quite the same shape with food as we were before. My people will be eating leanly for a while, and I assume the same is true with yours."

Roland glanced between us. "Leanly enough that the boy might get it into his head to do a little supplementing from the human world?"

I started to deny it but reconsidered. As Roland had said, Pagiel had done all this before. Maybe the Oak Land wasn't in the same dire situation, but those Pagiel cared about were still suffering. Pagiel had made it perfectly clear he thought humans were overweight and had too much— which was true to a certain extent. Really, his feelings on the matter had never changed. He'd only stopped his actions because I'd brought him with me to the Yew Land.

Jasmine joined us shortly thereafter, not looking thrilled that she'd been summoned by a guard. Her face brightened when she saw Roland since he usually brought her little luxuries from the human world.

"Jasmine, when was the last time you talked to Pagiel?"

She looked startled by my harsh tone. "Uh, I don't know. Not since we all got back. He was supposed to get in touch but never did."

"You mean that?" I demanded. "You're telling the truth?"

Hurt shone on her face, and a bit of that old dark temperament leaked through. As our relationship had grown, we'd established a lot of trust, and me asking a question like that was insulting.

"I'm sorry," I said before she could answer. "I don't mean to accuse you of lying. I just need to be sure you don't know anything that's going on with him."

"I'm sure," she said, looking slightly pacified. A note of bitterness laced her next words. "I wish I *had* heard from him. I don't know what his problem is."

"From the sounds of it," I said, "he may actually have a few problems."

We told her what had happened, and I studied her face carefully as she listened. Her shock was genuine; she'd been telling the truth. Unlike me, however, her initial response wasn't a denial or insistence that there was a mistake.

"He talked about it a lot," she said with dismay. "While we were on the road. All about the wealth humans had and how it was our legacy—you know, from when the shining ones walked the earth. He never wanted to hurt anyone, but he didn't think it was right that we're denied the surplus in that world."

"A classic Storm King sympathizer," mused Dorian. "No wonder he was so eager to serve you, Eugenie."

I made a face, not liking the implications. "He's a confused boy, caught up in propaganda and stories of greatness he hears from others. And, unfortunately, he's also a boy who can easily cross worlds."

"He's not bad," exclaimed Jasmine. "Or evil. Or even . . . stupid. He just wants to help people, that's all. He had to take care of his family growing up, you know. His dad died early, and the only person around to help his mom was that witchy grandmother of theirs. He had to be the man in his family. No one else would do it."

Dorian gave her a kind smile. "Easy, there. No one's doubting Pagiel's bravery or devotion. I've heard a little about his early years too and can understand why he'd have some of these beliefs. That doesn't make them right, however."

I shot Dorian a questioning look. I don't know if he just didn't see me or if he was ignoring me, but he kept his attention on Jasmine. Before, Dorian had been rather blasé about Pagiel's raids, and I'd kind of expected more of the same this time. I let it go because honestly, it was kind of nice to have him on my side.

"Speaking of his family life," I said, "that's the place to start. We need to find him, and I have a feeling he's lying low in whichever world he's in. Ysabel and Edria might know where he's at."

"And I know where they're at since I saw them just before I left," replied Dorian. His forehead wrinkled with a frown. "Which brings up the disturbing realization that they've probably known about this and weren't telling me." Dorian's seemingly carefree attitude often fooled people into thinking he was a lax ruler. He wasn't. He didn't like having his authority undermined or people keeping secrets from him.

"I'll go back with you to talk to them," I said. Leaving my kingdoms wasn't easy, and the only reason I'd imagined doing it had been because of Isaac and Ivy. A trip to the Oak Land to investigate the return of Pagiel's Robin Hood ways had never been on the table. I turned to Roland. "You want to go?"

He shook his head. "You two are better suited for that. I'll go back and do damage control if they strike again. There's no real predicting where they'll be, though, and I'm usually too late. If I do find them . . ." He hesitated and studied me carefully. "What would you like me to do?"

I grimaced, but it was a question that had to be addressed. "Ideally, banish them to this world. If something happens . . . I mean, if there are innocent human lives in danger . . ."

I couldn't finish, but Roland gave a curt nod. "Understood. I'll do what I can."

We all made preparations to leave that day. My kingdoms were back in capable hands, and it was a relatively simple affair to head over to Dorian's—especially now that I wasn't under the constant threat of attack. Traveling to the Yew Land had made me a pro at horseback riding, and I felt pretty confident my body had returned to its former state. Thinking of that made me think of making out with Dorian earlier. Yeah. My body was definitely recovered. *Watch it, Eugenie,* an inner voice warned me. *Look what happened the last time you did that. Besides, aren't you mad at Dorian?*

Watching him sidelong as we traveled, I really didn't think I was anymore. My feelings for him were muddled, and I was glad that he was too preoccupied with Ysabel and Edria's deceit to pay much attention to my pensiveness.

When we arrived, I saw that the Oak Land was well on its way to healing too. Most startling was how green everything was. It was the first time (aside from the blight) that I'd seen Dorian's land not in the throes of a magical autumn. Instead, all the plants and trees bore the look of late summer, green and bursting with fruit.

I received a lot of curious glances from his staff as we entered the castle. I was well known to them, and the ups and downs of our alliance and romance had been a source of gossip that rivaled Hollywood starlets. People never knew what to expect when Dorian and I surfaced together. This was no exception.

He was all business and ordered his guards to bring Pagiel's family to one of his receiving chambers immediately. Before Dorian left for his own rooms, he gave me a once-over. "Damn. Should have had you bring a dress."

"What's wrong with this?" I asked, gesturing to my jeans and Peter Frampton T-shirt.

"Nothing really," he said with a small smile. "As always, I like the view of your legs. But I think it'd be better if we carried the weight of our full royal status when staring down Ysabel and Edria. You, come here." A servant passed by and immediately came to a halt at Dorian's command. "Take the Queen of Rowan and Thorn to someone who can dress her properly. Then bring her to the east room when she's ready."

"What about me?" grumbled Jasmine as she and I followed the servant. "He doesn't care how I look, apparently."

I patted her back. "You're already in gentry clothes. Besides, if you want something nicer, I'm sure they can rustle a dress up."

We were escorted to a group of maidservants who were all too eager to dress Jasmine and me. I didn't know if they were in the service of some noblewoman in Dorian's court or if he just always kept them on hand to beautify women passing through. I decided it wasn't worth pondering too much.

I traded my jeans and T-shirt for a long dress with a lace-up V neckline. It had short sleeves, which I preferred to the latest gentry trend in bell sleeves, and was made of a light material perfect for summer. I kept calling the color "lightish greenish," but Jasmine and the maids kept correcting me and saying it was "celadon." Whatever. My hair was pinned up in a simple bun—nothing like the crazy towers of hair from the Yew Land—and I had to admit the final result was rather queenly. Jasmine wore a similar dress in dark blue.

Dorian nodded in approval when we were taken to him. "Celadon. Excellent choice."

He was also in regal attire. He'd traded his traveling clothes for a robe of black with silver embroidery. His attire usually consisted of pants and linen shirts, paired with rich, flamboyant cloaks. Apparently, he'd been serious about throwing around his royal status.

"That's a badass robe," I said as I sat down. "Dorian, Slayer of Souls."

"Well, I did tell you I was envious of that nickname," he said, stretching back in an ornate armchair. "You two are lovely, as always."

I glanced around. "Aren't Ysabel and Edria here yet?"

He waved dismissively toward the door. "Oh, yes. We found them right away. I just like making them wait. Like I always say, the more you can unsettle someone, the better."

"Oh? I don't think I've ever heard you say that," I remarked.

He flashed me a smile. "That's because I'm usually practicing it on you, my dear." Jasmine rolled her eyes, and he turned toward a sentry waiting near the room's entrance. "All right. Go fetch them."

The brief levity faded, and dresses and robes suddenly seemed irrelevant compared to what we had to contend with. I couldn't believe Pagiel was back in the human world. Worse, before Roland had left, he'd told me that

Pagiel's range had actually expanded last time. He'd been spotted in New Mexico too.

Ysabel and Edria were soon ushered in, with an unhappy-looking Ansonia. Much like before, I got the impression she'd been dragged along against her will. Her mother and grandmother displayed an interesting mix of emotions. Irritation, fear, and . . . a trace of guilt.

"Goddamn it," I said, not even letting Dorian start whatever grand, intimidating speech he had planned. "You guys *do* know. You've known for a while."

Ysabel gave me a tight smile. Her lips were painted as red as her hair today. "I beg your pardon? I'm sure I don't know what you're talking about." The fact that she was being polite convinced me even more that she was lying.

"Before you say another word," said Dorian, with a terrifying look I'd rarely seen him wear, "you will show the proper respect to me and Queen Eugenie. The lot of you have gotten lazy and disrespectful in your time here, and you'll be lucky if I just turn you out and don't imprison you for treason."

Ysabel's smile vanished, and she and the others quickly dropped into the lowest, most respectful curtsies I'd ever seen.

"Your Majesty," said Edria. "I don't understand this talk of treason. We are your most loyal subjects, and you need only ask us to serve."

Dorian rose to his feet and stormed over to Edria, leaning only a few inches from her face. "If you were my 'most loyal servant,' you would've told me immediately that Pagiel had resumed raiding humans! Now. Where is he? And I warn you, I'll know if you lie, so save yourselves while you can."

Ansonia was guileless and wide-eyed and probably would have spilled whatever she knew then and there.

Ysabel and Edria were a different story, and I could practically see the wheels spinning in their heads as they tried to figure out what strategy would get them in the least trouble.

"We thought Your Majesty approved of such actions," said Ysabel at last, apparently deciding truth mingled with faux ignorance was the way to go. "After all, you've always spoken out in favor of Storm King's prophecy. We didn't tell you, simply because we thought it didn't matter. We certainly weren't trying to hide anything."

Dorian had backed off and returned to his chair. "Yes, I'm sure that's all there was to it."

"You never answered the other question," I pointed out. "Where is Pagiel now?"

"We don't know." Belatedly, Ysabel added, "Your Majesty."

"Ysabel . . ." warned Dorian.

She blanched. "It's the truth, sire. We've hardly seen him since he returned from the Yew Land. He comes back every so often from the human world to distribute his goods—only to those in need, I assure you—but otherwise, I don't know where he stays. Perhaps here, perhaps there."

I weighed the truth in her words and knew Dorian was doing the same. Studying all their faces, I actually believed Ysabel was being honest. She really didn't know where Pagiel was. Perhaps that was intentional on his part. Plausible deniability.

Dorian's voice was very, very quiet when he spoke, which added a surprisingly menacing feel. "If he makes contact, you are to let me know immediately. If he actually surfaces, you will alert my guards and restrain him until they can seize him."

"Restrain him?" exclaimed Ysabel. "He's my son! And to be frank . . . I'm not sure any of us *could* restrain him.

He . . . he's far more powerful than we are, Your Majesty." She actually sounded uneasy about that.

I wouldn't have believed her if I hadn't seen Pagiel in action myself. He'd grown much stronger in the time I'd known him, partially thanks to me since I'd helped him better his magic in our travels. I hadn't asked Roland much about the dust storms in Arizona, but I knew how large that type could grow. That was serious magic.

"Nonetheless," said Dorian, "you will do what you can. Is this understood?"

Ysabel and Ansonia murmured assent. Edria cleared her throat. "It is understood, Your Majesty . . . but begging your pardon, may I ask *why* this is so troubling to you? What do you care for humans? You know they took our world. They have much while we have little. Pagiel is only doing what many—including yourself—think we deserve. I don't believe there's anything wrong with it, so I'm just having trouble understanding your commands, sire."

Dorian hesitated only a moment before answering, his eyes flicking briefly to me. "You don't need to understand my commands. You simply need to obey them. Now. Is there anything else that you have to tell us about Pagiel— aside from your justifications? Any idea of his plans? Who his followers are?"

They swore they knew nothing of his plans but did give us a list of several accomplices. Dorian dispatched a guard to find them, though none of us were optimistic about the success of that. After a few more threats and warnings, he sent the family away. Once we were alone again, his fierce countenance faded and he leaned back with a sigh.

"By the gods," he muttered. "What a mess."

"Ansonia knows something," said Jasmine. It was the first time she'd spoken since before the audience. "I can see it."

"She definitely looked scared out of her mind," I agreed.

"No surprise with that group. They sure do push her around a lot."

"It's more than that," Jasmine said. "I swear, there was something she wasn't telling us. I have really good intuition, you know."

I hadn't known that but didn't push it. "I can believe that she doesn't know where Pagiel is," I said. "And that's our biggest issue right now. I'll go back to Tucson tomorrow and see what I can uncover there. You want to go?"

Jasmine shook her head, still lost in her own thoughts. "I don't know. Maybe. I'll let you know."

Dorian could hardly resist the opportunity to show us off at dinner. We were gentry celebrities and dressed up to boot. Dinnertime at his castle was always a huge affair, a big party in the dining hall. His court liked the novelty of having other royalty around and was too excited by their own boisterous celebrating to notice the three of us just weren't into the festive atmosphere. Jasmine left early, and Dorian and I followed shortly thereafter, going to his rooms so we could debrief the Pagiel situation in private.

"You don't want to go with me, do you?" I asked him, settling down at a little table. I was reminded of that dinner he'd arranged for me ages ago, the one with the Milky Way cake.

He poured wine for both of us, the first alcohol I'd had since the twins. "In theory, yes. But I'm not too proud to admit I can't function in that world as efficiently as I'd like." Dorian was strong enough to cross over intact, but he suffered the same adverse reactions to technology as most gentry. "I trust you and Roland can deal with the situation initially. I'll deal with Pagiel when you get him back here."

I sipped the wine. It was fruity and strong, reminding me that I should probably exercise caution since I was out of practice. Then again, if ever there was a time to drink, it was now. "Why are you helping me?" I asked after taking another gulp. "I mean, I know you help me all the time, but Edria had a point. Why are you helping me with *this*? You've never had any qualms about invading the human world. You still call Isaac Thundro and talk about him conquering humanity."

"Thundro really is an excellent name." Dorian drank some of his own wine, composing his thoughts. "As for the why? It's simple. You don't want Pagiel raiding that world."

I waited for more. Nothing came. "That's it?"

"What more is there?"

"I . . . I don't know. It's just . . . it's just hard for me to believe." I downed my glass of wine, hoping to hide how flustered I felt. I actually could feel the start of a buzz, driving home that I really had lost my tolerance. I used to take down half bottles of tequila. With as confused as I was, the buzz was welcome. Once, Dorian offering to do something for me would have made me suspicious of ulterior motives. Now, I wasn't so sure.

Dorian set down his goblet and walked over to me, surprising me by kneeling so that he looked up at my face. "I told you earlier. What wouldn't I do for you? I don't know what else I can say to convince you. I've tried to make amends for the Iron Crown, Eugenie. I guess I've failed."

My heart lurched, and I sank to the ground beside him. I caught hold of his hands. "No, you haven't. It's not your problem anymore. It's *mine*. I'm the one who has to get over the past and start trusting again."

He ran his fingers over mine. "With everything that's happened to you, I don't blame you for not trusting anyone."

"I trust lots of people," I said. A memory of this afternoon came to me, and traitorous lust coursed through my body. "Including you."

I brought my lips to his and was flooded with that warmth and sweetness from earlier, that sense that Dorian and I belonged together. He wrapped his arms around me and pulled me so that I practically sat on his lap. I increased the intensity of the kiss, nipping his lip with my teeth. He responded in kind, reaching up to grab my hair and jerk my head back so that he could bring his hungry mouth down to my throat. I wondered if I'd have marks there tomorrow but didn't really care one way or another.

His other hand slid up to the bodice of my dress, deftly undoing the laces. He pulled back the fabric, exposing a breast, and brought his mouth down to it, finishing what he'd started this afternoon. I cried out as his teeth and tongue played with my nipple and shifted so that I sat up right on my knees and gave him better access. He freed the other breast and sucked on it while also attempting to hike up the dress's skirt. I tried to pull him on top of me and lie back on the floor, but he stopped me.

"No," he gasped out. "Not here. I need to take you to . . . somewhere else . . . the bed or something. . . ." He started to get up, and I pushed him down.

"No," I said, wrapping my arms around his neck. "Right here. Right now. Just like it used to be." I don't know what urgency drove me. Maybe it was the wine. Maybe it was the fear of another interruption like we'd had earlier. Maybe it was just the constant threats I seemed to face that made me want to grasp on to this moment before it could slip away. Or maybe I just hadn't had sex in too long.

He studied me for a moment, and I thought he might refuse. Then, he made his decision and came forward to kiss me even harder than before. His body pushed me down so that my back was on the floor. That ridiculous "slayer" robe turned out to be pretty easy to get off, and so help me, he was completely naked underneath. He pushed my skirt up over my hips and *tsked* when he saw I had underwear on. This had been a longtime debate between us, seeing as gentry women rarely wore any with dresses.

He quickly took mine off and then lowered his body on

top of me. His hands caught hold of my wrists, pinning me to the floor with the same domination he'd always shown in bed. A moment later, without further warning, he was in me, just as hard and long as I remembered. I let out a small cry of surprise, a cry he muffled with a kiss. My body seemed startled at first, seeing as it hadn't had a lot of action in a while. It didn't take long to recover, particularly since I was wetter than I'd expected.

He held me down and thrust himself in and out of me, awakening the desire we'd once shared. I grew lost in it, and soon it was as though no time had passed at all between us. I think he would've gone slow and easy if I had asked. I didn't. I urged him on to take me harder and not hold back. My body reveled in it, loving the feel of him in me. I arched up when I finally came, and he pushed me back down, thrusting harder still as the orgasm wracked my body. He came almost immediately after, his face exquisite in the throes of ecstasy. I had a feeling it had taken every ounce of control he had to wait for my climax.

He collapsed down on me when he was done, panting and sweaty. I pulled him to me, running a hand over that brilliant, fiery hair. In the afterglow, lying half dressed on the floor seemed a little ridiculous—but only a little. I tried to think of something funny to say, but my brain was lazy and tired with bliss and affection.

"I feel like I might have just been used," he said with amusement. "But I don't think I mind." It was a fair point, considering my earlier talk about not knowing where we stood.

A knock at the door interrupted any response I might have made. Dorian groaned and nuzzled against my breast. "Ignore it."

The knock sounded again, this time more urgently. When the knock digressed to what was obviously kicking at the door, I suggested that maybe Dorian should answer it after all.

"I don't think that's a servant," I said. "And hey, at least they waited until after we were done."

With a sigh, he got up and put the robe back on. I managed to do the same with my dress as he walked to the door, though anyone with a sharp eye would guess what had been going on. At least the gentry didn't judge much.

"Well, well," he said when he opened the door. "Very unexpected."

Jasmine and Ansonia stood there. Ansonia's face looked as scared as before, but it was Jasmine's that truly alarmed me. She was so pale, so terribly distraught that I thought she was going to pass out. I jumped up and hurried over to them.

"For God's sake, sit down," I exclaimed. "What's the matter? Are you okay?" There was no water in sight, so I poured two glasses of wine, figuring underage drinking was better than nothing.

Jasmine took a sip, though hardly seemed aware of it. There was a robotic quality to her.

"What's the matter?" I repeated. "Jasmine, talk to me. One of you, say something!"

"I'll send for a healer," said Dorian.

That seemed to wake Jasmine up. "No, wait. That's not—that's not the problem. I'm just . . ." She shook her head and drank more wine. "I don't know what to think. Ansonia, tell them. You have to tell them."

Ansonia regarded us with big scared eyes that were a lovely shade of gray-blue, almost the same as Jasmine's. "Do you know where Pagiel is?" I asked hopefully.

Ansonia shook her head. Her hands trembled so much that I thought she'd spill the wine, so I took the glass from her.

"You have to tell them," Jasmine urged. "They have to know."

Ansonia opened her mouth to speak, but nothing came

out. A few moments later, she tried again. "A . . . a few days ago, I overheard Mother and Grandmother talking at night. They thought I was asleep. They—they were talking about Pagiel and his raids."

"Damn it," I muttered. "They do know where he is."

"N-no." Ansonia shook her head. "They don't. Truly. None of us do. But they were talking about how they'd been expecting this from him but never thought it would happen so soon. Grandmother said it wasn't the right way, that he needed to go in with a real army and that he was acting without even realizing what he was doing. Then they started talking about you too, Your Majesty." Those nervous eyes flicked to Dorian. "About whether you'd support him."

"Support the raids?" asked Dorian, puzzled. "They know I don't. It's why they didn't tell me."

"No, support Pagiel. Fulfilling Grandfather's legacy."

I tried to dredge up what I knew about their family, vaguely remembering how Ysabel's father had run out on her and Edria. "What legacy?"

Ansonia swallowed. "I swear, I never knew! I never knew who he was! Neither did Pagiel. He still doesn't know."

Jasmine had recovered enough to no longer have patience for the length of this story. "Damn it, just spit it out!" Not waiting for a response, she turned to me and Dorian. "Ysabel's dad was *Storm King*. Our dad. Edria's been hiding it this whole time."

I could only stare. Even Dorian was speechless.

"Don't you see?" said Jasmine. "You aren't the oldest, Eugenie! Ysabel is. And Pagiel is Storm King's first grandson."

Chapter 25

There were only a handful of moments in my life where my world had been so irrevocably altered that time stood still and I was trapped in my own shock. I could count those times on one hand. Discovering I was pregnant had been one such moment. Another had been learning I was Storm King's daughter.

And now . . . this.

"No," I said at last. "That can't be right."

There were tears in Ansonia's eyes. "I *heard* them," she said. "And when I look back . . . there were a lot of conversations I never understood, hints of something big between my mother and grandmother. They didn't make sense . . . but now they do. It started, I don't know . . . maybe a year ago. I remember one day my mother was in shock. She wouldn't speak to anyone. I think that's when she found out. I don't think Grandmother told her until then."

Dorian pulled up one of the chairs and sat down. He still looked stunned, but it was fading as his quick mind began analyzing everything. He picked up the wine I'd snatched from Ansonia and took a gulp. "The whole family works weather. Or at least wind and air. Ysabel, Pagiel . . . you?"

Ansonia nodded at the query. "But not as strongly as them."

"That may not mean much," I said. "Magic isn't always passed down in families."

"Not always," Dorian agreed. "But often. And certainly in Storm King's line, if you and Jasmine are any indication. She got water. Ysabel got air. You were the lucky one to inherit it all, furthering our thoughts that you'd be the heir's mother. But look . . . look at the resemblance. You and Ansonia were mistaken for each other."

He was right, I realized with a sickening feeling. Up close, Ansonia and I didn't look alike, but from a distance we shared similar features. All of us did: me, Jasmine, Ysabel, Pagiel, and Ansonia. I'd thought it was funny that the clinic in Ohio had accepted my siblings so easily. Suddenly, that was no longer a joke.

"Oh God," I said.

Dorian's gaze was far away. "And Pagiel's power has grown—considerably. We haven't noticed it because of everything else going on."

"He's my *nephew*," said Jasmine in despair. No one paid much attention.

I closed my eyes as something else occurred to me. "And he's already begun his invasion of the human world. None of us knew it. He doesn't even know it." I opened my eyes. "Kiyo was right. Prophecies do fulfill themselves in unexpected ways."

And speaking of Kiyo . . . the most startling thing of all hit me. Isaac and Ivy. If this was all true—and I was beginning to think it was—Isaac wasn't Storm King's heir. He wasn't the first grandson. He really was an innocent, not a conqueror of worlds. He was free of the prophecy. Free to live his life.

Hope and joy blossomed within me, though I kept it to myself. This revelation was dearer to me than anything else we'd discussed . . . but it wasn't relevant to the larger problem. There would be time to bask in this news later.

"His raids just got a lot more serious," I said. "If there really is truth to the prophecy . . . well, then. What he's doing has the potential to develop into a lot more."

Dorian said nothing, and I wondered what he was thinking. He'd agreed to stopping Pagiel before, as a favor to me. Now that Pagiel's activities had become something more . . . what then? Where did Dorian's loyalties lie? He'd just professed all this devotion to me, swearing he'd do anything for me. But that was before he'd found out the cause he'd long supported was under way. I couldn't read him, and that made me nervous. My walls went back up.

Jasmine used the silence to again interject, "Pagiel's my nephew. Isn't anyone else freaked out about that? We were practically dating."

"Did you sleep together?" I asked bluntly.

She looked taken aback. "Well, no . . . but you know, we like kissed . . . and did other stuff. . . ."

I decided not to investigate the "other stuff." I shrugged. "I think you're okay then. Seems like it could be a lot worse." Jasmine's expression said she didn't agree, but she let the matter go.

The situation escalated after that in a way I never could have imagined. The first order of business was to call in Ysabel and Edria again to verify Ansonia's story. Dorian put on his tough face, but I think even he was amazed at the casual way Edria talked about having been one of Storm King's mistresses years ago. She acted as though being at the center of a prophecy was no big deal and she thought Pagiel's actions were a justified part of his legacy. Ysabel— my *sister*—stood by her mother's side and defended her son too . . . but I sensed a little uneasiness from her. I remembered Ansonia saying that Ysabel had only recently learned the truth. Despite Ysabel's love for attention and status, I wondered if perhaps this new development was a bit more than she'd ever wanted.

Nonetheless, once the cat was out of the bag, Edria had no qualms about spreading the news in the gentry world. Like so much gossip, everyone seemed to know in a very short time. The kingdoms were abuzz. People were shocked to learn that not only had my son been superseded, but that the new heir was already fulfilling his destiny. Divisions that had been quiet in the wake of the blight began to form again, those vehemently against and for Pagiel.

So, it was no surprise when, a couple days later, Kiyo showed up at Dorian's castle wanting to speak to us. There was some delay before Dorian agreed. Kiyo's last visit had involved a spectacular attempt to kill me, and Dorian had consequently banished him with strict orders for the guards on what to do if Kiyo surfaced again. Dorian and I conferred and decided I was safe, though my feelings toward Kiyo hadn't changed much, even after our Yew Land alliance.

"I assume you're going to do something?" Kiyo said immediately, once we were in a private room.

"I'm going back to Tucson today," I said. "He's not going to be easy to find, though. From what Roland told me, by the time you hear about one of his raids, he's already gone."

"I'll find him," growled Kiyo. "I'll find him and put an end to this."

I felt my eyes widen. "What's that supposed to mean?"

Kiyo met my gaze levelly. "What do you think? We need to stop this before it gets worse. Unless you had other plans." That was directed to Dorian, the subtext obvious.

Dorian had been very quiet on his opinions of everything. He'd supported my intentions of finding Pagiel but hadn't elaborated on what was to be done after the fact.

"Pagiel doesn't even realize what he's doing," I said. "There are other ways to stop this."

"You just touched on the problem," said Kiyo. "*He's doing something.* You berated me over and over about going after your son, about how he was an innocent and had done nothing. Well, here we are. Pagiel's pretty much a grown man, with a lot of power, and he's doing exactly what the prophecy said he would do. You can't claim there's a chance to change fate now."

"There's always a chance," I said stubbornly. "We aren't destiny's pawns. Pagiel can still change the future. He's smart. He's compassionate. And I believe he'll do the right thing. He deserves a chance. I'm certainly not going to kill him outright without talking to him!"

Nothing Kiyo did should have shocked me anymore, but I was amazed at how lightly he referred to his efforts to hunt down Isaac. No remorse, no apology. No "Hey, Eugenie, I guess I was wrong. Sorry about the grief I subjected you to for the better part of a year."

Instead, Kiyo's focus was solely on Pagiel now. "You talked to him before we went to the Yew Land. That didn't stop the raids. I really doubt anything you can say or do will change things now."

"I have to try," I said.

Kiyo shrugged. "And I'm going to stop you."

Dorian stiffened at the subtle threat. "And suddenly, I regret offering you hospitality."

Kiyo rose. "Don't worry. I'll show myself out. I've heard all I needed to."

He stormed out, eyes flashing with anger. I kind of agreed with Dorian and wished I wasn't under the bonds of hospitality either. "I could send guards after him, once he clears the entrance," Dorian remarked.

I shook my head. "Don't bother. He'll turn into a fox and

slip away before they can do anything. All we can do now is make sure we find Pagiel first."

"Of course."

I eyed him uncertainly, hesitant to speak my mind. "Dorian . . . when I find him, are we going to have the same goals?"

He arched an eyebrow. "I think we can both agree we don't want that kitsune to kill Pagiel."

"Yeah, but what about after that? Are you going to help me talk sense into Pagiel or give him an army?"

Dorian's expression was still damnably unreadable. He took a long time to answer, which didn't reassure me. "I told you before, I stand with you and support you. I should think the events of the other night would have convinced you."

I almost smiled. "The events? Mostly that convinced me we can still have good sex."

He shrugged. "That was never in dispute. But I wasn't the only one who made pledges, Eugenie. You said you trusted me. Do you trust me now?"

Now I was the one groping for an answer. "I want to."

"Then do."

He started to reach for me, then pulled back. I didn't know if I was disappointed or relieved. "What do you need before you leave?" he asked, back to all business.

I need you to touch me, I thought, deciding I regretted his reticence after all. *I need you to hold me and make me feel like you really do love me more than any prophecy.*

Instead, I matched his serious air. "Nothing on the other side. But once we get back . . . well. Then I'll need your help to talk Pagiel down."

Jasmine came to Tucson with me. Her reaction surprised me. I'd expected her to go wildly in one direction, either to adamantly support him or else hate him for the familial confusion in their romance. But she adopted neither attitude.

She was serious and focused, united with me on talking sense to him.

The hardest part about being in Tucson was the waiting. I split my time between Roland's house and my own—the latter delighting Tim and Lara. Jasmine, Roland, and I scoured the news obsessively, waiting for any sign of Pagiel's band of merry men. The whole time I wondered if it would be futile, if we'd hurry to wherever he was and be left with only a trail of dust. While he had been recently spotted in Arizona, his range also meant he could very well appear in another state. If he showed up in Texas or something, we'd never reach it in time.

While the grocery store and farmers market thefts didn't go unnoticed, most of the media attention was on the haboobs. They were big and sensational—and not common here in such great numbers. They were great distractions from the paranormal nature of the robberies and gave rise to all sorts of theories. Thankfully, it was a human trait to find "reasonable" explanations for weird events before jumping to crazy ones. Well, kind of. There were those who thought the dramatic sandstorms were a sign of the coming Apocalypse. Others blamed climate change and warned of worse to come. No one had suggested a supernatural invasion.

I thought a lot about Dorian in my free time as well. I missed him more than I expected and was torn over whether I could trust him. I wanted to. Badly. He seemed so sincere in his change . . . but I'd believed him before, only to be deceived. I'd loved him once and wanted to again, but how could you love someone without trust?

"Eugenie!"

Jasmine's cry rang through my small house, making me jump. I had been sitting in my bedroom one afternoon, trying to soothe my troubled thoughts by putting together a narwhal jigsaw puzzle. Footsteps came tearing down the hall, and Jasmine appeared in my doorway.

"Eugenie," she gasped. "On TV . . . a haboob."

I ran to the living room nearly as fast as her. I was just in time to see footage of the haboob, as it rolled over a small city south of Phoenix. Even as someone who had done insane things with the weather, I was a little taken aback. The sandstorm was huge, stretching high in the air and spanning nearly forty miles. The cloud rolled into the city, engulfing it. The storms caused little direct damage but could be lethal for drivers suddenly deprived of visibility. The storm was also an excellent cover for a raid.

"This is live," I said. "He's got to be there right now."

"It's over an hour away," she said with dismay. "He'll be gone before we get there."

My mind raced. "Yeah, but gone where?"

Fishing through my kitchen drawers, I dug out an old map of Arizona that Roland and I had marked up with gates a long time ago. I had most of them memorized but wanted to double-check. I put my finger on the city Pagiel was in and then looked for the closest gates.

"The nearest is in Phoenix proper," I said. "Whether they're on horseback or foot, they probably aren't going to risk going through the city. There's another north of Phoenix that goes to the Willow Land, but they'd have to ride around the city. This one, though . . ." I tapped my finger on a spot closer to Tucson but off the main roads. "It's remote and easier for them to get to."

"You think they'll jump back to the Otherworld?" she asked.

"I'm positive. They won't risk being caught by humans, and we know they give away their goods to the gentry."

"Pagiel's probably strong enough to jump without a gate," Jasmine reminded me.

"His followers aren't," I said with certainty. "He'll go to

the gate. And we'll be waiting for him. We can beat him if we leave now." This was a chance we weren't going to get again. Any number of places would have too many gates to choose from or else be too far away.

Jasmine followed me as I grabbed my car keys and headed for the door. "Where's the gate open up?"

"The Thorn Land, actually."

"Ballsy," she said.

I laughed. "I suppose so. But I think it's a pretty remote part of the kingdom. Easy for him to hide out and also close to an Oak Land border."

I wanted to double the speed limit but knew a ticket would slow me down. Still, we made good time on the interstate. It was once we had to turn off and head into the desert that we slowed. I watched the clock anxiously, constantly running calculations on how long it would take his posse to get there. The odds seemed in our favor, but I'd learned not to assume anything when it came to the Otherworld.

We reached the gate, and I parked the car a little ways from it. Pagiel wouldn't know it was mine, but I didn't want him getting spooked if he thought humans were in the area. It was late afternoon, in the middle of desert country, and the heat was in full effect. Jasmine and I had had the sense to bring water bottles, but they didn't stop the sweat from rolling off of us as the sand radiated back the sun's merciless rays. We found a spot near some saguaro cactuses. They didn't offer much shade, but they gave us a sheltered view of the gate. Again, I didn't want our presence to be obvious to Pagiel.

The afternoon wore on, and I began to doubt myself. Maybe I'd guessed wrong on the gate, especially if Pagiel decided not to risk crossing into one of my kingdoms. Or maybe he'd somehow made better time than I expected and was already gone. Our water was running low, though both

Jasmine and I could pull water out of surrounding plants if necessary. I felt bad about that sometimes, but it occasionally had to be done for survival.

"There," said Jasmine, straightening up. I followed where she was pointing and saw sand being kicked up as a group of horses and riders came into view.

"Unbelievable," I said. "They rode horses from Phoenix. He really is a modern-day Robin Hood."

Pagiel was in the lead, easily visible with the way the sun lit up his red hair. There were about a dozen riders with him, which made my heart sink. His initial raids had only contained a handful. A dozen was hardly an army, but it still signified an increase in support. After seeing the passionate reactions back in the Otherworld, I had a feeling he could have recruited more if he wanted. It was a small mercy that the majority of gentry had trouble crossing over to this world.

I waited until he was closer but not close enough to cross through the gate. I jumped up and strode forward, Jasmine right beside me.

"Pagiel!" I yelled.

He flinched in the saddle, and instantly, I felt the wind pick up. It stilled when he saw us, though the wary expression on his face clearly showed he didn't quite trust us as friends. His riders regarded us with equal caution, and I saw the flash of a few copper blades.

"Your Majesty? Jasmine?" Pagiel glanced between us. "What are you doing here?"

"You already know," I said, trying to present an air of peace and calm. "We need to talk about these raids you're on. Pagiel, you know they're not right."

"Humans have plenty!" exclaimed one of his followers. "We're entitled to reap our share."

Pagiel silenced him with a look, and the guy cringed.

Somehow, the boy sidekick I'd befriended had become more of a formidable leader than I'd suspected.

"The people in my kingdom are hungry," said Pagiel. "They are in yours too. Can you honestly say you don't want to help them?"

"No one's starving anymore," I argued. "We're on rations, yeah, but at least we're surviving honorably."

Pagiel shook his head. "We talked about this before. Honor doesn't enter into it—only survival. Besides, isn't this what I'm supposed to be doing?"

I winced at the bitterness in his voice. So. He knew. Somehow, I wasn't surprised. If he'd been back and forth between the worlds in the last few days, word would have gotten to him about his heritage.

"You aren't 'supposed' to be doing anything," I said gently. "You make your own choices."

"That's not what I hear," he said. "I heard what everyone said when I was back there. They've all got plans for me. Even my grandmother does. Why else wouldn't she have told me?"

"I don't know," I admitted. There was a raw pain on his face that broke my heart. Maybe he'd technically reached manhood by gentry standards, but he was still a boy in many ways. He'd been thrust into a world he wasn't ready for, had his life irrevocably changed. I knew the feeling, and I ached for him. "Let me help you. Come back with me so we can talk."

That set off alarms for him. The wind rose again, whipping my hair around. "'Talk'? I'm not stupid. I know what that means. You'll put me in iron and lock me away."

"Stop that," I snapped. With barely a thought, I killed his wind magic. He might be strong, but Auntie Eugenie was stronger. He cringed a bit, feeling my magic dwarf his. "I'll win if we fight, and I don't want it to come to that. We're family, Pagiel. And in a lot of ways . . . it feels right, you

know? You've stood by me since we met. I want to do the
same for you. I swear to you, I won't hurt you. Neither will
Dorian. We'll work this out together."

Indecision warred on Pagiel's face. He didn't know who
to trust, and I didn't blame him. I'd been in that position. In
a chaotic world, he'd carved out this outlaw niche for himself, one that at least gave him control of something.

"Pagiel, please," I said. Panic was building in me. I was
afraid it was going to come down to a fight, and I really
didn't want that. "I know what you're going through. I've
been fighting the destiny that was allegedly laid out for me
too. *You* are your own master, not some prophecy made
before you were born."

Pagiel still didn't respond. It was Jasmine who cracked
him. "Pagiel, please," she said, echoing me. "Please come
with us."

His gaze flicked to her, and I saw a new pain cross his
features. Like her, he'd come to realize the family connection that had killed their romance. Nonetheless, I knew that
as he studied her, he still cared about her and probably
always would.

"All right," he said at last. He turned his attention back
to me. "I trust you, Eugenie."

It was the first time he'd called me by my given name,
and I smiled. It was fitting, since we were related. A few of
his followers grumbled about this decision, but again, a
command from him silenced them. I also noted that a few
of them actually looked relieved. I wondered if maybe what
had started off as a fun, madcap adventure had become too
much for some.

Pagiel glanced back to where a couple of horses simply
carried packs and supplies. "Distribute those goods among
everyone so that my aunts can ride," he ordered.

His riders jumped to obey. I hoped desperately we could
work out all of this because he had so much potential. He

was powerful in presence and personality. If he was put on the right path, he could become the kind of leader who did great things in the Otherworld. He could inherit a kingdom someday.

I hoped my abandoned car would be okay and crossed with Pagiel's riders into the Otherworld. It wasn't one of the strongest gates I'd ever used, but none of his party seemed to have difficulty with it. He'd picked a strong group. We reached the Thorn Land and then turned down the road for the Oak Land. As we rode, I occasionally saw the other gentry going through the packs of stolen goods. A few of them started munching on candy bars, like Butterfinger and Heath. *Once Pagiel's stopped his raids*, I thought, *this will all be funny someday.*

It was still weird seeing the Oak Land so green. The trees held the fruits of both summer and autumn now, and I hoped Pagiel would soon realize there was a lot to love here in the Otherworld. He and his followers didn't need the human world. This was where they belonged.

We reached a part of the road that I knew well, a bend that would soon put us in sight of Dorian's castle. I breathed a sigh of relief. We had done it. We would bring Pagiel home and fix all of this.

Suddenly, seemingly out of nowhere, an arrow zinged by Pagiel, only just barely missing him. It was followed by two more, one of which took one of Pagiel's riders in the chest. I pulled out my athame and gun. The air swelled around us—a result of both my magic and Pagiel's—and his riders drew weapons. Shouts from the trees around the road told me we were rapidly being surrounded, but I couldn't see by whom yet. I looked around frantically, trying to decide how we could best defend ourselves.

Before I could say anything, Pagiel gestured to me and Jasmine with his sword. "Seize them! Use them as hostages! They've led us into an ambush!"

Chapter 26

"What?" I exclaimed. "They aren't with us! I don't know who they are!"

Pagiel didn't seem to hear me. Neither did his followers. A few of them advanced on me, which was pretty foolish on their part. I held out my silver athame in a warding gesture and summoned a sudden rush of dark clouds and flickering lightning above us that was mostly for show. I didn't want to hurt them, not when a third party was attacking us. The trick worked, and his riders hesitated.

"I'm not your enemy," I told them. "Deal with me later. Worry about *them*."

Our attackers conveniently chose that moment to finally show themselves. They were a mixed group of warriors, with no real uniformity to their attire. They could have been ordinary brigands, but on a few of them, I caught the flash of a golden willow tree pin. To round out the mix, they'd recruited a few wandering spirits and trolls.

"They're Maiwenn's people," I said to anyone who would listen.

Finally, one of the riders was smart enough to realize the danger. "The Willow Queen has sent her assassins to kill our lord!" he exclaimed. "Attack! Defend Pagiel!"

Many of his followers were his age. *So young*, I thought sadly. But from the fierce looks on their faces, they were more than willing to defend their leader. I respected that. Me, I didn't have much concern for Pagiel. He could take care of himself, so I left it to others to fret over him as I charged forward to help thin out the opposition.

Most of Pagiel's warriors could handle one-on-one physical or magical combat with the Willow attackers, so I focused on the monsters and spirits. A lot of them I could dispatch with shamanic magic, keeping my distance and ousting them before they even realized what was happening. I traded my athame for my wand. It was a *real* wand, not the homemade contraption from the Yew Land—though I had kept that as a souvenir.

Some of the spirits sensed what I was doing and attacked me directly. It occurred to me then that I hadn't really been involved in a true fight for a while. Despite all the dangers we'd faced on the Yew Land journey, there'd been very few physical confrontations. The closest had been when I freed the monarchs, but even then, my storm magic had kept most of them at bay. I hadn't gotten down and dirty in a while.

Like so much after the birth of the twins, I was excited to see that I really had recovered. Part of my fear when pregnant had been that my body was lost to me forever. Time had healed everything, and I was just as fast and effective as I used to be. Sure, I got a few bruises and burns from the spirits (this group had an acidlike touch), but I took it in stride and fought my way through.

Our group was making good progress when a group of Oak Land warriors, led by Dorian himself, came charging down the road. That pretty much cinched the odds for us, and in a very short time, Maiwenn's people were either dead or had fled.

I wiped sweat off my brow and put away the wand as

I rode over to Dorian. Having come at the end, he looked remarkably fresh and energetic, though I saw blood on his sword. "Well, well," he said. "What's all this?"

I grimaced. "Ambush. I found Pagiel in Arizona and convinced him to come back with me to see you. Then these guys showed up. Kiyo acted like he'd be hunting Pagiel, but my guess is he knew I'd have better luck and simply had Maiwenn's forces stake out likely places we'd return."

Dorian glanced around, a small frown creasing his features. "Where *is* Pagiel?"

"He's right—" I turned around and stared. There were all of Pagiel's riders, alive and well. But no Pagiel. "Where the hell is he?" A moment later, I noticed something else. "Where's Jasmine?"

His disappearance was as much a surprise to his followers as it was to me—well, most of them. A couple exchanged knowing looks, and I could see mild guilt on their faces.

"What is it?" demanded Dorian. "What happened?"

One of them gave a half bow from his saddle. "Forgive us, sire. When the attack started, we thought . . . well, we thought it was a betrayal." He shot me an apologetic look. "We urged Pagiel to leave since we knew he was the target. And . . . we, uh, encouraged him to take the Lady Jasmine with him."

"He didn't run away," added the other guy hotly. "He's no coward. He would've stayed if not for our insistence." His friend nodded fiercely.

I stared in disbelief. "He took Jasmine as a *hostage*?"

"Smart thing to do when you're scared and think you've been set up by those you trust," muttered Dorian. "I doubt he'll hurt her."

"He'd better not!" I exclaimed. "How'd he even subdue her? She's strong."

"And he's stronger," Dorian reminded me. He turned toward Pagiel's compatriots. "I trust you're convinced we're on his side now. Which way did he go?"

They hesitated only a moment. "I believe he cut across the woods, Your Majesty," one said, pointing. "I think that way."

"Then that's the way you and I will go," Dorian told me. "Nonetheless, we can't be certain he didn't change course. The wounded will go to my castle. The rest will split up and fan out in other directions to find him. If you do, convince him of our support and bring him back." He gave a sharp look to those gathered. "Do you understand?"

There were meek murmurs of agreement. They might support Pagiel, but most were Oak Land subjects. Dorian was impressive, and it was hard for them to refuse him.

"Damn it," I muttered, once Dorian and I had split from the others. "And damn me for not thinking Maiwenn and Kiyo might do something like this. I should've known they wouldn't take the proactive approach. They're riding off of our success."

"Well, they were proactive enough in setting up these ambushes," Dorian pointed out. "I'm guessing similar parties are waiting elsewhere on our borders. This group got lucky."

"Not lucky enough," I realized. "Kiyo and Maiwenn themselves weren't here. They were only guessing at which group might catch Pagiel on his return."

Dorian nodded agreement. "Their presence would have added an extra complication. Ah, this is promising." He stopped and pointed to where some grass and bushes had been recently trampled.

"I wouldn't have even noticed that."

He flashed me a grin. "That's why I'm here. An excellent hunter of all manner of difficult prey."

I rolled my eyes at the double entendre, and we continued on. Joking aside, Dorian did have a good tracker's eye for small signs of Pagiel's passing. And, the farther we journeyed, I began to notice some signs of my own.

"The air's not natural through here," I said, for lack of a better description. "It's faint, like residual effects, but magic's altered it recently."

Dorian gave me a concerned look. "Do you think it's a trap?"

"No," I said, after a moment's consideration. "Not nearly strong enough. If I had to guess . . . it's probably part of what he used to carry Jasmine off. Even if he's stronger, she wouldn't be easy to just slip out of there. Air can be used for binding, if you know the right tricks. You can almost create a kind of 'air rope' or—in extreme cases— cut off someone's breathing enough to make them compliant. I really hope it hasn't come to that."

"Well, like I said, I don't think he'd hurt her. I think she was just an easy choice, one he thought would hold you off."

I nodded, knowing that he was right. Even at a brisk pace, it seemed unlikely we'd catch up with Pagiel anytime soon. He'd undoubtedly taken off as fast as he could to avoid pursuit. Our one stroke of luck came when we found Jasmine's horse nibbling on some grass.

"Too difficult to bind her and force her on her own horse," I guessed. "He must have just pulled her onto his."

Dorian's eyes were aglow the thrill of the hunt. "This will slow him. It's our chance to catch up."

We continued off at that same fast pace for a couple more hours, hoping we could take advantage of them riding double. The residual air magic grew stronger and stronger, giving me hope, until we finally emerged into a clearing and found Pagiel and Jasmine sitting on logs. He jumped up when he saw us.

"Don't come closer," he warned. "I . . . I've got her."

There was a tremulous note in his voice, backing up Dorian's assertion that Pagiel would have trouble hurting her. Studying Jasmine, I saw that she sat nearly immobile, her arms held tightly at her side. I'd been right as well. She was bound with ropes of air. Meanwhile, the wind around him stirred.

"Pagiel, I told you before—you won't win in a fight. Especially against the two of us," I said. "Please let her go. I know you care about her and don't want to hurt her."

The earlier pain and confusion returned to Pagiel's face. "You lied to me. You arranged the ambush."

I shook my head. "If you'd stuck around, you would have seen that they were Maiwenn's people. We got rid of them. Your riders put up a great fight. They're really loyal to you and fought for your honor, even with you not there."

It was a subtle dig. I didn't actually blame him for leaving but knew it troubled him. If he was confused enough, I hoped he would come back with us and listen to reason.

"I can't trust you," Pagiel said. "I can't trust anyone. Even those who claim to support me . . . they ask so much, more than I'm ready for."

"Pagiel," said Dorian gently. "Have I ever given you reason to doubt me? Haven't I always been there for your family?"

Pagiel wouldn't meet his eyes. "Yes, sire. Once I would have trusted you implicitly, but now . . . now I know your loyalties are with *her*. I don't question your choice. It's your right. But it also means I can't believe you'll always act in my interest." He sighed and then looked up with a grim and unhappy resolve on his face. "Forgive me," he said.

That was my only warning. He wove his spell too quickly, more so than I would have imagined possible. A forest hardly provides the right conditions for a haboob, but he created a complex wind pattern that was nearly the same. And it was *strong*. Dirt flew up from the ground. Trees were ripped up. We were affected as well, blown backward and forced to scramble for our footing. I caught hold of a tree whose roots were still holding it strong and managed to keep myself upright.

Pagiel used the diversion to flee. I couldn't address him right away because I devoted all my energy to stopping the maelstrom he'd created. My magical senses burned, and I could detect every thread of magic, every molecule in the air around us. The magic was a mirror of my own, courtesy of our shared genes. I matched it, answering each glimmer of the magic with a nullifying force. It was a complex process, like trying to unravel a tapestry. I hated the delay but needed to undo this magic before it killed me, Jasmine, and Dorian. When I finished and the world stilled, I glanced around, expecting to find Pagiel gone.

Instead, I found him encased in a prison of earth and stone that had risen up from the ground, cocooning him up to his neck. I sensed him pulling his magic to him, probably in an effort to blast Dorian's handiwork away. I quickly slammed up walls of air, turning the air pressure up to crazy heights that were uncomfortable for the rest of us but ensured Pagiel wouldn't bust out anytime soon.

Pagiel fixed his eyes on Dorian. "Your Majesty. Please let me go. You said you would help me!"

"I am," said Dorian, a hard expression on his face. "I could easily keep building this structure until you suffocated. I don't want that. I want you alive."

"Then free me," Pagiel begged. "You always supported the legacy in my family. Will you really drag me back like a prisoner?"

Dorian hesitated long enough to glance briefly at me. "Things change. This is the better fate."

My heart swelled, and the last piece of fear within me shattered. Dorian had been telling me the truth. He could have easily let Pagiel go, letting him continue on with the prophecy. Instead, Dorian had stood by me. His love for me really was greater than the dreams of conquest he once held.

My epiphany was short-lived when a giant fox came tearing out of the woods. He leapt straight for Pagiel, jaw open for the boy's semi-exposed neck. In an instant, all the plants and trees in a huge radius withered and water shot from all directions toward Kiyo. It wasn't enough to incapacitate him, but it did throw his attack off course. He harmlessly hit the side of the rock formation and was knocked back, skillfully landing a short distance away. He blinked the water out of his eyes and then shook droplets off his muzzle.

Jasmine, who had been freed in the earlier storm, was on her feet and allowed the water she'd summoned to fall to the ground. "Let him go, Dorian!"

It was probably the most conflicted I'd ever seen Dorian. Letting Pagiel go might mean we'd never catch him. Keeping him imprisoned made him an easy target for Kiyo.

"Do it!" I cried.

Like that, the walls of rock and earth shattered, giving Pagiel just enough time to dodge Kiyo's next attack. The boy fell to the ground, but by then, I was back in control. I pulled up the water Jasmine had called, turning it to a mist that swirled in the wind. I moved the whole creation, surrounding Kiyo in a thick cloud he couldn't see through. A moment later, I felt the wind and air pressure intensify. Pagiel, whom I'd expected to disappear, was still around, adding his magic to mine. Maybe he didn't trust us, but he also wouldn't leave us to Kiyo's attack.

As the mini windstorm increased, I could sense the pressure closing in on Kiyo. That was Pagiel's doing too, and I realized there was a very good chance Pagiel would kill Kiyo in the process. In fact, I had no doubt that was Pagiel's goal. I was still a gray area for Pagiel, but he knew with black-and-white certainty that Kiyo was a threat. I could've counteracted the magic but was struck with a dilemma: Should I? After all the problems Kiyo had caused, wouldn't it be better to be rid of him? And wasn't it Pagiel's right to defend himself against an assassin?

I had once loved Kiyo and had a connection to him. That was a hard thing to overcome, but I daresay he'd done plenty to make it possible.

These thoughts flashed through my mind in the blink of an eye. Before I could act, Pagiel fell to the ground, eyes wide. The magic supporting mine abruptly stopped. Pagiel clasped his neck, gasping for air. For a moment, all I could think was that air magic was suffocating him . . . except, there was no one who could wield it here except me and him.

"Pagiel!" Jasmine hurried to his side, where he was twitching and flailing on the ground. Still keeping my hold on Kiyo, I joined her and fell to my knees. Pagiel was no longer making a sound, which was a bad sign. He was clearly still desperate for breath, and I could see now that his face and throat were swelling, like some sort of anaphylactic shock.

I tried to steady him, frantically wondering what I could do. But I possessed no healing magic, no modern EpiPen. His face was turning a weird purplish-pinkish color, and I knew we were losing him.

"Dorian?" I asked. He had joined us and looked down at Pagiel, anguish all over his face.

"This is beyond me," said Dorian. He lifted his head and gazed around the clearing. "There's someone else here." He got back on his feet and began to make the ground ripple and shake, in the hopes of scaring out whomever we couldn't see.

But despite his efforts, it was a little too late. Pagiel had stopped struggling for air. Pagiel had stopped struggling altogether.

Storm King's heir was dead.

Chapter 27

"No!" screamed Jasmine. Tears ran down her face as she shook him. "Can't we do CPR or something? Use the air! Give him some!"

I stared mournfully down at the boy. His face and neck were so swollen now that I knew there was no way I could force air into him, not when all the passages leading to his lungs were so blocked. I couldn't control the body.

A smooth voice suddenly came from the woods. "I'm right here, Dorian. You might as well stop with the showmanship."

Maiwenn appeared, gliding forward in a silvery blue dress that seemed out of place in this scene. Her golden hair cascaded down her back, and she looked like the California girl I always thought of her as. Dorian did stop the earthquake, but I could tell from his rigid stance that he held his magic at the ready. She released a tree she'd been holding onto.

"How did you do that?" I asked. "Your magic . . . it's healing magic."

She gave a small shrug. "It's all part of the same system. My magic understands the way the body works. It's as easy to hurt as to heal."

I was appalled at how casually she could speak about it after what she had done. Dorian had no such qualms. "Will it be easy," he asked quietly, "to sleep at night knowing you've killed an innocent boy?"

"There was nothing innocent about him," Maiwenn replied bluntly. "I've saved both of our worlds a great deal of trouble. You should be grateful. Now, if you'll release Kiyo, I'd be much obliged. I'd like to be on our way."

"Grateful?" I hissed. "*Grateful?* I'll show you gratitude!"

In an instant, I pulled the charges in the air together and created a bolt of lightning to send straight toward Maiwenn. Just before I released it, I heard Jasmine scream behind me. I had no idea what had happened, but I was just able to barely divert the lightning in time so that it struck a tree inches from Maiwenn instead. Thunder cracked deafeningly around us, and the tree exploded in a spectacular show of fire and wood. My ears hurt, and Maiwenn's were probably bleeding from the noise.

I immediately turned toward Jasmine and saw her writhing on the ground. Her face was contorted in pain. "It's like . . . pins and needles . . . like my body's on fire. . . ."

"Damn it!" I glared at Maiwenn. Dark clouds rebuilt up above, and the wind swirled restlessly around us. The elements answered my anger. "I should've let it hit you! Let her go."

"No. You were actually wise to spare me," Maiwenn said. "I've already worked the spell. Her body's right on the edge of tearing itself apart. Only my control right now keeps it in check. Kill me, and the spell will seize hold with nothing to stop it."

"Damn it," said Jasmine through clenched teeth. "Why . . . am I . . . always . . . the hostage?" I watched her worriedly, but thus far, the spell mostly seemed about pain.

She didn't seem in danger of dying as Pagiel had just done—yet.

"Now," continued Maiwenn. "Please don't make me ask again. Free Kiyo."

Without Pagiel's added pressure, Kiyo had simply been trapped in my misty whirlwind. Inconvenient, but not lethal. Angry and frustrated—but out of options—I let him go. He was still in giant fox form, his fur soaked in water. His eyes assessed the situation quickly, and then he trotted over to Maiwenn's side. She rested a hand on his head. He stayed in fox form, and I knew from past experience that the larger the fox, the longer it would take him to switch back.

"We're going to leave now," said Maiwenn. "I can hold on to the spell a fair distance and will nullify it once I feel secure. If I see any sign of you following me before then, I'll release what's holding it back. The only good thing that will happen then is that she'll die quickly."

"When did you become such a monster?" I demanded. It was hard to believe she and I had once been friends and allies. "*Both* of you? What you've done is worse than anything Pagiel could have accomplished. Even if you escape today, do you really think I'm going to let you get away with this?"

"What will you do?" she asked, with an amusement that made me want to rip her hair out. "Declare war on my kingdom?"

"I certainly could," said Dorian coldly. "You've killed one of my subjects within my borders. That's certainly an act of war by most people's standards. In fact, you sent a force of armed men on my land just hours ago."

"Perhaps," she agreed. "But are either of you ready to plunge yourselves into war again? None of us have the resources for that, not after the blight. And I doubt you'll find many allies, not even from those who supported the prophecy.

Pagiel thankfully hadn't established himself enough for anyone to pursue revenge on his part."

"I don't know about that," I said. Around us, the air burned with the rising storm that had responded to my emotions. "There's one person who would do it right now."

"Two," said Dorian.

"Three," gasped Jasmine.

Maiwenn smiled again. "As you wish." She began to back up, Kiyo at her side. "Remember—any sign that we're followed, and she dies."

The two disappeared into the trees. I caught hold of Jasmine's hand and gave her as reassuring a smile as I could manage. "It'll be over soon." I glanced up at Dorian, and my smile disappeared. "She was bluffing, right? Her range can't be that far. We can go after her once she releases Jasmine. *If* she does. She's hardly given us reason to trust her."

Dorian brushed some hair out of his face. He looked weary. "No, but I think she'll avoid another kill if she can. She had some brave words about how killing Pagiel was nothing, but she knows each offense carries consequences."

"Pagiel . . ." I murmured.

I looked over at where he lay near Jasmine and felt a sickening sensation in my stomach. I reached out and closed his eyes, then ran a finger over his cheek. It wasn't fair what she'd done to him. None of this was fair. He was technically older than me in human years, but for all intents and purposes, so much younger. Young and so full of potential. He'd been thrust into a fate he hadn't asked for, confused by what he wanted and what others expected of him. He'd been killed because of words spoken long before he was born, and now all the wonders he might have done in the world were extinguished.

Dorian slipped an arm around me and kissed the side of my head. "I know," he said simply.

Jasmine suddenly gasped, like she'd been under water and could only now take a breath. "Shit," she said, examining her arms and legs critically.

"Better?" I asked, brushing aside my tears. It only freed up space for more.

She nodded, but her entire face crumpled when she looked over at Pagiel. "No," she said. "It can't be true. Not really . . ." She shook his arm, willing him to wake up, but as the truth slowly dawned on her, she burst into sobs that made my stray tears look like nothing. Moments of true affection had been rare in our relationship, but I knew then that she was young and she needed me and that I would be there for her.

I wrapped my arms around her, and she cried into my shoulder. "It's okay," I told her, stroking her hair. "You're okay. Everything's going to be okay." I didn't really know if that was true or not. At the moment, it seemed unlikely. But as I held her, I realized I was grateful that she was alive and still in my life. Her words about "always being the hostage" echoed in my mind, and I met Dorian's sympathetic eyes.

"My loved ones are always used against me," I said softly. "Why?" It had been a recurring theme. Varia had used it to keep me in check in the Yew Land. Jasmine had been held hostage twice today. It was again one of those moments where I marveled that I could still control a storm above us and be so helpless in other situations, especially when it came to those I cared about.

"Because that's what heartless people do," Dorian said. "They prey on those who love."

Taking Pagiel back to his family was one of the hardest things I'd ever had to do. I couldn't hold animosity against Ysabel and Edria, not for their bitchy personalities and not even for withholding the truth about Pagiel's heritage.

Their grief was too great, and underneath all their schemes, they were ordinary women who had loved and lost someone. I would've wailed and lashed out at the world too if it had been Isaac in Pagiel's place—which it very well could have been.

It was understandable that part of their grief would transform to rage. They wanted to blame everyone for his death, me especially. The thing was, I'd already beaten myself up over the events of that day, wondering if I could have done something differently. Dorian talked them down, finally convincing them that Maiwenn was the culprit here. The method of Pagiel's death, gruesome as it was, was proof of that, at least. Ysabel and Edria demanded war on Maiwenn's kingdom, but he kept his own counsel on that.

I kept my own counsel on him. There was a lot to contend with in the aftermath of Pagiel's death, giving me little time to talk to Dorian. I watched him a lot and found that I missed the time we'd had together. I hadn't forgotten that he'd stood with me in the end. He'd proven himself time and time again. Now it was up to me.

Still, the timing proved difficult. We were both always so busy. The most I was able to talk to him was the day I left for Tucson, and even that was short-lived.

"I have to go back for a while," I told him. "I don't know how long. There are a lot of loose ends to tie up."

Dorian nodded. "I understand."

I glanced away. "I wanted to say . . . well, thank you. Thank you for everything, for standing by me. I never should have doubted you. And I know there's still a lot to figure out—"

He cupped my face, forcing me to look at him. "Eugenie, Eugenie. I told you before. There's nothing for me to figure out. I know what I want. I want *you*. Not just as a bedmate or war ally. I want you with me, always. I want to share the same jokes and look into your eyes when I wake up. I think someday—hopefully sooner rather than later—you'll want this too. Until then, I'll be here, waiting for you."

He gave me a light kiss, and that was our good-bye. It left me breathless and continued to haunt me as I returned to Tucson. Even so, I still had plenty of other things to distract me. Mom and Roland and I were making plans about bringing the twins to Tucson, something that filled me with eagerness. I was anxious to see them and had little patience for all the things that needed to be done first.

Not all of my loose ends were unpleasant, though. Although I was sure Candace and Charles would happily give us all the baby gear they'd acquired, my mom and I still spent a lot of time stocking up on our own. Those moments were some of the most peaceful I'd had, and I would spend ages in stores touching and examining baby clothes, wondering how big Ivy and Isaac had grown.

I was at an outdoor mall one day with my mom, scoping out cribs. They'd all looked fine to me, but she'd gotten into a lengthy discussion with the salesperson, grilling him on every safety detail. I'd begged out to grab a cup of coffee, promising to return soon. I don't think either noticed I had left. I found a coffee shop on the other side of the shopping center and had just received my latte when a familiar voice behind me said, "Eugenie."

I spun around so quickly that half of my coffee sloshed out. Kiyo stood before me.

The throngs of people around us disappeared, and the focus of my world narrowed down only to him. All the anger and grief I'd felt, as well as watching others cope with their own sorrow these last couple weeks, surged up in me. Maybe Kiyo hadn't dealt the killing blow, but he might as well have. I couldn't believe he'd even had the audacity to cross my path. I'd figured he was smarter than that.

"Watch it," he warned, glancing upward. I was doing the subconscious storm thing again, and a few people had stopped to stare in amazement at the dark clouds that had literally come out of nowhere. "You don't want to create a panic."

"Wouldn't be the weirdest weather phenomenon that's happened around here," I said. "Neither would you being struck by lightning."

He smiled without humor. "You won't do it, though. Not in this crowd."

He was right. I could call lightning with pretty perfect precision, but even so, we were in the thick of humanity, with people brushing past us to get where they needed. I could hit him but might inadvertently hurt someone else along the way. *These aren't even people I know or care about*, I thought bitterly. *But once again, my hands are tied.*

"I suppose you arranged this," I said. "Waited for a chance to approach me in public?"

"Yes, actually. I figured I wouldn't get a warm reception at one of your castles."

"You figured right."

He sighed. "Eugenie . . . there are a couple things I need to tell you. I debated a long time about whether I should, but . . . well, I don't know. I feel bad about what happened with Pagiel . . . and everything else."

I had to repress the urge to slap him. "Yeah? Maybe you should've thought about that before your fucking girlfriend killed him!" My profanity got a few surprised glances from passersby.

"I'm sorry it turned out that way," he said. "But it was better for everyone."

I started to turn away. "Maybe I have to let you live today, but I don't have to listen to your 'greater good' bullshit again."

"Wait, Eugenie—" He grabbed my shoulder. I immediately jerked his hand off but did come to a stop. "Please. There are two things you have to know."

I crossed my arms over my chest. "Hurry up."

He took a deep breath. "First . . . your children . . . they may still be in danger."

"I . . . what? How?" I demanded. "Isaac's no longer part of the prophecy."

"Maiwenn's not so sure. She's afraid that maybe the prophecy will simply roll to Storm King's next oldest grandson."

I couldn't even speak right away. "Out of all the fucked-up things I've heard—and believe me, I've heard a lot—that has got to take the prize. Do you know how nuts that sounds?"

"I didn't say *I* felt that way," he said. There was enough uncertainty in his voice to kill his credibility.

"If you didn't feel that way, you'd stand up to her and stop running her errands."

He shook his head. "I can't abandon her. Not yet. We agree on a lot of other things, and I'm not going to go hunting your kids anytime soon. I'm just trying to warn you that others might."

"Again, that means little when you can sit by and still be pals with the woman who very well may hunt them," I growled. "What's your other 'important' piece of info? Is it just as crazy?"

Kiyo look distinctly uncomfortable now. "I . . . well, it depends. Yes. No. I don't know." He took a deep breath. "Eugenie, I should have told you this a long time ago. I don't know why I didn't. I mean, I had reasons . . . but well, I don't know."

I had no patience for this, no matter how pathetic or conflicted of a show he was putting on. "Kiyo, I'm tired of hearing about your 'reasons' because they all suck. Just get on with it."

Resolved, he gave a quick nod and rushed forward. "Eugenie . . . I'm not the father of your children. Dorian is."

Chapter 28

Alabama reminded me a bit of the Oak Land—or rather, the old Oak Land—when my plane touched down. Autumn had come since my last visit, bringing rain at last to the grass and shades of red and gold to the trees. It was beautiful, but I only spared it a brief thought before my mind returned to other, more pressing matters.

Two weeks had passed since Kiyo found me at the mall. I'd lived those two weeks in a daze, reeling from what he'd told me. I hadn't believed him at first, of course. I had stared at him in disbelief and then laughed outright. It was hard not to. His words were too ludicrous.

"Of course you are," I had said at last. "I didn't sleep with anyone else around that time—I mean, except Dorian. But that was before I took the antibiotics. Then I was with you." I wouldn't trade Isaac and Ivy for anything, but it still bothered me that I'd gotten pregnant from the idiotic mistake of mixing antibiotics with birth control pills.

"What was the total time span there between us?" Kiyo had asked calmly. "About a week?"

I'd nodded. "About that."

"That's enough time. Even if you weren't fertile at that exact moment, you can still conceive shortly thereafter.

Find a health book and read up on it." His lips had quirked. "It probably mentions antibiotics in the same chapter."

I hadn't liked his smirk. "Supposing that's true, how can you know for certain that it wasn't you instead of Dorian?"

"Ah, well. Because I, uh, had a vasectomy."

That had been the moment my life transformed from a fairy tale to a daytime talk show. It wouldn't have surprised me if the crowd around us had turned into a studio audience and a host with a microphone had appeared, ready to show us paternity results. It was too unreal. Too out there, even for me.

Kiyo had told me the story. Shortly after Maiwenn had gotten pregnant, he'd decided to ensure there were no more unplanned pregnancies in his life. This had been particularly important while he was dating me. Our relationship had been pretty serious, and we'd both expected to be together for a long time. As much as he had wanted that then, he still couldn't risk me accidentally begetting Storm King's heir.

"I can dig out medical records if you want," he'd added. "Or I'm guessing if you just look at the kids, you won't see much of me."

Yes . . . I had already noticed that. I'd simply assumed the twins had taken after me, but if Dorian really was their father . . . it would be hard to say whose genes were dominant, seeing as we both had red hair and pale complexions.

"I don't know which is the craziest part of this," I'd told Kiyo. "That you were so adamant about birth control while we were together and never mentioned that you couldn't have kids *or* that you let me think you were actually going to kill your own children!" Not that him killing someone else's children was much better. It was horrible any way you looked at it.

"I thought . . . well, Dorian was already on your side.

But I thought—no, I *knew*—that if he found out they were his, I'd have a much harder time of getting to them."

No doubt. Dorian would level a city to keep his children safe. Still, the fact that Kiyo could have been sitting on a lie like this was mind-boggling.

"Then why are you telling me now?" I had asked. "Why tell me any of these things?"

Kiyo had shrugged. "It's the right thing to do, especially after you helped me on the Yew Land trip. Besides, some of the pressure's off now that the prophecy's immediate threat is gone."

"Not according to your pal Maiwenn."

"No. And probably not in the eyes of others. Even people who don't care about the prophecy are still scared of you, Eugenie. Those kids are leverage against you."

Kiyo had left shortly after that, disappearing into the throngs of oblivious shoppers. I'd let him go, both because I could do little to him in public and because I was really too stunned to react anyway. When I'd finally recovered enough of myself, I'd immediately sought out a book on pregnancy and learned he'd been telling the truth, that having sex a week before you were fertile could still result in pregnancy. I learned more about eggs and sperm than I'd ever wanted to know, but with my track record, maybe a little education wasn't so bad.

And so, here I was, about to see my children at long last. We were pushing nearly three months since my last visit, and some part of me half expected them to be all grown up and on their way to college. I hadn't told anyone the news about their paternity. I was keeping that close to my heart, unsure what to do with it. It could have a lot of consequences.

I rented a car and drove out to the country to see Candace and Charles. The little house looked the same, aside from its landscape no longer being dried and burned out.

I'd given them a heads-up about my arrival, and they were practically waiting at the door when I arrived. Candace whooped with joy and barreled into me with a huge hug. Even normally reticent Charles embraced me. Evan was with them too, equally welcoming.

Isaac and Ivy were everything I could have hoped for and more. They were bigger but certainly a long way from college. They looked like the kinds of roly-poly babies you see on TV. No more tubes, no more oxygen masks. Just chubby cheeks and curious eyes that were constantly learning something new about the world. Those eyes made me do a double take. They'd been the dark blue of most newborns back in the NICU. Now, they were still bluish, but I could see hints of green coming in—green like Dorian's. I almost started crying then and there.

"Look how much they've grown," said Candace proudly, putting Isaac in my arms. There were no attempts at gender equality in this household. Isaac was in pajamas decorated with rocket ships. Ivy was in a frilly dress. "The doctors said the early birth might put them behind in developmental milestones, compared to other babies their age. But look—they can practically hold their heads up."

I'd never thought of holding one's head up as a milestone, but as Isaac's little neck muscles fought to accomplish the feat, I saw that it truly was an amazing thing.

"They're not really behind in anything," she continued. "The doctors are kind of amazed at how well they've turned out."

Was that the result of gentry blood? Once they passed out of the dangers of early infancy, gentry were remarkably hardy. It was hard to know for sure what was at work here, but I didn't care. The twins were healthy and happy, which was all that mattered.

They hardly left my arms for the rest of the day. I even stepped up to change diapers because I didn't want to be apart from them. Everything about them was perfect. Every coo, every toe, every breath. Small talk abounded, but always, the discussion wound back to the twins. No one asked where I'd been. It was obvious the Reeds worshipped everything about Isaac and Ivy, and they never tired of telling me even the smallest details about the twins' lives. I never tired of hearing about them.

Candace finally convinced me to put them in their cribs later that night. Both had fallen asleep, and she cited some book she'd read about the early stages of infant sleep training. I didn't follow it all but figured she knew what she was talking about. The twins had matching cribs in a bedroom that had been converted to a full-fledged nursery. There were lambs and rabbits on the walls and pastel colors everywhere.

I stayed there after she left and watched the twins sleep. Every tiny movement enchanted me. I was so caught up that I didn't hear Evan enter the nursery until he was standing right behind me.

"I'm about to take off for the night," he said quietly. "I wanted to say good-bye. Will you be around tomorrow?"

"Should be."

"I'll come back then." His kind blue eyes drifted over to Ivy's sleeping form. "Pretty amazing, huh?"

"Amazing doesn't even cover it," I said truthfully.

"What will you do now?" he asked. It was his usual easygoing tone, but there was a trace of worry under it. "Still thinking you might stay here? Or will you take them with you?"

I watched Ivy's fingers twitch in her sleep and felt an ache in my heart. "I don't know," I admitted. "I thought when I came back . . . well, I thought I had this all figured out. I thought the danger would be gone, but it turns out maybe not."

Surprise lit Evan's features. "If they're in trouble, you know we'll do anything to keep them safe."

"I know," I said, smiling. "Believe me, I know."

And that's where things got difficult. I'd intended to bring them back to Tucson with me. When I'd finally accepted what Kiyo had told me about Dorian, I'd even begun plans for introducing Ivy and Isaac to their Otherworldly heritage. Then . . . as time passed, I began to doubt myself. Kiyo's words came back to me, about how Maiwenn still thought Isaac might be a potential threat. Worse than that were the insinuations that the twins could be at risk simply from those seeking to make a power play against me.

I could almost dismiss that last fear. After all, with the Otherworld still recovering from the blight, conquest wasn't on many people's minds. And yet . . . I knew enough of gentry nature to know some might think it an acceptable risk to take advantage of weaker kingdoms. I also had the haunting examples from recent times of those I loved being used against me. I'd scoffed at Varia's attempt to blackmail me for the Iron Crown, but what if she'd held Isaac in her arms when she'd made the threat? What if she'd done that weird mind melting on him? Yielding the Iron Crown's power to her and helping her conquer kingdoms would have seemed like very unimportant things in that moment.

Dorian's words came back to me, when I'd lamented about those I cared about being used as hostages: *That's what heartless people do. They prey on those who love.*

"I can probably protect them if I take them with me," I told Evan. "I have lots of ways to keep them safe." A castle, rings of guards and magic users . . . the Otherworld was filled with all sorts of protective means. "But I'm almost certain they'll be safer here. I also think they'll have a more normal life here." Safety, as I'd found with my pregnancy, had come at a cost. Isaac and Ivy would spend childhoods in the Otherworld tailed by guards. Most royalty did. But did I want that? Here, in obscurity, they could run around outside without shadows looking over them. "How do you choose as a mother? How do you choose between 'probably safe' and 'safer'? It's really only a tiny difference, but . . ."

". . . but you feel like that tiny bit is crucial," he finished.

I nodded and sank down into a rocking chair. "It's hard not to. I really can't ignore even the tiniest detail when it comes to their safety."

He put his hands in his jeans and strolled over to lean against the wall near me. "You could visit anytime you want."

"I know," I said. I'd taken another convoluted path to get here. That would likely be the norm if I left the twins in Huntsville. Not ideal, but worth it. "These last couple months have been awful, you know. I thought about Isaac and Ivy all the time."

"Of course you would."

"I don't want to go through that again, especially since we'd be talking about a much longer time." It could be years before I felt they were safe enough to emerge from this retreat. "And yet . . . I keep thinking I could make that sacrifice if it'll help them. It'll hurt me, no question. And I'll hate it . . . but I can do it. The problem is their father. . . ."

There it was. After the joy of realizing my children hadn't been fathered by someone who wanted to kill them, a few realities had set in. Dorian wanted children of his own—wanted them fiercely. Part of me wanted to run to him right now and tell him the good news. He would be ecstatic—beyond ecstatic. It would be a dream come true.

It would also be a dream he would not allow to hide away here in the human world.

He would want to bring them to the Otherworld—not for any grand schemes, but simply to love them. I'd noted earlier that he would level cities to keep them safe. He would exercise every power he had to protect them in the

Otherworld, and I doubted any argument I could make about safety here would win him over. He hadn't believed that when my safety had been on the line. He wouldn't accept it for his own children. Once again, *probably* they would be safe. But if something went wrong, our enemies would then have two powerful monarchs to blackmail.

I could already foresee the arguments that would come when I told Dorian I was leaving Isaac and Ivy where they were. I doubted he'd have any luck finding them. A search in the human world was difficult enough for someone like Kiyo and nearly impossible for a gentry. But there would be no peace for me. Dorian would never stop trying to get me to tell him where they were. Any attempts at rebuilding our former relationship would always be affected by this, and that hurt me in a different way.

"Is he a danger to them?" asked Evan.

"Huh?" It took me a moment to remember I hadn't elaborated on why the twins' father was "the problem." "No," I said. "Absolutely not. He would love them. He would do anything for them—except leave them here, even if it's for the best. He would want them too badly."

"I can understand that," said Evan earnestly. "You keep using 'would.'"

"He doesn't know he's the father." I sighed. "If I tell him . . . it'll be the happiest day of his life. If I don't, I'm the only one who suffers from being apart from them. He'll be in blissful ignorance."

Evan shook his head. "That's an ugly choice."

I stared off at the dark window without really seeing it. "Not telling him now eases a lot of problems—except, one of the biggest issues between us has been about the importance of honesty and rebuilding trust. I'm especially always going off on that. What kind of hypocrite would I be to push for that and then keep something like this from him?"

Evan was silent for a few moments. "So . . . you're getting back together."

I looked up at him, only then realizing what my words meant. Evan still wore that everything-is-okay look, but I caught a glimpse of disappointment in his eyes. There'd been no promises between us, but he'd still had his hopes pinned on me when I returned.

"Evan, I—"

He held up his hand and gave me a kind smile. "Don't worry about it. It's what you want, and I'm happy for you. It has no effect on what I do for these kids."

I still wanted to apologize but instead held back and respected his wishes. Going on and on about how sorry I was, making excuses . . . well, that wouldn't make him feel better. It would only make me feel better. He would have to process this in his own time.

"How long would you keep them from him?" Evan asked, returning to my dilemma.

"I don't know. Years. Maybe until their teens." I groaned. "God, that sounds awful just saying that. What kind of person even considers something like this?"

"Someone who loves their children," he said bluntly.

"Would he forgive me when he finds out?" I asked bleakly. "Would *you*? You wouldn't be happy to find out your girlfriend had been hiding something like this for years."

"No," Evan agreed. "I'd be pretty upset. But I'd also be overjoyed to see my children healthy, safe, and well."

I stood up and paced toward the cribs. "Would that be enough? Would it make up for the lie?"

He thought about it. "I don't know."

I looked between the two sleeping forms, and that's when the tears started. I wasn't a crier. With Pagiel's death and even in some of the more hormonal moments of pregnancy, my tears had been pretty minimal. Now, they were an onslaught as all the hurt I'd been holding within me for so long burst out. I cried for Dorian, for the secret I would have to keep from him. I cried for Isaac and Ivy, who would spend a good part of their life never knowing the truth about their parents. And I cried for myself, because I was going to hurt every day I was apart from my children.

Evan put his arms around me and let me cry into his chest. He didn't try to tell me everything would be okay, and I was grateful for that.

"I don't want to leave them," I sobbed.

"I know," he said.

I sniffed. "I've never had to make decisions this hard before . . . and believe me, I've had to make some pretty tough ones."

Evan nodded. "That's because they were always about you. Everything changes when someone else's life is in your hands."

Chapter 29

My kingdoms welcomed me back, both the lands themselves and the people. Everyone was in good spirits. Most
of the destruction had been repaired, and increases in both
our own crops and those imported from the unblighted
kingdoms were making rations less strict. In the Otherworld, the relationship between monarch and land was
viewed as a sacred bond. In many ways, people saw their
monarch as an extension of the land—which perhaps
wasn't so far off. What it meant was that much of the credit
for the land's rebirth was laid at my feet. I wanted to brush
off the praise—particularly since I felt a lot of our success
was the result of my clever servants—but I was told it was
a futile goal.

I'd spent a couple joyous—but bittersweet—weeks in
Huntsville before a quick stay in Tucson led me back to the
Otherworld. I'd left Alabama with a gift from Candace: a
baby book with records of early development, pictures, and
even tiny locks of the twins' wispy hair (which definitely
looked reddish). Through a system nearly as complicated
as my travel there, she promised to send regular pictures
for my book so that the twins wouldn't be strangers when
I saw them again. Dorian might not find out about his

offspring for a while, but I planned on checking in on them when I could.

No one mentioned him at all in the Thorn Land, so I finally cracked and brought him up to Shaya while we were inspecting a garden filled with flowering cacti. The mesquite trees were also in bloom, filling the air with a sweet, heady scent. Tucson was heading into winter soon, and while that was a pretty mild season for them, it made me appreciate the Thorn Land's perpetually perfect climate that much more.

"Has Dorian, um, asked about me?"

She'd been studying a retaining wall with a critical eye and looked up in surprise. "No, not that I know of. I've only seen him once since you left. Someone else asked him about you, though, and he simply said that you had important things to tend to and would return in your own time." She hesitated, never one to really advise on my personal affairs. "I think . . . I think he's waiting for you, Your Majesty."

He's waiting for you. He'd told me that before I left. Dorian had laid everything out for me. He'd proved his love and loyalty over and over. I'd told Evan I was getting back together with Dorian. I'd even sort of accepted it in my head. But something inside me kept holding back. I had yet to act and needed to. Dorian had opened his heart to me. It was time for me to answer.

I skipped protocol and traveled to the Oak Land by myself. My safety might not be an immediate concern anymore, but status said I should have an escort. I liked the alone time, though, and smiled when I saw some of the Oak Land's trees touched with the fiery hue of autumn. Dorian wasn't quite ready to let it slip into the season he loved, but it was getting closer.

As I approached his castle, I spared a brief moment to wonder if I should have worn gentry attire. I was in one of my favorite outfits, jeans and a Def Leppard shirt. No,

I decided. This was who I was. I wouldn't try to create an image that was more than that. Just before entering the castle, however, I did put on a crown he'd once given me. It was a delicate little thing, tiny gold roses and emeralds. I liked it because it was from him and because it wasn't too showy.

I received a warm welcome from the guards and was led outside through one of the back entrances. I expected to find Dorian in one of the many courtyards he spent his time in but was instead taken farther out on the grounds, finally ushered into a small, pretty clearing ringed in the trees that had given the Oak Land its name. Several members of Dorian's court sat around in the grass on blankets, making a picnic of the sunny day. Their focus was on the clearing's center, which contained a medium-sized pond. A path of very small stepping stones extended across the water, stopping at about the middle. There, balancing on one foot on the farthest stone, was Muran. He was sweating visibly, but I doubted it was from the heat.

Dorian stood near the edge like some kind of mad ringmaster, the sunlight setting his long hair ablaze. With an elegant gesture, he made a rock float through the air and settle in the water in front of Muran. The servant—who had been starting to waver—gratefully jumped onto the new rock with his other foot.

"Eugenie, Queen of Rowan and Thorn," announced the herald.

Dorian looked over at me with surprise that quickly turned to joy. It was such a rare outpouring of affection from his normally lazy smile that I felt weak in the knees.

"My dear," he said. "You're just in time. I was demonstrating the amazing bridge feat we conducted on our journey to the Yew Land. Muran is assisting me." Another rock landed in front of Muran who immediately jumped on it one-footed.

It was perhaps one of the more ridiculous things I'd seen Dorian do with Muran—and I'd seen some pretty ridiculous things. I laughed out loud. I was suddenly so happy to see Dorian, I thought my heart would burst. Our life had been filled with so many complications that I hadn't allowed myself to really feel or acknowledge how I felt. I had loved him for some time, I realized, and wasn't going to deny my feelings anymore.

Ignoring propriety, I ran up to him and threw my arms around him. I kissed him hard, a kiss he didn't hesitate to return with equal ardency. One of his hands rested on my hip, the other on my hair. He pulled me as close as we could possibly get while clothed, and my whole body turned to fire from that kiss. I felt like it would consume me, and I welcomed it.

Public displays of affection were perfectly normal among the gentry, but I had never made any secret of my disdain for them. I'd always rejected them, no matter how much Dorian tried to coax me. Right now, I really didn't care who was watching. It was actually kind of a surprise that he was the one who pulled back from the kiss, though his grip on me didn't lessen at all.

"This," he said, "might be the most astonishing thing that's happened in a while."

I gazed up at him, momentarily caught in the green of his eyes that our children were already starting to inherit. "I missed you," I said simply.

His lips twisted into a smile. "Even so, I'm not quite sure what I've done to deserve a welcome like that."

"What haven't you done?" I asked, echoing his constant "What wouldn't I do for you?" rhetoricals.

"Um, Your Majesty . . ."

Muran's voice was tremulous, and glancing over, I saw he was dangerously close to falling into the water. Dorian studied my face a few moments longer before finally turning to see what his servant wanted. "Eh? Oh, that." With an impatient gesture, Dorian sent a whole set of rocks across the water, completing the path. Muran sprinted across it, sagging with visible relief when he reached the other side. Dorian returned his attention to me.

"I wasn't sure if you were coming back," he said. "I figured you had a lot to occupy you in the human world."

I smiled back. "Yup. But I have a lot to occupy me here too."

"So I see." Dorian traced my cheek and then touched the edge of my crown. "Jeans and emeralds. Quite the fashion statement."

"Story of my life," I said. "I don't think I can give up either world. And I can't give you up either."

"Well, of course not," he scoffed, as though I had just said the most absurd thing in the world. "Who could?"

I silenced any more witty Dorian quips with another kiss. His court sighed happily, as though it were the best thing they'd ever seen. It was certainly one of the best things *I'd* experienced in a while. My life was split by two worlds, but he kept me whole. Lost in his arms and his kiss, I could see a whole glorious future with him. The secret of Isaac and Ivy burned within me, and I regretted that dishonesty. At the same time, now that I was with him again, I had serious doubts about whether I'd actually be able to keep the truth from him. Dorian was kind of irresistible.

Whatever decisions I made, however, would be because *I* chose them. I chose to be with him. I chose to be an Arizona shaman. I chose to be Queen of Rowan and Thorn. My future was mine.

And not some prophecy's.

Discover the fabulous fictions of
RICHELLE MEAD

'My kind of books – great characters, dark worlds, and
just the right touch of humour'
Patricia Briggs

The 'Succubus' series, featuring the fashion-conscious
shape-shifter Georgina Kincaid . . .

SUCCUBUS BLUES
Being a succubus seems pretty glamorous. A girl can be
anything she wants and mortal men will do anything just for a
touch. OK, they often pay with their souls, but why get
technical? Seattle succubus Georgina Kincaid feels her life is
far less exotic. Her boss is a middle-management demon and
she can't get a decent date without sucking away part of the
guy's soul.

SUCCUBUS NIGHTS
If Georgina so much as kisses her new boyfriend, she'll drain
his life force. But it's not just her personal life that's in chaos.
A colleague has started behaving very strangely and Georgina
suspects that something far more demonic than double
espressos is at work.

SUCCUBUS DREAMS
Someone – or something – seems to be preying on Georgina at
night, draining her energy and offering distinctly disturbing
visions of her future.

SUCCUBUS HEAT
As Seattle's supernatural population starts turning on itself, it
seems to be up to Georgina to rescue her boss and figure out
who's been playing them – or all Hell will break loose . . .

SUCCUBUS SHADOWS

What with her ex-boyfriend's wedding to plan, another succubus in town intent on seducing Seth and her new roommate Roman cluttering her apartment with sexual tension, Georgina has her hands full. And that's without the mysterious entity that is trying to take over her mind . . .

SUCCUBUS REVEALED

Seth Mortensen has risked his soul to become Georgina's boyfriend. Still, with Lucifer for a boss, she can't just hang up her killer heels and settle down. In fact, she's being forced to transfer operations . . . to Las Vegas.

The 'Dark Swan' series, featuring shaman-for-hire Eugenie Markham . . .

STORM BORN

Eugenie Markham does a brisk trade banishing spirits and other entities who cross into the mortal world. Mercenary, yes, but a girl's got to eat. Her most recent case, however, is enough to ruin her appetite.

THORN QUEEN

Eugenie's now queen of the Thorn Land. That said, with her kingdom in tatters, her love life in chaos and Eugenie eager to avoid the prophecy about her firstborn destroying mankind, the job's really not all it's cracked up to be.

IRON CROWNED

Saving two worlds, one from trespassing entities and the other from a brutal war, is no easy task. Eugenie's only hope is the Iron Crown, a legendary object even the most powerful fear . . . But who can she trust when those closest to her have their own agendas?

All available in Bantam paperback and eBook